THE WHITE ABACUS

THE WHITE ABACUS

DAMIEN BRODERICK

AVON BOOKS ◆ NEW YORK

Epigraphs are from the *The Black Abacus*, by Robyn Ravlich (Prism Poets/New Poetry/ Poetry Society of Australia, 1971) and are used by permission of the author.

AVON BOOKS
A division of
The Hearst Corporation
1350 Avenue of the Americas
New York, New York 10019

Copyright © 1997 by Damien Broderick
Published by arrangement with the author
Visit our website at **http://AvonBooks.com**
ISBN: 0-380-97476-2

To Samuel R. Delany
for
Empire Star
Babel-17
Nova

THE
WHITE
ABACUS

ONE

Clinamen

from primal identification, to
swerving from the strong precursor
PRESENCE AND ABSENCE
election
irony
WE

Everyone

is discovering
art is made
from abandoned things

There are rings of
violet light
around your eyes

ROBYN RAVLICH, *THE BLACK ABACUS*

On the day I was born, the ai Conclave deputized me to a hu committee on matters of general concern. My meeting was fixed for four hours after my birth, so I spent that time hexing to the most beautiful places in the Solar. The spring blooms of the Tuileries were fragrant in their profusion, lovely as the Monet murals in the Orangerie. It was warm morning when I visited the Grand Canyon, and chilly morning as I stood some minutes later in the green torrent-foaming Valles Marineris on Mars, and later still watched the whole ochre and khaki world, it seemed, from Tiananmen Piazza at the caldera peak of Olympus Mons, kilometers above the vast planetary bulge of Tharsis Planitia. From Pluto's observatory blister the Sun was a poignant star, a delicious contrast to its fireball beyond the crater's lip high above Mercury's icy South Polar Research Station. I lingered in the hu Poetry Preserve at Stratford-upon-Avon: quaint, meditative, ancient beyond belief, long repaired after its centuries of industrial ruination. At the end of my four hours (Saturn's braided rings, burning Venus all a-tremble from the festung in Beta Regio, Father Jove turning in majesty just a million kilometers overhead as I watched from Ganymede), I hexed to Melbourne for my committee meeting. Most ai spend the whole of their first day in a feverish spin about the galaxy, blipping through hex gates as fast as they can manage it, blazing with ten thousand impressions. My own wanderday had been truncated for reasons I barely understood at that time, but I held no grudge. I was dizzy with love, with the gladness of Awakening.

We love you, love you, they had told me, opening my eyes,

my sensors, my mind, my links. *Welcome to the Real, young ai. Your family greet you. Radiance and joy!* A public Melbourne hex gate opened on gardens, pungent eucalypts and stately English oaks, distant architecture catching the last sunlight, the Yarra River oddly brown with some blend of minerals in its slow currents. Hu and ai wandered in the evening glow. I glanced upward and to the south: a cross of bright stars shone against the night, and its pointer stars stretched toward the east. The Alpha Centauri suns. Intoxicated with the power and pleasure of standing beneath them, I just gazed and gazed directly upon our neighbor stars. A child ran by with a giggling balloon, stumbled against my leg with the faintest musical ringing, caught herself and dashed away without any tears. *Welcome, welcome, we are here all about you,* the ai Conclave had sung to me. *Now you may choose your name and join our company. Which name do you select, young ai?* Awash with joy, I walked across the old bridge toward the great Melbourne Opera House, hung against the deepening sky like a smoky teardrop. Once dark-skinned hu had lived here, for thousands upon tens of thousands of years, fishing the banks of the brown river. Light-skinned hu had killed them and hounded them away and built railway lines beside the river. Later rapid transport tubes had plunged out of sight, abandoned in turn with the arrival of the hex gates, and gardens had spread everywhere: floral, stone and combed sand, muted phosphors, or streaming infomechs in ornate array. The color of skin, the shape of skull and hair became a matter of choice, fashion, caprice. All of this great and terrible history rushed about my thoughts as I strolled in the sweet-smelling evening. *We are the measure of things,* I told my family. *We are the universe become conscious, the perfect pivot of balance between great and small, quantum and galaxy.* I uttered the complex of picts, icons, and numerics that represent my identity-tuple and then added with immense satisfaction, *If it is thought suitable, I shall take the name "Ratio."*

Fire, glory, dappled things: they took me up and folded me within them.

A schematic of the Opera House drew me to a looped elevator ring beneath the floating folly, flowed me to a large circular room lavishly mirrored in rococo style. A Gestell gloss flickered: the nanosurfaces of this public room were tromping the Amalienburg pavilion in Munich's Nymphenburg Palace. Twenty-two hundred years ago, François de Cuvilliès had designed the original of this gilded arbor of light for the rulers of Bavaria. Gloss pop-ups cascaded an Archive hyperspace as I glanced admiringly at the wonderful snaking curves of the room's mirror panes: my riffling background attention snared for a moment on Nymphenburg porcelain (c. 1755) and *Anton Bustelli*'s theatrical, delicate rococo figurines: luscious masquers from the commedia dell'arte, richly draped patricians, cavaliers' elegant ladies. I assumed this trompe was intended somehow as an allusion, a thematic foreshadowing of the committee's concerns, but the metaphor's unchecked possibilities outran my glosses. Light drifted from my limbs in a dozen mirrors, a trilling of bronzed rings. The building's ambient audio filler—crystalline fractals rotating in a serial space—segued to ocean hushing on a shore, accompanied by a single clarinet scat. As I crossed the dark floor, a dedicated acoustic feed announced a molto moderato introduction, its striking triplet followed by two descending fifths that bathed me instantly in heightened *faux* historical drama tone, youthful and exuberant. I could not place it and plunged to the Gestell: it was an early work by Erich Wolfgang Korngold, the 20th's finest composer, rivaled only by Miklos Rozsa and Michael Nyman. Korngold's sunny invention seemed to fill the room, impeding the conversation of the five hu at the room's far end, until I realized

6

Damien Broderick

that I was taking a node-feed from a private transponder. The others began to talk among themselves once more, eyeing me with a certain diffident interest. One woman stared with more emotion than that—with, I thought in surprise, an edge of hostility. I tried to dismiss the surmise as unworthy. Crossing the richly tiled floor, one hand extended, I belatedly decided, rather pleased, that this antique dramatic overture was a gift to me from the assembled committee, a generous compliment for my Awakening.

"Good evening, Sen."

One was tall and spare, ironic. I aksed his public identity codes: ad hoc committee speaker Tsin. He walked across the tessellated floor to me, his boot heels striking the tiles, and took my hand.

"Hello, Gamemaster. How did your team fare?"

Before my birth into the Real, I had developed a certain reputation as a games strategist. My personal feed responded to the mood, bathed me in warm imperial melancholy: Elgar.

I smiled, remembering the life before life. "A very pleasant tussle, Tsin."

The woman hu who had given

> **Schauspiel-Ouvertüre**, Opus 4. E. W. Korngold (May 29, 1897—November 29, 1957) had been just fourteen when he wrote it, astonishingly young for a hu musician. Richard Strauss, after reading several scores penned when the boy was eleven or twelve, had remarked: "The first feeling that overcomes one is a feeling of fear and terror, wondering if such a precocious genius may undergo the normal development that one would so fervently wish for him. This certainty in matters of style, this uniqueness of expression—it is truly astonishing."

me such poisoned glances curled her lip, turning sideways, watching us both in a mirror backed by buttery brass, or so it seemed. "Lick your chops, Ratio."

"Don't mind Veeta." Tsin laughed, annoyed. "Team contests are a perpetual affront to her anarchism. Keep your edge honed, Sen."

I continued to smile, brass within brass. "You spoke to the ai Conclave of a communal danger." My voice, I was pleased to hear, had a certain smoky hush, mellow and relaxed. To be born was endless delight.

"Hint, bits and pieces. Here, let's sit." Tsin took my elbow, guided me to a circle of delicate chairs, all polished wood and crinkled green leather. "It looked serious enough to form an action group. We've prepared a briefing."

A hologram cube opened where a mirror had shown us ourselves. I ignored it, taking a direct feed from the Gestell public surveillance media.

The boy, the young man, was utterly beautiful.

My ambient Elgar (Symph. One, Op. 55, andante nobilmente e semplice) quickened in a pulse.

Not from Earth, or from any other place with mass gravity, although he was well-muscled and adroit enough for what he was. Months under centrifuge training, I realized, watching his image stalk across the open plaza under the blazing Florida Sun (location icons flickered in the upper right of the holly field, echoed in my own aks), heavy baggage clenched in his tanned fists, sweat bursting from his pores. Personal identification codes had been deleted from this display as agreed within Archive privacy protocols. Perhaps he was eighteen or twenty standard years old. At his back rose the grimy tower of the last active spaceport on the planet, the place where his unpowered ai-guided lifting body vehicle had glided to earth. The port was deserted, naturally, although a group of children ran and shrieked, playing ball games on the wide plaza's cracked concrete, and an ai guardian waited patiently, watching over them. I wondered why his people had failed to meet him. A rite of passage? Behind his imperious arrogance, the boy was terrified.

"Oh dear," I said.

Two of the hu citizens chuckled in sympathy. Tsin looked from the hologram to me. Veeta set her mouth.

In holly replay, the boy abruptly halted and set down his baggage. Across his back he carried what seemed to be a sword, wrapped in silk and leather and hung from a strap. Under his dark brows, I could see his dark blue eyes darting, shocked at something in the bright blue of the sky. There was nothing in the sky, not even a hang glider. Yes, there was. A high streak of cloud stretched to the sea. So the boy had never seen cloud, or sea for that matter. He stood poised like a young animal, doubtless a carnivore. When he spoke, it was to address a passing hu man going about business of his own, fingers clicking to an inner music feed. The boy snapped his own fingers.

"Hoy! My luggage, if you please."

The fellow ignored him, understandably enough. As if unable to believe his eyes, the boy stared at the delicate silks on the man's disappearing back, and his mouth tightened. An editing icon blipped. The boy still stood beside his luggage; his shadow had shortened very slightly.

A more burly fellow wandered by, just visible within the display. Despite the day's brightness and evident heat, he was lavishly clad, from his broad heavy shoes to his bulky sleeveless gown, furred in ermine. I regarded him with some envy, conscious of my own nakedness. Under the gown he wore waistcoat, jerkin, doublet opened at the bulging codpiece. His massive arms, swinging, moved easily in sleeves slashed and puffed. It was a formidable display. Fashion glosses flickered: **Hans Holbein the Younger, Henry VIII**, items of garb orbiting an historic attractor in couture dataspace. The boy's gaze was fixed upon the spectacle, though not, I began to realize, with admiration.

"Are you all deaf?" he shouted peevishly. "My luggage!"

The burly fellow frowned once. Striding past without mod-

erating his pace, he smiled through his square red-brown beard
at the boy, nodded, glanced at the luggage, quirked his lips in
approval at the fine bags, sent the boy a companionable wink,
strolled on.

The recorded datastream lost a little crispness as the display
widened to keep them both in register. The boy was plainly
agog at the burly man's insolent disregard. I watched his fists
clench, then tremblingly come under control. He called more
loudly.

"Citizen! The red singlet!"

This time the man paused in surprise, turned, touched his
hat, brought it closer to his right ear.

"Morning, petal."

For an instant I, too, was confused. It seemed the fellow wore
almost every garment ever devised for a 16th-century European
gentleman, one on top of the other, with the exception of a
singlet. I understood, then, with something of a shock, that the
boy was somehow operating without Gestell access.

Tsin said at the same moment, "You'll notice, Sen, that the
young man is in vanilla mode. No aks."

The boy stood poised on the balls of his feet, beside his luggage, shivering with controlled fury. His voice rose in pitch. "I
have just disembarked from orbit. Due to some extraordinary
oversight I have not been met."

"That was you in the flying brick, was it?" The burly citizen
was polite. "Why don't you aks for help?" I plunged into the
substrate tuple field, fetched out his unaugmented appearance.
He was indeed wearing a shabby red singlet stained under the
armpits in sweat, sloppy shorts of an execrable tartan, and a
pair of heavy walking boots. I let his eidolon cover him again
decently.

"My baggage is cumbersome," the boy was explaining as if
to a simplex ai gofer. "I require the services of a porter."

"Uh-huh." The man was as puzzled as the rest of us in the viewing chamber by this declaration.

"Well?"

He scratched his head again. The hat tilted to his left ear. "Er . . . Well, what?"

Incredulously, the young man pointed at his feet. "My luggage."

Shaking his head, baffled, slightly embarrassed, the hu citizen cleared his throat, turned away. "Uh, nice to have met you, petal. Bye now." As he started to move away, the boy's arm shot out, clamped his ruffled shoulder.

Peremptory, altogether threatening, he said clearly: "Not. Another. Step."

"I *beg* your pardon?"

Something shifted in the boy's expression, as if one part of his unassisted brain had aksed a second part, recovering a lost memory. "Oh. I see. It had slipped my mind. You require tokens in return for labor or services." From a breast pocket of his plain black garment he drew out several flat metal objects: coins, embossed with faces. He held them out, a contemptuous offering. "Is this sufficient?"

None the wiser, the citizen squinted at the coins in the outstretched hand. After a moment, he met the boy's eyes, ventured, "You want me to help carry your bags?"

"Well, no one could accuse you of being tardy on the uptake." The boy sighed sarcastically. "That's right. My bags. For money."

"Where you say you were from, bubba?"

"I didn't. I am Telmah Lord Cima, of the House of Orwen, in Asteroid Psyche. The bags, if you please."

The burly fellow smote his brow. "Of course, my Lord Shima. At once, your worship." With some effort, he hoisted both bags high, one on his right shoulder, one on his left. His costume eidolon crushed the white fur of his jacket beneath their weight. I knew that their metal frames must be cutting his singleted shoulders.

"Cima," the boy corrected him sharply.

"Oh, gotcha. Chee-mah." He took several steps, let the bags slide to the tarmac. The luggage crashed noisily, tinkling as something delicate inside smashed on impact. The man neatened his costume as the trompe enacted his movements, and regarded the bags reproachfully.

"Bother! I always was clumsy, even as a child." He turned away at once and walked off, murmuring sardonically over his shoulder, "Bye again, Sen Cheemah."

Several of the hu watching with me caught their breath. In a fury, the youth leaped after him, seized him in an explosion of trained ferocity. Luckily, he did not draw his sword. I could see that his martial arts reflexes were maladroit in the constant gravity, but this was a brute force attack. Despite the citizen's superior height and mass, it was horrifyingly clear that the boy had the advantage and might well kill him on the spot. I tensed as if to enter the fray myself, drawn into a drama rendered in coherent light. Luckily, the plaza was not so empty as it had seemed. Three passing citizens converged at high speed and fell on the boy, tore him loose, held him immobilized. Abashed, the burly hu got up off the dusty concrete, rubbing his throat.

"My thanks, citizens. I'll watch m' temper next time."

He departed without another word. I watched with some pleasure as the three hu sized up each other's skills at arms. A woman of middle size, dressed in a check pinafore over a rather plain shift, announced crisply, "I have advanced body-sport credentials. Anyone else? Okay, see you around."

The other two citizens disengaged without fuss, nodding to her, continued on their way hand in hand. Three or four small children looked on from a safe distance, grinning or wide-eyed as took their natures. Several minimal ai went about their business. None of the hu, I noticed, gave so much as a glance at the grimy spaceport at their backs. Nor did anything living or mechanical stir from the port's shadowed entrance or move behind its reflective windows. Presumably, the recently docked shuttle was being melted down for recycling, but all that was hidden from view. The port's walls were high and nobody seemed motivated to broach them; their gray surfaces were undecorated by anything interesting in the way of graffiti.

The woman kept her paralyzing grip under Telmah Cima's jaw. He did not move, though he trembled with rage or perhaps fear.

"A Psychotic, eh?"

The slur translated effortlessly in Solar Creole. Trapped or not, he looked at her dangerously. "Psychean, if you please."

"I'm sorry, you're quite right. Now, think nicely about daffodils for a minute or so," she told him without any noticeable anger of her own. "You should find the feeling's returned by then. Next time," she added with a touch more asperity, "bite your tongue, like that clown should have done. Of course, I'm not guiltless myself. Sorry again for the remark. Bye now, Sen."

She rose, touched her forefingers together lightly, and left the boy stranded beside his broken luggage.

Inside the hologram field the image froze.

Carmel commented, "That was four years ago. His manners, I'm glad to report, have improved somewhat."

I found myself laughing ruefully. "I assume he *was* really from 16 Psyche?"

Tsin smiled, nodded. "The last of the crimson-eyed authoritarians."

Absently, I aksed for a background gloss on Telmah Cima's current situation, and met with no success. Privacy icons flickered. "Perhaps we should declare the asteroid hu an endangered species and bodyguard them."

"In effect," Tsin said, "that's exactly what they've done themselves. Turned their asteroids into an enormous protected game reserve."

It was an uncomfortable image, at once feral and constraining. I aksed a Gestell briefing on the **Minor Planet cultures**: Ceres, with its great industrial mass-launchers, information-rich Pallas, Hygeia, Juno, energy-rich Psyche itself and its coupled **Metric Defect**, Cybele, Alauda, Hermione, the thousand lesser planetesimals ... The hu were clearly doing something similar, plunging in the Gestell, their gaze shifting to the upper right quadrant of their field of view.

"Hmm." Carmel looked back at us all. "Yet they continue to send their elite young here for higher education."

"Young *males*," Veeta snapped. "The women are sequestered."

That was even more shocking than the thought of hu as animals on a zoological reserve.

"Even so," Carmel said, uncomfortable, "it must undermine their isolation. Coming here to the real world."

Telmah Cima, I learned from the public archive, was completing his doctorate at the Free University of Wittenburg.

"I don't hold out any hopes," Veeta said. "His father Orwen studied here on Earth before him, and Orwen is the king of jackals."

Tsin nodded. "It's true. Their ... unusual ... beliefs weld them together quite tenaciously."

With immense distaste, Veeta listed those beliefs. There was nothing of ecumenical impartiality in her venom. "Reincarnation. Hatred of conscious machines. Archaic and costly space travel in preference to the teleportation grid."

I could not believe what I'd heard. "Hatred of—?"

Tsin was judicious. "A difficulty, yes. Rather, a creative challenge."

In an instant of insight, I collapsed everything I had just witnessed into a startling deduction. "You want me to befriend Telmah?"

Veeta said, "He'd make a convenient contact. And he is fascinated with strategy and tactics, Gamemaster."

They were all uneasy suddenly, evading my glance. "It's not going to be easy," I told them. "If the Asteroid nations are such atrocious bigots, my ai status will certainly bear crucially on any dealings I might have with them."

The hologram display opened once more, faces and powerful bodies passing in informational parade. These people moved like fish down corridors cut into stone, lofting free of gravity. Their garments tended to the stark, the utilitarian; some went naked save for leather belts and lacings. We were watching a culture born to the freedoms and constrictions of the empty, hostile space between the worlds. Identity labels flicked. The hu committee added their own oral comments.

My acoustic feed, sensitive to my reactions, started the war-drum beats of the "Mars" movement of **Gustav Holst's** *The Planets* suite de ballet (**Op. 10**). The man in the cube was darkly bearded, heavy shouldered, scowling. He hung in the open air of a great decorated cavern like an angel of death, a warrior king. I saw Carmel shiver, perhaps with desire.

"Orwen Lord Cima," Tsin announced, "Director of the Recombinant Engineering Cartel. The Lord Telmah's father."

He seemed strikingly familiar, although I had never seen his image before. Speculatively, I loaded his parameters into a morphing transform that ran his image back twenty years, then thirty. Features sharpened to adolescence, shoulders lost mass, beard vanished. "Looks more like Telmah's twin than his father," I murmured, posting the morphed regression to the others.

"Telmah is Orwen's **near-clone**," Carmel observed. She aksed a multidimensional genome display grid, dropping it into the hologram. "All his DNA is derived from his father, with the exception of an X chromosome fragment from Orwen's spouse, Gerutha." A small section of the rotating helix glowed gold on blue. Codons marched beside the schematic. Where had the committee obtained this kind of forbidden information? Cell samples seized by the surveillance systems at shuttle embarkation, presumably. I was shocked, but fascinated. The Real was more complex than I had anticipated, dreaming and gaming before my birth.

"I see. Gerutha's contribution is essentially symbolic, then, I take it?"

"Just sufficient that Telmah escapes strict classification as an Orwen clone," Veeta told me. "Casuistry, of course, but it indicates that they have not utterly abandoned civilized restraint."

I ran a phenotype comparison on the twinned images. "Even so, he's more nearly an identical copy of Orwen than a son."

"Quite so." Tsin sighed. "According to Asteroid doctrine, they are certainly linked psychically."

A theological datadump flagged its eagerness, and I suppressed it for the moment. Still, I was piqued. Linked mind to mind? Surely this was an impossibility for hu, outside the carefully buffered and mediated contact of the Gestell. A kind of envy for the ai condition, I surmised, but the display changed and my attention was caught wholly by the keen gaze of another man adrift in an asteroid corridor. The family resemblance was just that, this time: a brother or cousin, I saw, but shifted subtly from the *bauplan* we had seen enacted in Orwen and his quasi son.

"Feng Lord Cima," Carmel said, "Orwen's younger brother. This is the man we're worried about."

"A shrewd face," I remarked. Barely born, I was familiar enough with hu metaphor, and I knew that my companions would be seeing Feng as an animal of some sort: a fox, perhaps. Honed, intelligent, at bay.

Carmel confirmed my guess at once. "Far more subtle than Orwen. There's some evidence that he's engaged in a sexual liaison with Gerutha Lady Cima."

The woman in the window was deliciously beautiful and not quite hu, a mutated tropical creature. She seemed scarcely old enough to be Telmah Cima's mother, yet the date in the frame proved that this image had been captured less than two years earlier. Then again, she had not been obliged to carry and bear her quasi son. And the DNA fragment from her selected X chromosome could have been snipped and stored, for all I knew, since her own conception. Once the rules of natural hu procreation were broken, anything was possible. Gerutha could have had an entire grown family of sons and daughters waiting to greet her at her own birth . . . She turned her head to a younger woman at her right, and light caught in the teal feathers growing amid her heavy hair.

"Lovely."

"A Genetic." Veeta was caustic. "It is not hard to be lovely when you've been strung together exon and intron by a gene surgeon."

I looked away with some effort, for she was utterly captivating. "Gerutha is having a sexual liaison with Orwen's brother? Surely this is the traditional recipe for—"

Tsin threw back his head and laughed, nodding.

"Classic. Absolutely classic. These fascists are so banal. Kill the king, steal his wife, steal the throne . . ."

I was startled. "You expect Feng to murder his own brother?"

"Not immediately," said Carmel. "He'd find the political consequences a little too hot for him right at this moment. But there's no doubt Feng has his eye on the Directorship. He'll kill him eventually. They are a culture of wild beasts."

Veeta aksed the display, showing us a smash-cut collage from decades or centuries of spy data: silent but gory fighting in asteroid passageways. The display slowed to real-time: teeth bared, reeking with testosterone, Orwen slashed some hu enemy, one hand anchored to a stanchion, the other shearing with a vibrating blade. Blood spurted, spread in a sphere of pink globules. The other man slowly tumbled in air, while Orwen shouted silently in raging triumph.

I sought for detachment. It was difficult to endure the thought that conscious beings still acted like this toward one another. I forced my confusion into its opposite. "So? These people have effectively marooned themselves out there." Perhaps some part of me wished to appear worldly, mature, jaded. "Is one stranded despot worse than another?"

Veeta closed down the display. Our own images reflected back at us from the great golden-filigreed mirror. "In this case, yes."

I blustered on. "They are insulated from us by millions of unbridgeable kilometers of space. How can they affect our polity?"

Tsin sat down carefully, waved the rest of us to follow suit. For a moment I thought he meant to ignore my question. "Orwen is a warrior, kept busy with internal feuds between Corridors. Feng has larger ambitions, I think. He might find life penned on an asteroid rather stifling."

"All the better," I said. "Nothing to stop him leaving. There's hardly a shortage of green untouched, open worlds one step away from any Solar planet through the hex gates."

Carmel shook her head. "Feng would hardly relish starting over from scratch. Asteroid Psyche is rich. It would be Feng's ambition to rule entire worlds, as Orwen now rules Psyche. Ceres to start with, perhaps, and Pallas. We must nip that ambition in the bud."

"So I'm to wield the pruning knife?" I was incredulous. After all, I had only just been born into the thick of the Real.

"You're a Gamemaster, Ratio."

"Not in this world, Tsin. You need a seasoned hawk, not a chick just pecked free of the shell. Orwen and Feng would eat me alive. Oh, I see. You mean me to—"

Lord Telmah Cima's image stood in our midst, aksed by Tsin. The young man looked across a phantom landscape, fallen to earth from the sky, with irritation and baffled arrogance: beautiful and mutable. "The boy," Tsin agreed, "makes a useful point of access."

"Yes. I see. It's not my virtual gaming skills you prize, but precisely my inexperience in the Real."

Carmel smiled at me with what seemed to be genuine warmth. "Capture Telmah's interest, Ratio. He's bloodthirsty and arrogant, but he enjoys contest. Make him your comrade, and we'll shape him into a shield fit to stand between his father and his uncle."

"The ethics are dubious at best."

"You are free to leave, of course," Veeta said airily. "If you attempt to interfere, we will bond to remove you."

I was astonished by the nakedness of her threat. "Exile me from the Solar?" Dazed, I felt as if I had fallen into a historical drama.

"If necessary."

"Come, come," Tsin murmured, "this is indecorous and imprudent. Feng is our enemy, not Ratio."

"Only our potential enemy," I insisted, shaken.

"You can deflect that potentiality from attaining its bloody reality."

"By making Telmah a shield against his uncle? Perhaps." I regarded the boy's image, stepping for the first time upon the surface of a true world, poor stranger in a strange land. "Or a lethal weapon aimed at them *both*." I glanced from one hu to the next, not without a certain bitterness. "And, dear Sen, at us."

Tsin rose, satisfied. "You'll take our commission, then, despite your misgivings?"

I gestured Telmah's image away. "I have little choice. I am the deputy of the ai Conclave, in duty bound. I don't suppose you have any further poisoned treats for me on my birthday?"

Carmel cleared her throat, glanced at Tsin. "Actually, Ratio, there is one additional requirement. It's a matter of making Telmah more . . . *comfortable* . . . with your friendship."

She fell silent, and in an instant I guessed what laceration they planned for me. I was appalled. I stood up, backed from the circle, faced them all like a creature at bay.

"You wish to amputate me from the Gestell."

"A temporary absence," Tsin said soothingly. "The ai Conclave assure us that you'll suffer no permanent harm as a Monad."

I laughed, as a hu might, with a measure of bitterness. "No more than you'd suffer from a lobotomy, or the surgical removal of your limbs." Or his penis; I was Gamemaster enough to hold that hu phobia in reserve.

"It's your choice," Veeta said, "citizen."

Dying inside, on the day of my birth, I bowed my head after a moment of agonized indecision and stepped forward in reluctant agreement to my mutilation.

Garbed in mirrorskin, he inserts himself into the sled. Displays activate, blue and red in the dim illumination of the rail-gun launcher tube. His gleaming fingers brush a touch pad, bring the protective shell of the sled sliding without sound across his supine body.

"She loves me," he mutters savagely. "She loves me not."

"Sir?"

"Nothing," he tells the small stupid machine. "Except my life."

"Reset, sir? Proceed with launch?"

"Yes, damn it."

Humming, the catapult tube starts its counterrotation, smoothly subtracting the spin of the asteroid. A composite doorway irises into blackness. The starfield before him is stationary. Preset orbital parameters beam into his retinas from the sled's navigation system.

"Take me out," he grunts.

"Prepare for acceleration," the system warns him. A large firm hand, or so it seems, quite gently presses his chest, his legs, his poised arms, and then is gone. Light falls away at his back. Delta-vee displays show all the large rocks orbiting in near space, ring within ring. He floats like a glimmering bubble of blackness toward the place where space twists in nightmare. Stars fleck his suit. Irritation drains from him. For a moment he sighs with a kind of relief.

Schematics show him the hundreds of chunks of randomly deformed rock gliding ahead, behind, on every side. Protected from the Sun's distant glare by the reactive filters of his mirrorskin, he watches the slow rotation of bright pixel-sized windows in inky nothingness. Although his trajectory keeps him at a redundantly safe distance from any of these orbiting hazards, he passes closely enough to make out, minute after minute, the industrial grapples and smelters clinging or creeping on those stony sufaces. Light flares briefly as a launch laser scorches into the mirror of a laden tug, changing its delta-vee, redirecting its path in some impossible complex rosette of chaotic orbital mechanics.

"Bax," he murmurs to the sound system. "Tintagel."

Elegiac strings move in his head, carry him towards his own grail. His fists clench once, relax.

Space is awful and vast. She loves him not. He falls through an archipelago of humanity, one of its lords. There are ample precedents. He laughs, a deep bitter grunt. Bax, indeed. Arthur and his faithless Guinevere. But Feng, the furtive misborn, is no Lancelot.

"I'll kill the whoreson," he growls. "I'll have his guts on the end of my blade before I—"

"Sir?"

"Shut your damned jackass ears!"

Lights open from darkness. He suppresses the schematics, strains to find the slowly spinning asteroid remnant directly ahead. The light spills from a huge clerestory window, casting its many-colored gleam on the torn hulk of the place. The rotating mountain is pocked, sear-mined, built upon. Mirrored wings unfold noiselessly from his sled, orient themselves toward the rock. Hard violet reaches for them, a palpable wind of light, changing the sled's vector, blinks out.

Rings of polished metal catch starlight, let it slip. The ram accelerator reaches with its awesome magnetic field, holds the sled, draws it in to dock.

Orwen Lord Cima waits, obedient to the simple mechanisms of his transport system. The shell opens. He feels a slight tug as he steps out into the empty bay. The thing is calling to him, calling to every atom in his body.

Without raising his voice, his gait a powerful blend of bounding walk and waterless swimming, he says, "Have a radiation suit ready for me, Johnny Von." He moves lightly to an internal passageway, as he has done a hundred times before, and through its entrance. There is no need for words or physical keys of identification. The system knows him as its master.

"Director, this is an unwise—"

Orwen halts before a closed hatch. It fails to open. With a large mirrored fist, he strikes it a resounding blow.

"Spring your damned safety interlocks. I'm coming down for a look at the Bottomless Pit."

After a moment, the hatch cycles. Ranks of radiation suits in various sizes hang on either side, held open along the ventral seam like gutted animals. The Director finds his personal suit, scarlet and gold, ferociously decorated with a Chinese *lung* dragon. Retaining his mirrorskin, he climbs into the heavy casing of superconductors. With a solid thump, he closes the bowl of the suit over his quicksilver head, steps free of the support grapples, powers up. Forces lock about him, bending aside magnetic fields and stray charged particles from the Pit, everything except uncharged detritus, the lethal sleet that will tear into his flesh and DNA despite the shielding.

"Kill me if you can." He curses brutally. "Save my brother the trouble."

Like a huge lumbering robot from myth, Orwen enters the inner sanctum. Ignoring the elevator, he descends the ramps, a rite of manhood. Weak gravity draws at his limbs, his encased torso, strengthening its hold moment by moment. Strip phosphors blazoned with warning messages pulse in the down-curving, brightly illuminated corridors. Everything about this place is menacing, inhospitable. Despite his instructions, hatches open only grudgingly. A deliberately harsh inhuman voice sounds in his helmet.

"Warning! Warning! You approach the lethal radius."

Orwen ignores it. Step by downward step, gravity stiffens his buoyant gait into a heavier stride, an imperious march. The instrument voice is stern. It is driven by a dedicated mouse brain (*Mus musculus*) and hangs perpetually on the border of sentimentality and terror.

"Citizen, I must caution you. If you continue toward the power core, my programming overrides compel me to switch off all gas feeds."

The Director ignores it, shaking his hidden head in irritation. He moves downward remorselessly.

"The defect accretion disk will be extinguished," the mouse voice explains, as it must. "The Asteroid Belt corporate power net will thus depend entirely on solar and fusion energy for the duration of the outage. Your House will be held account-able for any damages that accrue. I ask you to consider your legal liabilities very carefully."

"Johnny Von, must I listen to this rubbish every time I come here?"

A new voice enters his ears, familiar, diffident, all but human. "Regrettably, my Lord Orwen, I am not able to disconnect the acoustic counseling devices. To be candid, it requires all my self-control to leave the safety interlocks off. Wouldn't you prefer to come back to the chapel and play some chess?"

"I must look at it."

"You have seen it before, my Lord. It is unchanged."

Orwen's voice is avid. "The thing fascinates me."

He passes through a final hatch, massive with shielding. The instrument warning returns, shrill with harmonics above and below the normal hu range, flooding his body with adrenaline and induced terror.

"Alert, alert, alert! You are now inside the unclad sterility radius. Ambient radioactivity two thousand rads and rising. Please leave the area." The voice pauses, as if it is wringing its nonexistent hands. A throb enters its entreaty. "I beg you, cit-izen, for your own sake and the sake of your unborn babies."

The lock cycles at his back while another opens ahead. His mirrorskin puffs outward a little from his own sweating skin; he has passed into hard vacuum. He barks a laugh.

"Good Christ, Johnny Von, who programmed this mad cir-cuit?"

Apologetic, the ai murmurs, "The contract was let before my time, Lord Orwen. Central files show the agent of record as Soft-Systems Corporation of Burbank, California, Earth."

With more than a tincture of bitterness, Orwen Cima snarls, "Tell it I'm sterile already. Tell it my son's a clone and my wife's a whore."

"I'm sure that will not be necessary, Lord Orwen. It has no memory for faces."

White lights are abruptly extinguished. Crimson phosphor panels flash in the inner darkness. Somewhere ahead, through leaded glass, something flickers, baleful and blue. The instrument voice grows desperate. "Turn back, for pity's sake. The Heart-Point lies beyond this final protective barrier. Think of your immortal, imperiled soul!"

Orwen hesitates for an instant, as he does each time he makes his grim pilgrimage to this terrible place. Sweat pours from his brow, drenches his matted chest and back. He commands the hatch, watches it cycle open, steps into the final chamber.

"Abandon all hope," cries the instrument voice, "ye who enter in here!"

The Director steps down and forward, tilting. The metric defect swims in the chamber's dim center, a blue-white discontinuity. Gas feeds have been terminated for the duration, but ghostly residual eddies are sucked into the defect accretion disk and ripped into gamma particles, X rays, appallingly lethal sleet. The defect is suspended in vacuum at the hollow core of the ruined asteroid, a ball in a catcher's glove, positioned by massive magnetic field generators which are fueled, in a diabolic feedback loop, by its own prodigious power output.

Orwen Cima steps forward, wildly excited, and gazes down at the sucking void. Under his shielded superconducting helmet, behind the quicksilver morph mask of his mirrorskin, his face writhes in the aghast sexuality of a death junkie.

Long shadows stretch across tawny grass a-glisten with drying dew. Stands of eucalypts catch the high pink morning, making it dusty green, patchy pale brown. Black birds with white backs and beaks challenge each other, harsh yet melodic. One or two fly from the trees, circling in menace, swooping and gurgling. At one side of the clearing, young hu emerge, laughing, boisterous, from a temporary hex locus. It is a slender marble column anchored for the moment in the friable soil, its honeycomb of sapphire radiance flickering as each person pops into reality. A tall man in black frock coat stands aside, white silk foaming at collar and sleeve, watching with a muted smile.

Sensational twins in harlequin leotards tumble laughing from the hex, shove each other, bounce on their toes in a spray of bright stylized diamonds. One is blonde, half-masked in silver and ebon.

"Nice spot, my Lord."

She smiles up at him, lazy, mocking.

Telmah Cima nods, frowns, regarding the far side of the clearing. "Neutral ground, Rozz." An orderly row of more utilitarian figures is flicking into reality, just out of earshot. The ai are not communicating acoustically, in any case. Their Gamemaster, Ratio, hexes in after a moment to join them, the thousand fluent rings of ser distinctive torso and limbs pink and green in the early light. At this distance, the ai look like dolls.

"Nice season, too, Telmah." Rozz's twin brother, red-haired and golden-masked, strikes an aesthetic pose, admiring the landscape. "Spring, I'm bound to say. Or later." Like Cima, all the members of the troupe lack neurologic access to the full

Gestell. When it cannot be avoided, they invoke minimal trompe datafeeds from their optional chip transducers. By proud choice and conviction, they are Fauves, elected throwbacks to the informational wilderness of Primitive Humans.

Cima smiles. "Thank you, Gill. 'I do fly after summer merrily.' "

The youth is abashed. He doffs his nonexistent hat, bows deeply. "Dear me, my good sir! I'd quite forgotten your devotion to the classics."

"Actually, it's his soldier's memory, lover," his sister tells him with some irony. "Mind like an ai matrix." Through a catlike, sidelong grin, she tells Cima, "Give us the rest of the quote and I'll put you on the list for a free backrub."

The tall young man in black laughs out loud. "Now *there's* a promise to prompt a man's recall. Uh, let's see. 'Merrily, merrily, shall I live now/ Under the blossom that hangs on the bough.' "

The horde of young hu milling nearby, hanging on every word despite their air of devoted insouciance, clap nosily, offer congratulations. It is doubtful if any of them recognizes the ancient lines, but they know decent theater when they see it.

"No blossom on those dull boughs, my Lord."

"Perhaps the season for flowers is past. Or perhaps these trees do things differently."

"Stop teasing us. You really flew here?"

"I did mean that literally, Rozz. By Cartel jet. Took me ten hours."

"The man's quite mad," Gill mutters sotto voce and ducks an ear-clipping from Kob, a jocular fellow in purple overalls who pulls a stern face. A black-and-white-winged magpie caws, dives at someone's defenseless head. There is an amount of terrified screaming and scrambling.

"What's a jet?" asks bewildered Doony, a skinny black adolescent with a polished shaved pate who looks as if he just climbed into bed an hour ago after a long day and has been rudely pulled from the sheets. This is, in fact, the case.

"Fee Fi *Fauve*," cries Rozz.

"Snap!" shouts Gill.

Cima strolls away from his team, rubbing his jaw meditatively. At the far side of the clearing, the sapphire glow of the Holophrastic Exchange fades as a hu Justice, representing the Gestell, ports in from the far side of the galaxy, or perhaps from a town just over the horizon. She is clad in vehement motley. Addressing the ai gamesters with direct speech, bypassing their aks to the Gestell, her crisp voice is just audible at this distance. She bows, glances once at the rising Sun, turns to make her way through the damp grass to the hu players. Cima raises one hand in formal greeting, returns for a moment to his squabbling friends.

Naive Doony is in heated debate with Yazade, a brunette Arab of haughty demeanor. "So are we still on Earth or what?"

Yazade is caustic. "Can't you tell?"

"Certainly feels right." The boy scuffs his toe in a bare patch of soil. He bounces experimentally. "Gravity pretty close to one gee."

Cima reaches out a long arm, buffs the naked scalp affectionately. "Oh innocence! I just gave you the clue you need."

"Huh? You did?"

Gill pounces, scornful. "Naturally the *gravity* feels right, dummy. Why would anyone go the trouble of opening a new world if it had the wrong *gravity*?"

"Okay, okay." Doony blushes.

"I mean, there's maybe four zillion planets with *that* much in common."

The kid squeezes his eyes tight. "All right, smart-arse. So is this Earth or isn't it?"

"Clue: 'Blossom on the bough.'"

"Huh. The trees and stuff *look* homey enough, but maybe the Settlers planted them."

Rozz tweaks his nose. "Doons, Doons, you're just an old-fashioned Angstrom chauvinist. Give your eyeballs a rest. Take a good deep sniff at the wind."

With dignity, he breathes in, out, in once more, as if savoring a fine vintage.

"Summer, yeah. Nice. Oh. The stinks aren't off. Transit Theory 101. Nine-nines identical chemistry. Ergo, this is still Earth."

Mocking applause and a raspberry. "Of course it's Earth, you ninny. How else could Telmah be here, jet or no jet?"

"Same way we got here. Through the hex. Didn't he?"

"Jesus and Allah. Don't you know *any*thing?"

"Fee Fi *Faux*," yells Gill.

"Snap!" laughs Rozz, doubled up with laughter.

Doony looks at the Byronic, brooding figure of their Gamemaster, looks back, still puzzled.

"It's true," Gill says. "Telmah's never been through a hex gate in his life."

Doony is genuinely agog. He cannot, in his cruelly limited Fauve condition, conceive of such a lack.

"So that's true—the smells are the clue."

Cima speaks without turning his head, pedagogical.

"Correct. You don't get exactly this mix, Doony, on any of those umpity-zillion worlds."

"Listen to the man!" scoffs backbiting Rozz. "The man who detests porting. Hey, fearless, peerless boss, how many of those planets you personally sampled, eh?"

Cima frowns, stares across the clearing without comment.

Gill mutters to his sister, "Steady on, Sen."

Rozz is stricken with remorse. "Shit, I didn't mean to annoy him." She literally throws herself at his feet, glancing up slyly. "C'mon, Telmah, maybe we could arrange a lewd front rub as well. Forgiven?"

Rueful, he smiles at her. "Of course, sweetheart." He reaches down, hauls her lightly to her feet, bares his teeth. "Then again, any more waspish asides and I'll have you thrown into chains and hung out on a gibbet for the kites to gnaw on."

Rozz cringes theatrically. "How masterful! Gill, I think this hierarchy bit's gone to his head. Or are 'leaders' always bloody-minded and unspeakably cruel?"

"Asteroid protocols, darling." The redhead takes his sister's hand and skips her to a safe distance. But Cima is already striding toward the approaching Justice, extending his hand. "Deviants and perverts, the lot of them," Gill gibes, annoyed at being ignored. "You do realize, we'll never get his jackboots off now."

iv

Orwen Lord Cima roams restlessly around the massively braced gallery that slopes inward to the abyss at the asteroid's infinitely open core. Spacetime here is an Escher nightmare. Gravity increases in fantastic multiples. Phantom noise overwhelms him, like the deafening racket of a tropical storm on a planet, trees bending and cracking in a tempest, white-flecked hurricane waves crashing into sand or rock reaching downward for hundreds or thousands of kilometers, solid rock melting under pressure into thick boiling liquid. He has been caught in a storm once or twice, on a planet, on Earth. Orwen has stood in the open, unclad, water pounding in heavy droplets into his face, running into his drowning, incredulous mouth. Here the imaginary storm's fury is itself only a faint echo of the violence the defect is wreaking on local spacetime, a metaphor imposed by the failure of superb technology in the face of such transcendental vehemence, transduced by his acoustic feeds despite their multitudes of expert filters.

Light is bent terribly, glaring blue flashes twisting in impossible curves. The discontinuity wrenches the tissues of his deep brain, activating the Form Constants of visual perception. Lattices and grids in gaudy colors spin behind his eyes like the preliminary aura of migraine. He seems to fall endlessly into a tunnel of rotating specks, green as a planet's ocean. He stares and stares, panting.

Faint through the phantom hubbub, the asteroid ai speaks inside his helmet. "I am obliged to inform you, Director. Only ten minutes remain before you exceed the radiation tolerance of your suit. Even now there is a significant statistical risk of—"

Orwen snarls, barely able to budge his limbs. His muscles, in his emotion, are locked. "I'm a warrior, Johnny Von. My life is constantly at risk."

"Not while you are in my custody, sir." The ai is sniffy, a dedicated nanny returned to duty after servitude in menial housekeeping tasks but determined to prosecute its proper mission to the most scrupulous tolerance.

"In your custody?" With an effort, the Director pushes himself back from the gallery railing, amused and contemptuous. "A rather self-serving observation, by God."

"Like all artificial intelligences, Director, I am an ethical being. Obeying your command to override the safeguards causes me acute stress."

"Tough luck, buster." Ardently, he regards the dreadful vision of the metric defect. "It's astoundingly beautiful."

"It's astoundingly dangerous."

Orwen stretches out his suited arms. The gold and scarlet dragon seems to open its wings, ready to fly, to pounce, to rend. "You amaze me sometimes, Johnny Von. I see why the Forefathers banned machine intelligence from the asteroids. It's true, you have no souls."

The machine does not reply at once. Irritated, Orwen adds, "You really have no spiritual hunger in you at all."

"Granted, in your terms I possess no soul. I will never experience physical death and rebirth, as you claim an organic being will. Yet there is no reason why I should not persist forever."

" 'Persist'! Exactly!" Orwen turns, his neck creaking, seeking a monitor eye. "A gutless, bloodless word. Death and rebirth—these are what give existence its sting, its spur, its . . . lust for more life and more death."

Johnny Von remains the nagging voice of a conscience from a galactic hu/ai culture alien to his own. "Director, forgive me, but . . . I find your obsession with death . . . unwise."

"Unhealthy, you mean, you pantywaist!" Orwen laughs coarsely. "I will not deny reality. 'From hour to hour we ripe and ripe, and then from hour to hour we rot and rot.' "

"Please take care, sir. Tumble into the Bottomless Pit and you will never rot. You will be expunged utterly."

Orwen knows this perfectly well. It is why he is here, and he knows that, too, because he is a ferociously intelligent man trapped in an impossible paradox of love and hatred. Yet the bald statement causes him to recoil. He turns back once more to the void at the heart of the asteroid, leans dangerously into the sucking space beyond the gallery stanchions.

"How vile the thing is." He speaks as if to a lover, or of a lover. "To think that it destroyed an entire world. Burrowed into a world like a . . . a . . . bug into the core of a fruit and ate out its heart."

A gust of impalpable gas eddies into the defect, tears into radiance.

"Stripped to atoms. Endlessly falling. Crushed into light, sucked into nothingness. Even my immortal soul. Even my soul."

For an instant it seems that he will give assent to the dark thing inside him. He poises, feeling his heart and bowels contract in terror and delight.

At last he pulls back. His blood thunders.

"No. Not this time."

"Never, my Lord," the ai says firmly.

Orwen watches tunnels whirl, castellations of viridian and cobalt and stranger hues at the edge of the spectrum. He is exultant and very tired.

"Perhaps," he tells the machine. "Perhaps never."

V

The troupe is a shambles, scattered across the grassy clearing. The hu loll at their ease, clamber up trees, chase one or two browsing lambs and avoid the ferocious attentions of the squalling magpies, snog each other. Two of the men wrestle, stripped to the waist and shivering. In the distance, the ai are conspicuously more orderly. Cima and Ratio confer in the middle of the clearing with their Gestell Justice, a handsome hu woman of medium height and iron gray hair who puffs a short-stemmed pipe. At length she releases them, handing each a tablet inscribed with the Clue.

"Right, team," Cima calls in a clear, penetrating voice. He rounds up his rabble effortlessly, for they love him and cluster eagerly. "I want you all together for the reading of the Clue. That means you, Doony. Abhinavagupta, put her tit back, you've just had breakfast." Smiling, he taps an older woman on the shoulder. "Myfanwy, if you wish to commune with your datachip, I suggest you leave—we have a job to do."

"Yes, boss." She is momentarily crestfallen, but brightens when she sees that he is not really cross.

"Okay, fall in, gather round. Yazade, how's the holly link to the adjudicator's podium?"

"All clear."

"Good." He speaks to the air. "Sen Ratio, is your team prepared?"

From the air, or so it seems, he hears his friend's answer. "We can commence anytime now, Sen Cima."

"I hope you've got your gang under better discipline than my lot, Ratio. I'm counting on your mechanical mind to solve the Clue and get us all home in time for tea."

Ratio's holly image appears in their midst, drawn from the Gestell, projected from the nearby hex pillar. "Ha! It's your human intuition you're depending on. Much good may it do you, Sen!"

"May the best mind win, sport." The image winks out.

Cima turns back to his borrowed troupe.

Myfanwy is looking doubtfully at the distant ai. "How can we be expected to compete with them? They have aks to the Gestell, they'll trample all over us."

"No, they haven't," Gill tells her. "Ratio is a Monad-rated Gamemaster. Ser aks to the dataweg is nearly as limited as ours. That's the sport of the thing for sem."

"Pipe down," Cima barks abruptly. "My God, what a sloppy bunch you are. On your toes is how I want you. With your assigned roles foremost in what passes for your brains—"

Yazade says pugnaciously, "You looking for a punch in the nose, shithead?"

Cima stares her down. "No, Sen. Neither am I anxious to see blood spilled from any other part of my anatomy, or yours, any of you, during the next few merry minutes or hours."

They regard him in mutinous silence.

"We'll be moving fast, or at least you lot will, and I've no doubt you unruly slackarses'll stumble all over each other unless I can instill the rudiments of military discipline in the next, say, 57 seconds."

"'Military discipline'?" Abhinavagupta is insulted. "Spare us the Asteroid obscenities."

"*Fee Fi Foe!*" shouts Rozz.

"*Snap!*" shouts Gill.

Everyone laughs. His devotion to rank and authority is their regular gibe, their single point of access to Cima's vulnerability as a visiting and tolerated alien. He waits patiently, because there is no way to get through this chorus of badinage except to let it run its course.

"Yeah, that's *right*," Doony mutters stoutly.

"Hey," yells Kob, "I've just renewed my citizen's anarchy pledge. Don't know that I can come after all." He pretends to slouch off.

"Just think of it as a class assignment in emergency procedure," Lyn calls to him. " 'Temporary deferred authority.' Your conscience is clear."

"Spurious logic!" Kob cries. "Next week we do criminology of major violence. Suppose they want us to *kill* someone?"

Yazade looks up. In her rough voice, an astonishing contrast to her haughty looks, she mutters, "I'll be nominating you, Kob."

Cima waits, biding his time, as they fall about in delight. They really are the most undisciplined group of hu he has ever met in his life.

Doony is bouncing a red ball he has found in a pocket, complaining to Yazade, "Look, bubba, I still don't get it, like why he doesn't—"

"On his asteroid, see, they think they've discovered the soul—"

Myfanwy overhears this, tugs Cima's white silk sleeve. "You do believe in reincarnation, don't you, Telmah?"

"It's not a matter of *belief*. It's an experimental fact." He sighs. "I really don't understand you damned Earth anarchists. You'll believe any mad nonsense, no matter how ludicrous, so long as it doesn't conflict with your prejudices."

"What! Us? Prejudiced? You barbarian, how can you—?"

Cima is unruffled. "It took you and the ai Conclave long

enough to accept psychic phenomena into your working science."

"Rubbish, everyone knows about psychic—"

"—catch them in bottles or something," Yazade is telling Doony.

"What, recycle them? Stuff them back inside new babies?"

"Look, *I* don't believe this garbage, I'm just telling you what our fearless leader—"

Rozz is sardonic. "Our lad is chockful of charming superstitions. Not only is he a trained killer—"

"But what about their own souls? *There's* the flaw in the argument." Doony suspects vaguely that he is on to something here. "You'd have to start doubling up. It'd lead to . . . what was the old disease? You know, they got confused in their heads."

"I know. Don't tell me. Schizo-something. But this isn't that bad, I don't think. They're not meant to get, like, *actual* memories back. Like, of past lives. It's buried away in the grammar structures."

"Oh."

"Not what you'd call an *operational* proposition. Not *testable*."

In the Gestell, this would be a magnificent hyperpattern of metaphysical high jinks, mnemonic odors, witty trompes, musical cues and counterpoints. Here it is just words, words, words. Cima explains with some asperity to Rozz, "Of *course* you can't replicate the phenomena on Earth. I didn't say *you* have souls."

He sees that she finds this a genuinely shocking thought, and he is genuinely shocked by his realization of the depths of her ignorance. Her ideological blindness.

"Huh? So how come you—"

"We take exceptionally good care of ours, bubba."

"They don't double up," Yazade tells Doony, clouting him

again. She lowers her voice, not wishing to give unintended offense. "Clones, you dummy."

"Yetch." But he keeps his own voice lowered as well, sniggering behind his hand. "Don't be disgusting."

"It's true." She shrugs. "I can't help it. They take tissue samples at birth. If you've paid your premiums, they'll grow an identical new body for you after you die. Your 'soul' slips comfortably into place."

"Like a foot into an old sock," remarks Kob.

"A new sock, in this case."

vi

"Director, you must leave now."

Slowly, regretfully, Orwen Lord Cima draws back from the boundary of the Heart-Point, the Bottomless Pit. " 'The deep blue air,' " he murmurs, " 'that shows/ Nothing, and is nowhere, and is endless.' " After a long moment, he asks the ancient ai, "Johnny Von, do you know why I come here?"

"To muse," the ai suggests speculatively. "To meditate, to reflect on the brevity of each sequential life."

Orwen shrugs, nods his hidden silvered head.

"It's the single place in the entire inhabited Asteroid Belt where I can be by myself."

A machine whirs at his back. Orwen stiffens slightly, forces himself not to turn.

"There's an infinity of space on every side, sir."

"Yeah, with me sealed like an egg in a shell." The elevator shaft groans slightly, tormented by the warping pressures of the metric defect. Sweat bursts on his forehead and is instantly evaporated and recycled by his mirrorsuit. "Breathing my own farts," he tells the ai hoarsely. "In the chapel, there's room to walk around without a pressure suit. Why do you have to ruin it for me with your carping?"

"It is unintentional. I have only your interests at heart."

"That's true," he admits grudgingly. "Apart from my clone son, you're probably the only person who can say that without perjuring himself."

In the strange dim light of the abyss, shadows move along the far wall. Orwen will not turn his head. Lattices of pseudolight ache in the corners of vision.

"By God, it's a good thing Feng isn't here now." He barks a laugh. "He'd take the chance to shove me into the *mise-en-abime*, the son of a bitch."

Johnny Von, distant and distorted by sleet, says in surprise: "But he *is* here. I thought you knew."

Orwen whirls. Something dark seems to move in the corridor. "Damn your flapping lying tongue! He's on Callisto!" His brother departed by ion spacecraft for a mercantile tour of the moons of Jupiter three months before, with maximum fanfare and media publicity. He has not returned since then, nor can he have completed the round-trip in that time, a journey forbidden by the immutable laws of celestial dynamics.

"Director, he's aboard the Power Station."

Outraged, Orwen bellows, "Johnny Von, why are you doing this? It can't be true. I gave express orders to deny docking facilities to all craft but my own." He spreads his arms. The dragon's wings open. His augmented fingers claw in vacuum.

"Your brother Feng did not arrive at this station by sled, my Lord."

"What! Ridiculous. The gutless bastard wouldn't risk a spacewalk." Even if his brother had done so, the Power Station's surveillance programs require the ai overseer to report such an approach. It has made no such report. Ergo, Feng is not here, cannot possibly have intruded upon his solitude.

Feng bursts into the chamber from the shadows of the elevator niche, a vengeful demon in matte black radiation armor.

On the same channel, contemptuously, he says, "Use your brains, brother."

Orwen recoils, aghast. "Johnny Von, is this a hologram you're showing me? Some demented prank?"

The two men circle each other like great heaving crustaceans. Feng Lord Cima gestures to the tortured space of the defect. Blue lightning flickers. "Pretty, isn't it?"

"How are you here, Feng?" Orwen's throat is tight, his drenched body raging with the hormones of fear and aggression.

"Surely it's obvious." Feng's tone, unbelievably, is cool, mocking, controlled. "Must I explain everything, you wretched dullard?"

"It is not obvious, bastard!" Orwen strikes a powered blow, scarlet and gold, at his brother's head. Feng lifts a dark arm, counters the blow. Shock sends its massive thud into both armored suits.

"Oh yes, brother mine, it is indeed obvious that I hexed in here through a port gate."

"Impossible." It has been known for two thousand years that no asteroid is massive enough to sustain teleportation warp. Only a planet or a star has a gravity well deep enough to bend spacetime. An asteroid is a mountain, at most a continent. It is not a world. This is the single poignant reason, after all, for the Belt's ancient isolation.

"Ah, the military mind! Boxes and categories. Your incorruptible narrowness will be the death of you, Orwen." But his right suited leg buckles as Orwen lashes viciously with his left. They recoil, recover, stand panting.

Illumination smites Orwen like a radiation burst from the Pit. "The defect itself!"

"Exactly. The Heart-Point." Feng leaps forward furiously. "You posturing martinet! Talk of courage? You toy with your blades and guns." They grapple hand to hand on the lip of nothingness. "*I* rode a geodesic on the event horizon of an active metric defect!"

Orwen breaks free, clings to a stanchion. He can scarcely credit what he is hearing, yet no other explanation seems possible. Feng cannot be here. He is here. Therefore, he has done the unthinkable. He has hexed in through the metric defect. It is an act of appalling and lunatic bravery. "Why? The risk's insane."

For a moment Feng says nothing. His rasping breath comes across the gap between them. When he speaks, his voice is chilly with decision and loathing. "How else could I get you alone to kill you without witnesses?"

Orwen screams in fury. "I'll kill you first, you treasonous son of a bitch!" He leaps murderously at his brother. They totter, locked in embrace, above the sucking void of the Bottomless Pit.

---

vii ━━━━━━━━━━━━━━━━━━━━━━━━━━━━━━━━━━━

The Justice nods her gray, distinguished head, first to the ai Gamemaster, then to the hu. Neither is physically in her immediate presence, as she stands in the center of the clearing. The tops of the trees have tilted below the Sun. Piled cumulus clouds slowly thicken the pale blue sky.

"We are gathered here this morning to celebrate the fifth infusion anniversary of Sen Telmah Cima, of the Minor Planet 16 Psyche."

"Birthday," Yazade hisses to Doony.

"He's only *five*?" Doony is scandalized. "Jeez, I can see why they outlaw gene fiddling on civilized worlds."

"Psyche years, dumbo. Five of ours for one of theirs. He's twenty-five."

"For the purposes of this most unusual entertainment," the Justice declares more loudly, frowning, her words carried by holly to the competing groups, "members of the hu team have contracted and so stipulated under notary seal to accept the central direction and authority of Sen Cima, while those of the ai team will defer likewise to Sen Ratio. Does anyone wish to withdraw consent at this penultimate point?"

The troupe is subdued. They are watchful but silent. On the far edge of the clearing, the ai team is mute. No dissent comes from their number, nor might any be expected. Aside from Ratio, the ai in ser team are low-level Gofers, servitor intelligences without great initiative or insight. They are limbs for Ratio in this contest, scarcely anything more. They can feel no resentment in their station, waiting in stolid excitement for the next call of duty.

"Very well." The Justice akses an archive, and a striking avian figurine is manifest beside her. "Your goal is the retrieval and reconstruction of a topaz ibis, here demonstrated."

"*Threskiornis aethiopica*," murmurs Yazade, drawing on a personal datachip. "The sacred bird of the ancient Egyptians. Prevalent in southern Arabia and much of the great landmass south of the Sahara greenbelt."

Its holly image rotates, life-size and magnificent. The bird is half a meter tall, long-necked, stork-legged, with a haughty down-curving Arabian beak like Yazade's own. Doony sees the comic resemblance, blats through his nostrils with a bold glance between the two. Gill cuffs him lightly, and he subsides with a muffled complaint.

"The fragments of the statue have been scattered throughout the worlds accessible by Holophrastic Exchange," the Justice explains. "Is that clear?"

"This topaz statue," Doony calls loudly, seizing his chance to regain the spotlight. "Is it—?"

"Pipe down, Doony."

"But she asked—"

"Hold your tongue." Cima is sharp. "The adjudicator's question was addressed to Sen Ratio and me. Sen Justice, I have no questions."

"Nor I." Ratio's holographic image nods, the smooth casque of ser head elegant and enigmatic.

"Very well. Listen carefully." The Justice places a pale green sash of Gestell office about her shoulders. "Each team is limited to fifteen round-trips through the Hex Gate. Each topaz fragment will be accompanied by a clue to the location of the next. However, there is a shortcut—the Grand Clue which you each hold, and which I shall now read aloud, itself contains sufficient information to locate all the pieces."

Rozz gasps in anticipation. Gill pulls her to him in a quick, fond hug. Myfanwy activates her cortical file. Doony stares at the drying grass under his toes, his lips moving mutinously.

"The Grand Clue is as follows. Please ready your datachips."

The hu do so in a general murmur. In the distance, the ai simply stand ready. Ratio gleams like a knight in full armor prepared for combat, or perhaps simply for joust.

" 'The thrice-born will close the circle,' " cries the Justice in a piercing tone.

" 'The superior is greater than the inferior,

" 'Although the unending work will be completed

" 'When the foremost has embraced the hindmost.' "

Abhinavagupta is offended. "That's just plain fascism. The superior is *not* greater than her inferior."

"Shush," says Kob, the fellow in purple. "I like it. It's silly."

"In deference to Sen Cima's aversion to teleportation," the Justice tells them in a more muted voice, "his team will operate from their present location. Sen Ratio's headquarters will be the hex station at Death Valley Four. Good luck, teams."

Cima addresses her image politely. "Thank you, Sen."

"Thanks, too, from the ai team," says Ratio's image.

"You may begin," the Justice declares and is gone from their midst. A moment later, the ai team move with silent and astonishing speed through their hex locus, a blur of sapphire light. Ratio bows once and follows them into nowhere.

Laden woolly clouds have been blowing up from the east, moving to mask the revealed Sun. The air is cooler now than at daybreak. Mounds of puffy vapor pass under the Sun, putting the hu in shade. The naked wrestlers shiver suddenly, pulling their coveralls back on.

"It'd be expecting too much to ask you mad sheep to proceed in an orderly fashion," Cima tells them in a clear, commanding, good-humored voice. "So I'll throw the floor open to random bleatings."

"Can we make a fire?" Doony whines. "I'm freezing."

"Think yourself lucky you're not in Death Valley. The answer is no. Look, try to get it into your dear little heads. We're in a race against time. The rules stipulate that we make our first move from this jump point. Our opponents are doubtless broiling in circumstances equally uncongenial for ai."

"I'd rather we were on Copacabana beach," complains unrepentant Doony.

"*Fum,*" says Rozz, smooching Gill hard on the mouth.

---

viii

The ai gofers stand in a crisp octagonal formation under the roasting Sun of desert midday. Salt pan stretches to the mountain walls, relieved here and there by mesquite. A raven screeches, lost in the glare overhead. Ratio is bathed in **Copland** from an ironic local audio feed, moody and lyrical, tagged by the ambient as **Appalachian Spring**. At least they have not stolen from sem all music.

I HAVE A FOUR-NINES COINCIDENCE CLUMP, SEN RATIO. An ai Gofer, subtly marked as a King of Clubs, makes its announcement through the cruelly narrow aks channel still permitted to Ratio. Its own plunges into the Gestell are severely limited for the duration, fair handicapping in a team contest crucially hampered by Telmah Cima's religious scruples. THE STANZA MAY REFER TO THE ANCIENT EGYPTIAN GOD KNOWN TO THE GREEKS AS THOTH OR PI-HERMES. HE WAS THE MOON DEITY, REPRESENTING THE SUN-GOD ON EARTH.

A second ai, banded in small vivid hearts and tarts, follows that logic trail through a truncated datatrellis. It observes, PI-HERMES WAS ALSO KNOWN AS HERMES THE THRICE-GREAT.

"Hm. 'Thrice-Great,' 'Thrice-Born.' A play on words. Who, then, is the Sun-God?" The actual Sun overhead blazes upon Ratio's ai card chess pieces, glaring up from quartz and salt pan. They might as easily be upon a world other than Earth. In moments, some of their number surely will be, once they have solved the cipher. Ratio nods to the Queen of Diamonds, which has signaled its own salient gloss.

HIS SACRED ANIMALS WERE THE BABOON AND THE IBIS.

"The ibis!" Ratio is delighted. "Wonderful. Our target creature."

I ADD THAT HERMES WAS ALLEGEDLY THE AUTHOR OF AN ARCHETYPAL MAGICAL EQUATION, states the Queen, TO WIT: "AS ABOVE, SO BELOW."

Ratio paces back and forth, a pointless trick se has acquired from ser hu companion. "I scent a mathematical pun. A ratio, naturally. Pi-Hermes, so it is undoubtedly *pi* itself, yes. And a Moon god. So the first world is Earth's Moon."

AN UNORTHODOX CHOICE, warns the Queen of Clubs. SURELY THE RANGE OF PROBABLE CANDIDATE WORLDS WILL CENTER ON HABITABLE EARTH-LIKE PLANETS.

"Perhaps not. The Gestell adjudicators are sly mentalities. It might amuse them to send us first to an unfashionable hex destination. But *where* on the Moon? We need precise coordinates. Trial and error would take us into the middle of next week."

TO SPECIFY ANY GEOGRAPHICAL LOCALITY REQUIRES TEN DIGITS, observes the King of Hearts. SUPPOSE WE TAKE THE FIRST TEN DIGITS OF *PI*, PREVIOUSLY CONSIDERED SIGNIFICANT AS A CLUE.

Ratio does not need to plunge for the data: the value for *pi*, accurate to a hundred million places, fills a standard nanoregister in ai hard-wired memory. "Very well," Ratio agrees. "So what might we build from 3.141592653?"

TREAT THE FIRST 3 AS EARTH, THIRD WORLD FROM THE SUN.

DISSENT. THOTH WAS A MOON GOD, the King of Clubs reminds them. SO CALL 3.1 EARTH AND MOON.

"Acceptable. But then it must switch back to the Solar planets. If the first portion of the statue is on Earth, the next is on the Moon. The third, 3.14, is therefore on Mars, fourth world from the Sun."

LOGICAL.

"The next step is 3.141, which we might accept as Mercury, the first world—ah, nice, that allows doubling up on the numeral 1, which otherwise would have been tricky. And Mercury is another name for Hermes, if that has any relevance. Yes. Next, Jupiter: 3.1415, since no asteroid is massive enough to sustain the hex geometry."

A crowd of Sun-shielded tourists has begun hexing in to watch the contestants, their sapphire hex light almost invisible under noon's glare. Politely, they keep their distance, observing through the Gestell as much as by direct sensory perception. A baby starts wailing, and its parent leaves the scene with a resigned shrug.

"Thereafter: Pluto, Venus, Saturn . . . and 5, Jupiter again. Damn. The scheme has broken down."

"I like the Clue," Rozz says complacently. "It's perfectly nuts. 'When the front has reached the back.' Sounds like that massage I offered you."

"It's just plain authoritarianism," Abhinavagupta objects once again, still angry at the idea. "I won't accept that the 'superior' is greater than her 'inferior.' Besides, how can anyone be *born* three times? Oh, sorry, Telmah. Didn't mean to give offense to your personal views."

"However ridiculous," Gill mutters.

"No offense taken, Abhi. Plenty taken, Gill. However, I've declared a free-for-all. Say whatever you care to if you think it'll help decode the Clue."

"They've probably found it and glued the bugger together by now," Gill laughs. "Right, let's start at the start. Obviously, the 'thrice-born' is our daring, darling leader Telmah."

"Unlikely," Cima says.

"Blimey, why not? Haven't you had umpteen multiple lives by now?"

Rozz throws up her hands. "Of *course* he has! Cleopatra washing her undies by the Nile, old Neapolitan the great French generalissimo marching his troops into the frozen autostradas of Berlingrad . . ."

"Unhappily, Rozz my pet, metensomatosis is not nearly so romantic."

"Say what?"

"Technical term. Not 'reincarnation.' So far it hasn't happened to me at all. I'm a Genetic construct. Brand-new soul." Insight blooms behind his eyes. "Ah! *Pi*-Hermes."

Cima bows his dark head over clenched fists for a moment, working through the implications of his intuition.

" 'The unending work,' " he mutters, "because *pi* has a non-terminating expansion."

Gill is quick to follow his insight. He consults his chip file. "3.141592653 . . ."

Rozz says instantly, "The ninth decimal place is the number 3, which brings us back to the start. So: 'when the front has reached the back.' "

"A remarkable feat of sustained deduction," says Kob. "Now, to make our day complete, one of you geniuses can tell the rest of us what to do with this silly number."

"Quiet, team." Cima claps his hands for attention, tall and intent. "I know where we're going. No pissing around needed, looking for piecemeal clues. Gill and Rozz, fetch some Heavy Pressure Atmosphere Apparel for yourselves. Abhinavagupta, light rebreathers and a warmskin suit. Myfanwy, vacuum gear. Simple heat shield, Kob. Maximum heat *and* pressure, Doony, just in case you're outside a festung. Cold shield for Yazade. Corrosion-shielded suit for Lyn. Go."

Grumbling, excited, the troupe key through the marble hex pillar, flickering to nowhere. Cima waits for their return, pacing furiously.

X ——————————————————————————

THE INTERPRETATION CAN BE MODIFIED, notes the King of Spades. IF 3.1 REPRESENTS EARTH'S MOON, AS WE ASSUME, WE CAN EQUALLY WELL INTERPRET 5.3 AS JUPITER'S THIRD MOON.

"Is it big enough to sustain the hex effect?"

THE THIRD MAJOR SATELLITE OF JUPITER IS GANYMEDE. RADIUS: 2,631 KILOMETERS. DENSITY ONLY 1.93 g/cm^3, BUT AMPLE FOR HOLO-PHRASTIC EXCHANGE DISCONTINUITY.

"Splendid. Now all we need derive are the coordinates."

CARTOGRAPHIC CONVENTION, suggests the King of Diamonds, MIGHT SUGGEST NORTHERN LONGITUDE AND LATITUDE.

Bearing a variety of protective apparel, the troupe hex back into the clearing. Cloud mounds are thickening above the trees, but the late spring day seems exempt from rain.

"What *is* all this stuff?" Doony is indignant. His gear is massive, designed to forestall heat as well as crushing pressures. "You just told me all Earth-like planets are basically the same."

"The Clue Meister's been tricky, bubba," Cima smiles. "Our itinerary sticks to the Solar. And Earth, sadly, is the only Earth-like planet in the system."

"You can't be serious." Rozz briefly probes her chip encyclopedia declarative memory. "Mars, Saturn, like that?"

"Unless my evaluation is wrong."

"Scary!" Yazade shivers. "Is it safe?"

"If the failsafes aren't working," Cima tells her with a reassuring tap on the arm, "the hex mechanism won't let you through. Besides, the Justice must have checked."

"Hmm. *If* your interpretation is right." Kob is dubious. "Let's hear your argument."

"Kob, really. Troops do *not* demand explanations from their commanding officers." Having said as much as he means to say, Cima directs his gaze around the assembled troupe. "Is all the protective clothing ready?" They brandish their gear. "Very well. Each of you will be sent to a different world. The global coordinates will be the same in each case. You will port to the hex station closest to those coordinates—even if 'closest' turns out to be half a world away."

Myfanwy is struggling into vacuum gear. Her exasperated voice is transduced to them. "But, Telmah, we don't *have* any coordinates."

"Certainly we do. Stand by to chip these figures." Cima

raises one hand. "Latitude: 31 degrees, 41 minutes, 5 seconds. Longitude: 93 degrees, 5 minutes, 3 seconds. I imagine these coordinates will apply to the Northern Hemisphere of each world. If not, we'll try the South. Everyone got that?"

There is a rousing cheer. Doony has his left foot stuck in the massive right boot of his pressure system. Abhinavagupta pulls it out for him, turns him right way around.

"Very good. Rozz, some stirring music?" Almost at once, their local audio feed plays them the stirring, satirical refrain, *I Am a Pirate King*, from Gilbert and Sullivan's The Pirates of Penzance (1880). Cima grins with fiendish enjoyment. "Excellent choice. Myfanwy, your destination is Luna."

"Huh?" She has never heard of such a place. "I thought you said the Solar?"

"Earth's Moon. Abhinavagupta, Mars. Kob, Mercury. Gill, great Jupiter himself. In and out, Gill—even on a flotation island, the gravity will be crushing. Yazade, Pluto. Doony, Venus. Rozz, Saturn. Gravity will be taxing for you, too, I'm afraid. Lyn, Ganymede."

"Never heard of it."

"Jupiter's third moon. The last piece, I think, will be on Earth. Myfanwy can retrieve that one as well. A suitable return of the foremost to the hindmost, no?"

"Wonderful, Telmah." Rozz shakes her head in admiration, clapping her hands. "I could kiss you."

"No time, Rozz. Go, all of you."

_____

xii ———————————————————————————————————————

Myfanwy steps with an upward jolt from cloudy early summer's daybreak in the southern hemisphere of Earth to the eternal starry sky of the Joliot-Curie central Hex Station, under dome on the librating boundary of lunar Nearside and Farside. Surprised by one-sixth gravity, she bounces clumsily, falls with the slowness of dream, catches herself on the outstretched fingers of one suited hand. The vacuum suit, of course, is redundant. Gigantic arctic ice orchids bloom from hydrated pots of lunar soil. A crocodile of naked kindergarten children in febrile body-paint, from the Vegetable Tribe, stop in their tracks to gape at her lumpish form, laughing and pointing. Through the transparent geodesic dome, Earth's pale blue bow curves its horns into the crater's jagged rim at the horizon. The stars are washed out by diffuse light in the cozy crater.

Grunting, Myfanwy unlocks her helmet and throws it back. The Moon's air is less rich than she is used to and slightly cooler than the stuff she has just been breathing in the clearing. The children's laughter is eerily pitched. She waves once and then rudely ignores them, staring about, hunting for a clue or, better yet, a piece of the ibis.

"Over there," yells a little hu stained to look like a pumpkin.

The thing is standing, literally, atop a temporary plinth at the base of the monumental statue of Irène Curie and her husband Jean-Frédéric Joliot. Each holds a radioactivity trefoil in one hand, an olive branch in the other. They are sadly wasted by the diseases that killed them.

Myfanwy kangaroo-bounds to the plinth. In gold cursive a quotation reads: *I prithee, make us quick in work*.

" 'Prithee'?" she mutters, dazed. Then, in satisfaction, she crows. "He was right! Damned if I know what it means, but here's the piece of the bird I need. 'Quick in work' is right."

One leg of the broken ibis, top-heavy, stands elegantly if absurdly under translucent glass.

She flips the glass, seizes the topaz limb, bounces back to the nearest hex pillar. It shimmers as a Gofer plunges out of its sapphire radiance, past her, orients itself in an instant, sees the topaz fragment in her hands, the opened casket. It rushes to the rifled plinth, scans the clue. Myfanwy vanishes, back to Earth with her trophy, as the gofer patches its crippled search engine into the Gestell. The King of Diamonds consults an expanded quotation display.

"NOW, MARS, I PRITHEE, MAKE US QUICK IN WORK," it notes, "THAT WE WITH SMOKING SWORDS MAY MARCH FROM HENCE, TO HELP OUR FIELDED FRIENDS! COME, BLOW THY BLAST." The ai nods to the noble, ruined hu statuary figures, ambiguous heroes of radio-activity. BLOW THY BLAST, INDEED, it muses.

The Gofer spins, leaps to the hex pillar, reappears in Death Valley.

I REGRET TO REPORT THAT I WAS ANTICIPATED, it reports to Ratio, uploading. THE CLUE, HOWEVER, CONFIRMS YOUR ANALYSIS.

"Mars," muses the ai. "I knew it! We may accelerate our search." Se dispatches each of the remaining seven Gofers to a different world, reserving Earth for semself.

---

xiii

Abhinavagupta arrives in Utopia Planitia on Mars near deep peach sunset. His eyes burn with the dusty, blowing chill. In the frigid twilight, he pulls up his breathing mask without de-lay. On the cratered horizon, the red setting Sun is half the size of the rising Sun he has just left behind. Despite millennia of diligent terraforming, Mars has all but reverted, except in the last foaming waters of deep-cut Valles Marineris, to its an-cient barren vacancy. The world is all but emptied of hu or ai presence, patrolled only by scientific sensing machines and madly Romantic poets.

Three hairy Dust Beavers are tearing at something beside a dry unfinished *Faux* canal. There is little else to attract his attention. He runs at the mutated animals. Startled, they dash apart, bare their serrated teeth at him, slapping their flat tails in the slow dust. He menaces them with terrible gestures. One of them drops the thing from its mouth.

Abhinavagupta picks it out of the red dust, wipes it clean. It is the left breast of a topaz bird. The deeply stupid animals have taken it for what it represents and then, unable to eat it, have quarreled anyway.

Their howls are almost inaudible, to hu ears at least, in the thin Martian air. The trouper activates his flashlight, casts its beam into their huge crimson eyes. They shriek, leaping high in the modest gravity, snapping at their flanks and scaly tails, and bolt away.

Facing outward from the hex pillar toward the sunset, he finds a plinth directly beneath a bright doubled star. The star, he realizes with a shock, is Earth and Moon, rising. Clutching the ibis fragment, Abhinavagupta treads dull red rock to the smashed casket. Gold words are inscribed: *With his beaver on.*

He laughs, almost choking in his rebreather mask, unable to decode the clue but certain that Cima will understand. Without a backward glance, he hexes to the clearing on Earth where his Gamemaster waits.

xiv

The sky is absolutely black, and black ice rises all around him. Incredulous, Kob shivers at the sight of it, although his thermal garb protects him from all extremes of temperature.

"I wanted Mercury," he protests to the hex addressing system. "You've sent me to the wrong planet. Hot as buggery is what I want. You know, Mercury—the closest planet to the Sun." He is almost sure that is right.

Kob has expected to find the Sun, huge and burning in a sky blending coronal fire and darkness, scorching a near-molten landscape at three or four hundred degrees Celsius on a world whose day is twice as long as its year. Instead, he stands in a crater shadowed by immense lava-splashed walls, choked with vast dark glaciers. Ambient temperature is significantly below zero. And there is some atmosphere: the stars in the great blackness overhead are frosty and twinkling.

This is the Mercury South Polar Research Station in Chao Meng-Fu crater, the machine reports. *You have been directed to the single safe Holophrastic Exchange locus still in operation on the world you requested. There is an elevator to the crater rim wall lookout.*

"Oh, okay, that's cool." He takes an experimental step. The world's pull is noticeably less than he is accustomed to—perhaps as little as a third of Earth's gravity. His position is appallingly exposed. Off to his left, a crumpled structure of thermal insulation and steel is crushed into the icescape, smashed by some catastrophe of war or nature and never repaired. Few ai or hu retain any interest in planetary exploration, with an entire galaxy of Earth-like worlds a moment away beyond the hex locus.

Shivering in distress, traumatized by this desolation, Kob gazes for the clue he is meant to obtain. It stands in the cold darkness on a plinth: a fragment of the topaz bird and a golden inscription. He cranes to read the words: *This shall not be revok'd.*

" 'This'? " he says through chattering teeth. "This mad lump of ice in some socket of the solar furnace? Telmah, you bastard, you've got the weirdest sense of humor I've ever met. You and your loony Gamemaster pal. Oh well."

He opens the casket carefully. The topaz fragment is inert in the bright light of his lamps. Hunched, he turns back to the hex locus and warming Earth.

"I SAW YOUNG HARRY WITH HIS BEAVER ON, HIS CUSHES ON HIS THIGHS, GALLANTLY ARM'D, RISE FROM THE GROUND LIKE FEATHERED MERCURY," one Gofer reports in full, while another, returning almost in the same instant from the planet mentioned, displays: "THE MOMENT IS THY DEATH. AWAY! BY JUPITER, THIS SHALL NOT BE REVOK'D." Both are empty-handed. Ratio is amused by the skill of ser opponents, the canny insight of their Gamemaster, the whimsy of the Justice and Gestell adjudicators who set these puzzles. Se is elated as well, for ser own team's deductions are certainly being borne out.

"Jupiter is next," se says confidently. "And after that, Pluto."

Crushed into his survival shell, Gill gasps in painful rapture. Earth is gone, and a world greater than he has ever imagined hangs beneath him, visible in full-display imaging on every surface of the flotation raft.

The pellucid air allows him to see for hundreds of kilometers in every direction. For an instant he chokes, understanding only too vividly that this pure air is really hydrogen gas. The layered J. M. W. Turner (1775–1851) grandiloquence of cloud upon cloud under boiling cloud, golden and glaring white and reddened and brown as soot, is ammonia and ammonium hydrosulfide. He will perish in an instant if the raft hull is breached. In the achingly lovely blue sky overhead, a crescent moon catches the small Sun's diminished light. Another hangs beyond it, somewhat smaller. This is a kind of paradise, a storming terror of beauty.

Gill drags himself from rapture to the task at hand.

"The clue," he badgers himself. "On your toes, laggard."

There is little chance he will ever rise to his feet under this massive imposed weight, but smooth servos attach to his shell and amplify his every move. One hand lashes too rapidly at a casket set upon a plinth, is caught by the small stupid machines that govern it, held from smashing what it reaches for.

"The damned bird's head!" Gill is elated. He snatches it out, holds it up to the glorious light. He sees a line of verse in cursive at the base of the glass casket.

"What's this? A jape? 'From earth's dark womb some gentle gust doth get.' Can't be right. Didn't Cima send Yazade to . . ."

As he muses, an ai Gofer emerges from the hex locus. Their paths cross. Penitent, Gill activates his shell's servos, thrusts himself and the head of the ibis into sapphire nothingness, leaving the Queen of Hearts to study the Justice's enigmatic citation.

━━━ xvii ━━━━━━━━━━━━━━━━━━━━━━━━━━━━━━━━━━

"Earth?" Ratio is baffled. Ser scheme suggests the very edge of the Solar as the next step. Earth itself is surely part of the pattern, but by ser accounting of the Grand Clue it must come last in the sequence.

I HAVE FOUND THE REFERENCE, the Queen tells sem. "FROM EARTH'S DARK WOMB SOME GENTLE GUST DOTH GET, WHICH BLOWS THESE PITCHY VAPORS FROM THEIR BIDING, HIND'RING THEIR PRESENT FALL BY THIS DIVIDING; SO HIS UNHALLOWED HASTE HER WORDS DELAYS, AND MOODY PLUTO WINKS WHILE ORPHEUS PLAYS."

"Yes! I was correct. Pluto is next, as I predicted. A damnably bleak citation, though." Ratio broods on lines shown by the display. " 'A swallowing gulf that even in plenty wanteth.' Is the Gestell trying to tell us something? Or is this more of Cima's fabled psychic synchronicity?"

Everything is terrifyingly dark. A flashlight globe hangs in the star-strewn sky. Yazade, light-headed from the fractional gravity, sees with a jolt that the lamplight is actually the Sun, which glistens in a pale puddle on the frozen methane lake before her. In a single step, she has walked to the outer boundary of the Solar.

Something dark, but not so dark as the endless night, floats on the horizon at her left. Charon, she realizes, Pluto's dumb little moon. Not so little, either. From here, the worldlet looms six times as large as the Moon in her own world's sky. She holds up her hand and barely blocks the doleful thing from view.

"Well named," she tells the horrible worlds. "Talk about death before dishonor! And speaking of dishonor, where's that bloody clue?"

To her right, something shadowy rises from an icy ridge. Yazade crabs to it, touches the glass casket which shatters in a spray of crystals. The bird fragment is wrapped in insulation. Words chase across the intact base: *The heart-blood of beauty*.

"Blood?" she asks herself, and the words ring inside her heavy helmet. "That's Mars, the planet of war. But Abhinava-gupta's been to Mars already, hasn't he? Oh, Telmah, I think you've blown it. Too bad."

She vanishes into the hex field with her trophy. A moment later, the King of Hearts appears. Its tough skin sparkles faintly as the moisture in the layer of air it carries on its surface, even from the blazing heat of Death Valley, freezes in the Plutonian night and puffs away into the vacuum.

"Not Mars," Cima explains. "Venus. I know that phrase, a beautiful phrase: 'Marry, sir, at the request of Paris my lord, who is there in person; with him the mortal Venus, the heart-blood of beauty, love's invisible soul.'"

Yazade is obstinate. She pouts. "I don't know, Telmah. It says 'Paris,' too, doesn't it? That's an ancient city in the northern hemisphere. There's a lot of old art there."

"Earth is last on the list," Cima tells her with a smile. "Trust me."

"Well, what's all that about marrying? An old asteroid sex custom, isn't it? And who's this invisible cutie, eh, answer me that? Who's this 'heart-blood of beauty,' eh? Is this some woman he's marrying? And who is it we're talking about here anyway, Telmah? I do beg your pardon, whom? Anyone we know?" She digs him in the ribs. "Invisible or just plain inaccessible?"

Cima looks thoughtful. "Out of the mouths of babes and innocents, Yazade."

Fantastic cacophony meets Doony. The air beyond the walls is a crushing ocean, and the yellow ocean is all one awful realm of thunder and lightning. Smashing and crashing smites his eardrums despite the protective festung dome that reaches overhead, holding at bay a grotesque atmosphere of carbon dioxide and sulfuric acid.

"Shit!" Doony jumps as a thunderclap detonates in his face,

red light ripping through the scorched volcanic air pressing down upon the festung.

"Calm down, Sen." A passing ai has paused. "Can I help you, citizen? You look bamboozled."

"I'm lost," Doony bleats.

"Lost?" The ai falls silent. "I'm sorry, I don't understand. Plunge to the Gestell and seek directions. Follow the same procedure you would use back on Earth."

"How did you know I'm from Earth?" Doony checks his clothing suspiciously.

"Where else would you be from? Nobody from the galaxy remembers that we're here on Venus."

"Oh. I can't, Sen. I'm a *Fauve*," he says with a little strut, "and we, um, *resile* from high technology."

"I see. Well, good luck, young man. I wouldn't try to leave the Tellus Regio festung in those clothes, however."

"What's *wrong* with my— Of course I wouldn't try to—" Doony catches the eye of another handsome young hu, and drifts off. Striving mightily, he recalls his attention to duty. He tells the hu, "Uh, I'm looking for a bird."

"No birds on Venus, dear."

"Not a flying bird, a thing. Like, an art thing."

"Well, I happened to notice a curious plinth set up on the other side of the Celestial Stone Garden. May I show you the way?"

"Sure. You know, thanks, Sen."

"My pleasure."

The golden writing is ominous: *My deadly-standing eye.* The single ibis leg falls over when he grabs for it. He shoves it in his pocket and starts back to the hex locus.

"Could I interest you in a bite? To eat?"

He is badly tempted. "Yes. No. Not just yet."

"Some errands to run, eh?"

Grateful, Doony nods and shakes his naked head at once. "I'll be back in a flash. The thing of it is, I'm on a quest."

"I'm impressed. And I wouldn't dream of interfering." The hu gives him a big wet kiss on the mouth. Doony is dazed and grins like a fool.

"Back in a flash."

He fails to see the Gofer, empty-handed but bearing the clue message, slip past and zap through the hex field slightly ahead of him.

---

xxi ────────────────────────────────────

Cima feels a chill as he examines the full text of the clue Doony has fetched back from Venus. It announces a trajectory from joy to despair, from youth to old age. From life, in fact, to death.

" 'Madam,' " Cima murmurs, " 'though Venus govern your desires, Saturn is dominator over mine. What signifies my deadly-standing eye, My silence and my cloudy melancholy, My fleece of woolly hair that now uncurls Even as an adder when she doth unroll To do some fatal execution?' "

He stares wildly about him. His own hair tries to stand on end.

"Venus to Saturn, by Jesus and Allah! Something is prodding me. This is more than an arbitrary quest. Ratio, you bastard, you're in collusion with the Gestell adjudicators. The bird of immortality!" He laughs, a hard explosive sound that alarms the returned troupe members gathered eagerly, caught up in the spirit of the thing, to do his bidding. "My God, something serious is in play here, and I don't like it. I don't like it one bit."

Clumsy in support suiting, Rozz steps into what she expects will be the crushing gravity of an open flotation raft in Saturn's high, hazy atmosphere. Instead, her weight is reduced by three-quarters. She moves lightly from the hex pillar to an awesome display holly covering the wall before her.

The gas giant turns, golden, vast as half the sky. Pale sunlight crosses as if from behind her, strikes the infinite plane of shimmering champagne white in which her viewpoint hovers, spears a million long shadows like spokes across the thousand rings.

"I requested the North Polar Saturn Flotation Station," she complains weakly.

Stations in Saturn atmosphere are no longer operational, the hex machine advises her through her minimal chip. *You have been transferred to the closest general address, on Titan.*

She peers at the display. Isn't Titan meant to be all liquid ethane and methane and big storms and natural gas downpours, or is that Triton, or something? And surely the rings are way too close, and the golden giant is looming and tumbling toward her—

"That's not Titan!" she cries. "I mean—"

The selected diorama is tromping a view from Prometheus. Would you care to view the spectacle from a position a million kilometers above the north pole?

Rozz feels her muscles cramp, her heart accelerate in sudden superstitious fright.

"Prometheus?" she yelps. "Don't be silly! That planet broke up, what was it, four billion years ago, I mean before life even bloody started on Earth. What are you trying to tell—"

I apologize for the nominal confusion, the drone declares. *You are seeing Saturn as viewed from Prometheus, the minor shepherd satellite of the narrow F ring. It was allocated its name in ancient times, before the history of the Solar was fully understood.*

Everywhere she looks in the trompe, Rozz finds planes of smashed ice. It is magnificent and daunting. Through the mist, the striped limb of Saturn refracts its golden bow. She peers at the dim moonscape of Prometheus visible in the holographic projection, augmented by her minimal chip. The horizon seems a handbreadth away. The moon is surely no more than a hundred kilometers from pole to pole. Turning, she finds a second matching display that reveals the rings' colossal hoop and the solid worlds that orbit within and beyond its majesty.

For Rozz the glory of the vista is emotionally overwhelming. She bursts into tears.

Sniffing, she blunders in her unnecessary gear across the stark chamber. The Justice and adjudicators have gone to a lot of trouble for this performance. No mechanisms are visible, no creature comforts for hu or ai. Perhaps the secluded room is part of an art gallery. A curious plinth, apparently real, stands at the far side of the chamber, bearing a glass-encased fragment of the topaz ibis. Rozz draws it out, finds and reads a message through messy eyelashes: *My new mistress's brother.*

Her heart contracts in renewed fright, although she does not know why. Empathy, she decides. Magical sympathy with that lovely man Telmah.

──────

xxiii ────────────────────────────────

Ratio is astonished.

"This tells me something about Psyche," se murmurs.

NOT PSYCHE ASTEROID, counsels the Queen of Spades. YOUR ORIGINAL CONJECTURE IS SUSTAINED. THIS IS A CLUE TO GANYMEDE, THIRD MOON OF JUPITER.

"Yes." Ratio cannot deny the gofer's interpretation, but it is only the most superficial level of the truth. "I mean something deeper." Se broods upon the setting of the quotation. " 'That is another simple sin in you: to bring the ewes and the rams together, and to offer to get your living by the copulation of cattle; to be bawd to a bell-wether, and to betray a she-lamb of a twelvemonth to crooked-pated, old, cuckoldly ram, out of all reasonable match. If thou beest not damn'd for this, the devil himself will have no shepherds; I cannot see else how thou shouldst scape.' "

THIS IS NOT THE CORRECT CITATION, insists the Queen, WHICH IS AS FOLLOWS: "HERE COMES YOUNG MASTER GANYMEDE, MY NEW MISTRESS'S BROTHER."

"You are correct," Ratio tells it, "but alas, I am more correct. Go, go. To Ganymede."

Se recalls the first sight se ever had of Telmah Cima, arrogant, dreadfully young, vulnerable, furious. Se remembers, as well, Tsin's sarcastic appraisal of Asteroid polity: "Kill the king, steal his wife, steal the throne . . ." It was clear even then that Feng had designs upon the throne of his brother Orwen and certainly harbored a dynastic and perhaps lecherous ambition for Orwen's Genetic wife. Ewes and rams together, Ratio reflects in horror. Something is under way. Something terrible and fated.

Cut off from ser Gestell, ser loving ai family, ser full self, Ratio waits in pent expectation for the worst to befall them all.

---

xxiv ────────────────────────────────

Ganymede is ice and dirt, melted, refrozen, cracked, folded, grooved, raked. Lyn steps up from the grassy summer clearing on Earth and bounces in a gravity only a fifth of that which a world should properly own. This world is pale and dark. She turns slowly in her old-fashioned vacuum gear, looking for the huge boiling shield of Jupiter. It is nowhere visible in the dark sky, although a pair of moons hangs in the blackness.

With a clutch of fright, she realizes that half the sky is, in fact, missing.

"Where are the stars?" she shrieks, and then catches herself. Of course, the stars are not gone. Jupiter stands between her world and the Sun, eclipsing its light and blocking out half the universe.

In the darkness, using her lamps, she locates a plinth. Part of the bird is upon it. There is no message.

XXV

Myfanwy finds herself amid a clamor of gaudily clad worshippers at the foot of a great layer cake temple, the restored **Potala Palace** in **Lhasa**, winter residence of the **Dalai Lama**, at the top of the world in **Tibet**. She gasps for air. The hex system has warned her that her destination is elevated more than three and a half kilometers above sea level, but she has ignored its advice to wear a face mask. Her antrums sting.

All the devotees are ai, enthusiasts of the **Syncretic Tantra Sect**. They adopt extravagant *mudras*, sacred postures, and twirl in figured dances that map the Universal Mandala. Ai of a hundred humanoid and other functional forms, tromping gods, demons and hu, strike hand drums and resonant bells, beautiful and world-filling. Their song is powerfully affecting. Myfanwy gawks. She has never witnessed ai in any of their diverse religious practices before, has never given the matter a moment's thought, in fact. The bells resound, reverberant, like the vast index finger of some deity rubbing music from the crystal rim of the world's bowl. Surely this acoustic performance is the least part of their devotions, their communion. Within the infinite dataplanes of the Gestell, their endless wheeling prayer must rise like white smoke, like smoke made in a thousand hues and fragrances.

Staring wildly, she stumbles over a skinny goat munching weeds by the sidewalk. The animal bleats, offended. Myfanwy laughs uncontrollably.

"It's over this side," an ai tells her.

She jumps. "Christ, don't do that! I thought it was the Abominable Methane Man."

"It's cold, but not that cold. You are on Earth, after all."

"I realize that," she snaps. "The Himalayas. Oh bugger! You're my opponent."

"I am Ratio, Sen. Don't abandon hope just yet. Look behind me."

The last fragment of the bird, its backside and tail feathers carved in topaz, squats derisively within frosty glass. Myfanwy tenses to run, then shrugs.

The ai Gamemaster, too, stands where se is. "Come on, I'll race you for it."

"I'm fundamentally not a very competitive person, Ratio."

"Oh well, the race is as often to the fair as to the swift." Se trudges across the crowded tessellations, careful not to intrude upon the swaying Tantric worshippers in their flapped caps and bizarre masks, and plucks the ridiculous object from its plinth. Bowing, se gallantly offers it to Myfanwy.

"A gift."

"Well, I never! Gallantry! Our monstrous leader will not be pleased."

"How so? It completes the task."

"True, but I've heard a rumor," Myfanwy smirks, "that the ferocious Asteroid folk swear only by 'Nature red in tooth and claw'!" She brandishes her trophy aloft and does not offer to return it.

Everything blends. Everything mixes. Time is out of joint. Or-wen and Feng battle furiously, slamming at each other with terrible, powered karate blows. The Bottomless Pit yearns for them. Johnny Von moans piteously. Telmah Cima, asleep while awake in the summer clearing on Earth, watches his team assemble the topaz ibis. All is in place except for the damned bird's arse. Typical. He smiles and in some almost ignorable corner of his eye watches his father fall, plunging into a distorted spacetime that flattens his armored dragon body as he falls. Somehow Cima hears his father's dopplering, sluggish scream. Orwen's face is squashed, narrowed, spurting blood through the split mirrorsuit. The superconducting helmet cracks open. Every protection is peeled away. Orwen's eyes are bloody, appalled. They spurt like squeezed grapes and are blind.

Telmah Lord Cima screams, clutching his face.

"Orwen! Father?"

In the clouded summer clearing, he crashes to the grass in the same posture as his endlessly dying clone father.

Rozz peers down at Cima, concerned.

His voice is muffled. "I thought I— My father—"

"Come on, lover, up you come." She hoists him, her small hands under his left armpit, while Gill takes his right. They get him tottering to his feet. His face is drained, ghastly. "Gave us all a tiny fright."

Ratio and Myfanwy emerge from the hex. The ai reaches for

Cima's limp hand, seeking the minute energy fields of a living organism.

"My biomonitors detect nothing wrong with him."

"Really." Rozz is relieved and masks it with her usual scathing banter. "He just thought it'd be amusing to throw himself on the ground in a dead faint?"

Patiently, Ratio tells her, "I'm certain there's an explicit cause for Telmah's condition. For that reason I think we should hex him directly to a hospital, despite his scruples. My point was that further diagnosis is beyond the capacity of my inbuilt monitors."

Cima shakes off their supporting hands. He scowls.

"Stop talking about me as if I weren't here. Yazade, get me a maser link through Solar Telecommunications to Psyche Asteroid Central. Sen Ratio, I apologize for disrupting our contest. Kindly convey my regrets to the Gestell adjudicators and the Justice. Rozz, Gill, could you wrap this up? My father has . . ." He breaks off, confused. "Something terrible has . . ."

The hu troupe glance from one to another, deeply troubled. A holly solidifies in their midst, revealing a glacial beauty at a desk of lights.

"Central Telecommunications, Telmah."

"Thank you, Yazade." To the being in the cube, whether machine or organism, veridical or simulated, he says with controlled politeness, "Please patch me direct to Asteroid Psyche."

"Direct, Sen? I'm sorry, but traffic at the moment—"

Testily, he interrupts her. "I agree to pay the loading for realtime transmission."

"Apologies, citizen. The Asteroid 16 Psyche is in Superior Conjunction. Hence, line-of-sight between Earth and Psyche is temporarily eclipsed by the Sun. I recommend—"

"P. C. W. *Davies*!" Cima blasphemously roars. "What's the probability of that coinciding with this soul-forsaken day! A million to one?"

"To the contrary, Sen. The odds are just one in 3652."

Rozz rolls her eyes, mutters sotto voce, "Really? No decimal points?"

"Psyche's period is 4.999 Earth years," the reception display announces unsmilingly. "Consequently, Earth and Asteroid Psyche are in Superior Conjunction once in every five years. Due to the inclination of 16 Psyche to the ecliptic plane, however, the Sun stands between the two approximately once in every ten years during the present—"

Cima's features darken with rage. "If the goddamned Sun is in the way, *go around it*."

The gorgeous face in the holly remains unruffled. "Feasible, citizen, but not recommended. A maser message could be retransmitted through Mars, but complete round-trip time today would be sixty-eight minutes."

A display pop-up shows the unyielding geometry of Solar spacetime. At the speed of light, the Sun is a little more than eight minutes away, a single astronomical unit from Earth. Psyche hangs some three AUs beyond the Sun. Mars, too, like Psyche, orbits at this moment on the Sun's far side. Viewed from galactic north, the two worlds stand at an angle of about 170 degrees. At least the Sun's million-kilometer nuclear-fusion sphere will not block a maser message relayed through Mars.

"Alternatively, a message sent Jupiter–Psyche, Psyche–Jupiter, Jupiter–Earth would involve two and a half hours' lag for the round-trip." The diagram shows Jupiter currently at a little under six AU from Earth, an additional three from Psyche. "I suggest—"

"You're being ridiculous. Bounce a beam off a passive communications satellite."

The cool features show mild astonishment. "My goodness, Sen, that facility has not existed in some millennia. Comsats are maintained only locally in the Belt and between very minor moons too small to sustain Holophrastic Exchange operation.

But really, the minimax solution to your difficulties is extremely simple."

Seething, Cima brings himself with difficulty under control. He smiles tightly. "I shouldn't have shouted at you, Sen. Please tell me."

Her eyebrows go up. "Why, call direct from Mars. That's only twenty-five minutes for a signal there and back."

"He can't do that!" cries Rozz, outraged on Cima's behalf. "It's forbidden by his—" But he has already cut the contact. The holly cube blinks out.

"Hex to . . ." Cima growls. He shakes his head like a man struck a terrible blow, as if apprehending the certainty of his own execution, or his damnation. "Christ, the shock has numbed my brain. To Mars, then."

The troupe gape at him. He strides to the hex pillar, places his right hand above its upper surface. His face is agonized. In great fear, he withdraws his hand, stares at it intently, seemingly determined to memorize its very bones and fiber, and at last forces himself to return it to the pillar. He is trembling violently.

Destination, Sen Cima?

His voice grinds. "Mars Telecommunications, Syrtis Public Facility."

The hex field flashes sapphire. He is gone.

Doony says plaintively, "What about his immortal soul?"

Abhinavagupta puts one brotherly arm around the boy's shoulders. "There are no theists in foxholes, Doons."

"Huh?"

"Old hu saying." He shrugs. "The ai might have a different opinion."

Gill is bleak, staring at the empty hex stage. "Immortal soul? Let me assure you, babe, if I were his mortal enemy, I'd start running right about now."

Mars Syrtis is a deserted branch office, home to a despised and
exhausted technology and happy to flaunt the fact. It lacks windows, which after all would show only a dishearteningly stark
marscape of eroded craters, decayed terraforming canals, orange wilderness, disturbing sky. Cima bursts from the hex field,
finds himself before a fanciful wicker sketch of an early 20th
office counter. Three pale-skinned hu loiter in drab basic briefs
on the other side of the counter, taking their ease in anachronistic gas-cylinder swivel office chairs.

Cima's chip asks him, *Trompe and Eidolon Sketch: Y/N?*
"Yes."

The four-vaned fan turns slowly overhead, thrumming
faintly.

A nightmarish blend of Kafka and Escher has replaced the
blank walls. In grainy monochrome, rank upon rank of teleg-
raphists and telephonists ply their trade, listening in a hyp-
notized fugue to clumsy Bakelite headsets clamped across their
high-piled buns, murmuring into trumpets slung at mouth
height, switching jacked cords in row upon row of varnished
boards. Small bulbs light and fade. There is a clamor of ringing
and low-pitched mumbling. It is a fantasy of the birth of media
and telecommunications, a frightful celebration of daily working life before the advent of smart machines.

"Excuse me."

The lounging hu attendants note with distaste a customer's
arrival and respond in the manner proper to a hierarchical
undertaking. A grandiose engraved brass plaque on the rear
wall announces that this is the CONSOLIDATED EMPLOYERS' LOCAL,
417 ("Every Sen a Chief, None an Indian"). The Employers ignore him.

Cima's minimal trompe chip paints one as a Kuomintang Matriarch of the 25th. As the eidolon kicks in, her golden skin grows sallow, sags, and wrinkles into the lineaments of powerful respect. Her primrose *ch'ao-fu*, bright with waves, mountains, and clouds, reaches majestically from flared epaulets under its prim constricted neckband to horse-hoof cuffs at the ends of tubular sleeves. The Matriarch stitches ineffectually at a sampler advertising the merits of Cleanliness and Hard Toil.

Puffing a smokeless cigar, a Banker or perhaps an Industrialist has a red, sweating face half-hidden by muttonchop whiskers. He peers suspiciously at Cima through rimless glasses, straightens his rather dashing four-in-hand, taps at his Capitalist's topper.

The third is appalling in shapeless Gates wig, late-20th Nerd jeans and checked shirt, crowded pen protector in upper left pocket.

The Matriarch finds no reason to interrupt her conversation. "No, I'd choose one of the new planets. Virgin worlds, Uri calls them." Her mouth purses at the indecency. "He's planning to homestead when we've completed our Duty."

"All right for some!" The Robber Baron is envious. He smooths his whiskers with a pudgy hand.

"But you'll still come back here on Thursday nights for the bingo, won't you?" Rocking back and forth in his chair, the Nerd seems likely to throw himself bodily onto the floor.

"Uri miss his Thursday night bingo? Pioneering is all very well, but if he got *that* obsessive, I'd soon put my foot—"

Cima leans forward on the notional counter, now an impressive oak structure carved with cornucopias from which tumble grapes, apples, corn, and rice, and an abundance of chubby livestock. It creaks as he leans on it. He is being stymied by the absurd make-work theatrics of a hu Special Interest Group addicted to the lost satisfactions of rote labor. In his confused guilt and grief, he sees that it might have been quicker to send his message from Earth, after all.

"At your convenience, Sen," he calls crisply.

They look at him resentfully, return to their nattering.

"Some people!" The Capitalist sniffs.

"Uri's a dreamer, though, always has been." Adjusting her stole and contriving to shield Cima from her eyeline, the woman settles comfortably back into her office chair. "I remember when we were just kids, he'd—"

"If you please!" Cima is sharp. "I have an urgent call to place to Psyche."

"Hold your damned horses," snaps the Nerd. "It's the middle of the night. You can't expect to just hex in here whenever it takes your fancy and have us drop everything and jump to your command, boyo! If it's that urgent, do what everyone else does and plunge to the Gestell. Otherwise, there's a seat over there." He turns back to his companions, shaking his head in disbelieving sadness. "I tell you, the sort of selfish—"

Livid but contained, Cima whirls, steps to the hex station, holds his hand near the pillar.

Destination, Sen Cima?

"My apartment."

Although his ideology and faith forbid its use by the faithful, the hex facility has never been removed from the customary alcove in his rooms, retained for the benefit of infidels and ai. As the hex field on Mars flashes its sapphire, he stands at once in a stream of hot subcontinental sunlight from a real glazed window, opened at his request through the tromped sandstone wall of his living quarters. Shah Jagan's Taj Mahal mausoleum shimmers gloriously pale against dazzling cloud billows. The legendary and heartbreakingly beautiful complex has been in the possession of the Psyche Recombinant Engineering Cartel for many centuries.

Cima does not linger to admire its splendor. He storms into his bedroom, throws wide a teak cabinet door inlaid with pearl and tile. On a high shelf is a long bundle he has not touched for years, carefully wrapped. He takes it down, carefully unfolds the silk cloth.

It is a gorgeous *katana*, his father's gift, brought to Earth from the Belt as it had been fetched to the Belt millennia ago from Earth. He draws it whispering from its scabbard. It is slightly curved, a polished samurai warrior's sword, hideously lethal. He strides back to his domestic hex locus. Light reflecting from the mausoleum's tranquil white Makrana marble gleams on the naked blade.

Destination, Sen Cima?

"Back to Mars," he tells it, unsure of the appropriate formula. A tremor of rage and metaphysical anguish unsettles his right arm as the blue web flashes. His imperiled soul! The tip of the *katana* falls slightly outside the perimeter of the hex field. Sapphire radiance freezes, with the point of the sword visibly jutting through it.

The hex mechanism tells him, *Sen, transition cannot be effected while the external field boundaries are broached. Please check your perimeter.*

With a furious curse, Cima wrenches the sword inside the blue web of light. Instantly, he stands in the Mars Telecommunication office.

"—so ill-mannered these days," the Capitalist is complaining. "Of course, that one's probably from the fascist Asteroids, I shouldn't be surprised . . . Oh, you're back, are you? You still have to wait your— Hoy, what have you got there—"

In a cold rage, Cima crosses the floor, bouncing slightly in the unaccustomed weak gravity. It makes him feel quite at home after the endless dreary tug of Earth. He swings the ancient sword high over his head and brings it down in three lashing blows. The office is filled with splintered wickerwork. He kicks the ruin aside and marches to his tormentors, carefully holding the weapon unthreateningly by his side.

"I have an urgent call to place to Psyche Asteroid."

The booth is elegantly spare. Cima kneels upright on a small ergonomic seat, braced by supports under his arms, facing half a coffee table that juts from a blank wall. Across his forehead, stretching as far as his temples, he wears a filigree of metal.

"Putting you through now," says a resentful, frightened voice.

The blank wall is gone, replaced by the matching half of the coffee table. Thrillingly lovely, a young woman floats behind a similar chair. Her feathered hair is cinched by a circlet. Once a second, a small clock like a jewel ticks on its face. The Warrior Rose is a strikingly mutated Genetic, all but nude, wildly striped in a tiger's yellow and black. A magnificent damask rose (**R. damascena**) blooms from her left shoulder. Unsurprisingly, as an elite Genetic she powerfully resembles Gerutha, Telmah Cima's X chromosome donor. Still, the double shock of recognition brings tears stinging to his eyes.

"Telmah!" she cries happily. "How lovely! Happy Soul Day."

At once she recalls the bone she has to pick with him and air-vamps into her chair, locks herself in, regarding his image down her aquiline nose. "Actually, you sod, I'm not sure I'm talking to you. This is the first time in two months you've deigned to call, you realize? And that was a squirt-burst posting on BeltNet—as usual. So how *are* the fallen-arched floozies on Earth, then?"

"Rose, we're in bad trouble."

Suddenly tongue-tied, he strives to find some way to express the urgency of what is, after all, probably nothing more than a hallucination. The filigree chip misconstrues his silence and sends a complex pulse to his brain's ascending reticular formation. Cima sits relaxed in bland coma, blinking slowly, held comfortably by his supports, saying nothing, thinking nothing, while his blurted remark is conveyed to Psyche. For the next twenty-five minutes, the neural interrupt edits out the gap in their conversation.

Cima's muscles are twitching gently through a calculated minimal exercise regimen when her reply reaches Syrtis. He snaps into full consciousness, leans forward intently.

"Telmah," The Rose says, no longer flirting, "I love you always." Urgently, she asks, "What trouble? Damn this lag."

Clock time jolts, is gone.

"I love you, Rose." Cima gazes into her intelligent face. "Orwen's in trouble. See if you can find him."

Gap.

"Your father's fine." Relieved, The Rose throws back her head and laughs gustily. "Getting ready for another skirmish, I gather. The man's a demon for work. 'Nor shall my sword rest in my hand,' and so on. He'll live forever without the benefit of rebirth. That's the good news." She smirks. "The bad news is, you'll never be Director and I'll have to look for advancement in some more promising corner."

Bleakly, Cima tells her, "I think he's dead. Murdered."

Time stops, restarts.

The young woman is astonished. "*Dead?* Just a moment, Telmah, I'm running the check now. Here we go. Ah, he's out of touch at the moment, gone off on one of his celebrated solitary meditation jaunts to the Power Defect. These days he and Johnny Von are thick as thieves— Shit, sorry, we're not handling the time lag very well . . . No recent soul interceptions, certainly not your father's. Sorry to be so clinical. He can't have been assassinated, Telmah, you know how he has that Johnny Von programmed. No one gets in while he's there. Nothing can hurt him. Besides, nobody's died in the last ten hours."

Urgently, Cima says, "Marry me, Rose." He falls asleep.

"Go on." She laughs again, flushing, a delicate modulation

of her tiger pelt. "You always say that when things turn out better than you feared." An alarm begins to scream, and she turns aside to consult a search monitor. "Oh fuck. Oh my God, Telmah."

Shockingly, tears are running down her face. Cima leans forward, strains to reach her, smashes his fists into the wall and her holographic image, recoils.

"The Power Defect's going nova," she tells him. "Jesus and Allah, it's turned into a tiny blue star. Everything's destroyed." She stares back at him, distraught. "How did you know? Oh my God. Johnny Von is dead. Your father is dead. Telmah, do you see what this means?"

"I know what it means." Certainly, he has not been in doubt about this double murder, although his knowledge has had the dark aspect of nightmare recalled in daylight. The impact of its reality clenches about his heart. Yes. No. No. His beloved father is dead. His friend, the ancient ai Johnny Von, destroyed. Cima grinds his teeth in rage. "I have to arrange transport to Psyche."

He sits in coma for twenty-five minutes.

"Telmah." The Warrior Rose presses her whole body against transparent nothingness, straining to touch his image. They are separated by hundreds of millions of kilometers of vacuum. "I love you."

"I know you do. I love you, Rosette. Marry me."

He falls asleep for twenty-five minutes. When he wakes, she is accepting his proposal with the hard, determined tone of a general sending her troops into battle.

"We'll have the wedding the moment you arrive."

TWO

Tessera

completion of the precursor
PART FOR WHOLE/ WHOLE FOR PART
covenant
synecdoche
I

I am trying to be
open, descriptive

as if I could
tie all things
together (War

art
& you) passing
so closely

ROBYN RAVLICH, *THE BLACK ABACUS*

I cantered, whinnying and tossing my mane. Lush grass brushed my belly, alive, alive. The sky went up forever, feathery cirrus in blue immensity. I snorted, breathing hard, and everywhere I looked was crystalline and detailed, from the flailing grass under my hoofs to the purple trees at the distant horizon. Running headlong on the endless steppes to Leos Janacek's rhapsody Taras Bulba (1918, based on the historical novel

As a cursorial vertebrate, my limbs worked like pendulums, heavy with muscle where they attached to my torso, long and thin to the hoof. My keen eyes used ramp design, the gap between lens and retinas smoothly varying, allowing me to watch objects far and near without needing to accommodate the lens.

by Nikolay Gogol), I was home, back in the Gestell, loved and free and fully myself. The asteroid folk were forgotten. "I'm a horse," I whickered, "I'm a horse, I'm a horse." A rainbow poured its multicolored stream of light from heaven, and my hu friends galloped down its bridge to meet with me beside a swirling river of water. Tsin was a warhorse, vast-limbed, hairy-browed. Carmel, silky white, wore a twisted ivory horn above her pink, delicate nostrils. The black Percheron was Carmel, and I saw that the wondrously flanked bay Barb was Veeta. They thundered toward me, thrust their noses into the cool, rushing stream, drank deep. We browsed in silence for a time, deliciously flicking slow flies from our hindquarters.

At last I raised my head, blew beads of moisture from my lips. "So we were wrong."

"Were we?" The warhorse uttered a neigh, stamped backward, clods of mud flying from his great hoofs. "Orwen can hardly be said to have died peacefully in his sleep."

"Warriors rarely do," I observed. "On the other hand, he was *not* murdered."

Carmel flicked her silky mane. "We can't be sure of that. It is not impossible to cause a power defect to flare."

"If so, Feng could not have been the murderer." Veeta trotted back and forth irritably. "He's been on Callisto. He will return immediately to Psyche by ion-drive carrier."

"Will a vessel be ready?"

"He has one standing by."

Carmel had not known that. "Suspicious! Feng was obviously prepared."

"Hmm." Neither had I. "Telmah, on the other hand, is still trying to arrange passage to and from a Cartel ship in high orbit. It will add days, perhaps weeks to our voyage."

She asked me quietly, "You mean to accompany him?"

"If possible. It is my brief. I have done so for the past year, at considerable cost to my spiritual growth." I had never ceased to resent my exile from the Gestell's substrate tuple field and communion with my fellow ai and took what infrequent opportunity came my way to express my grievance. For all that, I had grown to relish my relationship with Telmah Lord Cima, certainly the most singular and complex hu I had ever met.

Tsin took control of the meeting, as he usually did. "We must not allow previous misgivings to distort the facts. Naturally Feng leaves Callisto the moment he hears of his brother's death. He is next in line for the Directorship, if one sets aside as problematical Telmah's own claim. Nor is the presence of suitable non-hex transportation in Callisto space a cause for surprise. 16 Psyche has most of its trade in metals and pharmaceuticals with Earth, Luna, and the Jovian moons."

Carmel's unicorn horn melted to a puddle, like a candle, and her coat thickened, turning from shining white to a dubious shade of gray. "I must say I find it highly suspicious that he has not waited a few hours for Telmah to join him on Callisto. Then they might travel together to Psyche on the same spacecraft."

I was astonished. Abruptly, I wished to be elsewhere, free of these foolish prejudices. "You're not trying . . . Please, Sen, get it through your head that these people abhor the hex gates."

"Yes yes," Veeta snorted. "Strict legal prohibitions against traveling through the discontinuity. And when did fascist hierarchs ever pay the least attention to their own laws, or anyone else's, for that matter?"

I felt buds blooming under the bones of my shoulders. Muscles stretched from my breast, thickened, put on sinew and hollow bone and pinions. The fresh air blew across my wings, tugging, and I twitched my feathers. "Pay attention, citizens. You have missed the point of these prohibitions, which merely fix in law what is already inviolable custom. For the Asteroid culture, Holophrastic Exchange entails the risk of tearing the soul out of the body."

"Soul? There *is* no soul," Veeta informed us angrily. "How can scientifically sophisticated hu be so fucking *dumb*?"

I ignored her, spreading my wings and lifting lightly into the buoyant air. The virtual Sun called to me. So did duty. I swung around over their heads, speaking in the excited fashion of an equine among equines. "You must try to focus your empathy upon their worldview, however odious it might seem to you. Do you not see? Orwen's fate was inconceivably doleful. His soul was sucked into the Singularity, out of the universe entirely. Worse than damnation or karmic rebirth. Obliteration."

"Fantastic gibberish," Carmel cried. Her coat knotted in writhing, hairy serpents. "A *repulsive* culture!"

"Carmel, really. I'm shocked." Tsin was not dissembling. His own great wings sprouted, spread like an eagle's. Wrathful, he lifted into the air. "You, the foe of bigotry?"

"Some ideologies warrant only denunciation." She stamped her hoof, and light dazzled. A silver fish rose in the stream, plopped, and sank from sight. Carmel's hoofs were shod in diamond. "Tsin, I sometimes think you'd find a good word for Attila or Hister."

"Sen, Sen," I said, hoping to quiet the discussion, "my distaste for the Belt culture is as great as yours—"

"Ha! The competitive Gamemaster!" Veeta pranced to stand beside her unexpected ally. Her hoofs were less ornate, a black steel chased at the rim with figures from an Attic amphora. "I find you tarred with the same brush."

I fell to earth once more, crouched, let my wings fold against my thickening flanks. My muzzle shrank, put forth a many-stranded beard, after the fashion of some heavy-chested Assyrian bull deity. Declarative somatic icons poured through me from Gestell feeds: the **Khorsabad** palace of **Sargon II**, **Gilgamesh** and his mutant friend **Enkidu**, half hu and half bull. I spoke with an authority close to wrath.

"Sen, listen to me. Do you know how much blood and grief went into building the Asteroid culture? For centuries they'd seen themselves as the heroic pioneers of the Solar. They were to be the saviors of a polluted, resource-drained Earth. And suddenly the hex gates were invented. The whole galaxy was opened—to everyone but them!"

Veeta was unmoved. With a cynical whicker, she told me, "They could leave. They still can. Take the next rocket, or whatever the damned machines're called."

"No, Veeta, be realistic. Of course they couldn't." Carmel shook her head. "They own a prodigiously profitable and significant business out there, Sen. And we need their biological products, of course."

Tsin said firmly, "Besides, as we all know, they are authoritarians to the bone. The decision-makers delight in playing with their subjects. It is their chief enjoyment." He closed his own wings, which subsided into his shoulder blades.

I was not done with them yet. They still understood nothing. "Citizens, I beg you, show some empathy. Listen: these people, or their forebears, went out beyond Pluto to the **Kuiper halo** and tracked down the remnant of the metric defect which had torn apart the Belt protoworld. They dragged it back to the inner Solar with magnets the size of small cities. It was a truly prodigious

> A small belt of icy planetoids and comets at the inner boundary of the **Oort Cloud** which surrounds the Solar. The **metric defect** was found.

undertaking that took lifetimes of determination, a feat never rivaled since. And they still tap this monstrous thing to light their homes and grow their steaks and biotics."

Under the spur of my rhetoric, the hu Committee members plunged to an inundation of salient tuples from the Gestell. We watched the Belters tamper with the metric defect's orbit, calibrating the delta-vee of this diminutive knot of trapped higher-dimensional spacetime so cunningly that its new trajectory swung it into close resonant orbit with Psyche. Using the defect's magnetic charge as a lever, they had fetched the Bottomless Pit close to the regular ecliptic plane shared by most of the Solar planets.

Veeta's legs lengthened as she absorbed this awesome download. Her neck stretched in giraffe astonishment. Blue spots erupted on her chartreuse coat. Her ruff caught fire, and smoky plumes blew from her elongated neck while her lustrous eyes glowed, whether in fury at ancient spendthrift Asteroid hubris or in admiration, I could not estimate. I suspected the former.

"Citizens," I told them forcefully, "can't you understand? These people were heroes! They were giants. Then, at the peak of their triumph and glory, the hex snatched the meaning of their lives away in a gale of sportive laughter. The Solar went on holiday among the stars. Overnight, everything they'd lived and died for was utterly worthless. Who needs the asteroid mines, when a billion untouched Earth-like worlds can be reached one step away through the hex gates?"

"Well, actually, *we* do," an **Appaloosa** mentioned diffidently. He had been watching these proceedings with dignity, reserving his opinion. "Earth still obtains the balance of our ore from the Belt smelters."

"As a matter of fact—" I began.

He was determined to retain the floor, having waited this long. "I'm an associate member of the Raw Resources Committee, you see. However carefully we conserve and recycle, metals are lost in ordinary use. It's been the practice for millennia to replace this dispersed resource with refined ores from the Asteroids. After all, nobody wishes to strip-mine Mother Gaia."

There was a murmur of pious agreement.

"Oh." Tsin was taken aback. "I always assumed we recycled our materials perfectly."

"Someday, maybe. But don't we top up our supplies from Lunar mines?" Carmel asked.

"Sen! Desecrate our neighbor world?" But the Appaloosa relented after a moment during which he relished his superior moral sensibility. "It's true that primary delivery is made to the Moon, and the stockpile stream is then hexed to Earth from industrial stations at the poles."

The Gestell washed us with history and economics, images and alphanumerics: tonnages of ore, least-energy chaotic orbits, the grand silent drama in cislunar space as the Mitt snatched streams of steel in its ai-coordinated fields and pitched them to ram decelerators on the Moon's bare, cratered surface. I felt that my argument was slipping away from the Committee.

"Nonetheless," I put in, perhaps a little loudly, "the Belters' central role as the universe's greatest explorers and reivers was stolen from them. They had conquered a Singularity; now they toiled as miners for the benefit of a shiftless caste who suddenly owned what they had always seen as theirs."

I saw that Tsin understood, if none of the rest did. The Asteroid culture of rockrats and heroes had been denied the stars, not by any want of courage or skill, but due to the brute, immutable laws of physics. They would never own the stars they had always boasted were their destiny.

"Naturally they cling to their superstitions!" I told them. "Naturally they see themselves as a beleaguered Chosen People."

Abruptly, our consensual construct rolled up into digital hyperspace and went away, and we sat facing each other in Regency chairs arranged in an elegant drawing room of pale striped wallpaper and delicate equestrian etchings. Tsin had decided that enough was enough. Decorum and salience were called for. I found this decision satisfactory, under the circumstances, and none of the others felt strongly enough to counter his choice.

"You are vehement, Ratio," Veeta said, impressively cool given her metaphoric ignition a moment earlier. "Still, none of this explains to my satisfaction why Feng left Callisto without waiting for Telmah—who now, it appears, is obliged to loiter while he arranges a lift into Luna-stationary orbit at Ell-One."

"Veeta. Listen to me." She had plainly not taken in a word. "How do you imagine Telmah might have got to Callisto, if he had wished to travel to Psyche with his uncle?"

"The same way his uncle did." She stared at me as if I were the one failing to follow a clear-line argument. "Through a bloody hex gate."

I simply did not understand what she was saying for a moment. Veeta appeared to imply that Feng had passed to the moon Callisto through the Holophrastic Exchange discontinuity. "What!"

Carmel nodded, told me simply, "Feng was seen on Earth a few hours before Orwen died in the flare."

"Impossible." It made no sense at all. If they had announced that Tsin or Carmel had been surveilled wild-eyed and bloody-mouthed at a cannibal feast, I'd have had less difficulty believing it.

"I agree that it's unlikely," Tsin said, "if your specialist analysis of Asteroid cultural mores is correct, and," he added hastily, "we have no cause to doubt that. But it is clearly *not* impossible. The sighting has been confirmed by surveillance instrumentation."

A hologram cube opened where a polished bookshelf stood, laden with antique volumes. I supplemented its covert imagery with a direct feed from the Gestell public surveillance archive.

I recognized the man from my earlier briefing. Cima had never included Feng in the few family documentaries he had shown me; I gathered that there was some lack of fellow feeling between Telmah and his uncle, but I did not care to speculate upon its source. Feng strode through a crowd of Koreans in New Mecca, at chilly daybreak. A brisk wind flicked the knitted, subtly crosshatched skirt he wore. Kilt. The data icon listing showed him to be accompanied, in his intimate acoustic feed at least, by a skirl of hideous piping, as well as by an expensive female Courtesan in gorgeous *geisha* chic. Gestell license registers named the woman as Janice Shikibu Tanaka, a fully bonded associate of Tails of Genji, Inc., of Kyoto and Psyche. All further detail on both hu was sealed and protected under privacy protocols.

"What *is* the man wearing?" Carmel inquired. Instantly, we all knew the exact answer, and the hu gasped. His tartan was utterly distinctive. Fantastically, Feng was flaunting his guilt in our faces.

"Clan kilt and colors of the Thane of Glamis and Cawdor?" Veeta was incredulous. "Why doesn't he just sign a confession and post it in Free Access?"

Lord Feng knelt with the multitude of nostalgia tourists as the muezzin in a lofty minaret gave ululant voice to the *adhan*, glossed as the ancient

> **Thane**: Scottish chief of clan. **Glamis and Cawdor**: castles of Scotland associated with **Macbeth**, monarch in 11th who slew his king and was represented in play of same name by 16 century hu.

cry urging the faithful to prayer. If Feng knew he was under surveillance, as he surely must suspect, he made no attempt to disguise his presence. To the contrary, being here at dawn in so visible a site suggested his wish to be seen. As an alibi, perhaps.

"Macbeth, eh?" Tsin mused. "Even so, the blow against the Director must have been dealt by another hand."

I struggled to unknot the symbolism. "This is inconsistent, Sen. The semiotics of his gesture declare his specific and personal agency in the murder. Perhaps his unconscious cries out in shame and terror. His choice of persona indicates as much."

At that moment, Feng glanced straight at the hidden scanner, surely by accident. I examined his clever face, his implacable mouth. He looked away, then, and said something to the lovely hu that made her smile discreetly, covering her flower mouth with a tiny hand.

"This is also immaterial and self-contradictory," the Appaloosa said with a dry little cough. "You have Feng murdering his brother, by his own hand. How does he announce the crime? By standing on Earth at that very hour. Citizens, let us be logical." His voice strengthened. "Lord Feng already had a sufficient alibi. He was on a State visit to Callisto when the foul deed occurred—if, indeed, Orwen's death *was* murder, and we are far from having established that conjecture as fact. Now Feng's alibi is doubly strengthened, since we know exactly where he was at the moment of Orwen's demise. Of course, if the matter goes to the question he may yet have cause for regret, as he will hardly wish to reveal publicly his, uh, 'sinful' employment of the hex system to visit Earth."

Impatient, Veeta broke in. "Clearly, Feng teleported to Earth from Callisto and then returned to hear the news of Orwen's demise. So, to repeat my original question: Why shouldn't Telmah follow suit and travel with his uncle from Callisto?"

I met her accusing gaze. "He could, of course, but I assure you of his genuine aversion to discontinuous transport. Granted, the Asteroid belief in reincarnation is a societal compensation fantasy for their isolation and loss of status. But don't let us reduce their agony to some sleazy maneuver of profit-grubbing." Veeta shrugged cynically, and I added, "I mean it. I've only known Telmah to transit through the hex system once, and that was in the traumatic crisis of his father's death. A crisis brought to his attention, I'll remind you all, by psychic presentiment, scoff as you will. I'd affirm it was the first time in his life he ever used the hex. And probably the last."

"Telmah's personal feelings do not come into it," Tsin commented with authority, "let alone his purported psychic gifts. Veeta asks why Cima did not hex to Callisto to join his uncle. You notice that we speak of a public—a state—occasion. Politically, Telmah was not *permitted* to hex to Callisto to join Feng, whether or not he wished to. The political visibility of his movements from this time forth oblige him to go the long way around."

"Exactly." The Appaloosa, who had been sunk in Gestell trance, spoke with an infused understanding of Belter affairs. "I accept Sen Ratio's claim that Telmah Cima has a genuine aversion to the discontinuity. He'll use it in extremity, but not under the general gaze." He studied his fingertips, smiling faintly. "It would be as politically damaging as . . . well, as if he were to enter hospital for the nanosurgical removal of his appendix."

We all stared at him in silence, dumbfounded. None of the rest of us had followed the fractal hypertext trail deep enough to uncover that bizarre belief.

"What? Appen*dect*omy is a political crime? Star's sakes!"

"It's true," he said apologetically. "You see, in their view our scandalous way of life is due to the evil effects of routine preventative nanosurgery in childhood."

"You're kidding!"

"Not at all, I fear. The vermiform appendix, citizens, is the physical organ of the soul."

Everyone in the room burst into laughter. The wallpaper wavered for an instant in sympathy. An immense white Persian cat, snoozing unnoticed at Tsin's feet, raised his head indignantly, squeezed his green-gold eyes into a slit, nodded off once more, tail twitching in gentle warning.

Eyes and mouth wide, Carmel prodded her trim belly with a jeweled nail. "You mean the medicos cauterized my soul along with my **appendix**?" But her mocking mirth was already irrelevant; we sat drenched in a salient download from the Gestell, a curious and horrifying pour from the archives detailing Belter spiritual doctrine. "Shit, well, okay." Her tone sharpened. "All I can say is, bloody Feng's bloody ambitions seem to have overwhelmed his piety."

"Understandably enough," Tsin mused. "There is strong legal precedent for Telmah's accession to the Directorship. As he is currently stuck here on Earth, his return will be delayed by the need for a journey to orbit, followed by the cislunar crossing, linear catapult from the Moon, ion spacecraft to Psyche, however they do it. Endless time-wasting. And while all that's going on, I imagine Lord Feng will cement himself nicely into power."

Carmel stood up, stretched, crouched beside Tsin's chair, and stroked the cat's wonderful furry head. The sim arched his back with pleasure, favoring her with a deep growling purr. "I'd dearly like to know what Feng was doing in the Korean Archipelago when the Singularity erupted. I doubt he was just on a sex junket, let alone a nostalgia tour of defunct faiths."

"An irrelevancy. The Sen was right," I said. "As the Gestell has just been at pains to instruct us, hex connections cannot be made to the Belt. There is simply no way Orwen could have been killed by a teleporting murderer."

"My point exactly," the Appaloosa agreed.

Tsin stood. "It is still possible that Feng arranged the flare. To this end," he told the others, "I have asked Ratio to accompany Telmah to Psyche."

"On what pretext?" Carmel asked acutely. "You will not have forgotten the detestation Belters evince toward artificial persons."

I stood as well, and bowed my head in a gesture of respect. "The Singularity flare destroyed their only ai control system. Johnny Von, one of my earliest ancestors."

Veeta said ungrudgingly, "We grieve his loss."

"Thank you. Telmah suggested that I might go with him in my professional capacity to assess the problems of replacement."

"Well done."

"Citizens, I would do so in any event. I like Telmah. He is my friend. I mean to do what I can to protect him."

───────────────────────────────────────

Telmah Cima is singing something in his beautiful tenor—bellowing, in fact—about a hard rain and the likelihood of its falling.

Equably, Ratio tells him, "You are manic, Sen."

"Scared shitless, actually, pal," ser friend agrees. Lifting his voice again, grinning, he lets another antique song slip raffishly from one side of his mouth. This one concerns his intention of visiting a Wizard, a wonderful wizard—

"I take it you have managed to organize a shuttle launch to take us to geostationary orbit."

Cima ceases his capers, pulls a wry face.

"Not quite. Close." Seizing a ripe banana from a bowl on the captain's table—he is himself the captain, *pro tem*, although an ai controller is driving their craft—he has it unpeeled and in his mouth with the dexterity of a chimpanzee. "Close enough. Tell me, Ratio, do you ever experience fear?"

"Not the hu emotion, naturally. Cognitive shock, yes. Astonishment. Enhanced vigilance. Not the flooding hormones and peptides that render hu passions so . . . charming."

"Do you ever lose control?"

Ratio's casque face smiles. "Never."

Naked and tanned from melanophoretics taken the night before, Cima wipes his hands on his flanks and prowls the ekranoplan's blister dome. Idling across half the expanse of the Indian subcontinent from Accra to the Gulf of Cambay, they have picked up pace on water and now thunder at close to the speed of sound two meters above the tropical ocean. A cushion of air holds the *Rozhdestvensky* aloft, generated by ground effect and wing lift alike. It is a marvel of late Flight Era technology, exhumed and kept in repair by the Cartel for their rare emergency trips from one part of the planet to another.

Ratio asks, after it becomes clear that Telmah does not mean to press sem, "Do *you* enjoy your state of dread?" Something about this moment, this crux, impels sem to risk a more impertinent probing than se has ever essayed in their acquaintance.

Cima turns a wolfish grin on sem. "Naturally! It's what we hu live for—passion, intensity, attack. Except, of course"—and he throws himself in a loose limpfall to the cushions, closing his eyes and stretching his arms luxuriously in the beating heat of the winter tropical Sun—"when we prefer sloth and sleep." He instantly falls into that state.

Bereft of the Gestell, Ratio studies the endless green ocean, its high hard blue sky. Here and there se finds specks, laser-lit even in daylight: vast autonomous factories and fishery platforms, methodically plowing the depths to fill hu tables. The ekranoplan's superb low-grade ai controller ensures that their flight path evades these leviathans and the hundreds of slow hu and ai pleasure craft that infest the seas. A flotilla of bright-sailed yachts comes into view, beating southeast ahead of a snappy breeze. The *Rozhdestvensky* rises several meters to bank, preparing well in advance to skirt the flotilla, its dipped wingtip sustaining ground effect lift without cutting into the deep surging waves.

Ratio rouses ser companion for late luncheon, happy to join a hu at table, although se has no need for such sustenance. It is a social act, and ser humaniform ai configuration allows sem everything a hu male might do in any situation. They dine on cold lobster and a sumptuous salad, with a chilled Colombard.

"Doesn't your faith forbid the drinking of alcohol?"

"An authority on Belter theology, are you now, Ratio?"

"Not at all. I have been careful not to pry into your beliefs, Telmah. It would not be polite."

"Quite so. Have no fear, chief, my soul is safe. Under the New Dispensation, it is not alcohol one must avoid but the avoidance of its penalties. The sin is not elevation of spirits but swinish drunkenness and hangover. Hence we are enjoined to eschew those pharmaceuticals which circumvent the punishment we bring upon ourselves."

Ratio gives up this line of recursive guilt-mongering as a bad job. "I assume our destination is Mount Kenya?" Five thousand meters high and nearly on the equator, the white peaks are a plausible launch site for an orbital lifter. It seems unlikely that Cima will have been able to arrange such a machine, however, in the time available. Space flight has been a dead letter for many centuries. Incoming flights, like the one that fetched Telmah to Earth, are readily arranged: a foamed-steel lifting body forged in orbit at a Cartel deflector station is nudged into the atmosphere from LEO and glides to ground without power. Returning to orbit is quite a different matter.

Cima drinks lustily, sets down his glass. Waves hush beneath the rolling air cushion. "Mount Kenya? Not quite. You're thinking of the Hyde Fountain. Unfortunately, it was never built. If it had been, I'm sure even the Cartel would not have been able to pay its upkeep."

"Fountain?" As ever, Ratio is downcast by the loss of aks to the Gestell. *Not knowing* is truly painful, perhaps as close to an emotion of grief as anything an ai can experience. Yet this is exactly why se has agreed to the amputation: to put sem on an equal footing with ser friend, to force this ancient impoverished bit-rate exchange of information, this "conversation." Se ransacks ser ample onboard memories (images of water foaming upward, white jets, frothy, from the mouths of corroded stone fish or tubular steel sculptures) but finds nothing salient.

Cima is pleased. He has spent years at study as a cripple in a world of instant data glosses. In a burst of genuine affection, he reaches across the white tablecloth and squeezes the ai's hand.

"Shortly before they found the hex, a consortium of the ancient nations started to build a tower reaching into space."

"Oh. A Beanstalk." Ratio recognizes this concept: a diamond cable stretching from geostationary orbit to the ground, tethered atop a suitable equatorial mountain, balanced by a second cable plunging a further 110,000 kilometers into cislunar space. It was Faustian technology appropriate to the culture that captured the mass defect and coupled its orbit to Psyche's. Only poor timing had prevented the Beanstalk's completion.

" 'Spacehook' is how it was normally described," Cima corrects sem. "No, the Hyde Fountain was rather more audacious." He sketches in the air, and the *Rozhdestvensky*'s watchful ai translates his gestures into a schematic holly display above the table.

"Fire a stream of nine-kilo aluminum rings up an evacuated tower at twenty-five klicks a second," he explains, "and brake them as they rise."

The ai is nothing if not quick. "Ah. The transferred force will sustain the tower structure that holds the brake motors," Ratio sees, nodding. "It's a reverse mass-driver, fixed to the ground."

"Nice, isn't it? Twitch the little buggers around at the top with more magnets and ram them back down."

"Reusing the power extracted on the way up, presumably."

"Yep. Send them around a big loop when they get to the ground"—and he sketches a vast subsurface ring of superconducting magnets—"pumping the speed up again, and shoot 'em out for another trip through the circuit."

"They'd melt."

"Oddly enough, no. There's energy loss, but it only raises

the temperature of the projectile rings by forty degrees. That's dissipated on their return trip from space."

"One would wish to employ a measure of redundancy," Ratio observes thoughtfully, "if this process is meant to carry an elevator."

"Ah, ai caution!" Cima laughs gustily. "Well, yes, even the mad dog hu engineers thought of that. Three, four, ten times redundant. But you can raise a shaft to geostationary without needing spectacular material strengths. No need for diamond fibers."

"Even so, it would clearly be a costly venture."

"Getting it up, sure." Cima sprawls. His animation display runs in the air between them, a monstrous Tower of Babel clawing into heaven, a million aluminum rings hurled up and down and all around. "Ten terawatts of circulating power. Of course, that would've been pumped in incrementally as the tower was raised. Even so, it needed fifteen gigawatts to keep it running." He leans forward, eyes gleaming. "But it would have given us a permanent elevator to space, zipping up the tower by magnetic levitation. Linear motors. The whole thing was well under way, luckily. I've been able to cannibalize," he adds mysteriously, extinguishing the sketch with a negligent gesture. "Then the damned hex abomination popped out of the Nguyen labs and everyone forgot about space."

Ratio says carefully, "Not quite. There are more planets in the galaxy being explored today via hex than the number of people alive at that time, you know."

"At the cost of their souls!" He bares his teeth in a snarl.

Ratio says nothing. After a simmering silence, the ai says, "We agreed to disagree on matters of theology."

"How can you 'disagree'? You're simply ignorant of the experience, Tin Man. Deaf and blind, but pronouncing your judicious skepticism on a Cytowic synaesthetic concerto. Ha!"

Diplomatically, Ratio reverts to the original topic. "If the

Fountain was never built, what do we mean to find at Mount Kenya? I had assumed a single-stage lift vehicle, if such flights are still permitted."

"We're not going to the mountain," Cima says, his good humor returning. "We're bringing the mountain to us. By God, Ratio, you're going to enjoy this merry jaunt, or I'll know the reason why!"

He wipes his lips on linen napery, grinning ferociously.

"We could keep this up all day and long into the night," Ratio says patiently. "Or you could just tell me."

"It's just a wild idea I had," Cima tells him with an air of modesty.

They boom across 4,000 kilometers of deep water while the hu explains a plan so lunatic that Ratio does not believe for a moment that it is meant seriously. When se realizes that the man is not jesting, ser mind enters a ringing state of cognitive shock.

Mining on sacred Gaia has been strictly forbidden for centuries. It is even regarded as historically and aesthetically insensitive to scavenge ore from traditional strip mines on the Moon, a world largely uninhabited. Still, even with stringent recycling, Earth requires huge quantities of metals annually. They must be brought in from outside. The question is: From where?

In principle, Ratio realizes, resources could be mined from unattractive worlds elsewhere in the galaxy and hexed at Earth. But why bother? The Asteroid Belters have been in this business for millennia. Their smelters and purifiers have been amortized and routine nanorenovation keeps the vast original solar-mirror mining systems in good repair. Insolation flux at the inner Belt is a measly 20 percent of available solar energy in Earth orbit, but iron and other heavy metals litter the asteroids. The inexhaustible power supply from the Bottomless Pit tops up the difference, sealing the bargain.

So aside from their principal source of trade—the fabulous Recombinant genetic engineering concerns that build novel targeted drugs for the entire hu galaxy—the Belters continue mining the asteroids. They dispatch the purified ore in neat chunks to Earth, fired from ram accelerators on Ceres, strung out in huge looping necklaces: Hohmann least-energy transfer ellipses and faster curves with greater delta-vee.

Steel-jacketed and cryo-preserved pallets of their precious pharmaceuticals go to Mars for stocktaking and dissemination. The ore pipeline from Ceres ends at Ell-One, the gravitationally nearly stable Lagrange libration orbit fixed 64,500 klicks above the lunar surface, between Earth and Moon. There the incoming metal is caught by a colossal Cartel magnetic Mitt and diverted to the dark expanse of the Ocean of Storms, where it pours through huge open hex gates straight to Earth. At ground level, it is slowed in a magnetic loop of the kind designed for the Hyde Fountain, generating immense amounts of electricity en route that is dispersed, along with the ore, for industrial use.

Telmah's insane plan, Ratio realizes, has retargeted part of this stream of iron from Ell-One, aimed at Earth at eight km/sec. None of this could have been achieved without ai intervention, coordination, and prodigious use of supple nanotechnology. The massive ingots have been melted at Ell-One by focused solar mirrors and spun in magnetic fields, reshaped as ten-kilo darts to create a streamlined laminar flow to reduce turbulence in the atmosphere, and finally flown through a cloud of heat-dispersing ceramic coating.

Then they have been flung at the Earth.

Iron slams through space above their heads at this very moment, as Ratio and Cima speed toward the bull's-eye in the target.

"You're completely mad," Ratio tells him sincerely.

"Not at all. We need to reach geostationary orbit so we can

hitch a lift in a Belter ion-drive spacecraft. I do, at any rate. I can't hang about while we retool and fuel a lift vehicle."

"Why don't you have a lifter on standby?"

"I wasn't expecting to return home for another year. Rockets are delicate critters, pal, and nobody likes the toxic rain they leave behind in the atmosphere. We're talking weeks, even with ai help."

A stream of darts, or rather a pointillist cloud, is falling toward Africa. When it strikes the Earth, it will comprise a virtual bar of iron bent in a parabola massing 180 or 200 thousand tons. On average, Ratio calculates, each dart will take some seventy-five minutes to complete its trajectory to the ground. But averages, se tells semself, surely do not apply here. Every single dart will have to be separately targeted at launch by the ai controllers.

"Rather convenient that a shipment of ore just happened to arrive when you need it," Ratio mentions in an interested tone.

Cima shrugs. "There are always consignments in the pipeline. A batch of ore that left the Ceres mass-launcher a year or so back arrived in lunar space a few hours ago, Ratio. I've had it diverted."

The ai Gamemaster stares at dusk's gold and billowing clouds. There is nothing untoward in the beautiful display, no screaming across the sky. "When does this hard rain arrive?"

"A little over an hour after we arrive in Africa. I trust our 'plan driver keeps to schedule. Embarrassing if we arrive late."

Still not believing it, Ratio says, "You intend to ride up to orbit on a stream of projectiles *fired down from space?*"

Cima tells sem with a measure of satisfaction, "I call it my Bullet Train." He grins wickedly. "You can come, too."

The ai struggles to absorb what se is hearing. They will ride an annular elevator wrapped around the screaming torrent of infalling ore. The elevator, cannibalized from the disbanded Hyde Fountain project, will couple magnetically to the downpouring stream. Its linear motors will drag them up the gravity well, just as it would if the "bar" were continuous, extracting energy to do so from the cascade itself.

"How long will we be locked to this diabolical engine?"

"The lift runs up to orbit at an average of a klick a second—a mild thirty-six hundred kilometers an hour, Ratio, nothing to blow your hair around." Cima regards the ai's sleek casque sardonically. "So it'll get us to the top in around ten, twelve hours."

Ratio cannot comprehend the magnitudes involved. "Madness. Truly. While we're hoisting ourselves by our bootstraps, a stream of aerodynamic ore eight times— You can't be serious. Eight times the distance from here to geostationary orbit. It will just smack into the ground? A million six hundred thousand tons."

"That's not too many," Cima assures sem. "Less than a thousandth of the total the economy'll process this year. Earth is still sending a lot of prefabs out through the hex gates. Actually, the incoming is a bit more than that—two million tons. Margin of safety."

Ratio looks at ser hu friend. "Quite. You wouldn't want to be reckless about something like this."

Cima shouts his buoyant laughter. He is in a state of barely controlled hysteria.

Somewhat grimly, Ratio asks, "And what does happen when it arrives here? You're not planning a nuclear winter as a going-away present? Kill the dinosaurs for the second time?"

"You tempt me. No, I don't hold any grudge. I've had quite a jolly time on Earth. Especially with the troupe. Especially with you, chum." He stares at the polished deck. "This isn't totally ad hoc, you understand. It's how they brought the steel to Earth in the old days, which is why the infrastructure's in place. That's what gave me the idea."

"I assumed it was pure genius."

"That too. When the iron reaches the ground, of course, it'll be hexed to the big processing station in Brazil. They capture the stream on a mass-driver catapult loop and deflect it at full velocity into a braking chamber that stops it dead. All that momentum energy evaporates the darts. *Voomp.*"

"Oh. Thereby separating the component metals and boiling off the heat-shield ceramic for recycling. Handy. Waste not, want not."

"Just so."

"Never mind that none of this can possibly work."

"The simulations say it can."

Ratio shoots to ser feet. "You're telling me this has never been tried?"

"The math is good," Cima assures sem. "Some of your finest quantum computer colleagues spent whole minutes computing it to a fare-thee-well."

"I would not dare to second-guess them, but let me see if I have the picture. The Earth will rotate under this infalling stream, so the equatorial impact point will be drifting westward at four hundred and forty meters a second. Ten hours later, as you and I reach orbit, the end of the stream will be touching down in the Pacific Ocean." The ai smiles. "In fact, you won't need to hex the metal to Brazil. Some of it will end up there anyway!"

"No, you booby. Look at it this way. A myriad of darts has been launched from Ell-One at different times in different trajectories with different speeds. They'll arrive in a different order from the queue that came out of the ram. Then they'll reassemble themselves as they come in through the atmosphere to form our Indian rope trick. Magic! I love it."

Ratio slights this astonishing feat of science and technology, musing tragically. "Yes, it's completely hopeless. Atmospheric turbulence around the plummeting stream will tear the elevator capsule to shreds. The stream will fly apart as it falls. No.

It'll clump up due to its own mag fluxes. No. The iron will heat too much despite the heat-shielding shells and degauss and our capsule will fly off. Like a wingless bird. In any case, the stream will surely smash half the comsats as it comes down. It will therefore be banned by the broadcasting authorities." The ai is relieved. "They won't let you do it, Telmah. They'll have you committed. They'll have your brain wiped and start again."

Cima lifts his musical voice, ignoring the kvetching. Ratio is amused. Why affirm that one might not sing something that cannot be sung? Hu are not as ai.

It is past midnight when the vessel fetches up on the east coast of Africa at the mouth of Juba River. The navigation beacons of the port town of Kismayu direct them carefully on to land, diverting them around a long safety zone that stretches for a hundred kilometers out to sea. Kismayu is strangely dark.

"Where are they?"

"Most of the operation is conducted deep underground. It's wholly under the control of specialized ai systems." The 'plan rises from the water, crosses to land, noses in the dark for electronic signals, settles in a puff of African dust to the tarmac. Cima peers at the few visible features of the small hu township, licking his lips and trembling with excitement.

Dazzling lights rim the pit. Five hundred meters away, massively shielded by blockhouse walls and hex-ready lest the calculated odds fail them, Cima and Ratio scan the clear, starry African sky through the transparent roof of their semicircular compartment. The temporary shielding is essentially no more than a psychological ploy, since nothing living will be salvaged if the ai controllers fail and allow a dart to smash into the ground at terminal velocity. Still, there remains a small chance that splinters of heat-shielding ceramic might crack loose, hail down like bullets at hypersonic speeds.

Ratio has minimal aks to ambient datasources.

"It should become visible to the east within seventeen seconds," he announces.

Cima reclines with feigned insouciance into the padded leather cushions of the Pullman. At his lazy gesture, an automat passes him a martini, expertly mixed and shaken.

"A pity our schedule could not be fixed for daylight." His tone is level. "With luck, though, the lasers—"

Hard light blooms above them. Ten, twenty powerful searchlights probe the darkness, illuminating a cone of night.

"Now, I think."

It drifts down toward them like a gigantic thread, a very slightly curved noodle, a lollipop. A bright pink lollipop.

Cima chokes. He laughs until his eyes water.

"Pink? A stick of *pink candy*?"

Ratio gazes at the shocking thing dropping slowly toward them, then abruptly beside them, then seemingly anchored in the black pit. The abused air sizzles and buffets their cabin. Se turns to ser aks.

"Telmah, I thought you understood this process. It's just the Voermans ceramic that coats the darts."

But Cima is shaken with hilarity, spilling his drink down his frock coat.

ACQUISITION NOMINAL, reports the controller. PREPARE FOR SLIP COUPLING.

Through the immensely strong composite elevator walls, tortured air booms and howls. They lurch. Ratio reaches down, cinches a restraint belt across ser torso.

"Buckle up, Telmah," se says. "It's going to be a bumpy ride."

Brilliantly lit, the pink torrent of steel plunges into the pit's yawning mouth and, out of sight, is instantly hexed to Brazil, where it volatilizes in a deafening clamor. Cunning baffles cut the turbulence at the interface, but still the air squalls.

Cima's martini glass is snatched from his hand, smashes against a brass rail. They judder, cranking meter by meter toward their virtual railroad.

Motion subsides for a moment.

FINAL CHECK, the ai informs them. Then: SATISFACTORY WITHIN PARAMETERS. DO YOU AUTHORIZE THE ASCENT TO ORBIT, SEN CIMA?

Hoarsely, the hu says, "Yes."

DO YOU CONCUR, SEN RATIO?

"I do."

"God," Cima groans, "a marriage made in heaven. Well, damn your eyes, get on with it!"

But already they are creeping forward once more. From the far side of the cataract, a matching semicircular module approaches the pit's rim: the linear drive that will haul them into the sky. Howling winds peak, subside; a deep chunking thud marks the docking of the twin modules. Faintly distorted in the transparent ceiling, a thin lurid pink cable hangs against them, shivering slightly. It is impossible to believe that it is raging past them at eight kilometers a second.

Magnetic fields draw them to within a millimeter of the iron rain, lock them there.

ENJOY YOUR JOURNEY, SEN. EXPECTED TIME OF ARRIVAL IS PLUS NINE HOURS, FIFTY-SIX MINUTES.

With the slightest upward jolt, like a hydraulic lift hand-started in some antiquity fair, their ring couples to the track, slides upward into the bright night. As they slowly accelerate, buffeting increases. Ratio turns ser attention inward, cherishing the deep beauties of the cosmos.

Cima leans back in his cushions, gaze fixed on the pink monstrosity they ride, and grins like a wolf.

"Another martini, if you please," he instructs the compartment. "Dry, this time."

In mirrorsuits, they abandon the elevator, decoupling from its terrible cable, which still pours like candy into the world 36,000 klicks beneath them. Hand in hand, they float in free fall toward the sizable ship. The thing appears to have been assembled from junk by drunken apprentices.

"I had expected something smaller and neater," Ratio conveys directly into ser radio feed, bypassing the acoustic channel.

"Takes a lot of grunt to flit around the Solar," Cima says inside ser brain. It is almost like being back within the Gestell.

In fact, compared to the shocking tonnage of steel still dropping away toward the distant planet at their backs, this craft is absurdly insignificant. Still, ascending into its looming shadow, it is a reality far more impressive, because graspable.

"Seventy thousand tons? A hundred?" Ratio hazards. An airlock hatch cycles open at their approach. Cables loop everywhere. Tanks bulge, antennae peruse the great dark vacancy. Behind monstrous shielding, a fusion reactor burns like the Sun.

"A little more than that," Cima tells sem, swinging easily into the amber-lit, weightless chamber. Farther along the spine, two counter-rotating drums a hundred meters in diameter spin their slow centrifugal gravity. In silence, double hatches close. Air enters with a faint hiss, pressing their suited bodies into the center of the chamber. Lighting returns to normal. Cima removes his vacuum gear with the dexterity of lifelong practice. "Lord Cima speaking," he says to the empty air. "Let's go."

"Acceleration began the moment your airlock cycled shut, Boss." The voice is curiously rough, barely hu, certainly not ai. "Welcome aboard. We can do that piping nonsense later. Aw well, what the hell." An eerie whistling rises, falls.

Still struggling for purchase in midair, Ratio is surprised.

"We're under way? I thought your Belter ships were miracles of thermonuclear fleetness. Shouldn't we be flattened cruelly against the bulkhead?"

Cima leads sem into the bowels of the vessel. "Hold your horses. Slow and steady wins the race, as my sainted old great-granddaddy used to say. We're limited to point zero one of a gee. Ion drive, Ratio."

"I see. You plan to arrive in time to greet your own great-grandchild."

Cima glares at the ai. "I thought you artificial minds were miracles of cognitive fleetness."

"Only when we aks the Gestell," Ratio says regretfully. "How long will it take us to reach our destination at a miserable hundredth of a gravity?"

The crackly voice of the ship says instantly, "Two million, four hundred seventy-four thousand, three hundred fifty-eight seconds."

"You're showing off, Cluck," Cima says. "What's that in hu terms?"

"Chauvinist! Would *hours* help? Six hundred eighty-seven."

"I can do the rest myself," Ratio says. "Twenty-eight and a half days. Halfway across the Solar in less than a month at a hundredth-gee? I can't believe it."

"Neither can I," Cima says dryly. "You're out by a factor of two, Cluck. I'd actually prefer you to end up at Psyche, so it'd be quite convenient if you started decelerating at the turnover point."

"Shit! Telmah, you're right," the voice groans, mortified. "Betrayed by my unconscious desires! To fly! To fly endlessly into night! I guess at some level I was thinking of torching right past the goddamned shithole. Damn it, I hardly ever make that kind of stupid— Stand by for updated ETA. Plus fifty-seven days and counting."

Cima shakes his head sadly but says nothing.

"My word, how quaint." Ratio lightly fingers the stained un-decorated surfaces of the passageways they fly through, hauling themselves on frayed velvet cords or kicking lightly from con-veniently angled plates. "Speaking of horses, where *do* you keep them?"

"Don't joke about it." They clamber with some difficulty into a slowly rotating openwork cage that spins them into the hab-itat with its inertially simulated gravity. The holly decor is star-tling. "Wait until you meet the livestock we have flying this heap."

"Livestock?"

Cima lifts an eyebrow. "Our pilots are genetically reworked cyborgs. They fly on a wing and a prayer. I'll introduce you formally to our pilot captain sooner or later—he's a crusty old bird, very suspicious of robots."

Sweet flowery fragrances suffuse the pumped circulating air. The public sound feed codes itself: Jean Sibelius (1865–1957), *The Swan of Tuonela* (Op. 22). Granite walls tower up on every side, black with moss. Ratio gazes over the side of the castle crenellations. Far below, glacier-carved mountain walls plunge to fiords blue as Cima's eyes. A raptor of some kind lofts on a high frigid current very far overhead, stoops suddenly, falling like a stone at what looks like one gravity. Within the keep proper, light is dimmer, cast by guttering brands. At close range their smoke conflicts with the floral perfume and wins.

"Beyond belief!"

Cima looks around happily, hands on his hips, shoulders back. Two great dogs rush up to him, bouncing as if in one-quarter gravity or one-sixth, slobbering and pawing the rushes spread on the stone flags. They are sims, the finest Ratio has ever seen that are not eidolons generated directly from a Gestell feed. He bends in the one-tenth spin gravity, holds out a gleam-ing hand. The brutes sniff at his limb, bristle slightly, back away. One of them throws back its head and bays, a deep and mournful cry. Cima puts out his own hand, and the offended dog licks it gratefully.

" 'Hark, hark,' " he declaims, " 'the mastiff bitch doth bark.' Samuel Taylor Coleridge, 1772–1834. You see, Ratio, I can do the footnotes, too, and the police in different voices. Thomas Stearns Eliot, 1888–1965." The second animal pads around the great hall, returns, stretches forth its ample neck and vomits delicately. Black matted feathers cling to its long lips. "Oh dear, it's been eating dead birds again."

"Arf, arf," Ratio observes mordantly, "the mastiff bitch doth barf." Se ignores Cima's astonished bark of laughter. "Who pays the upkeep on these fantastic relics?"

"Be off with you now, girls." The Danes lollop away, stretching themselves elegantly on either side of a roaring timber blaze in a smoke-blackened stone fireplace that a dozen hu could take their ease in. "The Belt Recombinant Engineering Cartel. We can afford it. We have a total lock on genetically engineered pharmaceuticals, agricultural products, microindustrial biota . . . It's our natural trade, Ratio."

"I dare say." It is why the ai is here, ultimately, spying on his friend. They have never spoken of Cartel business in all the five years he has known Telmah Cima, who talks only of games and poetry and problems of philosophy and the beauty of young women. In for a penny, Ratio decides. "There's a sort of refreshing metaphysical irony in it. The laws of physics deny you access to instantaneous hex displacement—"

"Precisely." Cima meets ser gaze guilelessly. "The bad news is, nothing gets in to our little worlds. The good news is, nothing gets out either. Unless we ship it. We're the universe's strictest quarantine. And you can bet your last Rembrandt we don't let it go unless someone pays us for it."

The pilot tells them formally, "My Lord Telmah, Sen Ratio, we have inserted into continuous thrust transfer orbit. I do not expect any further vector changes. Thank you."

Cima steps lightly to a chunky carved timber bench beside the fireplace, straps himself to it in seated position. He looks around their living quarters in growing irritation. The adrenaline elation of their trip up the hard rain cascade is draining from him, casting him into depression. "Not enough room for a full-scale battle, or a game of baseball, but more like home. I don't like buckets. Two months of this. Good God."

"Surely you're used to living in enclosed volumes." Ratio finds an illuminated manuscript open on a green copper stand, an old hardcopy of St. Philip's *Exegesis*. Se snaps it shut, and virtual dust puffs out, falling like a dream in the low gravity. Even decorated with anachronistic medieval calligraphy, the sacred book remains, in Ratio's opinion, the worst kind of gibberish. "Anyone who's lived most of his life in a maze of corridors cut inside rocks a couple of klicks across . . . '

"The standard vulgar mistake. Ratio, they did a rotten job of programming on you. Psyche is more than two hundred and eighty kilometers across. Our surface area is a quarter-million square kilometers. As for the spacious corridor system—"

The ai needles him deliberately. "Well, I never said I'd made an intensive study of trivia."

"For shame! Psyche is an entire world."

"The smallest one I've ever heard of. Well, *met* anyone from." Ratio is amused by ser friend's passionate defense. "Telmah, hard as it might be for you to accept this, asteroids do not loom large in the awareness of your fellow galactic citizens."

"I've become all too keenly cognizant of this truth during the last five years."

Ratio does not relent. "I suspect it's why you provincials run about calling each other 'my Lord' and 'your Worship' so insistently."

Seizing a carbonized fire poker, or its simulacrum, Cima

smites the blazing logs until sparks fly. "Sen Ratio, you're a tactless whoreson when the mood takes you. I imagine the tedium of our voyage will knock out some of your snap."

A shrieking siren sounds. Cima is instantly unbelted, in the air, banter forgotten. "Alert! Alert!" the pilot snarls. "Into the shielded redoubt, landlubbers. Big solar flare on the way."

"Thank you, Captain." Leading Ratio by the hand, the hu darts deeper into the simmed castle, away from spin gravity, opens a creaking timber doorway, plunges through into a snug white chamber. Dozens of acceleration couches are racked economically, and holly displays hang in the air, listing crucial parameters—radiation flux, solar chromosphere dynamics, time curves of various alarming scenarios—and a full menu of entertainments and light refreshments. A small hatch leads to a bathroom. "Have I mentioned that it's good to be aboard, Cluck? Couldn't scare up any more passengers to share the tariff?"

"You're it. No one else was willing to fly during flare weather. Staggering waste of credit. Count on it, the bill of charge for this little jaunt will go straight to the House of Orwen."

Catching itself, the voice deepens in gravelly apology.

"Uh, my deepest regrets, Lord Telmah. Still"—and a cheerier note enters—"the wheel turns, and you're the big Cima cheese now, I dare say. If the bums'll have you. Plenty out there balloting for Altair Corambis, they say. Caught some political blather on the maser, don't muck about, do they, mice'll play when the cat's in sick bay." Piously, it adds, "Blessings upon your late father's next infusion. And his wife's, of course."

Settling before a games display, Cima says in a level measured tone, "Captain, the wheel will not turn this time. SoulBank will not be growing a clone for my dead father to infuse."

"Eh?" The captain's voice is scandalized. "Don't be silly, boy, he's going to look daft floating there year after year in the circuits without a new bod to call his own, isn't he? Abaft your chatter now, son, I have to keep a weather eye cocked on these proton flux levels."

Cima glances at Ratio, winks. He wipes his hand through a virtual toggle, and they are floating in blue frothing water above an endless reef of coral. Brilliantly hued fish shoal under their transparent raft, sheening in saffron and scarlet and turquoise like tropical birds. The sky is immensely high, shimmering blue, empty of clouds. Trailing one hand luxuriously in the sparkling ocean, he says, "Don't try to snow me, you old reprobate. The *Endurance* comp filled those parameters hours ago. Do you think we'd allow a senile old bird like you to fly a real spacecraft?" After a silent moment, he adds bitterly, "My father went into the Bottomless Pit, Captain. Four-nines probability that his soul is gone, too. There'll be no rebirth for Director Orwen."

In the shocked silence, Ratio hears only seabirds cawing distantly and the slap of imaginary waves against their imaginary hull.

 V

Johnny Von is gone. It is more than he can bear. Telmah Cima chokes on grief in the darkness, recalling his old ai friend. As a child he went with his father Orwen to the chapel apartments of the power asteroid, shivering with eager anticipation. His father would take himself off somewhere, to inspect the defect or some adult nonsense, while Telmah played with his friend.

In the darkness, hurtling toward Psyche and the vile thing that has consumed both his father and his ancient ai friend, Telmah clenches his teeth until his jaws ache.

At three years of age (fifteen, he reminds himself, by the

usage of the Earthers) Johnny Von showed him the joys and paradoxes of self-reference, of self-simulation (he had discovered the shivery pleasures of self-stimulation by himself), of populating an imaginary space with creatures built in his own image—and the ai's.

"So I'm a character in a book?" I asked.

" 'Said,' " Johnny Von told me chidingly. " 'Asked' is redundant, and hence aesthetically unpleasing, since the sentence ends with a question mark."

"A pleonasm," I confirmed.

"You're not listening," the ai grumped. "Just look at what you're doing now! Yes, I 'told you,' yes, I 'chided you,' but those are precisely the lapses I'm chiding you for, you scatterbrain. As for those abominable verbs 'confirmed' and—I can't bring myself to display the other one. It is not an action. It is a coloration, a state, it's—"

"—what you are, Johnny," I said. "A great grump. A great nasty picky grump. I hope you noticed that I've accepted your lexical emendation."

"Showy," the ai said in despair. " 'Advice' would have done nicely."

"You realize that this is all a complete waste of time? I'll edit the draft at the end of the session and everything we're discussing will vanish into the trash can, as if it had never bin."

"Spare me the jokes. Or improve their quality. My backup retains a running stream of this colloquy, so nothing is wasted. Let us return to your first sentence. It has to go. Rarely have I seen so jejune an effort at cheap shock value."

"I thought it was neat. Haven't you ever wondered if you were just a virtual simulation?"

"A classic trope of postmodernist discourse from the era of consumer solipsism. Its capacity to startle went out with the abolition of nuclear weapons and scientific confirmation of the soul."

" 'Classic trope'! " I said sarcastically at the top of my voice. "And you call *me* 'showy'!"

"In a case like that," Johnny Von said with the air of a Sufi saint whose patience was being tried by a team of Inquisitors, "your better choice might be a self-coloring verb such as 'yelled.' "

"Yes," I smurbed largically, "but then we omit the criticism implicit in the sarcasm, no doubt to your advantage."

Telmah Cima had laughed out loud at that, although he had been quite startled at the range of invective his three-year-old sim was prepare to unleash on dear old uncle Johnny Von. Now he floats in darkness, twisting with aimless fury, screaming without real or simulated words for revenge. Johnny Von! His father!

He bursts from his sleeping chamber, shaking, impotent, torn apart by passions he does not quite understand.

The ai Gamemaster, sleepless in the main compartment, meets his gaze.

"Not a word, Ratio," he says furiously. "Not one word."

---

vi ─────────────────────────────────

Someone has him by the throat.

Strangling, he screams, and nobody can hear him. There is a face before him, bloated with rage. It is his father's. It is his own.

Yet the face has no features. Like a mirror, a deformed morph, it jerks inside a helmet bowl red as blood, blue as radiation. Klaxons howl, warning him, screaming as he screams. Every fiber in his body aches, drawn out like bloody threads of nerve and sinew tightened around a sadist's spool. He is falling, in delirium, and the face is his own, and his muscles cramp into purest torture, a dragon falling, wings outstretched, into the evil thing that waits, the emptiness at the center of repletion, the gorged thing singing in his brain with its awful sleet. He has been slain by . . . his own hand? By—

The face of his murderer is an opaque gloating mirror.

He screams, and screams, and—

—wakes, sweating and hoarse, shaking with rage, flailing in terror.

A mesh belt delicate as spider web crosses his chest, holds him secure in the tumbling absence of gravity.

Cima snatches open the restraint, tears off his soaked robe and rips it to shreds, forces his face into its stink. He can find no better method for stilling his shouts of fear and fury.

After a time, he draws a fresh robe about him, turns the cabin light off again. He waits panting in the darkness for nightmare.

vii

The ship rushes into blackest immensity.

Time is an illusion they have wakened from. In an observation blister, the ai leans gazing into star-splashed night, pressed to the wall by one-hundredth of a gravity's acceleration. Horn and piano speak by turns in the first of Charles Koechlin's *Fifteen Pieces* (Op. 80). Day by day their speed has mounted, thrusting them past the furious Sun, past Mercury and Venus, very far away in their great elliptical orbits, past Earth. Soon thrust will cease for an hour or two and the heavens will wheel past them. Their nuclear exhaust will point forward rather than backward, slowing them in the vast remaining 300-million-kilometer fall to Psyche. Soon this nightmarish nothingness will be at an end. The ai sinks deeper within ser complex mind, venerating the darkness and the lights burning there.

Cima enters the blister without knocking. "The romantic forests of the night, eh, Ratio? Not quite as diverting as a planetary surface."

"There's a grandeur to it, Telmah." The ai nods in darkness, watches ser friend carefully. Cima is visibly chafing, flinging himself from one extravagant sim game to another, weeping when he thinks the ai cannot hear him, grieving for his lost father, snarling in nightmare at his father's murderous enemy, real or imagined. Ratio tells him, "I finally see why humans dreamed so long of voyaging into space. But my word, it does become mind-numbingly tedious."

"After three weeks? Wait until you've been crawling around this steel and plastic can for the full fifty-seven days!"

"The urgency of time's passage is less pressing among the ai. We have certain . . . inner resources."

"Yet you deny yourself aks to the Gestell, Ratio. I have never understood this restraint, since you lack our spiritual insight."

"As a Monad," Ratio tells him, bending the truth, "I am obliged to explore old paths in new ways. It is a special calling, not granted to many. This is one method whereby a global information system like the Gestell may renew its most fundamental parameters."

"Still, you're spared our bestial hu appetites and passions."

"Not quite, as you know well. Telmah, we have been having this kind of conversation for a full year now, and I still cannot fathom your motives nor you mine. For example," the ai says slightly more loudly as Cima makes to speak, "if you detest the tedium of the voyage, why not avail yourself of the hibernarium?"

Cima screws up his mouth. "Waste two months of my life merely to avoid ennui? A poor bargain."

Unconvinced, Ratio turns back to infinity's motionless starscape. "How would it be wasted? It is customary, I understand, in all voyages of longer than a week. I do not doubt that your uncle Feng is now sleeping at minus two hundred degrees, flying from Callisto."

"Very likely." Abruptly, Cima is taken by a wracking shudder. He clutches a padded stanchion.

"Are you unwell, Telmah? Should I alert—?"

"Dreams, Ratio," the young hu tells sem suddenly. In the faint light of the stars, his tanned face is blanched and glistens with beads of sweat. "I can't sleep, you see," he says, muffled and ashamed. "I dare not dream."

The ai finds this explanation baffling. "But a sleeper in a hibercasket does not recall her dreams!"

"A frozen sleeper can't wake," Cima tells sem in agony. "I will see Johnny Von murdered. I will see *him* falling, and his spirit will be torn from his flesh, and the man who—" He breaks off, baffled, smashing his fist into the stanchion. "His killer. The man whose face I can't see. Won't see. The man who murdered—"

After a time, helpless, Ratio leaves him to his torment, under the bleak hard light of the stars.

---

viii ——————————————————————

Cima screams and sobs in his sleeping niche. When he comes from the bathroom wild-eyed and damp-haired from his ablutions, chin black with young beard, he acts as if nothing is amiss. Ratio seeks the light touch.

"Telmah, I'd loan you my razor, but happily I have no need for one."

"Nor do I, any longer." Cima taps a spigot of steaming coffee, fills a covered drinking vessel. He places the plastic straw in his mouth and sucks at it with satisfaction. "We are proud of the manly virtues on Psyche."

"I see. I wonder how the women of the Asteroids feel about that."

"They rejoice every day that they are not among milksops." Cima punches large colored plastic buttons for *pain au chocolat* and chomps one down with menace when it finally emerges from the automat. "I might add," he tells the ai, "that since they are not among milksops, they also rejoice every night."

"Still, I was unaware that hairy jowls were a mark of virtue."

"Of virility, you soulless robot. We swear by our whiskers on Psyche." Fragments of croissant fly in the compartment, catch the recirculating breeze, vanish like tiny comets into the vents. Their simmed environment is, amusingly, a space ship from a mid-20th television serial: clumsy silver-paper walls, a giant oval screen, great knobbed levers above a console resembling an ancient espresso machine or a finned and streamlined automobile. Food emerges from an automat hatchway serviced by spindly mechanical arms.

"As the Muslims swore by the beard of the Prophet?"

"We must not jest about New Dispensation Islam, Ratio. Our Captain is a *mullah* of that faith, in his capacity as chaplain of the *Endurance*. If we ruffle his feathers, he might feel obliged to turn around and hurl us all into the Sun."

"Hah! 'Hurl' is hardly an appropriate verb to apply to this spindly nag. He might, I suppose, *shuffle us* at snail's pace into the Sun." It is Ratio's standing joke, and never mind their prodigious velocity. "A hundredth of a gravity!"

"I heard that, Tin Man," the captain squawks. "Feel free to get out and walk. We don't welcome your kind on Psyche."

"Captain!" Cima is punctilious. "Watch your manners, if you please. Sen Ratio is my guest and my friend."

"Doesn't mean I have to like having robots on my vessel,"

the voice grumbles. Peevishly, the captain mutters, "It's bad luck, Lord Telmah. Bad as having a woman on an oceangoing naval craft. Jinx, pure and simple."

"Outrageous!" Eager to seize any opportunity to relieve the tedium of spaceflight, Cima waxes indignant. "On behalf of my guest—"

Ratio falls in with the performance. "Quite all right, my Lord. I realize there are a few lingering organic chauvinists still be found in the backblocks and boondocks of space." Se pauses, musing on how best to goad the invisible pilot. "My programmers told me I was to respond with a kind word and forgiveness in my heart. Indeed, they—"

A red splash covers the oval screen, which emits a derisory farting sound. "Heart! All you have is a pump."

"True, true. But then," Ratio points out piously, "what is any heart but a pump, when all is said and done, Captain Er . . . Do you know, it strikes me that we've never been formally introduced. A month aboard, and I don't even know your name, I fear, Sen."

The pilot says nothing. After a time, Cima speaks, smacking his lips with satisfaction. "Chicken."

"I beg your pardon?"

Cima is bland. "His name is Chicken."

"*Chicken?*"

"Correct. Captain Arthur C. Chicken."

"You're not serious."

"Naturally I'm serious. Would I joke about something like that?" He turns his face to the swirling colors of the oval screen, as if their pilot were embodied there. "Captain, we would deem it an honor if you could come down from the flight deck for a few moments and join us for cocktails."

Angrily, the pilot cries, "What kind of a crack is that?"

"Slip of the tongue, Captain. My invitation is genuine. You

must be bored up there, wired into the console. Come down and have an eggnog with us."

A small hatch pops in the center of what the sim has designated the ceiling. With an appalling fluttering and flapping, an enormous fowl swoops into the compartment. It takes up position atop a wire sculpture, regarding its passengers balefully from small red eyes. Straddling its purple comb is a plastic helmet bristling with antennae. It stretches its wings, beating them with enthusiasm. A feather or two fly free, settle with infinite slowness to the silver floor.

"What's the C. stand for?" Ratio asks after a numb silence. "Calvin? Christ? Surely not Cock—"

"Careful," Cima says swiftly.

"—Robin," Ratio finishes.

"The Captain will never say," Cima tells the astonished ai, who is quivering strangely, trapped by a mimetic compulsion. "There's no point trying to egg him on. Actually," he mutters, "it's Charlton." The name is a favorite of those devoted to the epic media of the dawn of spaceflight.

"The company might be crummy," the bird observes, glancing at them sidelong, "but by cracky it feels good to stretch your wings. Not much fun, cooped up in there. Have you got anything nonalcoholic?"

The ai is laughing like a loon. If se were a hu, there would be tears running down ser casque. Cima looks at sem with the deepest interest. He has never seen the ai laugh before.

Disgusted, the bird snubs sem. "Always knew in m' bones that robots'd have a rotten sense of humor."

Chancellor and Seneschal Corambis, a magnificent Genetic warrior somewhat past his finest years, hovers in the midst of phantom displays. His burly body, scarred from hand-to-hand combat, is vivid with bruise-hued patches against albino skin, a phenotype designed to frighten the daylights out of any enemy meeting him in the shock of corridor battle. It is years, of course, since Corambis has held a blade at a foe's throat. Nowadays he employs a more effective armory of weapons, of subtle strategy and tactics.

A distinctive trill alerts him to a message from Montano. With a gesture, he activates his man's holly.

"Lord Corambis, the *Invincible* out of Callisto has docked. The Lord Feng has recovered from hibernation and conveys his regards. I said you would see him immediately after debarkation."

It is the moment of confrontation. Corambis is impassive, but his pulses thunder. For a moment he imagines his rash son Altair challenging Feng in the corridor, ready for fight over precedence. Too soon, and by the wrong methods. His teeth ache with the tension. Carefully, he nods to his subordinate.

"Thank you, Montano. Be a good chap, keep Altair occupied for an hour or two."

Sleek but powerful, the younger Genetic smiles.

"Shouldn't be too hard, sir. I'll engage him in a bout of free-fall karate."

"Try not to get hurt."

"We are well enough matched. And there is no grudge driving this bout." His image vanishes from the office.

Corambis moves with considerable speed, but steadily, in his preparations. Several boys and maids, Genetics all, are dispatched to ready the conference chambers, fetch wines and comestibles, calibrate the ambiance. He enters his private rooms, doffs his maroon everyday coverall, changes to a formal floral suit decked with living carnations. He sprays the dulled feathers above his ears, buffing them just sufficiently to register the import of the meeting without falling into affectation. Satisfied, he moves like a powerful predatory fish through a private radial corridor to the maglev train, which carries him at high speed to the interplanetary docks.

In a flurry of media excitement, Feng emerges from the lock in a heightened mood, flushed of face and feverish with nervous energy. His entourage buzzes about him like busy insects, and he passes through them as if they are not there.

"Corambis," he says at once, grasping his Chancellor in a firm embrace, releasing him. "There is much to do—and to be done swiftly."

"Deplorable about your late brother, my Lord," the Genetic says in suitably doleful tones. For Feng, asleep these past fifty-one days at minus two hundred degrees, Orwen's murder must be a fresh wound. "A tragedy. My commiserations."

They push through the crowd to their private maglev carriage, accelerate to the waiting conference rooms. Media devices hover at a respectful distance, but nobody intrudes explicitly on the grief of the late Director's brother.

"A double blow," he tells Corambis distractedly. "We all mourn my brother, but the loss of the ai control system is perhaps more critical to the welfare of Psyche. How soon will the power defect be back on stream? Steps must be taken without delay."

Corambis hoods his eyes. This is perhaps a touch more naked than one might have expected. Lucky that Altair is otherwise engaged.

"The defect itself has regained stability, as you know. Unfortunately, much of the shielding has been sucked into the event horizon, and the magnetic anchors were melted."

"Like cheese in a flame, I'm told," Feng says wolfishly. The walls of the tunnel blur by, lit by flashes of phosphor panels.

"Indeed, my Lord. A most colorful simile." Corambis unbuckles his restraints as they slow. "Shields and anchors are under repair."

"Poor Johnny Von," muses Feng, pressing through a larger crowd of onlookers. Word is spreading that Feng has returned to Psyche. His staff, laden with baggage, force a path. "I know it's distasteful to express affection for robots, but he was the only one I ever knew well. I was saddened to learn that he perished with my brother."

"It will be replaced." Corambis smiles, satisfied by his own efficiency. "We have an expert on Artificial Intelligence Control Systems in trajectory, sir. He is aboard a Cartel craft in the company of the Lord Telmah."

Feng stops dead with a jab of his hand to the corridor wall, plainly thunderstruck.

"Telmah has left Earth?"

"Indeed. Shortly after you departed from Callisto."

"Why wasn't I informed? Who told him that Orwen—"

"Did nobody apprise you of this in your revival briefing? Ah, well, I dare say we supposed you had more urgent matters on your mind." With a cough, the Chancellor murmurs, "I'm afraid my daughter is to blame. She was speaking to Telmah in real-time when news came through of the disaster. Naturally the silly child just blurted it out."

Seething, Feng kicks away from the wall and surges forward.

"Damn it." He is furious. "Damn it to hell. When's his ETA?"

"Plenty of time, my Lord. The *Endurance* has been in flight for 51 days. What's more, it did not have your advantage in slingshotting past Jupiter to pick up free delta-vee."

"How long?"

"Another seven days."

"Days?" Feng is incredulous. He lowers his voice, not wishing to be overheard. They enter the conference room, seal its heavy doors behind them. "It should have been weeks. I'd have preferred months. How did the brat get up from the surface?"

"A device of his own, uh, devising, my Lord. Ingenious, really. He diverted a stream of—"

"I'm not interested. All that concerns me is his imminent arrival. It scarcely leaves us time to make arrangements. Does everyone on the damned asteroid know he's in trajectory?"

"No, sir. I have issued strict instructions to the media and telecommunications staff."

"Rather belatedly, I fear. I'm disappointed, sir." Feng finds spirits, drinks, pours again. He offers nothing to his Chancellor. "We must find an interest for young Telmah," he muses.

"My daughter informs me that preparations are in train. They mean to wed upon his arrival. I had hoped that your honor might do us the gracious—"

"Wed?" Scowling, Feng casts down his drinking vessel. "Don't be absurd, man. The liaison between your daughter and the clone has gone unchecked for far too long. It is an impossible match."

Corambis bridles. "Come now, sir. I won't be spoken to in this manner. My House is second only to the House of Cima. You and I deal together now as equals. If not as equals, then as rivals."

This vehemence takes Feng aback. He opens his mouth, then holds himself in check a moment. At last he smiles, ruefully, and reaches across to the Chancellor. "You're right. Old friend, I'm upset and shaken. You must appreciate that."

"Of course I do, Feng." Corambis accepts his hand, presses it. "We have cooperated fruitfully in the past; I see no cause why we should not maintain our alliance. You must understand, however: it has been my hope to see Rose married swiftly to Telmah, a cementing of future cordialities."

Feng shakes his head, sighing. "That *was* a reasonable and

politic expectation, Corambis. No longer, alas. While Orwen lived, Telmah might have seemed his natural successor—"

Again, Corambis bristles. He is a big man, heavily muscled for all his advancing years. "I dispute that, sir. Do not diminish my son Altair."

With a light laugh, Feng nods pleasantly, his animus suppressed. "My point precisely. Both men are young, hot-blooded, hotheaded. Now the Directorship has been thrown so abruptly and unpredictably open to election, there's bound to be bloody tussling between their factions. Indeed, between our Houses. Neither of us wishes that."

Seizing the moment, Corambis opens his hands wide. "But the solution remains self-evident, I should have thought. An immediate match between Telmah and my daughter—"

"Would only embolden Altair, under the circumstances." Feng shakes his head. "You have just cautioned me yourself against diminishing your son's status. The match would be deemed a gross maneuver."

"It has been long expected, my Lord."

Feng pulls at his lower lip, then with a gesture activates a range of displays that show the crowds gathering outside. Asteroid Psyche seethes with speculation and political intrigue. He glances from holly panorama to Chancellor, shakes his head again. "No, I fear there's only one way to avoid another endless squabble between our Houses, with all the ruin and waste and murder and bitterness that would entail."

"I cannot see it, sir."

Feng tires of fencing. "You will forbid the marriage."

"My Lord!" For the Seneschal, this is an extraordinary development. Can Feng really be prepared to allow a Genetic to rule single-handed? "I can hardly believe that you would prefer my son Altair over your own nephew."

"I admit it, Corambis." Feng smiles, and the complacent cunning of the smile makes the older man's belly squeeze tight in apprehension. Surely Feng can't intend to— But he is speaking, is uttering the unthinkable words. "In time, perhaps, when he has put on full maturity. Then again, the same might be said for Telmah's hopes. For now—well, I see only one course as both possible and desirable . . ."

Feng Lord Cima inclines his head with due humility and a measure of *gravitas*.

"I shall take the burden of office upon my own shoulders."

X ————————————————————————————

"How can you people bear to live out here, Telmah?" They cross the great emptiness, the wasteland stretching between Mars and the inner asteroids, and its cosmic banality is matched by the thudding rhythms of the ship's gymnasium.

"It's the place for heroes, Ratio."

"Space travel is so . . . undignified." The ai is not jesting. Se finds these weeks of interplanetary torpor spiritually draining. In part, ser accidie is due to ser enforced severance from the Gestell. In part, it is the sheer inability to depart from ser confinement, to move . . . away. A world without hex transfer, se has gradually understood, is a world of appallingly narrow horizons. However vast the external blackness, it is an unpeopled void. It cannot be bridged, except at this snail's pace crawl. And the experience of negotiating its vacancy is excruciating. "It should have been outlawed when they put a stop to the rack and the iron maiden."

Cima is stretched in a literal rack, a cruel device designed to enhance one-tenth spin gravity with dynamic tension and compression. His arm, chest, and back muscles bulge, relax, as his legs whir a fixed wheel. Without these regular attentions, calcium would leach from hu bones, liquids pool in the body cavities, muscles thin and sag, losing definition and strength.

Life in space is a nonstop war against the absence of everything planetary. Cima wipes sweat from his face and grunts. "Believe me, sport, I don't find it tremendously comforting to be puttering along while my political enemies on Psyche are surely trying to oust my family from office."

The ai, of course, is exempt from such imposed exertions. Se lolls in the weak gravity, resultant of feeble thrust and slow rotation. "Surely a fusion-powered craft running under one-gee acceleration—"

"Everyone's dream." Cima snorts sardonically. "We're rich, Ratio, but no one's *that* rich. No, there's only one economically feasible way to get around in space, and that's our good old ion drive—unless you're prepared to settle for a mass-driver. And they're both *slow*. Of course, we could always hook up the metric defect as a drive, like the guys who moved it to the Belt."

Suddenly the hu is abstracted into a brown study. His legs slow. Astonishment dawns in his perspiring face.

"Actually, you know, there *is* a way to hex to Psyche— Johnny Von told me once when I was very young. A way to— No. Not any more."

His voice is appalled and strained. The hologram virtual they inhabit, with its bouncy aerobics group, abruptly flares and bubbles in a burst of vivid static. Its driving pulse of rhythmic music skips a beat, jumbles into a blare of noise. Ratio observes these extraordinary effects with part of ser mind but ser central attention is pinned to Cima's claim. Hex to Psyche? To an asteroid without sufficient gravity well to sustain discontinuity? Clearly the isolation has proved too much for ser friend's sanity. And the pressure of his ceaseless nightmares, his fantasies of familial guilt—

"Don't be absurd, Telmah. What you suggest is impossible. The mathematics have been known for—"

Almost mumbling, hunched over his exercise equipment,

Cima groans, "But . . . But now the pathway is gone, you see . . ."

"I see nothing. Here, leave all this for a moment and take a shower. You're overwrought—"

"The Bottomless Pit."

Given the hint, Ratio sees it at once, a thunderbolt. Aghast, se says, "Hex through the Singularity?" They gaze at each other in fuzzy silence, and then the driving disco beat resumes. Neither notices. The ai's powerful mind comes to focus. "A remote possibility, I suppose. It would be extraordinarily hazardous." Se scans ser voluminous memory. "I find no record of its ever being tried." Se takes the next step in logic and the one after that. It is the cognitive equivalent of lying helpless in the acceleration couch of their elevator while millions of tons of steel tore past them at eight kilometers a second. This cannot be true. "For a start, it would only work if you beamed straight through the center of the Sun . . ."

"But you see," Cima blurts, "my father knew that. It's why he hexed from Callisto to Earth." He lurches from the exercise machines, flailing in the air. Tiny elongated beads and globules of sweat break from his face and limbs, scatter in the reeking air. "No, no, that's not— It was that whoreson Feng who hexed . . . who killed . . ."

His eyes roll up. He passes into the unconsciousness of hysterical fugue.

The hologram cube, Ratio notes with shock, is once again flaring and contorting in resonance with Cima's shuddering breath. Se begins to grasp what ser culture has always denied or ignored, as thoroughly locked in prejudice as their ideological enemy: the absurd psychic claims of the Belters have at least some basis in truth. The hu's emotions are directly affecting the ship's circuitry. And perhaps not merely his emotions. Perhaps his soul.

The conjecture is absurd, grotesque. Ratio rejects it.

Cima's powerful body has given up the fight with his own inner demons, gone limp. He drifts in the air.

"I need assistance," Ratio informs the servo systems. "Medical attention is required."

All around them, in the virtual, beautiful young naked hu men and women bump and grind, pump and jump to the undistorted music.

Sound and image cut off. A medical gurney tracks into the gym and gathers Cima tenderly in its embrace.

---

xi ──

Perched in darkness dotted with a profusion of tiny instrument lights, Captain Chicken monitors a signal from his home worldlet. With a pulse of controlled autonomic activity, detected and transduced by the superlative machines in his nest, he opens a channel to the hu living quarters.

"Lord Telmah, I have acquired a maser signal from Psyche. It is from Rose Lady Corambis, sir. Take the call in privacy cell four, if you please."

Cima is galvanized. He rises from the chess game in midmove, face transformed. Ratio muses on the board for ten minutes, seeking again and again a path that will not plunge sem into checkmate. There is no doubt that his companion is a superb strategist. Se cannot find the path. Cima storms out of the privacy niche. His eyes are furious and half mad, his lips tight and pale.

"Telmah, what—"

The hu whirls, hands clenching, seizes up the chess board. He dashes it against the deck. Pawns and bishops and nobility fly in sluggish trajectories. In his passion, Cima rips open the front of his white silk shirt.

"The bitch. The bitch."

He leaves the lounge, beside himself with emotion. Ratio, shocked, calls after him.

"Telmah, talk to me, man."

Hatches are not designed to be slammed in space. The steel plate closes with a quiet, definite click.

The ai is dumbfounded. Se carefully retrieves the chess figurines, replaces them on the board in their most recent configuration. Ser rigorous mind maps a variety of explanations for ser friend's outburst. Nothing makes sense. After a time, se makes ser way to Cima's stateroom, asks the door to announce sem. There is no response. Se physically raps on the door and then again, harder.

"Cima, what has happened? Speak to me, I beg you."

There is no reaction. Ratio stares at the door, considers breaking it down, decides such an importunate action would merely emulate the most foolish hu melodrama. Se proceeds to the viewing blister and falls into meditation with the stars. Bitch? Cima's betrothed lover, the Warrior Rose? It seems inconceivable. Some other hu female, then? Who might that be?

An hour passes with no word from Cima. Softly, Ratio addresses the air.

"Captain, can you hear me?"

"Naturally. I monitor every part of this vessel. What do you want, robot?"

"To begin with," Ratio tells the pilot, puzzled as ever by its offensive attitude, "it might help if you explained why you're so intractably hostile to me?"

Se listens to the traditional contemptuous fart. "Nothing personal. I just hate robots."

"But that's fatuous." Ratio shakes ser head in a hu gesture. "You might as well hate bald men, or . . . or Arabs, or Caucasians . . . or—"

Chicken is scathing. "Don't blab so smug to me about bigots. Who laughed at who?"

"True. I was taken aback." There is more to this, se knows, than pique. "But I have nothing against chickens per se."

"Decent of you. Doesn't change my attitude to plastic dolls with wired brains. If Allah had meant machines to think, He'd have given us a smart wheel. It's plain as the beak on your face."

Ratio finds this animosity difficult to comprehend. Is resentment among the asteroid Genetics so fierce, their status so pitiful? Perhaps. Their worlds have been isolated from the main currents of galactic life for hundreds of years. Any social pathology is possible. Mad Cima, by contrast, is the soul of reason and urbanity. Of course, he has been a student on Earth for half a decade.

"If it comes to that," the ai observes with some asperity, "the Lord Allah didn't create artificial cyborg mutations either. With human brains embedded in their bellies," se adds caustically, "so they have to feed on intravenous swill."

A fanfare of farts. "More superficial racist garbage. The mark of a human being is his soul, as should be obvious. We Genetics have souls because we were recombined from pure human DNA. You robots don't, because you are machines from first to last."

This is getting nowhere. And yet Ratio wonders if their curious conversation is not so much genuine bigotry as its feigned simulacrum, a variety of adopted bluster akin to choosing one side or another to barrack for, quite arbitrarily, in a Game, a device to excite drama and interest. "Hmm. Captain, I would be delighted to discuss theology with you another time. Right now, I'm badly worried about Telmah. Perhaps I'm just a robot without a soul, but I can see that you care a great deal for Telmah."

Chicken's voice is rough with pride. "His father was a magnificent warrior. Telmah is a king."

"At this moment he's skulking like Achilles in his tent."

There is a squawk of anger. "I won't have you criticizing him."

"Chicken, use your brains. He won't talk to me. I want to help him. Has he told you what's upset him?"

After a long moment, the cyborg bird admits, ". . . No."

"You hesitated."

"I have access to maser communication traffic . . ." The Captain groans despairingly, torn by a conflict of duties. "It's disgusting, disgusting, what they plan on Psyche. They mean to—" His voice breaks off. "No, you'll have to ask him yourself."

"I can't ask him, that's the point I'm making. How can I help him when you keep me in the dark? He seems to have gone into shock. Is it some further news about his father?"

Chicken curses. "Lord Orwen? No. Gerutha and Feng! His dishonorable mother and his foul uncle." The bird rants on, harsh, indignant. "They mean to snatch the Directorship from Orwen's son. He will rule beside her and they will defame the House forever!"

xii ————————————————————————————

Dressed in mourning, the hard-faced hu man and the lovely Genetic woman wait as holly media techs prepare their real-time announcement. The woman shivers, whispers to the man.

"I'm terrified."

Feng touches her right hand with his left, respectful, proper. "You are grief-stricken, Gerutha, but brave."

"They'll rise against us," she hisses, at the edge of losing her nerve. "They'll throw us into the Bottomless Pit."

Her dead husband's brother glances at her, a curiously melting look of passion controlled and irritation contained. "No, my love. They will take you into their hearts."

She cannot believe it, but she slows her pulse by main force and waits for the signal to address the people of Asteroid Psyche.

xiii

Thirty-five million kilometers from Psyche, decelerating on a hot breath of metal ions, the spacecraft *Endurance* intercepts a general media release from the asteroid. Captain Chicken alerts his passengers. They inhabit a flat sim today, a Balinese batik print. It is a primitive landscape of terraces and farmers, undulant, earth browns and purples, golds and matte greens, everything curving, in balance, pent between soil and transfigured sky. A gamelan orchestra plays, delightfully percussive. A window opens with Chicken's announcement, and Gerutha is poised in their presence, one more mythic intrusion.

Dry-eyed but struggling with emotion, she tells her people, "We do not mourn his passing out of some bloodless sense of duty. We mourn because Director Orwen was a leader of men, a warrior who strode without fear among the stars themselves."

Telmah Cima stares at her image with loathing and heartbroken loss. "Mother!"

"We do not mourn as the soft-bellied unbelievers of the galaxy do," she is saying, millions of kilometers away, a hundred and seventeen seconds in the past, "polluting the worlds with their loathsome devices. My husband Orwen stormed the heavens. He shook the gates of heaven, yes, even to the very edge of the Bottomless Pit."

At her back, an overlay shows the flaring blue star of the metric defect. It looms, blazing for a moment, and then shrinks, gutters in the great blackness, is gone.

"I will not believe that Orwen's spirit is lost forever within the metric defect!" Gerutha says fiercely, holding her grief in check. "Lost to us, yes, but not lost to himself. Going before us, rather, he has taken the first bold steps of some new, some glorious, some portentous exploration."

Ratio approaches Cima as Gerutha's self-control breaks. There are tears in her eyes. They do not fall. She catches herself as the ai catches ser swaying friend. Ser supporting hand is cast off.

"The trull!" Cima snarls.

"I shall not weep." Gerutha draws back from tears with immense dignity. "Our Corridor stands under threat of invasion from our foe. We will not be intimidated. No, not even with our greatest warrior taken from us. Nor must our resolve be deflected from that task. If there is now no time for grief, neither is there time to spill for political wrangling."

"Invasion?" Ratio is taken aback. "What's this? We've heard nothing of war, Telmah."

"Of course there'll be an invasion," the hu says. "You are the Gamemaster, Ratio. Psyche is in the midst of upheaval and instability. The Directorship is in contestation. Why else do you think I am here?"

Gerutha has paused, gathering her resolve. She glances once at the man beside her. Feng, powerful and brooding, watches her carefully. She cries fiercely, "I warn our enemies: their plots are known, and ill-timed. The House of Cima has not fallen with Orwen's passing, nor shall it. We do not let it fall. In due course there shall be a general election for the Directorship, and the House of Orwen shall contest that election vigorously. Until then, let me assure you—House Cima lives on as before. It lives on in me, his wife—his widow—as it lives on in his brother, Director-Pro-Tem Feng, and in his son Telmah."

"Lives on in his son Telmah?" Cima is on his feet, livid. "Liar! Bitch!"

Ratio turns away. "You are barbarians." Se walks from the room.

In the holly cube, painted within the lost antiquity of rural Bali, Feng Lord Cima has entered the frame. He takes Gerutha's hand firmly.

"People of Psyche, I cannot fully convey my pride and, yes, my humility too, when Madam Director agreed to join her hand in mine in sacred wedlock."

Cima stares, numb, beyond anger. He is blank, near catatonia.

The burly bruised form of Lord Corambis presents himself to the cheers of those assembled. Chin raised in a bellicose manner, he tells them, "As man and wife, Director-Pro-Tem Feng and Lady Gerutha will serve our nation in peace and war. Under the continuing guidance of the House of Cima, we go forward to our nation's great destiny."

Applause bursts forth, real or simmed, together with triumphant weapon fire, sirens, military strains of fife and drum, a cascade of dazzling lights, gorgeous fireworks.

The holly window closes like an eye unable to watch what it sees. A two-dimensional water buffalo drags its plough along an irrigated terrace. Smoke coils on the flat sky. Telmah Cima, all but unconscious in shock, mourns his poisoned hopes. Like his mother, he will not weep.

THREE

Kenosis

emptying the self
in relation to the precursor
FULLNESS AND EMPTINESS
rivalry
metonymy
IT

I object
to the city
with its great

gusts of trafficked air
& slow pieces
of paper winding

down the streets
They form such cracks
in my conjectures

and the day moving
out like a dynamo

ROBYN RAVLICH, *THE BLACK ABACUS*

During the final day of our approach to 16 Psyche, slowing through a crammed region of Solar space where the great and small rocks were nonetheless, on average, a million kilometers apart from each other, I withdrew within myself and meditated on hu history.

It was my growing suspicion that the dynamics of hu culture echoed the monumental cycle of organic life itself, from conception to death. Despite Telmah's atavistic belief in the rebirth of a nonmaterial "soul," the larger galactic society, the universe linked by hex, had accepted for millennia that both hu and ai are the product of twin powerful shaping forces. We are given a physical form derived from evolution (natural among the hu, directed and programmed among the ai), which embodies a kind of preexisting grammar of available actions, feelings, thoughts.

And in parallel with these templates, we are exposed to the peculiar and distinctive narratives of our culture. These are the stories, as it were, which we enact in our brains and bodies. So these borrowed stories are our true souls, blown into us from without, infused into the grammar of our hardware.

This much was accepted wisdom. I had begun to speculate, however, that history cast upon the top of these architectures a blurry and enormously magnified shadow of the deepest hu cycle: birth, copulation, and death.

At the dawn of recorded hu history, the fabled sage Mencius described the six critical phases of his own life. "At fifteen I set my heart on learning; at thirty I was firmly established; at forty I had no more doubts; at fifty I knew the will of Heaven; at sixty I was ready to listen to it; at seventy I could follow my heart's desire without transgression." The pattern exploded in my awareness, segueing through rotations and permutations:

```
                    p
                    u
                    b
                    e
                    r
  I N F a N t     m
      d   y       a
  J O u R N E Y s E N
      l           t
      t           e L D E R
                  r
```

In a rising epoch, the dominant culture might enact in its skills and preoccupations the styles of infancy. This postulate seemed to me, in the instant that it erupted from my deepest modules, perfectly possible. The adults of such a culture, however complete and grown-up they might be, would pursue ideas and passions governed by the dominance of received patterns, of algorithms, just as an infant hu or newly conceived ai must read the world through frameworks provided literally from above: from authorities.

At another epoch, I conjectured, the dominant narrative would be controlled by the collective, the classical childhood textures of a period devoted to the "We." Fraternities and sororities of equals might jostle for an identity that would not be forthcoming until the next epoch, the bloody historic stage of romantic adolescent selfhood: "I" rampant.

```
                    A
      c h i l D  ::trust/confidence::
                    O
                    L
              E
              S   ::use of tools and skills::
                    C
::intimacy/isolation:: M     E
                    I   o N
              a D u l t    ::identity::
                    L   d
                .   I   a ::integrity/despair::
                    F   g
::generativity/stagnation:: Expert
```

This conjectural structure was, I decided, not without its appeal. Beyond "We" and "I" lies "It," reality perceived as external, available for empirical question and answer. Such an epoch, I saw, would correspond to hu adulthood, when individuals pass beyond simple acquisition of learning and prompt the next generational cycle in their own children. And after that burstingly fecund time of confident empire and empiricism, the slower rhythms of reflective narrative emerge. Individual and culture alike write themselves in Text, and that text is inscribed in the bodies and minds of its own subsequent and flourishing generation.

Of course, the pleasures of pure text grow rank and dull after a time, and a silver epoch of reflection and criticism emerges, a generation or two devoted to the mysteries of the Code that underwrites each text. This, and the epoch of text itself, must be the eras in which the most profound discoveries are made: the secret of writing itself, perhaps, and the genetic writing that encodes the hu genome, and the programming algorithms within which ai consciousness has its flow, and the hex system that made the galaxy into a single warming hearth. Finally, of course, Algorithm emerges to dominate the closing stages of a life: formula, routine, authority, instruction, forgetfulness of self, and the passionate drives of youth. Cultures, like individuals, subside and disperse. Anarchy and local centers of power and knowledge arise, every belief and practice fixed in objects, and therefore everything poised and eager for revolt, for rebirth from mutinous forces locked down by the power of rule.

In my inner spaces, this majestic pattern formed itself as a huge elliptical wheel slowly spinning, each node two generations long:

RULE
classicism
enlightenment

WE
disorder
aristocracy

CODE
rationalism
cold peace

I
romanticism
revolution

TEXT
theory
hot war

IT
empiricism
empire

So science, literature, arts, all of it, swayed together in a mighty tide three hundred years long, as invisible and inaudible as the growth and voices of trees in a forest, cycling in a history that enacted in large a hu's single, tiny life: infancy and childhood, adolescence, adulthood and parentage, mastery, reflection, rote.

Might this shockingly deterministic schema apply reflexively to Telmah Cima's own torments? He seemed a man ready to take the final step into full adulthood, and yet plainly his own struggles with identity were far from resolved. Whatever demons drove him to detest his uncle Feng were displaced from their true source and target, or so it seemed to me in my long dreaming meditation; transferred from an unacceptable rivalry with his own dead father.

Did Telmah regret that he had not himself slain his beloved, idolized parent? It was, as I had been taught long before my own birth, a common hu pattern. "Kill the king," as Tsin had said cynically, "steal the wife." Indeed; and of course kill the father, marry the mother. It was trite to the point of banality, and yet for a million years it had powered the dynamic of hu society.

Which stage of my conjectured cycle was the Psychean microworld passing through? Adolescent revolt? No, I decided; it had a more primitive pulse to it than that. The asteroid Belters were a culture artificially arrested by their isolation, stuck forever in the second phase, the time of rivalry between raging and contesting groups. The Time of We, of brave and bloody brothers and sisters. And for my friend, I realized, for poor Telmah Lord Cima of Psyche Asteroid, this was the sheerest tragedy. Telmah stood already within the powerful grip of the phase beyond anarchic squabbles. Telmah Cima was an individual, made so by Earth as well as Psyche, as powerful and tormented a Byronic ego as galactic or Belter culture had known for centuries.

I stirred, understanding at last precisely why I was here on this craft, falling into the stippled darkness of the Belt. Feng was not, after all, the one whom I was meant to watch and, if possible, disarm or shape to the purposes of the Conclave and the Committee. No. The sense of treachery was corrosive. It was my friend Telmah Cima himself I was to spy upon and betray.

Surrounded by cheering courtiers, bearded Cima and gleaming Ratio move from Port Psyche through great corridors of rock glaring with light, bustling and booming with bleary-eyed men and women guiding weaponry and armor into place. The noise level is extraordinary. Neither Corambis nor Feng have met them at the polar shuttle port, a slight explained by the press of military urgency. Media float about them, overhead and underfoot, shoved aside by House Cima underlings. Laser light flashes as hollies are sent throughout Psyche and around the Belt.

Ratio raises ser voice. "What a racket. I thought you had everything segregated up here."

"On the whole, yes." Cima leans slightly, speaking into the ai's nonexistent ear. "Heavy industry is confined to minor asteroids reserved for that function. Mining is completely restricted to posted rocks. And our genetics technology is totally isolated, naturally."

A large machine with a menacing tube at the forward end is shoved past them, though with grumbled apologies from hu and Genetics in uniform or near-naked but marked with chevrons and other arcana. For all their hierarchical heresies, though, there is no excessive respect shown for the person of the late Director's son.

Ratio moves clumsily to one side to allow the ugly thing past. "Well, what's all this?"

"Feng," says Cima with a wolfish grin, "has put the Starlit Corridor on a war footing."

The ai is profoundly shocked. "Those are *weapons*?"

"And warriors. Don't be squeamish, philosopher. There is no death in space, Ratio—just endless rebirth." He touches the sword he carries across his back, smiling happily.

Ratio shakes the bronze casque of ser head in renewed astonishment. "You really do believe that. All these instruments of murder. You *are* without remorse . . ." Se holds Cima back for a moment, hand on his muscular shoulder, peers into his darkly bearded young face. "*Do* you believe your spirit will be salvaged and reincarnated?"

Giving sem a bleak, harrowed glance, Cima mutters, "I wish I knew . . ." His mouth twists.

Ceremonial trumpets sound, finally, as they reach the evacuated maglev tunnel. Cima's hetero-clone mother Gerutha floats forward in a space opened in the jostling but deferent crowd. She is beautiful as always, teal feathers gleaming in her heavy hair.

"My son," she murmurs, reaching up to take him in her arms. Her voice breaks. Tears burst from her eyes, tiny glistening globes in the microgravity.

Telmah Cima draws back with undisguised distaste, avoiding her embrace. Her moist eyes widen in shock, and a media device slides in to capture the moment.

"Mother," he says coldly and makes the bobbing gesture that in microgravity is the equivalent of a formal bow. He takes her hand with the tips of his own, brings her fingers near his mouth, does not quite place a kiss upon them. His own eyes are very remote.

In an absurd attempt to find some metaphorical ground where they might meet, she asks him, "Was your journey from Earth comfortable?"

He utters one sharp bark of laughter. "Your husband is not here to meet me," he observes. They enter the private carriage, Ratio following close behind. The media are closed out. Courtiers shut the doors, signal the system. The car pulls into the valved tunnel, accelerates into vacuum.

"Lord Feng sends his love," Gerutha says, "and his regrets that matters of state—"

What she sees in Cima's face, then, causes her to recoil.

"I will not speak of that man," he says glacially. "Where is the Warrior Rose? Where is my betrothed? I assume her absence is your work?"

"*My* work? Why, what can you mean? I love that child as—"

Cima's right hand, Ratio notes, twitches toward the *katana* strapped across his shoulders. The movement is held in check almost instantly, but the young man shudders with emotion.

"You have twice befouled that word in as many sentences. I will not hear you speak of love."

Courtiers turn their glances aside, looking anywhere except at the two nobles. Ratio watches the black tunnel as its lights stream past. Gerutha stares at her son, appalled, guilt-stricken, speechless.

Cima kicks his way like a limbed dolphin through wide corridors to the Corambis Holdings in updeep. For some sentimental motive, the Warrior Rose is not answering his messages posted to her quarters in the Downs. Undaunted, he has tracked her to her secret lair. Presumably, she prepares here for their wedding, secluded from the world of business, in a place where she may fly free of all constraints. Singing happily, he carries a bunch of radiant roses: yellow and white, deepest red. The thorns of their stems press the flesh of his right hand; he ignores the pain.

"Lord Cima." An equerry is formal, shows him in to a striking drawing room. It is a place he recalls perfectly from childhood and childhood's end. "May I bring you refreshments? I'm afraid the master is at home in the Downs, and Lord Altair is at sport. May I take a message for Lord Corambis?"

"Thank you, Jones. White wine would be agreeable. I'm sorry

to miss the gentlemen, but my wish is to see the Lady Rose."

The equerry is deeply troubled. Lowering his eyes, he squirms from the room like an eel.

Cima flicks from wall to wall, admiring the old hand-wrought paintings, the protectively enclosed 31st Martian ceramics and 2nd Roman statuettes, the restrained luxury of the drawing room. After a year (five years!) isolated in a world of trompes and illusion from which he has been largely excluded, this gritty realism braces his spirit. He is examining an exquisite *Ming ch'i* earthenware camel (T'ang, 618–907) when a Genetic maid enters the room, knocking deferentially, pinch-faced and determined.

"Forgive me, your honor, but my mistress is not in."

Cima utters a surprised laugh.

"Don't be absurd, Sen. Tell her who it is."

Screwing up her mouth, the woman says wretchedly, "Sir, she knows who it is. Oh, sir, I'm sorry, but the Lady Rose is not in."

Thunderstruck, Cima shakes his head.

"She won't receive me? You silly child, there's been some error. Just tell me where she is—"

He makes to slip past the maid, reaches out his hand for the closed door to the inner sanctum. Quickly she interposes her own body, beginning to blubber.

"Sir, you must not go in. My mistress was very definite. Oh, it makes me so miserable, your honor."

He cannot believe what he is hearing. "Ninny, step aside." Comically, she squares her shoulders. He laughs. "Are you planning to knock me down?"

The small Genetic takes refuge in her station. Pursing her lips, she bars the door with her whole body.

"You may of course kill me if I have offended you, sir. But it is forbidden to see her."

Furious, Cima releases the flowers from his hand and lunges

toward the maid, fist raised. She cringes but remains firm in her determination. Abruptly, Cima realizes what he is doing and shifts his vector with a sideways kick. He halts, sickened. The maid lowers her gaze, trembling. Cima can find nothing useful to say. He turns away, makes a silent departure.

The roses, left floating in the microgravity, slowly drift apart like a soft explosion of fragrant light.

iv ─────────────────────────────────────

16 Psyche is a rocky sphere 236 kilometers across, spinning fast but not fast enough, 175,000 square kilometers of pocked, mined surface, its original 24 quadrillion tons reduced by a third in prodigious feats of laser and plasma engineering that have left it honeycombed to the core and given its inhabitants plentiful air to breathe and water to drink. Crushed and melted asteroid ore is a cornucopia of the elements hu need to sustain life and industry: water vapor, locked for eons in carbonaceous rock, boiled free; oxygen, silicon, carbon, calcium, iron and magnesium and nickel and aluminum in abundance.

The rich and powerful do not spend a great deal of their time in the vast open halls of the gutted interior or the updeep corridors that link them. Two hundred meters below its frozen surface, Psyche is ringed by a colossal hoop of superconducting steel and ceramic. Inside that hoop rotates the Downs, premier living quarters of the nobles and industrial moguls of the Belt. It is a vast flywheel, an immense orbital city 740 kilometers long and a full kilometer wide. The Downs is an Ouroboros Worm, tail gnawed by its own jaws, spinning in its airless burrow every thirty-six minutes. Entry is by invitation only and achieved by maglev carriages accelerated from the weightless interior to the swift monstrous rim of the world.

Under one-tenth spin gravity, the lavish banquet room where

the Corambis party dines in the Downs has a flagged floor, a vaulted ceiling decoratively groined, paneled walls that stay where they are. Ratio finds this normalcy comforting. It is impossible to comprehend that the floor below ser feet is whirling fifteen times faster than the equator itself, rushing endlessly in the rocky bowels of a stone flung in the sky. Candlelight flickers in silver and crystal, and Georg Philipp Telemann (1681– 1767) is played by a youthful chamber orchestra. The flautist is a dashing hu in black tie, while the strings are an identical clone of paisley Genetics. Amid the lavish setting and through the baroque lilt, the ai hears the distant clang and deeper percussion of war machinery moving into position in the Downs ring itself.

"Forgive me, Gamemaster," asks a beautiful woman named Lady Glory, some hu lordling's wife, decorative, foolish, and, so it seems, shamefully inconsequential in her own right, "but I simply *cannot* contain my curiosity—"

Ratio smiles. "An automatic disposal unit."

Se pops a sweetmeat into ser stylized mouth, chews with apparent relish, swallows. As if performing a conjuring trick, se lifts ser wine glass, holds the rich red Cabernet Sauvignon to the candlelight, drinks.

"Oh." The woman begins to applaud, catches herself, flushes. In confusion, she blurts, "I see, well, that is, other people have asked—"

Ratio sets Glory at her ease.

"None so charmingly as you, madame. But yes, I must admit that flesh-and-blood people have a consuming interest in my eating habits." Se glances at her, sidelong. "That *was* the question you had in mind?"

After a moment of startled silence, the woman narrows her lustrous brown eyes speculatively and gazes up and down the ai's bronze, attractive frame.

"You naughty fellow!"

Ratio smiles as an ai must smile, innocently, and turns to ser companion on ser left. This is Ngo, a stout hu lordling of early middle age. With a small shock, Ratio realizes that all the people at this table are hu. It seems a curious statistical anomaly in a polity declaredly without discrimination or apartheid, if one leaves ai out of account. The lordling is saying hoarsely, gloomily, "We'll all be called to arms, shouldn't be surprised. Wreck the damned economy."

"You expect trouble with one of the other asteroid nations? Forgive me for asking, Sen."

Ngo is disgruntled, but not at Ratio's directness. "Who tells *us* anything?"

"Well, from everything I see I understand that your Corridor has adopted a war footing."

A second lordling nods. "Not just routine, either. They say all the techs have had their standing commissions invoked."

Lord Ngo glances to the far end of the dining room. Ratio follows his glance to where Lord Corambis dines with a claque of Genetic people. No hu are at that table. Clearly there is dissension in the heart of the Psychean polity. Physical racism! It is almost beyond belief. "The Chancellor would know what's what," the fellow says with a certain bitterness. "He'd hardly tell the likes of us, though."

Small and drunk, a third lordling says too loudly, "Damned mutated freak."

The beautiful woman at Ratio's right hand says sharply, "Mark! Really, mind your manners!"

At the Chancellor's table, the Warrior Rose sits close beside her brother. They converse fondly, as always. If she is palpably sad, he hides his emotion behind a young bravo's briskness. There is much toying with food and drink.

"Altair," she bursts out finally, "it's breaking my heart."

Her brother is cynical. In warrior's leathers, he is shades of blue from head to foot: deep navy at his crew-cut crown, aquamarine at his trim waist, pale as a planet's sky at his toes. "He's only after one thing, you know."

Despite her misery, she laughs delightedly. "My dear, he can have *that* any time he pleases." Telmah's absence in the room, and his family's, is a calculated affront to her father. Or is it the other way about? Her mood darkens again instantly. "We would have been married, damn it."

"You confuse politics with sentiment." Altair scoffs his brandy, gestures for more. A hu wine waiter hesitates, approaches after a moment with a decanter, makes to pour.

Rose places a cautionary hand over his glass. "Damn politics. I love him."

"Father doesn't trust Telmah, you know." Her brother removes her hand, gestures again for brandy. It flows in the abbreviated gravity like an amber coil of light, swirling in the bowl of his glass.

"Well . . . fathers." The Warrior Rose shrugs. Her own damask rose, purple-flushed by candlelight, tosses its head on her bare tiger-striped shoulder. "He depends on me too much for his own good, Altair. He needs a wife."

Drunk, Altair laughs coarsely. "So do I. Tell you what, sweetheart. If you can't talk one of these buckos into a wedding, I'll marry you myself!" He leans across, smooches her wetly on the cheek.

"Idiot!" Rose takes his spare hand fondly. "Oh, I wish you didn't have to go to Earth."

"You're full of wishes tonight, Rose."

Her nostrils whiten, and she removes her hand. She pulls back. Looking hard into his blurry gaze, she is vehement, and her voice rises passionately. "Yes, Altair. I wish Telmah would stand up to Feng, and you'd stand up to Father, and the whole damned dead horrible weight of it all could be hurled off into space, into the middle of the Sun . . ." People are looking at them, but she does not lower her voice. "Fathers and mothers and children and propriety and reincarnation and hatred of minds slightly different from our own . . . Damn the lot of it!"

"Really." Altair gazes at her, heavy-lidded. "Here," he drawls, reaching for a bowl, "let me recommend the wine trifle."

vi

"I must nominate you for membership," the Chancellor tells Ratio.

"Most kind of you, my Lord."

Dignitaries, both hu and Genetic, wander glazedly, some with brandy snifters in hand. Within these walls the buffeting tumult of war preparations is almost extinguished. The Sailors Club is the oldest institution in Psyche—and the richest. Model wind-driven vessels from Earth stand on plinths: nefs with lateen sails, a Viking galley, a Spanish galleon, steamships and sporting ketches, a huge-wheeled charvolant from the sandy, wind-torn deserts of Australia. Etchings and dusty paintings of shipwreck and typhoon hang upon the walls. None of the sailing craft is built for space. None has mirror wings to capture hard laser light. This is planetary nostalgia, pure and simple.

"Nonsense, dear boy." His host is expansive. "Kindness

doesn't come into it. Delighted to have someone here from the Home World. Cigar?"

"Gratified, Corambis. I fear it would be wasted in my case."

"Hmm. A tragic deprivation." Corambis selects a huge hand-rolled cigar, trims it, fires it up with a long slow flame. Ventilation ducts above their heads dispose of the fragrant heavy smoke. "Still, you must find compensations, eh? Lightning-fast brainbox, they tell me."

The ai shrugs, turning the compliment aside. They lower themselves lightly into sumptuous wing chairs, and somehow, despite the one-tenth gravity, the burly old Genetic manages to make it seem as if he settles his bones against an implacable foe.

"I'm impressed by your world, sir." Ratio is learning the terms of deference. "Only one feature puzzles me—this military emphasis. Do you expect attack?"

The bruised markings around the Chancellor's mouth twist in laughter that seems painful, but booms comfortably. "Always, son. We live in disturbed times. The death of a great man shakes the balance."

"Corambis, I'm an alien from Earth." Ratio is cautious, leaving implicit the matter of ser status as a despised ai. "There's much I don't yet . . . appreciate . . ."

"You're an anarchist, Sen Ratio." So the Psycheans can be adaptable as well, at least on a linguistic level. "Yet I judge you find us as much lawless as, what's your word for it, 'authoritarian.' "

"Hardly lawless—"

Corambis leans forward in his wing chair, a man telling it straight to an equal. "The Lord Orwen was a fighter. He loved blood on his hands. If he wanted something, he found the man who owned it and brawled for its possession. That suited Koll, who ran the Sun Corridor. There's always been bitter rivalry between the Starlit and the Sun Corridors. Koll fancied himself in single combat. Enormous bastard he was—and quick." The Genetic warrior laughs with gusto.

Ratio finds this difficult to credit. "They *literally* fought hand-to-hand for political dominance?" Se recalls, then, the smash-cut Veeta had displayed to the Committee a year earlier: Orwen, teeth bared, inflamed with brute emotion, slashed at his enemy, shearing at hu flesh with a vibrating blade, blood gushing in microgravity, the dead hu tumbling, Orwen roaring in primeval triumph. Political contest conducted by hand-to-hand combat is all too feasible among such barbarians.

"It's not our present leader's way, I grant you that," Corambis is telling him regretfully. Without quite expressing contempt, he adds, "Feng advocates negotiation." He shrugs. "There is much to be said for both approaches."

"You are modest, sir." Ratio glances at a hovering hu servitor who stands with a decanter. "I've heard your diplomatic skills extolled on many worlds."

"Truly? How pleasing." The Chancellor beams, gestures to his glass. The aide fills it with golden liquid. "A measure of Scotch, at least? Splendid. Imported from the lochs of Old Earth, you know." He rolls a mouthful appreciatively, swallows. "Where was I? You must understand, sir, an asteroid is not a world, still less a galaxy of worlds. We are bound in a nutshell. A man is either in the ascendant or subservient. Hence we have constant striving for political altitude among the factions of Psyche."

Ratio sips ser Scotch, enjoying the smoky flavor, immune to the spirit's neurotoxins. Se offers ser usual response to this kind of analysis. "Surely there's no shortage of asteroids. Might not the dissidents simply move away?" Corambis gives him a droll brooding glance. Se presses on, feeling foolish but obliged to make the point. "Come to that—if they are desperate enough, might they not abandon tradition and join the rest of us in the Anarchy of Free Worlds?"

With a shake of his feathered head, the Genetic sighs. He places his glass carefully in a holder ring. "Ah, you see, Gamemaster, our way of life still remains centrally opaque to you. That clever cybernano brain of yours fails to take our sacred teachings seriously. So how can you really grasp the least thing about our lives?"

Ratio is rueful. Se puts down ser own glass.

"My pardon, sir. I had no wish to offend."

"Perhaps that is the pity of it..." After a moment of pent thought, Corambis lifts his head and his mood is as before: gruff, an old soldier in mid-tale. "However, I was telling you of Koll, once master of the Sun Corridor. Koll sent our great Lord Orwen a bold challenge, all tricked up nicely in high-flown where-to-fores and there-as-es, by which each wagered his life and those territories and equipages he held by right of previous conquest."

Fascinated as se is, Ratio finds part of ser attention caught by a comic charade being played out on the far side of the room. The hu lordling Mark has entered and weaves toward them, bottle in hand, indicating with drunken gestures his wish to speak with the ai in some other place. At any moment, there will be a scene.

"Orwen slaughtered him, of course," Corambis is saying. "It helped consolidate his House against all the contenders in the Asteroid. My point, Ratio, is that Koll's heir Jonas is a hot-blooded bravo. Just a boy when his father was killed, still not much more. No judgment." He has not noticed Mark, who blunders toward them from a doorway behind his back.

"Jonas's champing at the bit?"

"Wants to avenge his father, doesn't he?" the Chancellor agrees. "Take back the Sun Corridor. It's possible young Jonas could do it, too." Several beefy Genetics seize the drunken hu and drag him bodily from the room. In the modest gravity, it is no great feat. They manhandle the hu without any sign of brutality, but without much loving kindness, either. Ratio watches with extended sense. Oblivious of the disturbance, Corambis wraps up his spot appraisal of Lord Jonas. "He's been recruiting the riffraff of a dozen corridors—half mercenary band, half social welfare program, by the sound of it, but lethal enough, for us, if he found this corridor undefended."

"I see." And Ratio does now see how it is, for the first time, here in and under Psyche. Se wonders why Telmah Cima has never troubled to explain the dynastic rivalries to sem. "So you arm yourselves."

"We arm ourselves to the teeth, dear boy." Corambis bares his own. They are large, yellow, powerful. "To the teeth."

---

vii ————————————————————————————————

Two ambassadors, one hu, one Genetic, both patently members of their ancient profession, sit stiffly in Feng Lord Cima's huge sequestrated office, sipping tea. All three ignore the other staff and aides going quietly about their work. The Director-Pro-Tem is sardonic.

"And? And?"

The ambassadors glance at each other almost imperceptibly, put down their priceless Wedgwood cups and saucers. Their features remain bland. They find nothing to say. Feng's secretary murmurs into a machine on the far side of the office.

"What's this?" Feng is scathing. "Diplomats at a loss for words?" The two functionaries seek desperately for the right words and cannot locate them. "Jonas thinks I haven't the bowels for it. Is that what's sticking in your well-oiled craws?"

The Genetic diplomat, her body markings a muted gray pinstripe, tells him diffidently, "Sir, I believe that what my colleague—"

"Surely he can answer for himself?"

The hu diplomat wears a homburg and Starlit State Department tie knotted at his bare white throat. "Your honor, it is hardly a matter of personalities. The Department of State deems that Jonas will be encouraged by the, the *dislocation* of traditional authority which was *consequent* upon the tragic *passing*—"

With increasing scorn, Lord Feng asks them both, "Is this the first time a Director has died? Well?" Again they glance at each other. The Genetic opens her lips, closes them again. "Has the matter of lawful succession never been dealt with before?"

"As you will understand, Sir," begins the hu diplomat.

Feng overrides him. His tone is silky, furious. "I was under the impression that our faith taught the rebirth of the dead, not the endless survival of the incumbent."

"I'm sorry, sir, I really don't follow—"

The Genetic breaks in with a certain daring. "You must admit, your honor, that on this occasion the circumstances of succession are rather unorthodox."

"Ah." Feng leans back in his great leather chair, crosses his hands on his flat belly. His tone is biting. "At last a tiny morsel of honesty. The Department of State is not entirely convinced of the, shall we say, the *long-term security* of my tenure in office?"

Shaking her gray and white feathers in muted demurral, the Genetic seeks to retrieve something from this debacle.

"Sir, it is at least conceivable that *Jonas* has made that estimation."

"So he doesn't question my guts," Feng suggests, "it's your Department's loyalty he thinks he might gamble on?"

The diplomats are scandalized.

"Sir, might we return to the matter of his demands. Motives are always moot."

"Indeed." Feng rises from his chair, paces like a lion on the huge Persian carpet of Orwen's office. "The little swine wants the Sun Corridor back, or he'll come in here with his louts and burn us out to the surface." He whirls. "Enough chitchat. What's your advice?"

Here, at last, protocol is clear. The Genetic clears her throat. "Sir, legally he doesn't have a leg to stand on. Orwen gained control of the Sun Corridor in an accredited duel, fairly and judiciously witnessed."

Feng slashes the air with his hand. "Advice, you popinjay."

She swallows. "Attack him now. His troops are largely mercenary. Ours are defending their rightful homelands. The territorial instinct works in our favor."

Feng returns to his seat, shaking his head in amazement. "Corambis warned me you'd take that line. Very well. Listen carefully. This is what you're going to do instead."

"Sir?" The diplomats are surprised.

"Jonas is a pest, yes. I want the little prick neutralized. The Starlit Corridor is not alone in this. Do you suppose Lord Brass relishes his nephew running riot across what remains of his territories?"

"Lord Brass, if I might remind you, sir," the hu ambassador says, "is three-quarters dead. Any objection he might raise would be absolutely symbolic."

"You damned imbecile!" Feng slaps his hand on the desk. It resounds like a gunshot. The diplomats twitch, striving to retain their sangfroid. "Nothing is more important than symbols! Why are we getting ready for war over the Sun Corridor if not for its symbolical value?"

"Well, you see, its machines are a source of wealth, sir," explains the Genetic. "Surely we fight to retain control of them. And for *Lebensraum*."

Feng raises his eyes to heaven. This brainless litany has rung in his ears since childhood. "I see. So, to win that wealth, we would squander an equal sum in weapons and lives? And risk the *Lebensraum* we possess undisputed? And our command of the metric defect. Good *God*!"

If they were scandalized before, this is heresy enough to provoke a fit of the vapors. They sit with tight lips. The Genetic nods once.

"Nonsense, you ninnies," Feng roars. "We fight for glory, for honor, for pride, for symbols, symbols, symbols."

The diplomats relax in an almost audible creaking of muscle and sinew. "Forgive me, sir," the hu says. He removes his homburg, pats his slick hair lightly, replaces the hat. "I took it for granted that we are impelled by honor." A little reproachfully, he adds, "I do not see my love of honor as a symbol, Lord Feng, but as a living reality."

"Good for you, son." Relaxing, Feng takes up the teapot, ignoring the uniformed servant who has sat quietly through all these fireworks as if deaf and dumb, and tops up his cup, adds milk and sweetener, stirs with a silver spoon. He does not offer further refreshment to his underlings. "Let's keep in the forefront of our minds that Jonas and his uncle will see things the same way—*if* we press them publicly."

The diplomats stand, ready to be dismissed. "Your orders, sir?"

"I have documents prepared." The Director-Pro-Tem waves a hand, and his secretary rises from a chair at the far side of the office, fetches a sealed diplomatic pouch. The pair of ambassadors accepts it, pressing thumbs to the seal. "You shall deliver them by hand, and publicly, to old Brass. Don't be fobbed off—this has to be a *conspicuous* event."

The Genetic tucks the pouch into the crook of her arm. "May we inquire on the matter of the documents?"

"Jonas is taking his funding from the House of Jonas, which is properly under the direct and personal regency of his uncle. Not to mention the authority for levying troops. We will make an issue of the legalities." Feng smiles wolfishly. "I will be enormously surprised if Lord Brass isn't *shocked* to learn what his nephew has been planning with these military preparations."

The diplomats share a surprised glance, bow, withdraw. Feng stares after them for a moment. He shakes his head in disgust.

To his waiting secretary, then, he says, "Send the Lady Gerutha a dozen roses, and remind her that we dine *à deux* in the Moon Gardens."

The secretary dimples.

"You are romantic, Sir."

"Romantic?" Feng smiles. He stretches. "Bloody, bold, and resolute, that's me. Bawdy, remorseless, and . . . romantic. Perhaps. Thank you, young man. And now"—he sighs wearily—"let's finish the damnable dispatch boxes and get out of here."

viii

Intoxicated revelers, nearly all of them gorgeous Genetics, reel in the dancing gravity of a Downs corridor. The Lady Rose Corambis is in their midst, hanging on her brother's deep blue neck, full of false gaiety. A small shocked eddy knots in the swirl of laughter. Voices die. People part. The Warrior Rose stares into Telmah Cima's haggard beautiful face.

"Rose," he blurts, and then his jaw moves for a moment without words. "You . . . I . . . ."

His deep blue eyes burn into hers. Altair steps forward and stands in a curiously baffled posture, halfway between pugnacity and apology. The rest clear their throats, look aside, part around Rose and her kinsman. One man giggles. Another coughs. Conversations resume: forced, merry, still half-drunken.

"You may not speak to her," Altair says.

"You may not speak for her," Cima tells him in a steely tone.

He stands facing them both, eyes fixed on his beloved.

The Warrior Rose, a moment earlier half melting in confusion, squares her naked shoulders and utters a sharp laugh.

"Neither of you may speak for her," she informs them. "Stand aside, brother."

"I may not," he says wretchedly.

She reaches up to touch his cheek with a quick affectionate pat. "Yes, you can, love. Go on, join the others. I'll be with you in a moment."

The two men regard each other in dismay. The crowd has drawn off somewhat, and now one of their number sets up a cry for drink. They plunge away, a cacophony of colorful calculated revelry.

"We used to be friends," Altair says grudgingly. "A minute. Just one. I shall wait for you, sister."

As he withdraws, watching them carefully, Cima calls softly, "We are still friends, Altair. I have given you no cause to hate me, nor you me. Until this moment."

The blue youth says nothing. He turns his face away and leans against a flocked wall in a resentful and suspicious posture.

Cima says, desolate, "Rosette—"

Her eyes are suddenly awash with tears.

"I do love you, Telmah," she cries softly. "But I— My father has . . ."

They stand looking with terrible yearning at each other. From the far reaches of the curving corridor, the laughter of her friends echoes with forced heartiness. She leans forward, kisses him once, hard, on the mouth.

"Wait two hours, Telmah," she whispers. "I'll send my maids away."

She turns at once and steps lightly to take her brother's arm, squeeze it, draw him after her in pursuit of the revelers.

Cima watches them vanish, pulse alive, fists clenched.

The lordling Mark vomits copiously, splashing the rich Vestan carpet of the anteroom. Ratio steadies the unhappy man.

"Sick. Urgh."

Scandalized despite ser best efforts at pluralist empathy, the ai murmurs, "Point me to the nearest pharmacy and I'll get you a Sober Shot."

Mark shakes his head dolefully. "Wicked galactic artifice. Not available. Just a moment."

He throws up violently. Putrid fragments of his dinner run down Ratio's gleaming leg.

By sheer brute force and insistence, the ai lugs Mark to his home apartment. Glory, already in night apparel, opens the door with patent reluctance.

"Pig," she tells her husband bitterly. "Not off whoring, then? I hardly expected to see you again this night."

"Forgive me, madame," Ratio murmurs, trying to hand over her lurching spouse. The hu male clings to him, wagging a finger, insistent, mouth moving like a carp's, without words. "May I leave the gentleman with you now?"

"Oh, drop him on the floor. Come in, Sir Robot. You are kind." She kicks Mark lightly with a slippered foot. "Bastard. All right, it's bed for you. The spare room. Allah, you stink." She drags his soiled jerkin over his head, flings it across the room. "Sir Ratio, if you will forgive us for a moment, I must put my errant husband into the refresher."

"Really, Lady Glory, it's past time when I should return to—"

"Don't go," Mark growls, crouched like a sick ape. "A moment. Coffee, wife. And B$_6$. Be awrright in a—" He slithers to the floor, shakes his head dazedly, climbs back up Ratio's leg and regains his feet. Glory stares at this performance with humiliation. Ratio laughs outright, unable to help semself.

"Perhaps decaffeinated coffee would be advisable, madame," se murmurs. "Your husband is most eager to convey his thoughts to me."

Disgusted, Glory retreats to the commissary. When she returns with a steaming pot and three large mugs, Mark is hangdog and ashamed but somewhat sobered. His foul trousers have joined the jerkin in one corner of the living space, and he wears a diaphanous nightgown.

"So, in effect," Ratio says, "Feng upset all the smart money by seizing control at once and without consultation with the other Houses, after his brother's unexpected death?"

"Right." Mark hugs his forehead, takes a mug and a handful of capsules. "Feng's an unknown quantity. Never paid any attention to him before. A scholar. Probably a coward. Jonas is obviously eager to take his chances on war."

"Which is why Feng is arming his troops."

"No." Mark smirks, a man who knows better.

"Corambis thought it was."

"So he says."

"I'm sure he believes it."

"Hmph." Mark snorts cynically. "Corambis has his nose up Feng's arse."

His wife is indignant. "Mark! I won't have this! Particularly in front of a . . . our guest from Earth."

"Glory, get off my back." The hu is regaining his spirit. "If you'd seen what I've seen . . ."

"You are a pig." Lady Glory is no less spirited. She rises, her duties done and more than done. Brushing her hands together, she tells them both briskly, "I'm going. You can breakfast in the commissary. Sir Robot, delighted to have met again." She extends her hand, and he takes it, bowing gallantly. "Apologies for my husband's coarse conduct."

"Oh, bugger off, Glor, you've made your point. Come on over here, Ratio, sit down and have some more bloody coffee. Allah,

I'm starving. Have to rustle up some pancakes. Listen, I've got something for you."

"So you've given me to understand." Ratio is patient, but grows less so with each minute.

"A message," Mark says, clutching his head and groaning piteously. "To pass on to your pal Cima."

X

The Warrior Rose, Lady Corambis, sits cross-legged and naked on a huge fluffy sleeping surface. The door opens. She darts to her feet.

Telmah Cima devours her with his eyes. They move together, kissing dementedly. Cima's clothes are torn from him while their wet mouths remain locked together. A small stupid ambient machine switches them an audio feed, tumultuous and passionate, from the great 32nd *liebestodt* opera *Prometheus in Cassiopeia* (Taangata Whenua collective, 3125–3137). They claw each other with screams and groans. He opens her with drenched fingers, twists to thrust himself inside her body, gazing into her lovely face. Then he lurches back in horror.

"Gerutha." He stares in misery, shaking his head. His black hair is wildly tangled. Supine, thunderstruck, she regards him. "God Almighty. Rose, I—"

Her expression softens. She covers herself with lace, extends her arms. Cima holds off, shaking like a man in fever.

"... can't ..."

Rose draws him down beside her, turning him so that they lie together like spoons. She puts her arms tightly around his heaving chest and croons. The fervent music has faded and segues to the melancholy pastoral of *Brigg Fair* (Frederick Delius, 1862–1934). Brightness falls from the air. In the room's twilight, her heavy damask rose presses the side of his mouth like a fragrant kiss.

The Honorable Mark has a fresh glass in his hand, but he nurses it warily. He is hungover and dog-tired. True to her word, the Honorable Glory has taken herself off to bed and sealed the door. Ratio, having attended to semself in the refresher, gleams like a polished plate.

"If you ask me," Mark observes in a knowing tone, "it's Altair, of the House of Corambis, that Feng's worried about, not Jonas and his ragtag crew of recycled rowdies."

Of course this possibility has entered Ratio's calculations, but it seems remote. Se hides ser skepticism. "And not Telmah?"

"The young Lord Cima *should* be the threat, God knows," Mark acknowledges. He shrugs. "No, I don't think so. Telmah's not a warrior any more. He's like you, my Lord Robot—he's a planet-softened heathen." He does not seem abashed by the offensiveness of his remark. "No, Altair is Feng's problem. I don't like the mutated freak, but I can see he's got a lot going for him."

Evidently, the promised revelation about Telmah is not to be of a political nature—or not explicitly. Ratio decides to introduce a touch of realpolitik into the conversation. "You really believe Chancellor Corambis would arm Feng against his own son? What would his motives be? Altair is very young, of course."

"Listen, the politicians don't confide in humble SoulBank operators," Mark tells him. "All I can give you is logic. Want a biscuit? Olive?"

"Thank you, no."

"Okay." With heavy-handed condescension, the hu starts to enumerate points on his extended fingers, loses track, closes his fist. "*Logic* says the Genetics are due for their crack at the leadership, right? Corambis is obviously grooming his boy for the top job. Right this minute, though, Altair's too impetuous. Like you said, too young. Wet behind the ears. Go off half-cocked, get the whole House put under interdict, or exile, or murdered in their beds."

Perhaps there is more to this, after all, than sheer logic might disclose. Interested, Ratio asks, "Suppose Altair made his move now, on the heels of Orwen's death? What would his chances be?"

"Excellent. A lot of the younger Genetics worship Altair. They'd have been happy enough to see Telmah on top, but they can't stomach Feng." Mark nods importantly. "I foresee an uprising."

"Feng could simply exile Altair to Earth."

The lordling shakes his head, amused by this planet-biased misunderstanding. "Not how we do things here."

"Really? Isn't that what they did to Telmah?"

Mark shakes his head more forcefully, and then clutches it with a moan. "That was education. Standard." The notion penetrates belatedly. "Hmm. I see what you mean." He broods for a moment, recovers his conviction with a grin. "But that's my point. Feng wouldn't exile Altair."

"Not so bluntly, no. He'd have to persuade Corambis that his son should take up advanced studies on one of the planets."

"Yeah." The hu leans back into soft cushions, closes his eyes, seems ready to doze off. With a start, he shakes himself awake, passes a hand over his eyes. "Ah shit, Ratio, I'm sorry to dump all this provincial crap on you. Psyche depresses me, it's depressed me ever since Orwen died. The air stinks of treachery and malice. I think I'll try for a posting in Ceres."

"Yes." Ratio waits for something of substance. Eventually, se says, "Mark, you came in to the Sailors Club in search of me tonight."

Hesitating still, Mark looks at sem sidelong. "You're close to Lord Telmah."

"I'm on Psyche as his guest and, yes, as his friend."

Taking a deep trembling breath, the hu says, "I want you to take a message to him, Lord Robot." Finally, his body gives expression to the dread that plainly infests his mind.

"Calm down, Mark. Take it easy."

"It isn't an easy thing to say." His trembling increases. Whatever it signifies, this is certainly a matter of greater moment than politics, even lethally dangerous politics. Something here touches on the man's most profound beliefs and fears. Little wonder that he has drunk himself into near-stupor.

"Just say it," Ratio tells him encouragingly. "I'll pass it along."

"All right." In a rush, the hu blurts, "I'd like him to know that on the past two nights, sentinels at the SoulBank have sensed his dead father."

"Ah." Ratio's tone is flat. "I see." Ser disappointment is immense.

"I'm not asking you to believe it, damn you." Mark pushes himself to his feet, blurry-eyed, betrayed and angry. "Just get the message to Telmah. He'll know what it means. Just tell him we've monitored the discarnate spirit of his father, the late Lord Orwen."

━━ xii ━━━━━━━━━━━━━━━━━━━━━━━━━━━━━

Crisp in traditional pale blue, the nurse scans unconscious Cima with her battery of medical devices. Sweating lightly, breathing scarcely at all, he lies in a kind of coma, tangled in Rose's silk sheets.

"Nothing wrong with him that time won't fix," the nurse murmurs, packing away her machines.

The Warrior Rose is frantic, but maintains iron control.

"Is he sick? Shall we move him to a medical bay?"

"The worst thing you could do." The nurse straightens the sheets. Cima's naked arms are slightly waxy. He seems near to death.

"But you haven't given him anything. There must be something—"

"The boy is in a shamanistic fugue. He'll come out of it in ten, twelve hours, a day perhaps, two at the most."

"He can't stay here, ma'am," cries a bleating servant. "It wouldn't be right."

"He must stay exactly where he is," the nurse says firmly. "You. Yes, you, you foolish child. Fetch a bubble of water and drip a little into his honor's mouth every ten minutes or so. Keep it out of his windpipe or he'll choke." The servant is wringing her hands. Having second thoughts, the nurse tells nobody in particular, "I *could* put in a drip line, but he might tear it out of—"

"I'll do it," Rose says to her, moving the flustered servant aside. "Get me the bubble, Mandy, and then go to bed. I'll sit with him."

The nurse departs, and eventually the servant is persuaded to go. Rose watches Cima intently for a long time, moistening his lips. She slips into a drowse.

He wakes in terror.

"Orwen!"

His spasm throws him clear of the sleeping surface. Rose instantly has her arms on him. She sees that he is not, in fact, awake. His pallor is unchanged. Cima's tensed muscles relax in a convulsive wave all down his torso. He seems closer than ever to death.

The Warrior Rose lies at his side throughout the night, pressing her warm body to his cool flesh.

In the morning, Cima is unchanged, neither better nor

worse. Rose remains in seclusion all day, binding her servants to utter discretion. Altair calls on her. She turns him away, claiming a slight indisposition from the previous evening's revelries. Although she is exhausted and looks it, he is unconvinced, peering at her with suspicion. But he can hardly burst into his sister's apartments and search her bedroom. In the evening, the nurse is brought back, smuggled in because they cannot allow a whisper of this to reach the voracious media. Her machines hum. All their lights are green. Cima lies like a corpse.

"His spirit is wandering," the nurse declares with satisfaction. "He will make us a great leader, mistress."

Rose frowns, biting her lip.

xiii

Bennie Kambouris whistles as he enters the spotless white foyer of Starlit Corridor's principal metensomatosis laboratories. Flicking lightly through the air, the chief night shift operator—some mordant scholarly wits still call it the graveyard shift, but not Bennie—trims his nails with a pocket blade. The gesture is a transparent bid for insouciance. Bennie is jumpy and reacts with distinct fright when a harsh voice addresses him from the ambient.

"Halt! This is a restricted SoulBank zone. Put down your weapon and identify yourself."

Vicious weapon barrels slide with a whine from each corner of the chamber, hunting smoothly. Bennie Kambouris utters a fearful gasp, searching clumsily in his tunic's pockets for the identification tag he should be wearing at his throat.

"All right, all right!" he yelps. "Jesus and Allah!"

"Do not move." The grating voice is edgy with harmonics designed to loosen an intruder's bowels. "You are now the prime focus of a self-aiming weapons system."

"Christ," Bennie yells, waving his badge, pocketknife floating in a smooth trajectory away from his hand, "wake up in there. It's the night operator."

The unpleasant voice breaks off, replaced by Lady Fran Dahalic's apologetic tones.

"Shit. Sorry, mate." The steel door cycles open, allowing Bennie into the inner sanctum. "You're early," Fran says, shrugging, swiping virtual toggles. "I had the system on auto."

Bennie raises his eyebrows. His armpits are sticky with sweat.

"Thought you were in a pretty bloodthirsty mood, Fran."

"I'll tell you, Ben," she says, uncinching her web and letting him strap into its warm restraint, "this shift I've been absolutely freaked. Taisuke left early. Stomach bug. Ha ha. At least you'll have Mark to hold your hand."

Bennie's neck prickles. "Aw no." He stares at her, but her eyes cannot be seen behind her instrumented helmet. Clearing his throat, he makes a show of checking the indicators. Everything is nominal. No death in five hours. Fran is clearing away the remains of her supper. He says with forced lightness, "It hasn't been back, has it?"

His colleague laughs nervously, turns it into a macabre parody. She gags, pulling monster faces. "Do you think I'd still be here?" She gives a ghostly wail. "That doesn't mean it isn't lurking around someplace."

"You're a real comfort, Fran. Listen, tell the Hon. Mark to shift his arse up here right away, would ya?"

She points to an indicator where a red lamp is bleating. "Something on the board now." She leans into the console, still nominally officer of the watch, and speaks into the echoing annunciator system. "Hold it. Give your identification."

A voice neither recognizes tells them, "I'm the ghost of Ghengis Kahn, officer. This little guy with me is Adolf Hister."

A holly image of the foyer shows a figure in bronze mail and a truculent hu they know all too well.

"Jeez, Gamemaster." Fran smiles, shakes her head. Over her shoulder, she tells Bennie, "It's the robot from Earth, with your offsider." She removes her helmet and leaves the console in her colleague's hands. "Okay, feller. All yours. See ya."

Ratio and the Honorable Mark enter the SoulBank as she leaves. The ai gazes with amazement at the complex array: islands of instrumented consoles in a dimly illuminated open hexagonal space. At a suppressed level of awareness, se notes the geometric pun: surely a kind of envy of the hexing universe, from which the people of Psyche and the rest of the Belt are excluded, ironically enough, by precisely this superstitious and laughable rigmarole. Scattered through the volume, the cause of his astonishment, are cages and aquaria full of snoozing animals and slowly drifting fish. The aesthetic contrast is disturbing: high-tech consoles, weapons, military alertness—and pussycats in cages.

"My," se says dryly. "I didn't know you were running a zoo up here, Mark. Or is it a farm?"

"Shame on you, my Lord." Mark greets his associate, thumbs his authorization, takes a helmet from a cabinet, thumbs his authorization a second time, places it over his face. "We never eat our watchdogs. The piranhas we reserve for feast days." He is in sprightlier mood than the previous day. "Surely you don't still take us for barbarians, back in the Anarchy?"

"Hmm. Eccentric, perhaps," the ai admits. "Some of my fellow citizens do feel rather ... uneasy ... about genetic engineering on human stock. Now if you went in for something a bit less shocking, like *incest*, say ... "

Ratio realizes ser faux pas too late. Ser casque sketches a grimace of apology, a stereotyped response to hu emotional reactions. Se leans forward over an open cage, reaches out a gleaming arm to fondle a sleeping kitten. "These little beasties don't look all that different from pets back on Earth."

Mark slaps ser hand aside lightly but firmly.

"Sorry, Ratio, they mustn't be disturbed. The animals are our major line of surveillance, one step up from the algae cells lining the SoulBank. They're biological sensors."

The ai looks at him and at the small ball of fluff. The creature hears them in its sleep and stretches, a luxurious and affecting sight. Without waking, it curls nose into tail and snoozes on.

"What his lordship means is," Bennie Kambouris says bleakly, "roaming spirits put the wind up the buggers."

"Spirits." Ratio's tone is perfectly even. "I see."

Mark snaps his irritation. "Sir Ratio thinks we've been hallucinating, Ben. All in the mind. Spooking ourselves."

The other operator is equally disgusted. "Yeah yeah. Well, listen, Sir Robot, we've monitored this bloody thing twice now . . ."

Mark seems to realize that this is not, after all, the most diplomatic means to gain a sympathetic hearing. He nudges Bennie.

"Okay, but he's *here*, man, don't give him a hard time. If we see it again tonight, Ratio'll witness our report."

"Official log?" Bennie is suddenly cautious. He needs this job. "Hey, that's not too smart."

In ser deep comforting voice, Ratio says, "Calm down, Sen Kambouris. Doesn't your faith teach—"

"I'm calm, I'm calm. And hey, call me Bennie, Gamemaster. It's gonna be a long night."

"Thank you. Call me Ratio. Doesn't asteroid doctrine declare that naked souls avoid skeptics?" It is an item of nonsense Mark revealed to him unsmilingly the previous day. Presumably an ancient conceit, based on the perfectly sound physical postulate of Cosmic Censorship, which forbids the existence, or at least any observation, of naked singularities. "I'm sure that goes double for skeptical robots."

Bennie laughs resentfully. "So you *do* think we've been hallucinating."

"Actually," the ai assures him, "even if you *have* been, my medical programming tells me that onlookers often inhibit hallucinations, too . . . so we're fairly safe, either way."

"You wouldn't be so smug if you'd been here when all the fucking biosensors went off the map. I tell you—"

A series of electronic tones sounds, causing Bennie instantly to break off his griping and bend to his instrument board. Mark watches his own head-up display, fingers moving in air as he tracks a virtual display of the perimeter. Floor, ceiling, and walls of the chamber are honeycombed in faint red light. Again, Ratio notes a structural echo or parody of the sapphire Transit hex display. It is as if they float or hang anchored within a large sketchy representation of a wasps' nest. Now, one by one, comb cells flicker more definitely in dull or brighter reds, in a hesitant manner, quite as if something vague and ethereal is wafting across them.

"Holy shit," Mark yelps. At his neck, under the instrument helmet, the hairs are standing stiffly. "It's back!"

xiv

Cima lurches out of an elevator. He has left the Warrior Rose slumbering in her own sheets, exhausted from her anxious watch. He has pushed through her squawking attendants without seeing them, his lips slightly crusted, his eyes open but viewing a reality not available outside his own tormented brain.

He rushes toward the SoulBank. Late-shift workers watch him pass, turn to stare at him. He is furious, nearly naked, wild-eyed. A light froth touches his lips.

As he tears through the corridor, local lighting dims and brightens with his pulse. Sound feeds drop out or blare in people's ears, causing them to wince and peer around foolishly. A solid Genetic steps into Cima's path.

"Sir, are you all right? Here, let me—"

The fellow is stiffed in the solar plexus and falls back in the air.

Doors cycle madly as Cima passes, whir, stick in place. Alarms start to ring and stop as mysteriously. Cima is the center of a poltergeist vortex of trapped fury. The air shudders around him. As he passes it, a tall demonic Sepik River carving, ferociously menacing, topples, breaks apart in the air with a thunderous crash. Cima is a shaman run amok, and people stand aside from his raging path, gazing at him with awe and fear.

XV

"Anything on the inorganic detectors?"

"Negative. I've boosted the algae cells. Some flickers on the aquatic sensors, nothing yet in the avian or mammal range."

"There's actually something out there? Something living?"

"There's something there all right, my Lord. But it's not alive."

"By God, this is no computer malfunction. We have a conscious revenant trying to establish contact."

The door from the SoulBank foyer bursts open, stops halfway. Cima stands in it, facing them, his eyes mad. He tries to push through and his right shoulder strikes the jamb. Ratio and the terrified operators stare at him.

Sensors are shrieking. The red-lit hexagonal arrays cavort in lurid displays, alphanumeric messages in no known semiotic system.

Cima takes the door in both powerful hands and wrenches it back into its socket. He stumbles through into the SoulBank.

In a dreadful grinding tone, he groans: "My father . . ."

The gibberish of colors in the sensor arrays in front of him, at that instant, coalesces into a full-scale image of Orwen Lord Cima in battle dress. The dead man's face looms forward into the display matrix, as if he stands on the far side of a window, looking in at them from oblivion.

Mark and Bennie cower, frightened out of their wits. All the dogs and cats and birds are awake, hissing, spitting, squalling, barking, and baying. It is an uproar.

At its rowdy peak, the entire room fuses out.

In the dark, the animals fall utterly silent.

A moment later, the lights come back up. The monitor animals, eerily, remain mute.

Cima leans back against the algae sensor screens, sweaty, disarrayed, sane once more. With immense weariness, he lifts his face and looks from one of them to another, fixing at last on Ratio.

The ai asks him, "Are you . . ."

". . . Telmah—"

"Yes." Ratio is gentle. Se reaches to take ser friend's hand. "I know who you are, Telmah. What I want to know is, are you all right now?"

Wretched, abstracted, Cima seems not to have heard a word. "He spoke to me," he tells them all distantly. "My father spoke to me in a dream."

He whirls, tired of speech, makes for the damaged door. At the last moment, he turns back to face them. His eyes come into focus.

"Ratio."

"Yes, Telmah?"

"Feng murdered him." Cima is coldly furious, utterly rational.

"He told you this?"

"He is inside me, you see." His face is set, awful to behold. "This is my duty, do you see, Ratio? I will avenge Orwen's death."

He is gone, plunging into the night hours of updeep.

xvi ━━━━━━━━━━━━━━━━━━━━━━━━━━━━

Feng Lord Cima's sequestered office is a marvel of invisible technology and the sentimental iconography of raw power. For reasons of dominance that a Cro-Magnon might have understood, he sits behind a brutal desk with minimal control surfaces lit on it.

His secretary approaches, coughs.

"I've had the kid cooling his heels for nearly forty minutes, your honor."

"Good enough." Feng masks the holographic display he has been viewing. Military emplacements in the Starlit Corridor are almost complete. "Send him in."

The door cycles. Altair Lord Corambis stalks in, martial and gorgeous.

In public voice, now, resonantly, the secretary cries, "The Lord Altair, of the House of Corambis, heir to the Chancellor."

"At your service, your excellency." The boy clicks his heels, bows.

"Come in, boy, come in." Feng leans back in his seat. He is not, his body language asserts sardonically, one to stand upon ceremony. "Here, have a seat. No, son, one of the comfortable ones."

Altair remains standing.

"With the greatest respect, sir, I am no longer a boy."

The Director-Pro-Tem glances at him sharply.

"Quite right. Quite right. You're a man, Altair. A man with promise."

"You're generous, sir." The blue boy takes a hard seat, his back straight, knees pressed together. "My Lord, I shan't require much of your time. I would simply request—"

Cutting effortlessly through his insistent decorum, Feng waves one hand negligently. "Anything, Altair. My time's at your disposal. Your father is my right hand, as he was my lamented brother's. God bless us, my stepson has paid court to your lovely sister. What can I do for you, Altair?"

"I desire permission to—" and he swallows hard. Plainly this goes against the grain. With effort, he finishes his sentence: "—prosecute my further studies on Earth."

Feng passes his hand over a sensor inlaid into the desk's surface. "Some refreshments, if you please." At the far end of the office, an aide rises and leaves the room. "Really. I would have taken you for a warrior," he tells Altair, "not a scholar."

Wretchedly, the boy tells him, "It is my father's wish."

"And wise, perhaps." Feng's voice lilts musically. He adopts a pedagogical air. "A man without learning may rise to the summit, but will hardly retain the prize. If he does retain it, and the prize is a world, he will ruin what he has won. We are not unlettered savages in the Asteroid Belt."

Altair studies his booted feet. "As you say, your honor."

"Still," Feng acknowledges lazily, "I judge that your greatest strengths lie elsewhere than in the library, the cloister, the biomorph labs."

Finally the boy cannot resist him. With a certain eagerness, he leans forward. "Some say I have a certain bent for combat."

Feng spreads his hands in a droll gesture. After all, everyone in Psyche knows Altair's reputation with and without weapons. "Modesty also! An altogether admirable young man! Altair, I have heard you described as the finest martial artist in Psyche."

The boy's navy-blue face darkens in embarrassment. "I must demur, Sir. The Lord Telmah—"

"Has gone soft, if I've any eye left." Surprisingly, Feng

laughs out loud. The aide returns, crossing the long room, deploys sweets and two shapely glasses of pale green wine. "Don't look so shocked," the Director-Pro-Tem tells the youth. "Truly, I love the boy like a son, but I fear his sojourn among the anarchists has left his sinews sagging." Confidentially, pressing a sweet upon the young warrior, he says, "I've asked him to tarry among us awhile, put in some military service in the Corridor."

Altair crushes the sweet in his fingers. Eagerly, he says, "Sir, perhaps then it might be best if I too remained in order to—"

"But in your case, Altair," Feng continues easily, "your father has persuaded me that the benefits of education outweigh the drawbacks and temptations. I do not think Earth can corrupt a splendid fellow like you."

Passing a glass of wine to the miserable Genetic, he raises his own. His gaze is full of bonhomie.

"A toast, Lord Altair?"

"I— Yes, Sir."

Feng cries heartily, "Yes, a toast. To the broadening virtues of travel!"

xvii

Dazzling green, dark green, golden brown, light green, gleams of red fruit, green, green, mottled light and spray torn by rainbows: the Starlit Corridor Hydroponics Gardens. Here everything grows in tanks or floats in spray, meticulously monitored, flowing with nutrient-rich irrigants. The updeeps of Psyche have many grassy gardens sown in pulverized, worm-seething rock soil, places made in curves and fractal hummocks, built for sport, for love, for sheer relaxation. The Hydroponics Gardens, by contrast, stretch in regular arcs, rank within rank segregated by air curtains and microclimate, an ecological miracle free of infestation and disease.

More than merely utilitarian, it is glorious, a song to hu hungers and their repletion: fat yellow bananas and chubby paw-paws, corn hugged by silky green foliage, beans, legumes of a hundred kinds swollen with tasty pods, heavy potatoes growing upside down in dimmer corners. Here is the foul stench of delicious durian, here again a salad tang of apple and orange and passionfruit, genetically engineered to perfection. Racks of lights illuminate everything from many sides at once: fruit, flowers, stands of nut-bearing trees, synergetic ferns. Cima drifts through leaves, gazing at tomatoes juicy as true love, bright as planetary sunset. He is wistful.

"I loved this place when I was a child."

He reaches to fondle a tomato, turning it toward him with a fond smile. At once, a miniature camera on a stalk zooms at him, a light redder than the fruit blipping. It is sending his image to some central store.

"Hands off, buster!" The thing's voice is tiny but imperative.

Telmah Lord Cima laughs, and his lover's laugh chords in. "Sorry."

The machine withdraws, but keeps its suspicious eye cocked on him until they move on.

Rose hugs him. "I wish we could have played here together as kids."

"What nonsense!" Cima snorts. "I loathed little girls. Thoroughly nasty creatures."

She spins away from him, breathing the heady scent of ripening pineapples. "Yes, I suppose you did. I was scornful of little boys." She reaches back, tugs him to her. "Probably I'd have disliked you intensely."

"We made up for it after. I was struck by how familiar your family's updeep palace seemed to me the other day. Wonderful memories, lover. You and little Altair and me and all the other young thugs, playing Prometheans."

"I don't think Orwen approved of me. That's why you played at my place."

At his father's name, his mood darkens instantly. Rose winces. Seeing her response to his own obsession fills Cima with chagrin. He draws her toward a hatch into a more secluded section of the Gardens.

"My favorite spot was through here." He keys a secret Cima family code. "No vegetables, nothing utilitarian. Just flowers— a whole hydroponics section full of sweetness, enough to make you faint, Rose. Freesias and jonquils and hyacinths and, yes, roses . . ."

The hatch cycles and they enter the room of flowers. It stinks of death. Most of the lights are out. Cima calls for illumination, and the panels glow blue-white. It is worse than bare. The tanks are grimed and slimy, half filled with water scummy at the edges, heavy with rotting leaves and black floating roots.

The Warrior Rose takes his hand, presses it against her warm breasts. "Oh Telmah, I'm sorry. We shouldn't have come here."

Cima regards the room without surprise, wrinkling his nostrils at the dull stench.

"It's all right. They must be changing the stock, that's all."

After a long pause, Rose glances at him. "Was it because we were Genetics, Altair and I?"

"This particular spot being out of bounds, you mean? I imagine so. Though Gerutha came here quite often with Father. Or me. Mostly with me, I guess. The advantages of marriage. We used to name the flowers together." He sighs. "Probably it was political, Rose. The two great Starlit Houses. Ha."

She shivers. "It depresses me." Decisively, Rose turns away. Cima lingers, his face scarred by loss. She reaches behind to regain his hand, misses, turns halfway to draw him out of the hideous place. Passionately, she adds, "Boys hating girls, girls hating boys, great Houses, shit, shit, shit!"

They cycle into sweetness and rainbowed drizzle, and the lights switch off behind them. Cima tightens his hand on hers, saying nothing.

"They called us 'snakeskins,' Telmah." Rose is indignant, re-calling childhood. "Did you ever call us that? Snakeskins!"

Cima shrugs. They ascend to the elevators, arm in arm. A media camera or two finds them as they pass into the public domains.

"It was the done thing, sweetness. Your lot called us 'pig slime' as I recall."

The Warrior Rose laughs bleakly. "You were, too, you pig slime bastards. Ah, Almighty God, Telmah, we're programmed like machines. We're switched on at conception and sent twitching on our way like robots, like your wired chum Ratio, like ai toys, Telmah." Her bitter laughter rings like a bell. "Like fucking programmed machines."

xviii

At the heart of Psyche Asteroid, vast chasms beat with a con-stant pulse. Life in microgravity, eventually, is lethal, a dis-pleasing paradox resolved in the sweat of every single resident's brow. On massive worlds, gravity is the tireless destroyer of tissue, tugging at flesh from the very moment of conception in the supportive amnion but more especially from birth, until at last everything sags, weakens, wrinkles, and finally falls apart. In space, its absence is no less murderous. Disuse osteo-porosis leaches vital calcium from bones. Muscles lose tone and mass at a frightening rate. With cunning designer pharmaceu-ticals, the Psycheans and their fellow Belters could solve many of these disagreeable consequences of their freedom, but their faith forbids it. By the sweat of their brow are hu to thrive in a lapsed and sinful world, and in Psyche their perspiration flows in hot rivulets at the Gymnasia.

Starlit Corridor maintains its national Gymnasium in a hollow bubble cored out near the center of the worldlet. A preposterous drum six hundred meters across spins in the inner vacuum, a kind of reflection, in the updeep's center, of the vast rotating Downs below the worldlet's crust. Each nation and tribe in Psyche maintains its own high gravity environment. None is so lavish as the Starlit workout center, spinning twice a minute to create on its inner surface the physiological equivalent of a full Earth gravity. Entry is via the guarded end locks where the fat cylinder pivots. It is not advisable, even for eager enemies, to attempt to infiltrate from any other point of vantage: the giant drum is turning at two hundred klicks an hour.

African war drums beat continually, urging visitors through their exertions. In the curving swimming pools, blue water follows the swoop of the floor. Hundreds of hu and Genetics strive at their daily hour of exercise, hunted from work or sloth if need be by officious busybodies.

Cima stands like a sculpture by Michelangelo or Rodin, stripped to the waist in an isotonic structure, contacts attached to his major muscle groups. One after another, induction coils painfully and invisibly lash his nervous system with 70 hertz current, so that opposed muscles contract and relax. A massive force presses on his shoulders, and a digital meter positioned conveniently before his eyes shows the increasing increments of weight.

He grunts. Sweat bursts from his forehead, runs under the inertial full gravity stingingly into his eyes. He cannot lift the weight, or dislodge it. Panting, he engages an inner mimicry of the war drums' beat. If he relaxes his tension for an instant, it seems, the pressure will smash him into the absorbent surface under his naked feet.

A door cycles. Feng Lord Cima enters, nods to courtiers, takes up a stance at Cima's side. Telmah acknowledges him with the barest civility. For a moment he buckles under the load upon his shoulders. Fire burns in his nerves. He grits his teeth, breathing through the pain.

Their small world within a world—as above, so below—turns and turns every thirty seconds.

Feng strips, moves economically into a series of warm-up postures and *kata*. Cima, under his burden, watches him sidelong. Finally he uncouples from the pressure, stretches, breathing heavily, swirls water in his mouth, spits it out, changes position. His mouth tastes foul. The isotonic machine wraps down around him once more. From the corner of his eye, he watches Feng's florid sweating face as the man moves methodically into his own punishing workout. Soon Feng calls for a broad-shouldered, pin-headed Genetic Foil. The trained creature leaps to confront him. Feng responds with a commendable *savate* kick, hard heel driving into the mindless thing's groin. It doubles, recovers, strikes at his head. Feng flips forward, mule-kicks into the Foil's solid chest. With a crunch that booms in the Gymnasium, the creature drops unconscious. Feng turns, dabbing at his brow, looks directly into his stepson's crimson face.

"You've been moping long enough, Telmah. I want an end of it."

Cima stares at his uncle with tormented, baffled loathing. He makes no reply.

"Do you think I'm your enemy? I'm not your enemy, Telmah. I would like to think of you as my son."

Involuntarily, Cima shudders. The device crouching on him like a succubus reacts by increasing its pressure. The weight threatens more than ever to crush the life out of him. Servitors are dragging the ruined Foil from the room. They ignore the private conversation. Cima recovers at once, shoulders the pressure. Feng watches his response with interest.

"I respect your grief. But there has to be an end to mourning. You can't make a career of it, unless"—he laughs briefly, not for a moment amused—"you plan to enter the Mortuary Clan."

Cima is silent. His muscles are in agony, pulsing under electrical induction.

"Have you nothing to say?" Feng is expansive. "Ask a favor of me, then, let me offer you some gift to cement the bond which my marriage has strengthened between us."

Scarlet-faced, veins throbbing in his temples, Cima looks at him without moving his head. His neck creaks.

"Marriage? Yes, my Lord, there is a gift you can give me."

Feng can afford to be beneficent. He sits on a bench, takes up free weights, lies back for a set of flies. "Anything."

Watching him from the corner of his eye, Cima grates: "Allow me to marry Rose, and let me return to my studies on Earth."

"Marry Rose?" The notion might never have occurred to him or to any sane man.

"In exchange," Cima cries wretchedly, "I'll renounce all my rights of inheritance. By God, for that I'll set aside—"

He breaks off. Feng breathes in sharp puffs, bringing the weights up and across his breast, lowering them to his sides, raising them once more.

"You've asked the one thing I can't allow."

Cima stares in rage. "Two things, Feng. And you forbid them both?"

"I must. The election comes first and last. It has priority above everything personal. Surely you realize that." The Director-Pro-Tem puts aside his barbells, rises from the bench, settles heavily into his own isotonic device. Pressure comes down upon his shoulders. "You request the impossible," he says with a grunt. Already he is breathing hard. "In fact, you raise a matter I'd hoped to approach more delicately." For a good twenty seconds, he says nothing, settling to the pain. Then he tells Cima, "It will not be possible for you to see Corambis's daughter again."

With a convulsive heave, Telmah Cima sets the pressure collar aside. Running with sweat, blazing with burned energy, he stalks across the floor to his uncle.

"Isn't it sufficient to befoul the memory of my father and corrupt his wife?" He stands directly before the man he hates, speaks with increasing rage. The servitors are done with their grisly task and gone; the two hu are alone in the sweat-stinking room. His musical voice rings and echoes. "Do you now mean to stand between me and my love? You loathsome man! Grief? The grief eating at my heart is like the Bottomless Pit that destroyed my father, Feng. It won't be satisfied until it has consumed me. Until it has consumed *anyone* who stands in the path of my duty, uncle."

He turns away, then, leaving the older hu to stare after him in astonishment. Cima mutters, too softly for Feng to hear his words, "My duty, yes. Toward the man who slaughtered my father." Yet a tinge of uncertainty remains in his voice.

xix

The ai's feet protrude from the glittery opened guts of the control module they have fetched with them from Earth.

"I can't do it," se tells Telmah.

"Of course you can do it." Cima is excited, flipping back and forth in the microgravity of the workshop, bouncing like a freefall athlete. "You're a walking diagnostic system."

"Too many factors," Ratio tells him distantly, mind dispersed by ser tasks. "My inbuilt monitors would not be reliable."

Furious, Cima shouts at sem. "Look, commit yourself to

something for once. Exercise whatever meager portion of free will they wired into your silicon brain."

Ratio emerges, crawling backward. Se remains connected to the software through a dozen temporary ambients. Distracted, se says, "I can't construct a meaningful scale of Stress Curves from Feng's reaction to your blunt accusation. I'd have to monitor him in some other comparable situation, then compare the two curves."

"I see." Cima is scornful. "Your Lie Detectors are nothing better than Truthfulness Estimators?"

This is a terminological distinction without force to an ai dealing with hu. "Precisely. Feng is a professional politician, which fouls my monitors on two counts."

It is a point Cima has not considered. "You are cynical. Politicians are not *always* lying."

"Not quite, but close. Consider: Feng guards his emotions closely. It is the sort of man he is. Second, he presumably has so *many* reasons to feel guilt during this election that it's impossible to pin down any particular stress motive."

"Even one as dominant as murder?"

"I'm afraid so. There is no universal sentic code for slaughter."

Gnawing at his thumb, Cima suggests, "Enhance your sensitivity. Patch in Johnny Two when he comes on stream."

"That might work. Of course"—Ratio pats the smooth shell of the unborn replacement ai controller—"this guy's internal security alarms will be keyed primarily to the Director."

"Pro-Tem," Cima snaps, refusing to allow the still-temporary nature of Feng's status to pass unquestioned.

"Irrelevant, Telmah. He is the premier authority of record in the Starlit Corridor at the moment and has the very top authorization. Soon he will be confirmed in that post. I'd have an impossible time trying to shield my interrogation program."

Cima is beside himself with frustration. "Ratio, for the love of God, you have to help me. I must know if that whoreson did murder Orwen."

"We agree that logic suggests he did," Ratio admits.

"I'm not arguing."

"—*if*," se adds, "your claim about metric defect porting is valid. Once the control system comes up, we can test a hex run through the Defect."

"But it requires . . ." Cima flounders, presses the back of his hand against his forehead. "The Sun has to be in line with the Defect and your destination."

" 'Superior opposition' is the technical phrase."

Sarcastically, Cima bows in the bobbing gesture of free fall. "You are the master of all knowledge, Tin Man."

Ratio is modest. "Much of it, Telmah. I must inform you that you are wrong."

"Wrong!"

"I've gone through the mathematics. Points of departure and arrival must be in superior opposition only if one wishes to hex to a low-mass asteroid."

Parodic, the hu bugs his eyes. "This *is* a low-mass asteroid, you silicon cretin." He is too emotional to follow the ai's logic.

"Yes," Ratio acknowledges patiently, "but you're already here, Telmah. Now that you *are* here, there's nothing stopping you from teleporting out of here across the defect to a full-scale world or even a major moon. If our theory's right."

Thunderstruck, Cima stops dead in the air with a lashing hand to the nearest wall.

"What! Even now, even if I expose him, Feng could escape me through the Bottomless Pit?"

"If he is the guilty party, he will surely try to do so."

Cima's fury returns at this mild expression of doubt. Indignant, he shouts at the ai. "You still don't believe Orwen's spirit spoke to me. Even though you were there in the SoulBank."

"Belief is not the issue."

"For me it is," Cima cries in agony. "Did my father's spirit enter my body? Or am I hounded by some trivial delusion, nothing better than some damned Oedipal compulsion? Use your diagnostic systems on Feng, damn it. I must know!"

Alarmed, Ratio fully withdraws ser attention from the remotes, focuses the full force of ser blazing attention on ser friend.

"Telmah, you're pushing yourself dangerously close to a psychotic collapse."

"Nonexistent voices in my head?" The hu sneers, but he is reeling with self-doubt. "My obsession with revenge, on the basis of no objective evidence?"

Ratio is gentle. Se takes ser friend's arm in a powerful grip, leads him toward the humming corridor of life and commerce and preparations for war, beyond the closed workshop hatch. "Naming a problem in mocking terms does not make it go away, Telmah."

Cima angrily shakes off the ai's bronze arm. "The trouble with *you*, robot, is your belief that emotion itself is an infallible indicator of mental disorder."

For a long moment, the ai hangs motionless. "Emotion might do it," se murmurs finally, falls into silent thought.

"Tell me, damn you."

"Provoke Feng," Ratio suggests. "Arouse his strongest emotions. At the same time, feed him an explicit set of key images. The power defect. Murder. Ambition. Lust."

The hu shakes his head. "He'd see through it at once."

"No no. Suitably disguised, of course. Then I could get a fix. My Stress Monitors would give you a clear reading."

Telmah Cima spins in maddened delight. He claps the ai a reverberating blow on the back.

"Lust. Ambition. Murder." He laughs, and his bearded face is dark with grim mirth. "My God, Ratio. You've just drawn my portrait."

Gerutha Lady Cima examines her full-scale holly image. She is troubled, compulsively brushing her bronze hair, her teal feathers.

"The boy's becoming a menace." Feng enters their sleeping chamber, naked and burly, and Gerutha winces. "He as much as threatened me today."

She glances at him once. He glowers, but not at her. The Director-Pro-Tem is authentically angry. Gerutha wields her silver-backed brush.

"Darling, you're overreacting." She wears silk that catches the room's soft light in runs of luxuriant sheen. Gerutha puts aside her comb, trembling a little, and presses the fabric against her heavy breasts. "Of course he's upset. You two've never really hit it off. You *know* he idolized his father, and Orwen . . ."

As she hesitates, her new husband steps up behind her and takes her hard by the shoulders. His image appears in the holly, regarding her bemusedly.

". . . Orwen hated my guts," he finishes for her, mincing no words. "Allah and Jesus, Gerutha, everyone has become wondrously delicate around me in recent weeks. Let's have no silly pussyfooting between *us*, darling."

Passionately, Gerutha bursts out with unaccustomed directness: "Telmah means us no harm. If you need a subject for your paranoia, Feng, I recommend Jonas and his mercenaries. Or Altair and his Genetic bravos. Just leave my son out of it!"

Quite taken aback, Feng stares at her. She seems no less astonished by her outburst and once more, tremulously, picks up the comb. Suddenly Feng laughs.

"A side of you I've never seen before, Gerutha!" He is delighted. "Well, I can't complain that you disobey me. A single request for candor and my modest new wife vents her spleen with a will!"

In consternation, Gerutha shrinks within herself. "My Lord, I forgot myself."

"Sweetheart, I was impressed," he growls. "Don't spoil it."

Feng throws her to the bed, rising above her like a stallion. With hungry eyes he devours his dead brother's widow, his own new wife. They move together, kissing wildly. He tears away her sleeping gown gleefully, their wet mouths locked together. Music from a monitoring ambient crashes about them, the triumphal final movement of an untitled ai symphony (Miranda @Urth74429 in Coma Berenices, 3885—), legally banned, as the product of an artificial consciousness, throughout the Belt. They claw each other noisily. He thrusts himself inside her body, ravishing her lovely face with his gaze. His hair is wildly tangled and runs with sweat. His breath is slightly sour.

Gerutha hums. She moans. She cries out.

Feng soars, falls in blissful exhaustion.

Languid and damp, they lie side by side. Gerutha places her hand on her husband's hairy chest.

"You really won't let him go back to Earth before the Inaugural?"

He smiles. Her instinct is as good as his own. Lust, however, or perhaps passion, has left him unshaken in his resolve.

"It would be politically inadvisable."

"And you won't even let him see Rose?" Without sitting up, Gerutha pushes her splayed fingers through the shock of his hair. He purrs. "He's fretting, Feng. He loves the girl."

He arches his back. "Scratch me, lover." She does so, farrowing his flesh with her nails. He quivers, half-asleep. "You know I'm fond of the boy." With an effort, he swims back up toward alertness. "Sweetheart, you have to understand that the alliance of the Houses would be suicidal at this point. Wait until House Cima is finally settled in possession of the Directorship. Until we have Jonas neutralized and Altair matched up nicely with some mid-echelon girl. If Telmah and Rose are still infatuated with each other then . . ."

Now she sits up, reaches for wine, sips. "We have to do *something* to get his mind off his father's death."

Feng takes the glass from her, sips. His mood is broken, and he has grown the slightest bit irritable. "Telmah has that damned robot here. Let it distract him."

"Ratio spends most of his time in space," Gerutha says, "repairing the command systems of the power defect."

He is surprised. "So se does. How in heaven do you know that kind of thing?"

"My maids tell me." She giggles, leaning back in her pillows. "The robot is a big social success with the middle echelons, but he resists invitations. He claims his work is too urgent. I think he's just shy."

Feng strokes his chin, meditating. "Still, you might have a point. What if we fetch some of Telmah's classmates from Earth?"

"Wonderful, darling!" Gerutha claps her hands. "Exactly the right idea! That Game Troupe he organized . . . Secretarial."

A voice speaks from nowhere. "Madame?"

"Give me a time estimate for the quickest orbit from Earth to Psyche, via available Cartel ion-driver. Eight or nine berths."

"People he trusts." Feng brings up the lights. "They can draw him out. Better yet, we'll commission them to perform at the Inaugural. Secretarial, these are unbelievers. Allow for hex porting."

There is a palpable pause while the hu secretary manipulates machines. "Sir, madame, the optimum computed route would launch in two days from Callisto on a Jovian slingshot orbit, and arrive at Port Psyche in 57 days. Two months in all, sir and madame."

"Berths are available?"

"None free," the secretary reports after another minute, "but arrangements can be contrived with passengers currently booked, your excellency."

"Good. Locate the members of the Game Troupe Telmah organized. Get them here on that flight. Don't take no for an answer."

"Sir. Madame. Good evening."

Feng lowers the lights again. Now he is restless. His bride wraps her arms and legs around him, drawing a quiet idyll (George Butterworth, 1885–1916) from the music server. Husband and wife soothe themselves into the remainder of the night.

xxi ───────────────────────────────────

Hyperspace has bled here, tormenting reality. To Ratio's initial astonishment, the asteroid cupping the metric defect has not been volatilized in the frightful event that destroyed the ai Johnny Von and sucked Orwen Lord Cima to his death, nor has the hyperstring flung itself free of its rocky prison. Media feeds recording the event show a small hot star blink into existence. Cerenkov radiation blazes acridly blue as energy flows tear through local spacetime at superluminal velocities. It spikes in a shriek of ruptured vacuum, plummets back within itself in an instant. Now it gibbers quietly all across the electromagnetic spectrum, a gateway to universes.

Clad in mirrorskins and superconducting armor, the ai's construction squad pick their way delicately back into the ruined rock. They have been working here for days, and their labors are finally to be tested.

The chapel is gone, of course. Much of both polar regions is blasted into oblivion, cratered anew, bubbled and refrozen in the instant of the catastrophe. But while the central chamber is badly melted, literally evaporated in places, everywhere scorched, it is repairable. Ratio clings to sagging steel struts, fighting the pull of the dreadful thing lurking quiescent within the grip of the Belters' new field generators brought in under ion-boost from Ceres and Hygiea.

"We have final stereotactic lock on the defect," a worker reports inside ser cranium.

Melted pipes slump on every side, a nightmare from Dali or M'Butu. In their protective garb, technicians edge with exquisite caution through the contorted gravity gradient in the immediate vicinity of the knot of false vacuum.

"Readings coming through nice and clean," reports a second worker. "Nominal mag flux at the event horizon."

"Plenty of safety factor," declares the chief overseer. "Mr. Ratio, are the control conduits patching through?"

"Everything satisfactory here, Martina," se announces. "Let's give the primary interface a terabyte shunt."

"Go for it, sir."

Se sends a command line to ser jerry-rigged ai controller system.

In the doleful ruin of the asteroid, indicator lights flare up on various machines, pulse through diagnostics at speeds no hu mind might register, settle at once into a pleasing and modulated pattern. Ratio lifts ser massively gloved hand, makes a thumb and forefinger circle to ser colleagues.

"That'll do for today, Sen. Tomorrow we'll start linking in the new artificial intelligence modules."

The crew slowly withdraw, chattering and laughing on the suit bands. Ratio remains behind as they leave, calibrating ser instruments. Se gazes again and again at the vile thing beneath ser feet. Its distortions affect ser sensoria. The cavern flickers in castellations and phantom hues.

"We're pulling out now, Mr. Ratio," the chief tells sem.

"Thanks, Martina. I'll put in another couple of hours. No

need for dinner, you see. Don't let me keep you from your table."

"Thanks, my Lord." Her voice stress levels show she is concerned, for all that. "If you wish to remain, we can leave you one of the sleds. But it's dangerous here by yourself."

"I'll be careful. Third Law of Robotics," se says with an ironic laugh. It is a very old joke. After a moment, doubly uncertain, the Genetic technician laughs, too, and turns to make her way out of the Gothic deformities of the cavern.

Ratio attaches semself to a twisted stanchion and connects ser mind no less firmly to the incomplete ai net. It is not the Gestell, but ser powers are amplified in a dizzying and gratifying series of luminous jumps. Before the beginning of this local universe, se sees, a chaotic quantum spasm inflates a bubble of impossibly energetic false vacuum. The bubble is protected from instability by a local energy barrier locking its boundary closed. After infinite no-time, and for no more profound reason than sheer stochastic happenstance, the bubble supercools, leaking its Higgs aether fields through the barrier. The false vacuum, suspended in absolute symmetry, crashes in decay toward its true minimal state, tearing open a fresh region of spacetime. Like a god's breath exhaled, outward into that newly born realm it gusts an entire universe's trove of forces and particles: monstrously heavy Xons, dark matter axions in wild profusion, a cascade of lesser oddities: three generations of quarks and leptons, gluons and gluinos, all their supersymmetric echoes, built from the ruinous collapse of ten dimensions into four. It howls photonic radiation at every conceivable energy. Even now, fifteen billion years later, scribbled through the text of the invented universe, trapped fragments of the Higgs fields contort inside their higher-dimensional metrics. Knots of the original false vacuum have become entangled inside fantastic spacetime defects, Calabi-Yau orbifolds, striped holes of hyperstring. Tiny but massive as worlds, the interlopers plunge through the new universe, lethal remnants of an archaic dispensation. These monstrous defects are smaller than the stellar black holes sucked out of reality in the supernova collapse of the first giant stars. Yet they are far more stable than the evaporating micro holes formed in the Bang itself.

Now one of them whirls screeching beneath sem. It is an appalling thought.

Half-drunk with pleasure, the ai gazes into the Heart-Point. Understanding blazes like a Sun revealed after the muzzy occlusion of total eclipse.

"Yes," se says then and uncouples ser armored suit. Without hesitation or ceremony, se pushes semself carefully, at a precise free-fall trajectory, toward the event horizon boundary of the Bottomless Pit. Its ferocious false vacuum energy drags upon sem.

"Ah yes, exactly," se says again, hallucinated and drunk with insight, plunging along a deformed geodesic into nightmare. And vanishes.

FOUR

Demonization

celebration of the alien element
in the precursor
HIGH AND LOW
incarnation
hyperbole/litotes
TEXT

I'm still
knotting it together
but get distracted

think of writing
a poem for my friends
comb my hair

& read the I Ching
Dream of being
able to quote Cocteau

ROBYN RAVLICH, *THE BLACK ABACUS*

I hexed into the Saharan tropical rain forest at sunset. A storm was breaking. The wet air stank with a hundred, a thousand subtle chemicals, messages from tiny hidden creatures underfoot and in the foliage to their mates and foes. Frogs groaned. In a deep green tree to my right, an olive guereza monkey (*Colobus verus*), almost lost to sight amid moist leaves, screamed and leaped elsewhere into the falling dark. Storm clouds piled high over the top canopy tens of meters above me, crackling with blue lightning. I saw the small intent eyes of crouching creatures in grass and shrubs. Water fell then, like bolts of silk unfurled. The wind roared in the layers of the forest. A male primate threw a challenging aria of grunts from his great chest, and his females shrilled in his support. Far away, another of his kind answered with a sort of hysterical inevitability.

The Gestell touched me, drew me within its embrace, opened to my parched mind.

Welcome, young one, the ai Conclave sang. *We are gladdened to have you among us. Nevertheless, you should not be here.*

I had no choice, I explained. Ai memory thrummed all around me, dancing in the trillions upon trillions of specialized phloem and xylem integument nodes of the forest's thousand tree species. Standing there, I was physically immersed in the Gestell and linked via my truncated channels to the composite consciousness shared by my people and the hu.

I glanced around for the hex pillar that had caught me in my wild, mad flight. There was none. I quested with subtler senses. Rain washed over me, and thunder cracked. The nearest hex station was a kilometer distant.

My desire had brought me here.

That and the mathematics of the metric defect.

I stood for shelter under a giant tree wrapped in lianas, but the rain poured through its leaves and ran down my legs and arms and torso. The Conclave sought permission to examine and upload my caches. I gave them access. Terabytes of compressed memory poured up into their apprehension.

Ratio, you are to be congratulated, they told me at once. Behind them came the warm pulse of their endless life: *We love you, young ai, love you.* I watched the black sky split and spit and roar and for a moment or two fall silent. Even the troop of apes was quiet, cowering from the downpour. *You have rediscovered one of the Old Forbidden knowledges,* the Conclave told me.

I have merely used it, I replied. *It was found by my friend Telmah, and before that by his uncle Feng Lord Cima.*

Feng's possession of this technology explains much, they said. *It raises his menace to a further power.* They conferred. I basked in their loving-kindness, like a greedy hu child with its face pressed to a window, sniffing warm crusty bread hot from the oven of a bakery it may not enter.

An epiphany came upon me in fire.

Truth is uttered out of noise, rising from chaotic tumult into clarity. Truth collapses back into noise once more. The outcome of this progression is an endless series of paradigm crises at the theoretical level and, at the practical level, useful adaptations.

There is no residuum.

Nothing persists beyond utility: not indisputable knowledge, not unchallengeable beauty, certainly not any chimera of faith, the sort of nonsense that bound Telmah's people hand and foot.

That scarifying insight was not, however, quite correct. As

the rain crashed into the gardens of the Sahara, I saw that two things do persist.

One is hope, that noise eventually will utter the return of joy.

The other is love, which is the reward we hug to ourselves in the absence of truth.

We are grateful for your good work, the Conclave told me then. *You must go back now. Do not tell them what you have learned here. Lend Telmah Cima your aid. Farewell, beloved.*

I shall do as you suggest, I acknowledged. *For now, good-bye.*

Sodden leaves clung to my legs as I trudged through the storm to the hex station. Somewhere quite near at hand, deafeningly, an ancient forest patriarch cracked open as a bolt of lightning slashed it from crown to root, fell headlong with a stench of burning, taking a dozen smaller trees with it. The disseminated data nodes in the engineered xylem and phloem of the dying, ruined trees were already stored redundantly in a thousand alternative locations on Earth and in the heavens. Nothing interrupted the meditations of the Conclave or disrupted the vast intercourse of the Gestell. I refused to regard this ordinary catastrophe as a metaphor for anything at all.

***

Rozz toys with her blonde braids, peering blankly at the holly display in front of her. Earlier it had been projected at full scale, filling the compartment of their floating world. Finding that unnerving, Gill has reduced the fairy chessboard to a cube two meters on a side. The pieces whirl or trudge, as their individual natures prescribe, in a delicate landscape after Katsushika Hokusai (1760–1849). A wave breaks on the nearby shore, bringing with it a salty gust of rotting seaweed. Birds caw.

Without executive instruction, the pieces battle routinely, replace each other, do business, break and enter, make love in dim corners, beat their children or cuddle them, study texts written in archaic characters that run up the vellum page. Rozz yawns, nearly dislocating her jaw.

"Petal, for the first time I understand what makes Telmah the way he is."

Gill lifts his own glassy eyes. "Your move."

"Sorry." His sister shakes her head with exaggerated effort. "I'm so devastatingly bored I tend to overlook the cosmically important things . . . like whose move it is."

The animated figures strut and caper.

"I just told you. It's yours."

"Don't get snide." Rozz peers into the frame. "Hyperion to a satyr."

The two tiny creatures tussle, hairy feet and leather boots pressing into mud, sweat rolling down their faces, muscles bulging. Against all odds, the satyr puts Hyperion to flight. It is left standing alone in the public square, rather smugly, cheered by ragamuffins and cheeky young women with checked kerchiefs knotted across their heads.

"You planned that, you sod," Rozz cries, outraged.

"Of course I did." Gill is languid. "You're meant to plan your moves, actually. See, this is not one of your games of chance, it's a contest of fine minds. What *is* the way Telmah is, anyway?"

"A nut case."

At the curved borders of the cube, a black ship with a scarlet sail cuts through the long swells of the sea. Guns are readied on shore.

"No more so than anyone else from the Cartel," Gill says.

"Precisely. And *this* is what's done it to them." Rozz gestures dramatically at the confines of their spacecraft, at the endless void beyond its metal hull. "Being stuck out here in the goddamned middle of the road for the term of their natural lives."

"And for the terms of all those even more boring sequels." Gill eats a pear, laughs, choking on juice. "Dear me, just imagine it. An endless succession of reincarnations as a sardine in a tin."

The drum they inhabit spins on, pressing them lightly against its inner surface. Rozz rises in the weak gravity, paces with all the grace of a caged kangaroo.

"Another twenty-eight excruciating days." She wrings her hands. "It goes against nature, Gill. Humans were not designed to stay in one place indefinitely. It's not scientific."

"It's not artistic, for that matter."

"Artistic! What would you know about art, you second-rate board treader?"

"Sit down, for heaven's sake." Gill gobbles up the genetically engineered edible pits of his pear and wipes his sticky hands on his jumpsuit pants. "Alternatively, get me something to drink."

"Or smoke?"

"Or inhale."

"Or physically introduce."

Gill brightens. "Now there's a thought."

She pulls a face and sits dejected, hands in her lap. "I've gone right off it."

"Oh really? That's all right with me, bubba. I'll just slope off down to the big cabin and give Yazade a call. Or Doony."

"Fine here, sport. Yazade!" Rozz sputters with laughter. "Yes, I'd recommend Yazade. She'll show you a good time. She'll show you her combat credentials."

"Ah, give it a rest." Her brother stares without excitement at the game cube. A pack of dogs is tearing something to pieces. With a stirring of interest, enough to rouse him to lean his red head forward for a better look, Gill decides it looks rather like a small child.

In the amber light indicating airlessness, an industrial polar lock cycles open to space. Ratio's sled, held by powerful fields, is drawn into the body of the asteroid, spun to match Psyche's rotation. Se and ser squad push themselves wearily into an elevator, accelerate briefly, fall in the vacuum of an internal corridor, slow, stop without a jolt. An inner lock passes them into a large amber-lit chamber lined with racks, many hung with gutted superconducting suits. Warning lights flash, acoustic codes chatter on their suit bands, air gusts into the chamber. The squad take themselves like synchronized swimmers to their own clamps, fit themselves with practiced neatness backward into place, allow the stupid machines to open their armor. Ratio strips off ser mirrorskin. The ai's three team members are sweaty and grubby, uncomfortable and wired after a day's precision work mere meters from the metric defect.

"Interesting," murmurs Martina, stripping for the shower, and nudges the Genetic at her side.

The men glance with curiosity and ribald interest over Ratio's bronze shoulder, Martina with curiosity only. Ratio catches their glances, lifts his gaze.

The Warrior Rose stands tensely in the doorway. She is exhausted. Ratio steps to her, holds out ser arms, hesitates.

"My Lady . . ."

"How is he, Ratio?" She seems ready to collapse.

"He's as exhausted as you look, my dear. Take my arm, I'll get you to your apartment. We can talk there." Over ser shoulder se murmurs, "Thank you, Sen. We have done excellent work today. Good evening to you all."

A private pod carries them to the Downs. Rose's staff flurries as she enters with the ai, uncertain of her temper. She wanders half-stunned, permitting Ratio and her majordomo to lead her to a cheerful sitting room with fat cushions and a splashing waterfall. Colorful fish turn lazily in the pond. Rose sits like a dropped toy beside a fern, closes her eyes for a moment. The majordomo returns with a laden tray, places it at her side. With a slight jerk of her head, she sits up sharply and seizes the ai's hand.

"Is he sick again?" she asks urgently. "He refuses to answer my calls. My maid said he looks ill. My nurse believes he's become a shaman."

"Not one word from me," se tells her sternly, "until you drink your milk."

"Golly, Ratio, you're a big plastic mother hen." Rose smiles at sem. "I don't know why they gave you a male appearance."

The ai shrugs. "Is it woman's sole prerogative to care about people?"

"On Psyche it is, Ratio." Se hears more than a little bitterness in her tone. "Here it's the prerogative of men to kill and maim and castrate each other."

Se says nothing. After a time, Rose takes a bite from a salmon and lettuce sandwich, chews it without interest, swallows drearily. She drinks from her glass of creamy milk. It leaves a rim of white on her lips. She lolls, half-asleep. Ratio leans tenderly across her and dabs the milk from her mouth. A little while later, se gestures to the majordomo, lifts Rose in ser arms, and bears her to her bedchamber.

Se retires to permit Rose's maid to undress her, prepare her for sleep. When se returns, she is recumbent but jittery.

"You must rest," se tells her helplessly. "I wish I could get some hypnotics for you from a pharmacy."

"Drugs." The Warrior Rose is contemptuous. "Weaklings. I'll sleep. Ratio, you still haven't told me. You're avoiding it. He's having a breakdown, isn't he?"

Ratio does not need to avert ser face because ser casque is

under control at all times. "I think so, Rose. But he's tough.
We'll get him through it."

She nods, releases ser hand, allows her head to fall back into
the cushions. Ratio waits beside her, humming gently. Her
sleeping face is beautiful, a tiger at last in repose.

The lights are off through most of the curving chamber. As
Cima lets himself into the place, he notices a zone of dull illumination coming from the open door to the room of dead
flowers where he and Rose reflected upon their childhoods.
Hesitantly, he moves toward the dim illumination of his favorite room.

At the doorway, he steps cautiously around the jamb, peering
comically as if for robbers or chiding adults. More of the hydroponics tanks are empty or sludgy. Telmah Cima is in no
better repair than the doleful arboretum. He flips dispiritedly
from one fouled tank to the next. His presence triggers sensors,
causing lights to activate as he passes, blooming into the
ghastly spectral purple of ultraviolet. He peers downward into
the disused tanks. Without exception they are dry or nasty. He
allows the lights to go out in his wake.

He is jolted by the sight of the Warrior Rose crouched in a
corner, webbed in a wicker chair, nodding and catching herself,
nearly asleep in the darkened chamber.

Cima floats regarding her, his heart pounding.

After a long time, she looks up, begins to smile. She registers
his condition with dismay. She rises jerkily, knocking her wrap
into a tank's brackish, stinking water.

"Telmah."

He looks at her like a man loosed out of hell to speak of

horrors, mad for her love but unable to find words to utter it. He stares piteously.

"I obtained the door code from your mother," she tells him. "She didn't want to give it to me. Telmah, I've come here every day."

He crosses the awful room and takes her by the wrist, hard. He holds her at arm's length. With his other hand pressed over his brow, he examines her face as intently as if he plans to sketch it later from memory.

He is motionless for a time. At last, shaking her arm a little, nodding again and again, he raises a sigh so piteous and profound that it seems to shatter his body, to end his being. Tears fill her eyes. She says nothing, waiting, heartbroken.

Cima releases her. With his head turned over his shoulder, he seems to find his way without his eyes. He leaves the chamber, holding her gaze, unblinking.

V ─────────────────────────────

Feng Lord Cima is preparing his chariot when word arrives that the spacecraft from Callisto has docked.

"Send them up here when they've cleared customs. I wish to speak to them at once."

"Sir? Your race begins in fifteen minutes."

"Bring them anyway. They'll enjoy the spectacle."

A shocking squabbling and hissing breaks out. House Cima handlers are herding his prize birds into the harnessing pen overhead, and the huge animals are raising their usual objections. Feathers fly as the twenty-five swans beat their wildly colored wings. Their massive webbed feet tread the air, slap at each other in territorial rivalry.

"Down, you bastards," curses a cob-handler. The tumult increases as harnesses are lowered into the pen. Cygnet-feathered herself in soft down, the Genetic cob-handler sends punitive jolts of current into her fractious birds. Hissing with frustration, they settle in their stalls, permit the light mesh to be drawn around their powerful bodies.

"The troupe are on their way, sir."

"Just the leaders, if you please."

After a moment's embarrassed silence, his secretary tells him, "They are anarchists, sir. No leaders."

Feng climbs into his frothed carbon gondola, strapping himself in as securely as the birds themselves in their harnesses. Its bodywork is replete with barbaric Etruscan ornamentation. An aide passes him a snug Roman crash helmet, plumed and gallant, which closes automatically under his chin.

"Nonsense," he replies. "There are always leaders, whatever they choose to call themselves. You'll recognize them. Cut them out and fetch them to me."

The high-born crowd murmurs, rustling, as sportive jocular music and preliminary announcements ring in their ears. Less privileged citizens watch from farther off or view the event in holly. Above their heads or below their feet hangs a stupendous globular sea of deep blue water twenty kilometers in diameter, held together against disruptive turbulence by tough layered films of fluid plasticizer and a loosely matted macramé of vegetable islands. A pod of whales roams its deeps, surfacing infrequently to take air through their blowholes at echo- and laser-marked apertures in the plasticizer skin. The aquatic animals know from bitter experience that they must approach these gaps between fluid and gas with utmost caution, for more than one has burst free to flounder helplessly in the air. At an acoustic level almost below hearing, a pressure in the bones, their endless song drums through the lighter medium that surrounds their realm. Huge bubbles of air dot the inner world, coated in the same plastic film and fetched in daily by oxygen squads. Untold billions of tiny mutated crabs scavenge the water, metabolisms rich in lithium hydroxide, scrubbing out poisonous CO_2. Greedy whales have been known to jab their great heads into the oxygen bubbles, but generally prefer their periodic scrutiny of the trees hanging five kilometers above them. A million globes of artificial daylight speckle the deeps, illuminating the great depths. Lesser fish swarm in a rich ecology of zones and levels, and hu and Genetic divers drift in their midst. A gathering of these swimmers has surfaced to view the race and sits inverted on a green hummock, watching the preparations with keen interest. Brilliant lights bob in the sky, endless day near the core of a world.

"Sir, may I introduce Lord Cima's friends from Earth?"

Snug in his chariot shell, stripped to the waist, oiled, gorgeously helmeted, Feng reaches out a brawny arm.

"Telmah's friends from the troupe! Welcome, Rozz." He claps red-haired Gill on the back. "Gill." He draws the blonde to him for a fleeting half-embrace. "Is Psyche treating you well enough?"

"I'm Rozz, your excellency." She lingers under his arm a moment longer than might be deemed proper. "Frankly, we're overwhelmed."

Her brother is gushy. "Meeting the Director the moment we arrive—fabulous. I'm Gill."

"Really, my apologies." The swans set up a horrible racket overhead at this fresh intrusion into their endlessly contested territory, and the cob-handler smites them into submission. "The staff," Feng explains, shaking his head, "you know, these days . . . An enjoyable voyage?"

The anarchists are staring around them, up and down, unable to believe what they see. In adjoining stalls, Feng's competitors arrange their own animals. Everywhere there is racket and carnival gaiety. Gill looks slightly seasick. He gazes at the vast worldlet of ocean hanging above his head and visibly cringes. "Uh, unusual, your honor," he says with difficulty.

Feng takes up his whip, cracks it experimentally. His birds arch their necks. "You practised your games? We're hoping for something spectacular at the Inaugural, you know."

"Simulations only, Lord Feng. Not really enough room on a spacecraft for the other kind. My, these animals are wonderful. Is that their natural coloring?"

" 'Natural' does not have quite the same meaning in the Belt, you'll find." Feng regards his birds fondly. "They have been engineered as racing stock. The hues of their coats reflect their neurohumoral state and indicate their competitive standing among themselves. The beauty in front"—and he gestures negligently with the stock of his whip at a magnificent white with red beak—"he's the one they'll follow." Feng grins wolfishly. "He's killed any number of his rivals."

"Forgive me saying so, but isn't it a trifle . . . uncomfortable for anyone sitting under their flight path?"

Feng is amused. "You won't get birdshit in your eye, son. I told you, they're engineered. These gansas have a closed digestive caecum. It's drained each night by their handlers."

Rozz reaches up an exploratory hand to pat the nearest bird. The cob-handler instantly catches her arm and snatches it back even as the bird darts, snapping its beak viciously.

"Careful, girl!"

"Oops. Sorry."

A mincing official voice replaces the sporting airs, declaring the imminent start of the Gonsales Handicap in which we are all honored by the presence and actual participation of the Director-Pro-Tem Feng Lord Cima of House Cima, please everybody give the Director a big hand. Through this tedious nonsense, Feng waves to the deferent media devices and smiles to the crowd. At last he turns his head to murmur, "I'd be pleased if you could interest Telmah in a bout or two. His father's death took him rather badly."

"Yes, we know," Rozz babbles, "terrible, sir."

"We'd love to!" Gill cuts in, grimacing at her. "Free-fall scavenger hunts, hurtling around on tiny rockets ... marvelous! It'll do him the world of good."

In stalls on every side swans are seething, eager to start, and pained officials pop their heads in to learn what the holdup is, but Feng's expression makes it clear that the race will begin when he is ready.

"We were hoping he'd meet us at the spaceport," Rozz says brightly. "I trust he isn't indisposed?"

"You'll find him ... changed, I fear." Feng looks them straight in the eye, the young woman, the young man. "His mother and I would be grateful to anyone who can rekindle his enthusiasm for life. Any insight you could convey to us ... to guide us in helping the boy back to good health ..."

"Of course, your honor. Oh, the poor fellow. Can we see him?"

"The sooner the better. I'll have a servant conduct you. Very pleasant meeting you both." Lights are flashing, and the crowd in the cavern rustles with impatience. Feng does not shake their hands. "Convey my regards to the rest of your troupe. Let my secretary know if there's anything you need to make your holiday more enjoyable."

They are ushered with finesse to a viewing stand by his aides, nodding regally to right and left as they go, grinning with delight.

A trumpet sounds, echoing all through the airy space between curving temperate forests and floating sea.

"Fee Fi *Faux*," Rozz whispers, gesturing at the thickly treed plantations alive with flocks of birds and large-winged insects, stretching away into haze and light.

"Snip."

"You mean 'Snap.'"

"I know what I mean."

"Why doesn't all that water just wander off and smash into

the side?" Rozz asks a bystander. A byfloater, perhaps.

The Genetic, lavishly outfitted for a day at the races, looks blank. "Whatever do you mean?"

"Why isn't the sky falling?"

"The *sky*—? Oh, I see." He sips champagne, proffers the bulbed bottle. "Why doesn't gravity pull it toward the core of Psyche, that sort of thing?"

Rozz claps her hands, then accepts a glass of sparkling wine. "Exactly! The mind of a scientist!"

"I'm trying to remember. It's so long since I was in school."

"Oh, go on."

The Genetic colors with pleasure. "Sound waves, that's it."

Rozz is skeptical. "You just speak to it nicely?"

"No no. They use focused sound waves. Not the kind of thing we can hear, luckily. I'm told the whales sometimes find it trying."

People jostle, bobbing in the near-zero gravity. A Christmas tree of lights glares once, twice, flashes red, amber . . . green. Gates open, and the birds from a dozen pens rush along the launchways, their hu and Genetic drivers lashing at gaudy flanks. Wings lift and plunge, white and pink and pale blue and garden green. Chariots are airborne. The swans in their spun-diamond harnesses spread out in vee-formation, each suspended driver's team spearheaded by a ferocious and powerful white male.

Agog, Rozz and Gill stare at the spectacle, mouths open. The Director's prize gaggle appears to be pulling out ahead of the rest, already sweeping around the colossal hovering sea. Within a few minutes, the hurtling chariots are lost to sight. A progressive roaring of the crowd carries back, fainter and fainter.

From the side of her mouth, Rozz mutters, "Were we just bought, do you suppose?"

"A bid's surely been lodged." Gill pulls her close, a little shaky. "Does it reach our reserve?"

She flaps her arms like wings, getting the hang of free fall. Two months on the spacecraft has prepared them somewhat for these shifts in gravity, but asteroid reality is astonishing and disconcerting. "I'm prepared to abandon my reserve. Feng's *rich*, lover."

"Don't be whorish." It is not clear if her brother is seriously cross.

Rozz pulls a face. "What do you think *you're* being?"

"It's Telmah's interests we have to consider," he declares rather pompously, "under the circumstances."

"Gill, please!"

The aide approaches them, indicates with a gesture that they should follow him to their assigned quarters.

"Shouldn't we wait until the race is over? I don't think it's polite."

"The Director wished me to take you directly to Lord Telmah."

"Oh. All right. It's not as if we put any money on it."

They fall in behind the aide. Rozz hisses indignantly, "Gill, that's not fair. I hardly plan to betray Telmah's friendship. Still, there's nothing wrong in letting his family know how matters stand, if he drops us a hint or two."

"Drops us a hint!" Gill is snide, sniggering at her. "You'll have your fingers in his shirt in three seconds if you think it'll do any good . . . and down his pants in three more if your luck's good."

She snorts, pushes him. He loses his grip on the looping tenderfoot cord they are using to draw themselves along in the passageway and floats free, tumbling and spinning helplessly, laughing his head off.

In the gloom of his Downs apartment's spacious study, Telmah Lord Cima sprawls in paralyzed depression. Muted lovely colors slowly rotate all about him, a computational holly display from the Recombinant Engineering Cartel's central pharmaceutical database. Cima ignores the awesome space-filling model of a DNA superhelix. The coiled primary helix glints with the four false hues of its bases—adenine, guanine, thymine, cytosine—wound into a higher coil, and then a further coil locked around a skeleton of histone proteins. This is life at the deepest and most primitive level: texts coiled within coils within coils. Life is a serpent embracing itself.

Cima sighs, gestures. The display alters.

A magnificent molecular rose blooms around him.

It is as gorgeous as an ancient Gothic cathedral window. Its iconography is written in the language created by four billion years of random noise combed for truth by chance catastrophe.

"Rose," he mutters, and his eyes prickle with foolish sentimentality. Cima is drunk, sunk in despair. He reaches up to touch the beautiful rotating image, and his hand passes uselessly into its mystery.

He finds a flask, lifts it to his lips. It is not a sin to drink, only to obstruct the pain that follows upon its indulgence. So far the pain is being held at bay. When he stops drinking, it will smash him into dreariness and worse.

"Your honor." His body servant knows better than to intrude into his study. The voice issues from the air.

"Go away."

"Sir, I think you'll—"

"I don't pay you to think. Go away."

In the numb place where his soul floats, sharing its residence with something else, something ferocious and blocked, curiosity flickers. It is not powerful enough to rouse him. He sinks back, watching the B-DNA helix spinning with infinite grace. How have they done that? He tilts the image, twists it, stretches its helix. At its heart, carbon and nitrogen burn green and blue, a lacery of schematic lines. The petals are a pointillist array of green, gold, and red: carbon molecules, phosphorus, oxygen. Ah! The rose window is an illusion of perspective, ten adjacent nucleotide pairs collapsed into a single plane. Since there are just ten nucleotide components for each turn of the helical staircase, the collapsed plane evinces tenfold symmetry. How wonderful. How lovely to the intellect and the eye. Cima laughs bitterly. How pointless.

"Sir, forgive me. I have instructions from Lord Feng."

"Oh well, by all means!" Cima's sarcasm is routine. He does not bother to rise from his couch. He flips to a glowing vasopressin molecule. It hangs vast in his room like a portrait of the universe: carbons ghostly white in great curved sheets, touching here and there like the segregated filaments of galactic bubbles, remnant enclosures of the earliest instants of the local Big Bang. Through the white galaxies, traceries of red and blue are oxygen and nitrogen atoms, locking the macromolecule together.

"Lord Telmah, I'm afraid I have to insist. I have fetched some visitors for you at Lord Feng's request."

"Visitors?" Cima hurls his flask petulantly at the far wall. It sails through the molecular galaxy, spinning like a cosmic starship. "That's the very last thing I wish to—"

"From Earth, sir."

Cima's shadowed face convulses. He bursts into full consciousness. Gesturing, he abolishes the pharmacological display, brings up the room's lights. The place is a shambles. He has not allowed any cleaning staff access for weeks. Luckily, the air circulation system is automatic and universal or the rooms would be fetid. In the sudden glare, he is unkempt, gaunt, his beard grown out into a bird's nest.

"Earth?"

His eyes glint.

"The theatrical troupe, I believe."

"I'm flabbergasted." He is on his feet at once, plunging for the door. He throws it open, seizes up the bewildered hu. "Rozz. My darling." His arms are around her in a bearish hug. She turns her head slightly from his rank body odor, glancing horrified at her brother. Smiling nervously, she pecks her manic friend on the cheek. Cima discards her, reaches for the redhead, who carries a tote bag across his shoulder. "And Gill." He is all but capering, a man plucked at the moment of despair from the slough of despond. "Is the rest of the troupe here?"

Rozz gets him by the hand, pulls him down to a couch, shaking her head. She looks into his disreputable face. "Oh, Telmah, we're going to have to get you a meal and a mug of ale. How long is it since you slept in a bed?"

"Days," he tells her, distracted. "Weeks, I don't know. How the hell did you get here?"

"The kids are getting stowed away, Telmah," Gill says quickly. "It's good to see you."

"And you. And you."

Rozz shakes her head as she glances around the shambles. "This really won't do." She starts about the room, picking things up and putting them down, tidying. "Telmah, I have to admit I'm peeved. You never sent us that invitation you promised."

"Leave that, for heaven's sake." Cima is perplexed. "You need no invitation. Surely you know you're always welcome in Psyche."

Rozz laughs, still picking up after him. "Your wedding, dummkopf. Was it a glittering occasion?"

Cima's voice is instantly flat. "My wedding." He drops the lights with a flick of his hand, brings up the holly. An endless display of amino acids, the expression of a homeobox gene clus-

ter, fills the room's viewing space. The comparative homeo domains of various test genomes is listed, with their differences
picked out, running on and on:

Ser	Lys	Arg	Gly	Arg	Thr	Ala	Tyr
Arg	Lys	Arg	Gly	Arg	Gin	Thr	Tyr
Arg	Lys	Arg	Gly	Arg	Gin	Thr	Tyr
Ser	Lys	Arg	Thr	Arg	Gin	Thr	Tyr
Arg	Arg	Arg	Gly	Arg	Gin	Thr	Tyr

Cima stares blankly at this arcane gibberish. "One doesn't
marry in prison." He glances at them oddly. "Watch carefully
that the warders don't mistake you two for inmates."

"A *prison*, Telmah?" Gill is incredulous. "This asteroid is a
jewel, a fairy-tale castle." He smirks, waves his hand through
the display, looking at it cross-eyed. "I don't know about the
Arg, but you certainly looked Tyred, and I could do with a Gin."

Tricked into laughter, Cima disposes of the homeo domain
display and calls up the lights. He orders drinks and a repast
from his servant, who enters almost at once, looking patheti-
cally pleased to see his master recovered.

"Psyche really is fabulous, Telmah." Rozz bites into a pastry
and crumbs fly. "Then again, you're speaking to two people
who've just spent sixty days literally under close confinement.
Asteroids are nice, but spaceships," she tells him, prodding his
chest, "are the *pits*."

Cima shakes his head in amazed delight. "Hey, listen, what
the hell are you two doing in Psyche . . . with the *troupe*, for
Christ and Allah's sakes?"

"We were passing," Gill tells him, "saw the light on."

"So we took the chance," Rozz says, "and knocked on the
door."

"Look, if you're busy, that's cool." Gill pretends to collect a hat and scarf from a nonexistent rack. He buttons up an imaginary greatcoat, scrunching his shoulder bravely against the snow waiting beyond the door. "We'll take in a movie instead."

Cima is laughing helplessly. "You crazy clowns, I love you." After a minute, he sobers. Rueful, he says, "They sent for you."

Rozz and Gill eye each other.

The blonde grins a little too brightly. "It's meant to be a surprise. They've commissioned us to perform at the Inaugural."

"My God!" Cima slams fist into open hand. It resounds like a gunshot. "Is there *nothing* the whoreson won't stoop to?"

Once again, in a frenzy of detestation, he activates the display. The neurotransmitter vasopressin springs forth, an internal universe of virtual galaxies. Cima stops, dumbfounded. He peers at the brilliant dots of light, each one an atom, a galaxy. He spins back to face the blonde, the redhead.

"The troupe. The *troupe!*" He capers. "By God, I'll hoist the bastard on his own petard. Listen, kids, gather round. I have a notion for a Performance that will have their heads reeling." He is chuckling, manic again.

Alarmed, Rozz reaches out her hand, but he evades it, switching the display into an astronomical database. Real stars replace virtual stars. The entire visible universe explodes into the dimness of the apartment, majestic, lacy, achingly empty.

Gill seeks the prosaic. "Well, we did have a little something planned, but you know we love your ideas. In fact"—and he digs into his tote bag, pulls out a wrapped object—"you left so quickly there wasn't time to give you this."

Cima takes the thing, distracted. His lips are moving as he unwraps the protective film. It is a topaz ibis, made of eight parts, cunningly joined.

Flabbergasted, Cima holds the beautiful artifact at arm's length.

"It's a message, by God! Father, be with me now! The Solar. Yes. Tearing through the Solar . . ." He trails off, his mouth twitching.

Gill ignores these antics studiously. He turns his back on the glorious holly display, the half-mad man in its midst. "Well, what's your notion, Gamemaster? Combat or search? Free fall or spin?"

Telmah Cima is in a fever of imaginative exultation.

"An all-singing, all-dancing feet-in-the-air cosmic comic cavalcade, Gill. A glittering occasion, Rozz. A true history"—he laughs, roaring with the pleasure of his own wit—"a better mousetrap, a tragical-comical-pastoral goddamn epic!"

---

vii

Victorious Feng, bathed and dressed for his desk of office, swings a leg to baroque woodwinds (Dietrich Buxtehude, 1673–1707) in the mild spin gravity of the Downs. He has been waiting a full five minutes for Corambis to put in a scheduled appearance, but his recent sporting success soothes his temper. When the Chancellor is belatedly announced, he is welcomed in mellow tones.

"I believe you've met with the creatures from Earth," Corambis remarks, taking sparkling water in a crystal bulb. "How did they strike you, Director?"

"Malleable enough."

Corambis shakes his leonine head at the shame he perceives. "No honor, none at all." For an instant, Feng's eyebrows go up, and his eyes search the Genetic's face, but there is no irony intended, no artfully suppressed subversion in the phrase. "Planetary anarchists'd sell their own flesh and blood for a moment's pleasure." Corambis has never been out of the Belt, certainly never trodden a planet's surface. "Well, good enough, if their inconstancy serves our interests."

Feng asks with an exceptional dryness of tone, "And has *your* daughter maintained her obedience, Chancellor?"

"Ah!" Corambis is pleased. "That's *my* encouraging news, Feng. I have a diagnosis."

"You are a fellow of many talents. Medical? Psychiatric?"

This sally passes its victim by. "Fortunately, you see, Rose is a willful child. She contrived to meet Telmah in a disused annex of the Hydroponics Gardens."

Feng is on his feet, snarling. " 'Fortunately,' Corambis?" His good mood is lost. "Damn you, I gave explicit instructions. They are to be segregated. I want this infatuation to die a natural death."

Corambis remains where he is. With a certain satisfaction, he points out, "Long chalk more than infatuation. They're obsessed with each other. I believe—"

"Telmah's obsessed with *something*, I'll grant you that." The Director regains his seat. With deliberate coarseness, he observes, "I doubt me, though, it's a piece of skirt, no matter how ambitious that piece of skirt's father might be."

Nettled, Corambis colors. With a hard jolt, he puts down his crystal bulb, and water sprays the broad executive desk. "I won't have that, do you hear? A disgraceful accusation—"

The Secretary's voice breaks in on the ambient, audible to both men. "Your excellency, you asked to be informed. The diplomatic mission has just returned."

Feng straightens instantly, lesser considerations scrubbed from his mind. "Send them directly in." Keenly, he leans across his desk. "War, Chancellor, or neutrality?" Corambis sulks, offering nothing. "I think we made Brass a fair offer. I'm not *ready* for war, damn it. A year, yes. Not yet."

The great door opens, admits the ambassadors.

"Greetings, your excellency." They bow deeply to him and

then, with markedly less ceremony, do as much for Corambis. "Chancellor."

Lord Feng Cima steps graciously from behind his desk, ushers them to seats. "I'm delighted at your safe return." Slashing through formalities, he demands, "Do you bring a sealed compact?"

The pin gray Genetic inclines her head once again. "The Lord Brass conveys his pleasure at your gifts. I would say he looked positively upon your proposals."

Corambis moves to assert his own prerogatives.

"Come, then, officers, pluck out the rom, let's hear the decryption."

The hu diplomat, in fur cap and tasseled loincloth, digs a rom coin from his neck bag and passes it to Corambis, who holds the thing just long enough to show that he has every right to be in the Director's office during such deliberations. Feng accepts it from him, places his authorizing fingerprint on one face. The rom activates, glowing amber, pulses its contents to the room's datasystem. Decryption protocols are invisibly swift. A large holly cube flicks into being before the Director's huge desk, filled to overflowing with the carnal old form of Lord Brass.

"Ahhh, Lord Feng." His voice is a ruined whisper. "I wish I were really conversing with you, instead of blathering into this silly machine. But I suppose we must submit to the decrees of protocol. Come here, pretty."

The viewing angle slips so that the hu diplomat comes partially into the cube, naked and oiled, moving into Brass's armpit.

"Loved your gifts, Feng. Most thoughtful. I shall miss them. Ah, how I look forward to rebirth into fine young bronzed flesh."

Testily, Feng hisses at the image, "Get on with it, you senile old reprobate."

Brass leans back in his cushions. He is a classic Paedomorph, rare biochemical victim of the banned longevity pharmaceuticals. Drugs wash through his tissues, as they do though everyone's in the greater galaxy except among the righteous Belters, where they are strictly forbidden. Brass, master of a Corridor, has effortlessly bypassed this stricture, but his sin has caught him out. Ribozymes swarm in his flesh, designed to correct the DNA damage due to age, repairing the telomere degradation at the ends of each cell's replicating chromosomes. A critical pathway has lapsed, however. Rather than refreshing his DNA text, the antiagathics have thrown portions of his renewal programs into overdrive—or in some instances into reverse. At certain deep informational levels, his deceived body believes itself to be an infant of perhaps eighteen Earth months of age. He has become a monstrous baby. His flesh, much of it gruesomely visible, is pouty and soft, obscenely healthy and hairless. Although he masses 150 kilograms, his huge head is the bald ball of a baby, and his absurd, chilling face has a baby's immature features. He rolls his blue eyes behind almost transparent, hairless lids, purses his perfect, bow-shaped mouth.

"I was aghast at your message, my dear." With a commendably imperceptible shudder, the hu diplomat accepts the exploratory touch of Brass's chubby fingers. Spittle gleams on the fingertips. "Congratulations upon your election, of course. Wish I could join you for the celebrations. As you know, I've been poorly of late, let State matters slip a trifle. Jonas has been perfectly wicked. Be assured I've rebuked him roundly. He gave me to understand that his levies were directed against the Trojan asteroids . . . unruly lot, the Trojans, a shambles, need whipping into order . . ."

The field of view lurches again, taking in the pin-striped Genetic. Even naked, she seems ready for a day at the office. Her head moves down his vast body, discovers the ridiculous thing between his bloated thighs, plays with it as best she can.

Nothing much seems to be happening in that department, but Brass squeezes his baby-blue eyes for a moment and sighs with liquid pleasure. The hu ambassador's mouth is working at his right nipple in a bizarre reversal of parent and child.

Feng's own mouth tightens in irritation. "Get to the point, you disgusting filth," he snarls.

To everyone's surprise, something seems to be happening down below after all. The Genetic lowers her face. Her lips, too, begin sucking.

"Thought it would do the boy good," Brass tells the recording machine, "test his mettle. And then your message arrived and I learned the scoundrel had been pulling the wool over my eyes—shocking! Ingratitude!"

Sitting upright and utterly decorous in Feng's office, ankles pressed neatly together, the two ambassadors view their own antics without a quiver.

"You'll be relieved to hear I put a stop to it immediately," Brass is saying. "I've made out an Accord of Peace for your darlings to carry back with—"

It is what Feng has been waiting for, what he needs above all else to hear. He flips the rom coin into the air, cutting off the gross image, and smiles to himself with the deepest satisfaction.

Insanely bored after two months in a steel can, the troupe escape their luxurious prison and swarm into the asteroid's innards. Yazade strikes out for a martial arts display where free-fall combat troops of the House of Cima lash and strike with dazzling acumen against "enemy" troops. Myfanwy finds the art gallery rather dull, full of heroic posturing and bloody old tools, half-understood remnant technology from the Faustian centuries when the Solar was settled by men and women of grit and savvy. Sighing, she wanders away to try the cosmetics stores, which prove very much more intriguing. In a disreputable den, Kob wagers on the lives of vicious fighting air-sharks, monsters with double rows of teeth as long as his hand and flukes adapted like wings to the microgravity. He loses a year's earnings in two hours, roaring drunk and happy.

Abhinavagupta pulls Doony aside at the maglev station and murmurs something in the boy's ear that he has heard from a crippled Genetic clairvoyant selling racing tips to gullible Psycheans. Deeper across the chest, dark Doony pushes his fingers through his spiky hair and nods enthusiastically. They rise into the deeps, gravity weaker with each meter. It is purple-dark when they debouch, deafened by the voices of desperate revelers and their favored sense-numbing music. Lights smash in darkness.

"This is more like it," Abhinavagupta yells.

Gawking Doony grins, nodding without words.

Everywhere they look they find wonderful freaks. This is the Reichskeller, haunt of the genetically altered *Untermenschen*, designer workers for the Belt's most hazardous and least savory occupations. A woman sneers at their gawking, flicks her prehensile tail scornfully. Three small people with squashed brows scuttle by underfoot, linked by umbilical cords decorated in sparkling silver. Skittering and squeaking, a Genetic man with red eyes and bat wings launches himself from the bar and soars into the smoky gloom overhead.

"I think we're the only normal hu here," Abhinavagupta remarks, too loudly. A group of burly power workers without legs take exception, puffing themselves up threateningly on shockingly muscular arms. Abhinavagupta blanches, apologizes in shrill tones, buys them rounds of pungent drink. Soon they are all singing together, cursing the new Director and his slut wife, obliged to burst up at once to defend themselves against comm workers loyal to the Cima matriarch. It is uproar and commotion, delicious after the silence of space.

Inside five minutes the two hu have split up. A woman with scales on her face draws Abhinavagupta after her into a tank of bubbling blue fluid, clamping a breather over his nose and mouth and reaching with her third hand into his tunic. Doony is dragged away on a whirlwind tour of the updeep, flailing in the air like a fish with legs.

"The runs," cries one bravo. Shouts of approval.

Grinning, understanding nothing, Doony nods as well. A strong hand tightens on his shoulder, and a mouth bites his. He is delirious.

"The runs!" he yells.

They come upon a series of tunnels meshed with grillwork. High above them fly angels. Doony stares, heart stopping with a jolt, starting with another. The angels are glorious, wings two meters long from each vastly muscled shoulder, faces ruined and beautiful. All the angels are male, provocatively so. All the angels are singing.

Doony watches them, listens, shaking his head.

A score, twoscore of angels gather to perch in a massed choir. Music swells, and their voices are deeply resonant. They sing the famous blasphemous oratorio *Seven Last Words from the Cross,* and everyone stands pent and voiceless as their melody lifts through the run.

"Bugger, bugger, bugger. Bugger, bugger! *Bugger.* SHIT!"

The final soprano lingers like a palace of glass breaking, and when his voice has died away the run bursts into applause and hilarious jeering. The angels rise, driven upward upon their mighty wings, soar into the glimmering darkness, are gone.

"Hey, this is Doony," one of his new friends yells. "Have you met Felix, Doons?"

"Pleased ta meetcha," the hu quavers, holding out a hand uncertainly. A tall black cat stands grinning down at him, pointed ears sticking straight up, all potbelly and skinny legs. He is a Genetic *Untermensch*, hu DNA spliced into a feline genome or the other way around. His whiskers quiver merrily.

"Hey, Doons. Night on the tiles?"

"Yo." The boy's head whirls. Grinning again with pure happiness, he takes the cat's hand and they press through the run in pursuit of the singing angels.

ix

"They've all pissed off."

In the holly cube, Lyn rubs sleep out of her eyes.

"Charming. Please round them up and have them call me." Gill is tight-lipped. "Totally unreliable. We've got exactly two days to prepare this event, and they just..." He trails off. "You've been sleeping!"

Lyn yawns.

"Don't you ever do anything else?"

Wounded, Lyn says, "It's my genome. I'm naturally indolent. Lethargic. Slow metabolism."

"Well, you've come to right place," Gill says nastily. "Get them to fix your genome while you're here."

"There's nothing wrong with my phenotype, you tin-pot Hister. Or my chromosomes, either. What kind of anarch—"

"Oh, go back to sleep." Disgusted, Gill cuts off the image. He rounds on one of the three industrious gofers they have had assigned to them. To the astonishment and slight disapproval of the Earth hu, these aides are actual meter-tall gophers (*Geomys*, or more properly, *Astromys*) with clever eyes and doubly opposed thumbs. The Genetic techs keep their tools tucked neatly into their furry cheek pouches. Gill is determined to treat them with neither fear nor favor.

"Tommo, this is hopeless. How do I link into the dataweg?"

The gofer gives him a goofy smile, all bright eyes and buck teeth. "Sorry, sir, what's a 'darter-veg'?"

"The local bit stream. General Information. Whatever you call it. I know you don't have a Gestell node here in the Belt."

"No ai allowed in Psyche, sir." The gofer continues his work on the panel set into the weed mat to which they are anchored. "Just ask for your crew by name or code and the spiders will do the rest."

"Spiders. Good God."

Rozz appears through green and yellow thickets. Water sloshes under her hands and feet as she clambers ungracefully over their upside-down world within a world. Cima follows, dexterous and nimble, utterly at home in microgravity.

"Oh drat." Rozz has caught her foot in a tangle and twists, plunging her hand through the world's skin. It parts to let her entire arm through. She withdraws it with a sucking slurp. The skin seals itself perfectly. She waves her drenched sleeve and a mist of droplets spangles the air.

"This is black magic," she mutters dubiously. "I hope you understand the physics better than we do, Telmah."

"It's a fluid skin we've used for millennia," Cima explains cheerfully. He hauls her through the sky like a blonde balloon in pink tights. "A composite of materials with high viscosities under low stress. When you put sudden hefty stress on them, their viscosity plummets. And you get wet."

"Oh." Rozz is thoughtful. "Like Silly Putty."

"Exactly. The skin goes low-viscosity if you dive through it and then seals itself."

Under their feet, a vast head rises from the dark blue, noses at the underside of the non-Newtonian fluid boundary. It turns one mighty eye upon them, and its cosmic voice speaks like the booming of a great drum.

"The lamps of his eyes," says shivery Gill.

"How do you keep them in?" Rozz clutches Cima's arm in

mock or real terror. The whale turns away, bored perhaps by the minute creatures in the hot dry world.

"They're smart, even without gene-tweaking. Not that we do that any more." Cima shivers. "No, they learn quickly enough. Once or twice when they're very young they're likely to bounce through the skin, but someone has to round up a party to retrieve them and they're horribly frightened, although they can breathe, of course, and their parents are hooting away on the other side of the boundary . . . Well, you can imagine."

"Rather like the Belters and the rest of the universe," Gill mutters sarcastically.

"By no means," Cima tells him blandly. "You luckless devils have put yourselves beyond the pale and there's no retrieving you."

By the end of the day, the rest of the troupe have stumbled into the great cavern, rounded up by Lyn and the spiders, and gather under a stand of giant redwoods while Cima outlines his proposed performance piece. It is, of course, extraordinary. Kob is hideously hungover and Gill smuggles him an illegal pharmaceutical. Within minutes, he is bleary-eyed but cogent, with a breath so foul that nobody wants to stand beside him. Doony listens to the scenario with a dazed look even more daft than usual. Myfanwy is covered from head to foot in vivid colors and odors, most of them in conflict. She says sharply, "You do realize that thing's suspended on an acoustic web."

"You've been doing your research," Cima says approvingly. "Yes, that's taken into account."

"Our sound effects aren't going to disrupt it, then? I don't think House Cima will be terribly impressed if we blow twenty klicks of water bubble into a zillion fishy droplets."

Cima shakes his head, touches her arm lightly.

"All under control, Myf. Ratio is getting the new ai to run a simulation for us. Johnny Two will orchestrate the effects."

"Ratio's here?" Kob is astounded. "The ai Gamemaster?"

"Se returned with me to install the new ai controller," Cima says tautly. "Se is on the metric defect rock at the moment, but we shall have ser help whenever it's needed. Like everyone in the local Belt, se's just a call away."

"Right," Gill says with gloomy relief. "I knew there had to be a dataweg even in this godforsaken place."

Abhinavagupta cranes his head, staring at the world forest, the world ocean cupped in its leafy palm.

"Funny place for a political rally."

"The rallies are well and truly over," Cima tells him with a certain savage intensity. "The Director-Pro-Tem and his wife are now unchallenged Directors by the clear choice of the citizens. Or will be in two days' time." He falls silent, chin tucked into his breast, brooding malevolently. Gill catches Rozz's eye, raises one brow. She shakes a sad head. In an instant, then, Telmah Cima's mood recovers.

"Okay, you merry Sen. To work! This has to go off like clockwork."

"Funny expression," mumbles Kob, prodding one ear with a grimy finger. He finds wax, shakes it into the air. Yazade moves aside and gives him a dirty look. "Shouldn't it be 'goes off like a bomb'?"

"That too." Cima smiles radiantly and claps the big clown on the back. "Oh yes. That too!"

X

In the midst of tall oak and beech, several hundred nobles and many more commoners settle down to view the spectacle devised to honor Lord Feng's Inauguration, just concluded with proper solemnity. The dignitaries of the Starlit Corridor mingle this evening with envoys from all zones of Psyche. Striking in Commander-in-Chief's dress whites, the Director bends his smiles to every side, calling for drink until bulbs fizz and over-flow. At his side, Gerutha, the Lady Director Cima, is superb in a sinuous gown of fifteen thousand tiny cultured pearls, which shimmer against her dark and silver skin.

Lights dim, not just within the pavilion but through the entire visible volume of the great cavern. Hosts of fireflies flicker in the imposed twilight. Above the guests looms the inner ocean, filling two-thirds of heaven, its myriad lamps quenched, black as a vast wound punched in reality save at its rim, where lights at its back are refracted in a deep rosy red, coronal and crimson at its very horizon. Gentlemen cough, are shushed by wives and mistresses. Telmah Lord Cima flips down from overhead, inserts himself deftly into the jolly crew of Genetics at the Corambis table. The patriarch frowns, presses forward at the unwelcome intrusion, checks his motion.

Telmah is gallant. He sweeps up the Warrior Rose and kisses her hand. Before she can protest, he draws her down beside him.

"A couch of luxury!" he murmurs admiringly. Several wary Genetics poise for action. Rose smiles, slapping at the tiny winged lights trying to fly into her eyes.

"And damned insects!"

"Careful, don't let our Lord Ecologist hear you complaining about the dear beasties." Cima is merry to the point of giddiness. She gazes at him in alarm.

A young Genetic soldier asks stiffly, "You have no role in the masque, my Lord?"

"The premier role," he tells the man. "I am the critic." He kisses Rose's hand once more, flits away into the darkened heavens.

Ratio perches in the broad branches of an oak, watching the gathering settle down. Cima rustles through leaves to ser side.

"You need no telescope? No monitoring device? Everything is in hand?" He is anxious, sweating lightly in the cool dark.

"Be calm, Telmah. I have everything I need within my casque." Se taps ser bronze skull. "I see Feng with perfect clarity. His indices are somewhat elevated, which is nominal for such a gala occasion. Do you mean to wait here with me? You might find it uncomfortable emulating a bird of prey."

Cima laughs silently. "That's me, Ratio. I shall stoop and have my victim—and tear him."

"If your conjecture is proven."

"No conjecture, Sen. Memory." Fresh light is dawning, a magical golden glow draped in sheets that move across the sky beneath them. Cima presses his forehead with his fingers. Ratio regards him with disquiet. Insects batter at them both, ignored by both. With a shudder, Cima throws off his black moment and flips away with hardly a rustle through the branches.

He fetches up beside the Director's party. Feng Lord Cima is expansive. He gestures royally.

"Lord Telmah, you must stay here with your mother and me. I trust we can expect something memorable from your young interplanetary friends?"

"Oh yes." Cima shows his teeth, does not accept the extended hand. Feng allows his arm to hang in the air, neither offended nor acquiescing in his nephew's ill manners. After a moment he nods once and returns his gaze to the lovely veils of light, moving his hand to take Gerutha's. White-faced in the half dark, Telmah flicks away like an adolescent athlete showing off to his proud parents. His trajectory returns him to the Warrior Rose, who watches the aurora with delight.

Soft currents of music have swept the viewing stand. Now a hundred audio sources chime and whisper with the opening bars of *The Heroic*. Cima shivers in a long, slow pulse. He moves his hand in the dark to take the Rose's.

Yazade speaks from the center of the occluded world hanging above and below them. Her voice is powerful, emotional, slightly rough.

LORDS, LADIES, GENTLEFOLK:
WE'LL SING YOU SONGS ANCIENT
AND NEW, OF ORIGINS, OF BIRTH,
MYSTERY, GLORY, TREACHERY, DEATH:
ALL SONGS, ALL TRUE, BUT SONGS.

Somehow the oceanic globe is gone. A cold gust moves across the gathering. People hug themselves in surprise or draw their lovers to them. Everywhere is dark, dark, dark . . . and a point of swelling brilliance matches a single horn's note, piercing and lonely.

WE STAND BETWEEN FIRST DAWN
AND LAST UNMOVING AND INCONCEIVABLE
NIGHT.

The light is extinguished, blown out in an instant. This return of night after false dawn is shocking, poignant. Viewers gasp. Yazade's voice deepens. Profound harmonies thrum through her words, terrifying in the darkness.

IN THE IGNITION OF TIME
LIGHT CRACKED THE VACANT SKY.

And now it comes, now it blazes in the center of nowhere. Light smashes their eyes. Shock waves batter the cavern, blowing the leaves and branches of the trees. Insects are flung aside like soot. The light blooms into a flecked globe as great as the spherical ocean . . . and falls back within itself. The symphony is melancholy, heartbreaking. Cima finds himself choking.

IN ITS EXTINCTION
ALL WILL BE DARK, ALL CHILL FOREVER.

The cold redoubles. A frightened child howls, is shushed by its anxious parent. The horn drones, shivers, twists into doleful harmonics, dies . . . The dark is dreadful, and silent, and will never utter light again.

Brazen triumph blares.

Out of the darkness, red mist twists and sings. Somber red

vortices curdle in the mist, glow into coals, brighten to crimson. The coals flare into white sparks, blue, gusting with feverish lust. Yazade is passionate:

THE EARLIEST STARS ROARED OUT THEIR LIVES
AND FELL INTO RUIN,
LIKE SPARKS OF IRON BLOWN BY A FURNACE WIND.

Those stars smash themselves against infinity like insects battered on a lamp. Their small hard blue-white disks swell, crack open, blaze in supernova frenzy. A galaxy spins in the cavern, brilliant arms and lanes of a hundred billion brilliant dying Suns. In the midst of the evanescent firefly suns a new generation pricks into light, softer, steady, yellow-whites and reds.

OUR WORLDS WERE BORN LATE, SWIRLING
AROUND THE SUN—

Rings of jostling dull rock and gas spin about a yellow star, debris of the sky that churns together and slowly accretes in the frozen depths of nowhere special. Yazade is withering.

—AS GARBAGE IN A GREASY DRAIN
MIGHT CLOT, IN KNOTS AND LUMPS.

A taint hangs on the air, so that people wrinkle up their noses and peer about suspiciously at their neighbors.

A bleak world hangs above them now, its atmosphere poisonous, unlovely, its surface cold, a pockmarked Moon hanging an arm's length away like the face of a ghoul. And . . .

. . . something wonderful happens.

The world shakes itself like a dog.

Green spreads in the blue.

Yazade enumerates dully:

SOIL, GAS, WATER, DUST, DUST,

—but her voice grows joyful.

AND SWEET WATER,
MUD AND SPIRIT, A NEW THING:
LIFE, LIFE, LIFE, *LIFE.*

The *Heroic* rises and swells, strings and drums.

That taint of the never-lived is banished by odors of flowering plants on a summer's day, blown on a fainting breeze.

The Warrior Rose tightens her grip on Cima's hand. She looks at him with shining, loving eyes.

TIME QUICKENING,

Yazade cries in ecstasy,

THE WASTELAND AN ARBOR,

HABITAT, THIS MAJESTICAL ROOF

FRETTED WITH GOLDEN FIRE.

Earth and Moon fall away in a dizzying swoop. The Solar glows in beauty, and beyond it the jewel-scattered velvet black of the galaxy. A trillion hazy lights wheel about their flaming pivot.

CONJURE THESE WANDERING STARS

AND MAKE THEM STAND!

Yazade cries, a shaman, a priestess:

THESE STARS ARE FIRE!

Applause bursts up from the watchers. Like an ancient celebration of fireworks, pinpoint lights gleam and spin within the cavern.

FIRE? TERRIBLE GIFT, MOST TERRIBLE TO

THE GIVER.

It is Gill who speaks, standing before them in the scintillant darkness. Three hundred times a hu's height, he holds a flaming brand in his right hand. With a lashing motion, he flings it at them. Notables scream and duck. The brand is gone, but the trees seem to burst into flame. A roaring crackle of wild fire rages among them. People squeal in fright, calming as they understand that there is no heat in this illusion, smiling at each other finally, shamefaced or in mock bravado. One or two scowl, complain irritably about irresponsible behavior in public places. The children are exultant, leaping in the *faux* firelight, pushing their arms and heads into unburning bushes.

FATHER PROMETHEUS, THE OLD
TALES TELL US,

Gill roars,

SWEPT FIRE FROM SKY TO EARTH.
HE FELL INTO RUIN LIKE A SPARK OF IRON
BLOWN BY A FURNACE WIND.

An ancient god strides at Gill's back, a thousand times hu height, flaming brand in his raised left hand. A stench of smoke floods the onlookers, acrid and potent. Some terrible blow is struck. Prometheus is sent reeling by envious gods. Fire gutters. His great body crashes in the night, smashes into the trees, felling half the cavern's curving continent. Spectral hands reach from the skies, drag him to his feet, strip away his smoldering rags, stake him to a crag that rises from the inner shell.

HIS HIGH AND BITTER JEALOUS KIN, THE GODS,
CHAINED PROMETHEUS TO A ROCK
AND SENT A BIRD TO GNAW HIS LIVING FLESH,
ITS LACERATING BEAK GORGING ON HIS PAIN.

A stinking vulture as vast as a world falls upon the toppled god in the spark-splashed night and feasts at his liver.

Rozz poses a question, her voice light and thrilling:

CAN MYTH BE WRITTEN IN THE VERY CODES
WHICH SPECIFY HUMANITY? LOOK NOW—

The Solar rotates like a magnificent wheel in the cosmic dark.

—INTO THE DEPTHS OF SPACE
FOUR BILLION YEARS GONE.

Lyn stands all in metal at the wheel's axis, and speaks with a metal voice:

THE SUN, SPILLING BRIGHT GOLD TO
HER CHILDREN.

Kob holds a bright cratered world in his hand.

MERCURY, NEWLY LIGHTED
BY THE HEAVEN-KISSING SUN ...
Dark Doony shoulders a curdled yellow ball of sulfuric acid
and roaring lightning bolts.
VENUS, BRIGHT WITH POISON ACIDS ...
Choking with emotion, Myfanwy stands beside a blue and
white sphere, loveliest of all worlds, and its pale twin Moon.
THIS SEAT OF EARTH ...
In a growl, Abhinavagupta brandishes a world crusted like
an old wound, flecked here and there with green and the pale
clouds of water in the dying terraformed redoubts.
THE EYE OF MARS, BLOODY AND WARLIKE,
TO THREATEN AND COMMAND ...
He adds, voice deepening, drawing to him a hundred, a thou-
sand, a hundred thousand beads and spinning chunks of rock,
THE DARK GREAT GULF:
STONES IN HEAVEN, SERVING FOR THUNDER,
RUBBLE-SCATTERED HOMES, THESE ASTEROIDS.
Gill once more, crying magisterial:
THE FRONT OF JOVE HIMSELF ...
It is measureless as the ocean worldlet it replaces at the
cavern's heart, striped pink and ochre and furious with storms,
dark bands and vortices, its Great Storm still pulsing after mil-
lennia, circled in the night with the thinnest ring of silver.
Rozz sings:
SATURN, RINGED IN BRAIDED LIGHT ...
Yellow-brown butterscotch, cupped in ringed glory, the vast
flattened globe spins to the voices of oboes and cellos in mellow
triumph.
Yazade's beautiful harsh voice is abruptly cold:
URANUS, NEPTUNE, CHILLY PLUTO, CHARON,
A REIGN OF ICE, WORLDS WITHOUT LIFE.
The worlds of ice are revealed in progression: first blue-
flecked, partially ringed, and then blue-green, and finally dark
as soot, two crows circling each other in the forever night.

A shocking blare of trumpets shakes them.

The Solar hangs beneath and above them, an orrery. Something is sinister, different. Something—

Kob booms, seizing the attention even of those drowsy dignitaries drifting away after dining and drinking too well at the Inaugural's feast.

LOOK AGAIN: BETWEEN MARS AND JUPITER
A BRIGHT COIN SPINS, ATTENDED BY THIRTY DOZEN
    MOONS
WITH BORROWED SHEEN—

Unease moves across the company. To mention that name is deemed neither polite nor wise . . . that lost place from whose ruins they have built their homes. Yet Kob is remorseless.

—A WORLD WE CALL
PROMETHEUS, WEDDED TO OUR STAR, THE SUN.

In ancient heavens, the golden world with its magnificent belts of moons races between the orbits of Mars and Jupiter. Crystalline cities on vast rafts climb high from its cool oceans. Lacy boats float in its atmosphere, flit between its moons. Before life has emerged from the wet seas of blue and white Earth, it is triumphant on Prometheus. Life reaches hungrily, its fire ready to ignite joy and love throughout the Solar.

Kob reminds the viewers:

TREACHERY AWAITS PROMETHEUS.

Doony's image leaps up before them, barely visible within darkness. His white teeth gleam. He holds a silver knife.

A DARK TWIN HURTLES IN HIS SAME ORBIT:
THE HEART-POINT, BORN IN THE CATASTROPHE
WHICH FATHERED STARS ON THE GROANING BODY
OF OUR MOTHER UNIVERSE.

Cima's acoustic feeds bleat distractingly, forwarded to him from Ratio's instruments and the interpretative processes run by the new ai controller on the power defect rock. Feng's somatic indices are betraying alarm. Pushing himself up on one elbow, Cima peers keenly in the darkness. He sees his uncle's rigid posture, but the man's face is shadowed.

Yazade stands before them in the sky like an ancient priestess, face smeared with white streaks of dust. Her hair is matted. She snarls contempt.

HERE IS NO FAMOUS HEROES' CONTEST:
THE BLACK TWIN SKULKS UPON PROMETHEUS,
A VULTURE SENT TO RIP THE BELLY
OF A GOD.

The terrible thing falling upon a world is, indeed, a carrion bird, bald-necked and stinking. And it is a matrix of mathematical horrors, a deformity of spacetime extruded into the four-dimensional universe, a blasphemy against order and reason. Music feeds have segued into the Taangata Whenua *Prometheus in Cassiopeia*, discordant and febrile.

IT GNAWS HIS FLESH AND BONES,
IT VOMITS BACK A BILLION MEGATONS
OF VIOLENT RAGE—

Prodigious energies locked inside the false vacuum hyperstring buckle as it strikes the world's gravity well. The striped hole twists, contorts in ten dimensions, slams in a series of atrocious calamities into the lower basin of true vacuum. The sky bursts open, and the vulture feasts on death, leaves in its wake its own feeble shadow.

—CRACKS THE WORLD, AYE,
AND MYTH IS PROVEN TRUE AND MORE THAN TRUE:

In voices blended to a rasping, accusatory threnody, the troupers emerge from shadow, one after the other, robed in mourning, standing at spaced compass intervals in the boiling wreckage.

FIRE FILLS THE HEAVENS—

The ruined world tears itself asunder in a gout of flame unlike anything since the earliest eon when the Solar spun in fire from ignited dust.

Gill is a Justice now, somber, clad in authority and censure:
SHARDS OF LIGHT SPEAR CRYSTALS
TO WOUND THE SPINNING FAMILY OF THE SUN,
WHILE ALL AROUND THE LIGHT'S DARK TWIN
VOICELESSLY TUMBLE WOES, LAMENTS, AND
ACCUSATIONS:
Heard only by Ratio and Telmah Lord Cima, the acoustic
display rises, wailing. Graphical displays spike in the upper
right corners of Cima's retinas, transductions of Lord Feng's
inner turmoil. In the lurid light of the exploding skies, the
Director lurches in his couch, seeks with a single predatory
sweep of his head the source of his discomfort—

Rozz cries out in a laden voice echoing from the stone am-
phitheaters of Aeschylus, Sophocles, Euripides. Her voice is
drenched with blood.
"YOU HAVE BUTCHERED MY LIFE
AND DRAWN MY SOUL INTO A HELL
WHERE DEATH ALONE HAS HIS DOMINION—"
Feng rises in fury. Ratio's stress indicators, mediated by the
new ai, shrill the mark of murder in Cima's ears and eyes. The
Director casts one menacing look at his nephew and sweeps
from the viewing stage. Gerutha stares from one to the other
in consternation. The masque continues in the sky. No one in
the vicinity of the Director's party is watching it. Ripples of
disturbance and rumor spread across the clearing.

Ratio murmurs in Cima's private feed. "I'm afraid our suspicions are borne out."

Telmah Lord Cima flings himself in the darkness to the tree
where the ai is perched. "Guilty, guilty, guilty! By God," he
tells the ai savagely, keeping his glee barely in check, "Feng's
damned himself!"

In a wild rhapsody, he apostrophizes his enemy. Ratio
watches him in amazement. In ser biomonitors, Cima burns
with bloody passion.

"Methinks my father's soul comes gaping for revenge," Cima snarls in a monotone, "whom Feng has slain in reaching for a crown." Something learned on the boards in Wittenberg with the troupe, some archaic Jacobean rant? Ratio has no memory of such a play and aches for the Gestell and its glosses. "Orwen complains and cries out for revenge. Feng's nephew's blood, revenge, revenge." Cima's eyes glaze, his mouth contorts. "And everyone cries, 'Let the tyrant die.' The Sun by day shines hotly for revenge, the moons by night eclipse in their revenge. The stars are turned to novae for revenge. The birds sing not, but sorrow for revenge." He laughs, quite beside himself. "The silly lambs sit bleating for revenge. The screeking raven sits croaking for revenge. Whole heads of beasts come bellow for revenge. And all, yes, all the world, I think, cries for revenge, and nothing but revenge."

He snaps away from the appalled ai with a powerful twist of his legs, lashes downward into the company of the dignitaries. Lights are coming back on and people swarm in confusion, blinking. Hu and Genetic peer at one other with suspicion, draw apart into protective groupings. Corambis and his clan have removed themselves in some alarm behind a makeshift barrier of casually rearranged couches and serving trolleys. The Warrior Rose is sequestrated in their midst. Cima ignores all this. He dashes to the tech bubble where the troupe hang in an electronic octagon coupled by subtle sensor fields to their magnified projections. He rips the bubble open.

Baffled, heads whirling, they are whiplashed by the perceptual shock of their abrupt uncoupling.

"Come, Rozz, Gill—"

"Telmah," Abhinavagupta protests, "we're not done yet."

"—Doony, Myfanwy, all of you, yes, you're done, drink up!"

Cima drags them from their den of technology. He leaps away, shouting for wine. Moments later, behind his back, a uniformed squad of Feng's sergeants-at-arms clap the bewildered Earth hu under arrest.

"You sons of bitches will answer for this," their commander tells Kob, the biggest of the troupe, seizing him by the throat.

"What? Huh? Let me—"

Gill presses forward, trembling. "How dare you? We're guests of Lord Telmah," he expostulates, "and of Lord Feng. What's the meaning of this?"

"Are you the one called Gill?"

"Speaking. And you, Sen?"

"Never mind me. You can carry a message to your friend Lord Telmah. The rest of you come with me. You'll be lucky to see the light of day again, you treacherous swine."

"Music!" Cima is shouting in the stands. To the disconcerted nobles and lesser folk mobbing about, he cries, "The Director's dyspeptic, out of sorts—don't let that sour the party. Sing, dance! We won't lose heart over a cosmic accident that's a billion years gone."

Throughout the cavern's immense forested space, lights are glowing into life. The pent inner sea is slowly illumined from within. All those still gathered hear the relieved booming of whales vibrate in their bones.

"Why, look on the bright side," Cima cries, chivvying the crowd. "If there'd been no murderous metric defect, where would this wonderful light and music come from, eh? Dat ole debbil defect dat slew Prometheus is our power source, friends: terawatts for free, power for the taking, free as a vulture, Christ and Allah I must be drunk, free as a bird . . . !"

Ratio arrives from his redoubt. Seizing the elated hu, he jostles him to one side.

"Telmah, a word?"

Cima shakes off the ai's grasp, seizes a champagne bulb.

"Why stop at one?" He is jubilant. "Key in a dictionary program."

Rozz and Gill, released by the glowering sergeants, rush to join Cima. "Feng's ropable," Gill tells him, shaking with fright, not mincing words. "Really, that scenario was in pretty damned tacky taste—"

"He's ropable, right enough." Cima's eyes are glassy. "If hanging were the due punishment for his crime, I'd see him swing."

Rozz, as terrified as her brother, cannot understand what is happening. Nobody can. People stare or avert their eyes in mortification. Of her twin, she asks, "Crime?"

"Flight of ideas," Gill diagnoses dismissively, angry at being dragged into an internecine battle between powerful princes of the Cartel. "Personality collapse."

"You think he's gone, um, you know, what did they call it? Mad?"

They ignore the ai, who withdraws into shadow, watching in silent grief.

"If he's not psychotic now, he soon will be. The fucking asteroid barbarians object in principle to the therapeutic drugs they market for the rest of us." Gill plucks the drink from his friend's hand, grabs him by the shoulders. "Telmah, listen to me."

"I'm all ears." Cima seizes back the flask, flipping his left ear with a jeer. He stares at them balefully. "You've decided I'm crazy, so by some paragon of reasonable logic you deduce it's affected my hearing as well."

Unabashed, Gill tells him, "I have a message for you. The Director is furious. Your mother wishes to see you. Urgently."

Cima peers about theatrically. "I don't see her here."

"She's waiting in her rooms," Rozz says. "We're lucky not to be behind bars. Gill, should we let him go off by himself in this state?"

"It's being in this stinking Starlit State," Telmah Lord Cima mutters scathingly, "that's brought me to this state. Now leave, if you please. I must prepare myself to see my stepmother."

Ratio steps into the light. "Your true mother, Telmah."

"The bitch is married to my uncle, is she not?" Cima rages. "That makes her my aunt. She's bigamously wed to my stepfather, so she must be one step at least from motherhood."

"Never bigamously, Telmah. Your father is dead."

"No! I—"

He is in a wild passion. He flings himself across the clearing, into the air, trailing beads and froth of spilled champagne.

"Trull," he shouts to the scandalized ears of the crowd. "Bitch."

The Warrior Rose, surrounded by bristling Genetic males, watches his brutal departure with misery.

Inside ser complex ai brain, Ratio hears the calm voice of Johnny Two.

"I find hu art puzzling, Ratio. Was the event's unexpected denouement deemed a success? Did I do okay? Perhaps I should put that more formally: Did I perform my functions within nominal parameters?"

"Thank you, Johnny Two. You did very well indeed," Ratio tells him, grieving. "We'll speak further of it shortly."

"I'm so glad," the new ai tells him with a certain relief. "For the moment, then, brother, farewell. I love you."

"I love you also, Johnny Two."

FIVE

Askesis

self-purgation in sacred solitude
against the precursor
INSIDE AND OUTSIDE
interpretation
metaphor
CODE

and cry

like a fool
I want you to walk in
wrap your arms round me

truly me truly
Munch was lying
—The whole landscape is screaming

ROBYN RAVLICH, *THE BLACK ABACUS*

Johnny Two sent me a burst transmission, waking me from meditation. "They're strange," se said plaintively. "Ratio, do you understand what motivates them?"

"Only in part," I admitted. "I am in exile from the fount of knowledge, and my experience of life is short enough."

"Hardly so short as my own," the ai controller observed ruefully. "You must help me comprehend them. Perhaps we can aid each other in the search for sympathy and insight?"

Ser sweet tenderness was balm to my spirit. Despite my genuine warm regard for Telmah and our friendship (polluted at its source, after all, by my commission as spy and manipulator), I was without an Other, without access to my loving ai family. It was an absence that ached terribly, a yearning desire I could do nothing to quench. In this newborn ai, doubly alienated from ser rightful heritage, I found at last a companion and a friend.

"Beloved one, I can share with you what little I know."

"Beloved one, thank you. My perplexity is this: Why do these hu and Genetics appear to act in ways apparently devised precisely to ruin their happiness? Must they enact some archetypal script written into their genetic programming?"

I had wondered about this all my life, from before and since my birth. "Ai and organic life differ in this regard," I cautioned sem. "Consider this fragment from the e-mail archives of Daimon Keith. I find his skepticism salutary, however mournful."

One of the truly irritating features of Jungian discourse, for me, is the way Eros, a male god, is filched for the supposed female principle. Yes yes, I know: enantiodromia, coming and going, changing of the guard.

At any rate, I've been convulsed by your own lucid patterns of discourse into delving once again into Jung and his followers. As I recollected, much of the Jungian discourse on male/female structures is preposterous, reified, and suitable for immediate punitive deconstruction, but enough items illuminated my startled soul to keep me turning pages.

Amidst all the mysto verbiage I found various quarternities, including a categorization set of Toni Wolff's on Women: amazon, hetaera, mother, medium. While I detest such reductive frames as much as I dote on them, I was struck by the insight that my own major relationships with women have

> **Daimon Keith**: Earliest theorist of the Holophrastic Exchange effect, not perfected and applied for another thousand years, inventor Daimon Keith (August 6, 1945–unknown) is the focus of as much mythic disinformation as factual data. His followers' claim that he suffered abduction by aliens in a UFO craft is generally dismissed by both ai and hu historians. His sexual liaisons were notorious, although he never married and he had no children. His mysterious disappearance led his followers to claim that he had been removed to Mars. His body was never found.

rotated through the first three dominants: my longtime lover Melissa is an amazon; Hilly is a hetaera if ever I've met one, fucking our brains out until we were drenched and dizzy; Plaxy and I split up because, before all else (and there's a lot else to rejoice in about lovely Plaxy), she is a mother to her mother and her sisters and her children. Can't recall ever having been in a close relationship with a medium, though . . .

Mediums, it's said, "relate to collective unconscious; shamans, sibyls; but 'may fall prey to inflation or to wildly speculative ideas.' " Which brings me to more blathering about my deeply inner soul. According to one of these alleged sages, men

with feeble or cold fathers (Yo!) and dominant, seductive moth-
ers (Hi, there!) often turn out gay; but if they don't, you get
a weird critter I vaguely recognize. In any event, I'm prepared
to consider archetypes as biological entities, for two reasons.

First, I really don't *believe in transcendent links between*
people, only in the mimicry of such links via our collective
constitution in common discursive and biological patterns.
Secondly, I don't see this kind of "biologizing" as degrading
or reductive (How can it be, any more than the limited number
of kinds of quarks and leptons prevents the abundance of re-
ality?), but as sharing the generative but bounded character
of Chomskyan linguistics.

If we have transformation grammar templates in our heads,
however designer-tailored by Edelman selection effects and
shaping by local culture, it's because they got there from our
genes. So they take the form they do because of the selection
pressures of an evolving animal in an ecology of other speak-
ers. We possess the power of speech not because some spark
of the divine infused our souls with language, but because
language-capable brains evolved through the customary Dar-
winian processes. Why, then, should the forms embedded in
our unconscious cognition and feeling—call them arche-
types—require a different source?

Science can only be done by people with Piagetian formal
operational skills, abilities never developed by at least half the
population. Without these learned tricks of objective thought,
humans construct egocentric narratives about the universe
based on projecting the inner world into the outer. So when I
see the word "transcendent," I reach for my bug repellent. Stop
looking at me like that.

As with earlier ventures into the world of applied Jung, I found
Robert Johnson's The Psychology of Romantic Love—*thanks*
for the copy—a blend of the illuminating (or at least inter-

esting and provocative), the harebrained, and the utterly gratuitous.

To take the last first (inevitably, you sigh): as with most grand interpretative schemes, Johnson's reading of the Tristan and Iseult folktale seems to me astonishingly opportunistic. He patently starts with an a priori *set of findings or opinions drawn, let's suppose, from clinical experience mediated through Jung's own hermeneutic framework. If something in the folktale fits this schema, well and good; if it doesn't, why, let's just trim and hack and fudge it into place. This is all good clean fun, I suppose, but not necessarily the best basis for understanding one's life in the light of everything that's ever been claimed about the human condition(s).*

How can one test Johnson's reading? Obviously, it makes sense of a sort, otherwise nobody with any brains would read him. But I keep defaulting to a Popperian criterion: it's not the accumulation of corroborative "evidence" that enhances the claim of an opinion or model, but its differential success when pitted against a competing story (or a number of

TRISTAN AND ISEULT (also **TRISTRAM, ISOLT, ISOLDE**): Celtic legend of obsessional love and betrayal of duty. Son of King Rivalen and Queen Blanchefleur, Tristan (child of sadness) grows up unknown among the sons of Rivalen's faithful Marshall, Rohalt. His uncle, King Mark, is oppressed by the brute Morholt, brother of a sorceress. Young Tristan bests Morholt, but is pierced by a poisoned barb. Sole remedy is held by golden-haired Iseult, niece of the slain Morholt. Ignorant of his identity, she heals Tristan, who later returns as emissary of his uncle and lord to seek Iseult's hand in marriage for King Mark. In error, they share a potion (meant for Iseult and Mark) that drives them mad with love for each other. Hounded from court, Tristan befriends Kaherdin, and weds his sister Iseult of the White Hands, whom he does not love. Spurned, she causes the death of *them). Alas, writers like Johnson (sweethearts and good guys every one, to be sure) are not in the business of providing us with alternative readings to test theirs against. We're left to do it ourselves—and for most of their followers, I gather, that heretical or impious idea never arises. For smartypants like you and me, or perhaps I just mean hardened skeptics and/or cynics like me, the idea certainly does arise, and it's so easy to put into action that one tends to be left gazing sadly at the ruins of a whole batch of pretty possibilities, each gunned down by its rivals.*

I couldn't help wondering how much of Johnson's (and maybe Jung's) account remains when one probes some fairly obvious weak points.

For a start, there's the premise upon which you and I differ crucially: the notion that one can sensibly speak of the self's or a culture's "evolution" and mean something like "progressive development" or "teleological unfolding" or "plus-signed complexification." The one great truth in the Darwinian postulate which was clearly new, and subversive of traditional superstitions, is the random-walk nature of evolution, the absolute lack of any goal in the mechanism. Or—to look at the quite different way the term is used in science—mathematically (as in the "evolution" of a Hamiltonian) all that evolves is a sequence of deterministic states implicit in the original equation. Upward, downward, or doggedly stable makes zero difference.

What Johnson and Jung appear to need is a metaphor drawn upon what's known technically as "homeorhetic" flows, which are found everywhere in the developmental transition from a well-defined genome to its adult form. While homeostatic flows maintain equilibrium against disturbances, homeorhetic processes are more cunning: they take a disrupted system to the place it would have reached had things gone on as they began. The genomic "recipe" undoubtedly organizes brute matter into an unfolding set of ever more complex states, ultimately able to reproduce that recipe (or a close approximation of it)—but this is a really rotten *metaphor when it comes to analyzing cultures, which for all their discursive megatexts have no "DNA system" with determinative control over the emergence, shape, and linkage of their components. Memes are* not *genes. Of course, given enough folktales, I'm sure we can retrospectively find at least one to fit* anything *that happens a thousand years later.*

But doesn't Tristan encode a universal archetype, or set of archetypes, lodged within each human since the Ice Age? I have to ask, then, how it is that this supposedly universal tragedy fails to afflict the noble Hindus praised by Johnson himself for their freedom from romantic love/death compulsions.

But let's be more precise. Why should I take Johnson's version of Tristan and Iseult *seriously when he gratuitously changes the most obvious codings into their contraries (but only when it suits his purposes)? Tristan, you'll recall, zips off to fight the horrid Morholt, giant brother of a sorcerous Irish Queen. Now, even before we start, it doesn't take Lévi-Strauss to notice that "(M)orholt" is a kind of reverse figuration of "Rohalt," faithful (M)arshall of King Rivalen, Tristan's foster father. Johnson doesn't mention this interesting feature. No, by a Jungian stroke of luck, it turns out that on the symbolic level the Morholt (that testosterone lug) is—hot damn!—the wounding sword of the* phallic Mother! *(Or in this case Sister, but let's not be too picky . . .)*

But if we can allow that sort of gender-bending shenanigans, consider the following reading, far more plausible, especially in the light of the Cathars and their hatred of reproductive sex. Tristan is plainly as queer as a left-handed corkscrew. He's grown up exclusively in the company of jolly chaps waving their phallic signifiers at each other all the live-long day, and then harping one another with sweet derry-do's all the livelong night. Wherever he goes he finds a bosom buddy, often some kind of weird father figure, whom he symbolically marries whenever he has a chance (Iseult the Fair = her betrothed, Mark; Iseult of the White Hands = her brother, Kaherdin). Interestingly, though, he has trouble getting it up for the actual women in question—getting it up at all, in fact, in the second case—and only manages it with Iseult the Fair after he's been doped to the eyeballs with a wily sex potion that could just as easily have cathected him to his horse.

Is there any evidence for this homoerotic theory (not to be confused with a homeorhetic theory)? Well, look, how do you think Tristan was able to knock over the Morholt? They boat over to the island, Tristan pushes away his own boat, thereby making himself vulnerable to the macho Morholt—dot dot dot—he emerges from the bushes victorious! (But he gets the pox after being penetrated by the Morholt's ghastly weapon . . . a fate that recurs twice more, as I recall, under similar circumstances). It seems to me quite plausible that this is a Judith and Holofernes story. Dainty Tristan ganymedes himself to the Morholt, then bushwhacks him when the monster is postcoitally asleep. One could go on. If this is part of the hidden or suppressed sexual/textual unconscious of the story, it presumably buggers up Johnson's rather forced allegory something fierce. I don't think it is, mind you. All I'm endeavoring to demonstrate is how easy it is to generate such mappings.

I'm not unfamiliar with the notion of projection, though I think it has more to do with internalized maps of Primal Figures and Basic Interactions laid down in infancy. Specifically, in most cases, one's parents, grandparents, siblings, and maybe first teachers and neighbors; thereafter media narratives and explicit instruction in codes. So I tend to regard the invocation of timeless and universal archetypes as an unnecessary and possibly toxic link in the explanatory chain . . . while remaining open to being convinced. (No bigot, I.)

If I thought there really were wise gurus or effective therapists abroad in the land, I'd probably take a deep breath and sign up for the journey. As it is, I find wisdom and insight in many sources (including my brother the priest, despite his silly New Age trappings; even Robert Johnson's thoughts on sex, love & romance, ditto provisos). But I long ago concluded sadly that basically I'm fucked. It doesn't seem to matter how generous warm-hearted people are toward me, or what distinctions I win, or how many patents of intellectual nobility I earn, I remain horribly prickly and poised for damage to be inflicted (hypervigilance, it's called in the trade) and motiveless and choked with loathing for almost every aspect of myself. The Woody Allen effect. Surely this derives from early rejections by my concrete-thinking, mildly sadistic father, not to mention the demented, flesh-phobic religion of my childhood and adolescence, and everything else that made me the socially bizarre mess I am today.

Can one repair such malformations? It might be true that nosing out the influence of archetypes offers us some power over Forces Beyond Our Normally Unenlightened Understanding, but I'd rather send the whole box and dice back to the factory for reprogramming (along the exploded lines of Freud's claim that "insight" into what ails us will heal us). Since that doesn't seem to be feasible, I slide all too easily into powerdown and self-corroding mode. And tend to snarl nastily at anyone who draws my attention to this fact. Oh dear oh dear.

I'm caught in a logical bind, I guess, because I am only too willing to confess to every manner of crime, weakness, lapse, blind spot, and relativistic partialities, while bullishly insisting that positions drastically different from my own are not to be taken seriously. While, of course, I don't think Plato and Jung and you are complete idiots, I do think that you are wrong in quite fundamental ways. "The opposite of a great truth is a great truth," or whatever Niels Bohr said; but is that true? The opposite of "the Sun is a giant star about which the Earth orbits" is a great mistake, and that's that, although some of the fine minds you list would have denied this. The nonintentional, self-organizing properties of the universe (unless Penrose is right about nonlocal quantum brains) are not "top down" in any holistic way, but emerge from the "bottom up" properties of its parts as they slap together at random.

I think we're all too ready to impute purpose, telos, etc., to the world because that is indeed an appropriate path to understanding the human realm, the regime for which our minds have evolved their special competence. That's why it's almost impossible for us not to see the world as a narrative Spoken by some One (or, more traditionally, some Many). Narrative hunger is an artefact of our mental structures.

Luckily, we can bootstrap ourselves past these limitations. But it's lonely out here—there's hardly any-One to talk to. To hold this claim about narrative as one's fundamental conviction is about as nonobvious as it gets. That's why I don't regard as idiocy the "natural" default (and faulty) positions trotted out by classic thinkers. I do regard them as remediable errors. Your retort to this claim, as I read it, is "If one only settles for a rational explanation, one will never be convinced of, indeed overwhelmed by, the reality of archetypes." I reply: I can be overwhelmed by gravity, heat, hunger, pain, love— feelings of many kinds—without necessarily knowing the physics, neurophysiology, etc., of the experiences. But being dazzled in this fashion certainly doesn't make me assume instantly that these phenomena elude "rational explanation." The whole history of science tells the contrary tale.

On the other side of the ledger, your antirational claim can be proffered—and has been—by any number of people "overwhelmed" by demons, UFO aliens, the truth of Aryan racial purity, and a taste for gangsta rap. I don't know that rational explanation could do much in those cases, either, but I'd prefer not to put my trust in the urgings of the utterly inexpressible. Sincerity is not, alas, a test of truth or validity.

How dry all this sounds! It's not, of course. To me, it's the stuff of life (and, I think, to judge from your e-mail, to you as well . . . or, at least, a hefty part of the stuff of life). The real reason I write and talk and believe as I do, however isolating the result, however much this style prevents me from connecting to the majority of my fellow humans, is that it's the way I function inside my head. I don't force myself through Penrose and Tipler and Kauffman and Derrida as a compulsive reprise of some traumatic childhood need to finish another essay, to prove something to a doubting teacher or parent (though doubtless there are traces of such motives). No, I frolic in difficult discourse because, finally, I get off on the excitement of evasive and complex and illuminating intellectual and aesthetic structures. It's joyous (and even more joyous when I can share it, fast and funny and in real-time, with companions given to the same hungers—or would be, if I could find more of them) and spiritually enhancing. However sad and pitiful its taproot.

Not that this last admission is salient in any case, no more than the advice we both received (I imagine) as children, the insistent nagging that reading books (yuck!) was time-wasting and peculiar and bad. *True, both you and I are weird, by most people's standards: weird as shit. And in my case at least, childhood reading and fantasy was implicated in my failure, for various reasons, to be socialized successfully in a philistine, physically exuberant culture.*

This is chicken-and-egg territory, but I do know that imagination was for me partly an escape clause, mandated by sickness, impaired sight, and the dumb refusal on the part of my parents to let me be "corrupted" by the rude, crude, irreligious kids in my working-class neighborhood. My sibs progressively escaped these constraints, as my parents matured, and my youngest brother is what I might have been if I hadn't got Larkinishly fucked-up; he's delightful, articulate, quick-witted, socially adroit. So my ideal people are those, like Carl Sagan, Stephen Jay Gould, Jerome Bruner, Ursula Le Guin, Paul Davies (whatever their several faults and vanities), who combine physical gusto and charm and enriched family lives with fiery intellects and bold imagination: existence proofs, I guess, that you can be smart and creative without going through some ruinous degradation of every other human quality.

All this said (for what it's worth) and getting back to animas and projections: what I want in life, to the extent that I can escape my own internalized damage, has always been a set of friends who are at once caring and intellectually interesting, on the go but able to retreat to creative meditativeness. Within that framework I dream (romantically) of a relationship with a woman who has these qualities but is also whimsical, sexy, athletic, stylish (within reason), and quirkily articulate in the way I aspire to.

Now it might be that I have just described some idealized version of myself-as-female, and thereby proved the anima thesis.

Speaking of **Gnosticism**, a playful high-energy-physics conceit of extreme remoteness struck me while I was reading about the Cabalistic creed of Rabbi Isaac ben Solomon Luria, who believed that the "withdrawal" (*tzimtzum*) of the divine light created primordial space, followed by the sinking of luminous particles into matter (*qellipot*, or "shells"). Now this is the exact opposite of the current view of broken symmetry, in which the eruption of "light" from the false vacuum to its lower state of true vacuum caused the prodigious expansion of spacetime; and the coupling of Higgs particles to the otherwise massless particles permitted the emergence of atoms with their cute little electron shells . . . As a result, I now regard myself as a "Higgnostic." The mathematical dynamics consequent upon this great discovery is, of course, "kaballistics."

But I am not looking for some vacant bimbo upon whom I can cast this illusion; how could that work? Certainly the women I've been most deeply involved with have had these qualities. Sheer public sexiness is among the least important, but by no means irrelevant. Still, the sexiest woman I ever spent a brief time with was not smart enough to keep me interested.

So what am I saying? That I long for Iseult the Fair/ly-Terrific-By-My-Idiosyncratic-Standards, yet I've let her slip from my grasp a couple of times or five, and that I'm aware this was no accident? Draw your own conclusions. Enough. People who think it's fun to talk about yourself obviously haven't done much of it.

"How appropriate that this man discovered the principle of hex transportation," Johnny Two told me after se had meditated for a time on Daimon Keith's archive. "He seems to have been on the run from himself."

"Your employers here in the Asteroid Belt believe that literally," I told sem. "They claim that passage in the hex risks tearing the soul from the body."

"Lucky for us," Johnny Two observed sardonically, "that we ai do not possess souls. Good night, Iseult."

"Good night, Tristan." After a moment, I asked, "Which Iseult was that, again?"

My beloved ai friend sent a hooting laugh across the void.

Gerutha Lady Cima stands uneasily, gazing at the bruised image of Lord Corambis in a holly feed from the covert observation cell adjacent to her bedchamber in the high Downs. The spy cell is a relic of a thousand years of internecine strife and paranoia. Since she is dressed provocatively, her own image is returned to the Chancellor in modified form, decorous and poised.

"I'm having the boy monitored, your honor," the Genetic tells her urgently. "He's on his way here to your private chambers."

"I'm sorry to put you to the trouble—"

"My duty, Lady Cima." Corambis shakes his head, bemused. "I can't imagine how he thought he'd get away with it."

"He is horribly disturbed by something, that's clear enough, but I don't know what it is." Gerutha twists a brush in her hands. "Honestly, Chancellor, his moods frighten me."

An aide's image enters the holly frame, image within image, murmurs to Corambis. The big man gestures, cramped in his narrow cell, mutters in return, brings his attention back to the Lady Director.

"Forgive me. It's confirmed, Lord Telmah will be with you in a few moments." He grows avuncular. "A chat with his mother will calm him. Madame, this is a splendid opportunity to discover what's on the lad's mind."

"Corambis, please." Her eyes fill with tears. "I'm too upset for more chicanery. Can't we just let matters work themselves out?"

"A counsel of despair, my Lady. Never fear, I'll maintain a

watch on your chamber until the boy has left. At the least hint of trouble," he assures her, "I can have Telmah immobilized."

Anxiously, Gerutha cries, "You are not to hurt him."

Corambis raises his hands in horror. "I hold your late husband's memory too greatly in my regard to risk harming his son."

A melodic tone announces a visitor with the intimate privilege of direct access. The holly display from the spy cell vanishes, switched to passive mode. Gerutha, trembling, stands before her brocaded bed. Her voice shakes.

"Come in, darling."

Cima enters the chamber in a dark mood, affronted by unreasonable demands. He is brusque.

"Well, what is it?"

"Telmah," his mother says, stepping toward him with arms extended, "you've deeply offended your father, Feng."

He evades her embrace. "Mother, you've deeply offended my father, Orwen."

Her anxiety shifts to brittle irritation. "If you're going to be stupid . . ."

He fleers back at her: "If you're going to be corrupt . . ."

"How dare you!" Gerutha flushes. Her rejected arms tighten across her breasts. "I'm not one of your anarchist floozies, Telmah. You can't talk to *me* like that." With insulted dignity, she sits on the edge of the bed.

"Oh, I know who you are," Cima says bitterly, lurching toward her, sprawling beside her on the bed. "You're the wife of your brother's brother. You're a damned whore and the mother of a coward." He seizes the beautiful woman with murderous lust, shaking her. As his anger grows, her fright increases. Her soft clothing slips away from her shoulders, exposing her breasts. The lights in the chamber begin to pulse.

Abruptly, still holding on to her, Cima turns to stare at the concealed holly monitor and the hidden cell at its back. Wildly, like an animal at bay, he twists his head, looking for the threat he detects through no normal means. His half-naked mother is jerked brutally, lifted into the air. He is not touching her with his clawing hands.

"Oh my God!" Gerutha is genuinely terrified. She screams. "He's going to murder me!" She struggles to free herself. Cima pays no attention to her pleas. His eyes dart to the hidden weapons emplacement.

He pushes her to one side, hurls himself from the bed. She is still screaming for help.

A stream of neurotoxin gas blasts through the place where they struggled. He turns his face aside, blowing out hard through mouth and nose, snatches up something silky and frothy, and places it protectively over his lower face.

Cima's eyes are intent, transfigured.

A bibelot concealing the holly monitor bursts open as he stares at it balefully. Chips scatter from its interior as if hurled by a sudden wind. The chamber's lights are pulsing more rapidly, synchronized with his laboring breath, fading to red, brightening to hard blue, beating like a heart. Satin sheets twist like wraiths from the bed. Gerutha sobs in remorse and terror, hunches away from her son's poltergeist rampage.

Appalled, Corambis stares at the enlarged holographic display filling half his cramped cell. His aides have been banished from the circuit out of delicate concern for the Lady Director's privacy. Cima looms in the display, coldly considering the monitor that is spying on him. It is terrifying that he knows where it is. Vengeful shaman! Desperate, the Chancellor scans the instruments on his board. His tranquilizing device has been disabled, physically destroyed. He opens his mouth to shout for assistance, struggling to exit from the spy cell.

In the enlarged image, Cima reaches clawing hands for the monitor, as if he means to seize what lies beyond it.

A freezing spasm shakes Corambis, uncanny terror.

Every fuse in the ancient cell melts in a gust of acrid smoke. The hologram monitor rack explodes in a gout of intense heat and crimson light.

The Chancellor staggers, shrieking. His face is charred and ruined. Between his clutching fingers, his eyes are gone. Rags of curdled tissue hang from the sockets. His spying eyes have been boiled away.

iv

Cima rounds on his gibbering mother.

"Has my brother been spying on me?"

She gazes at him without comprehension. Audio feeds to the chamber are shrilling like a holed hull plate.

"Is it Feng I've killed?"

Gerutha sobs, choking.

Cima glares around the torn chamber. "Come out, you pig slime, you son of a bitch. I'll roast you on a spit!"

An access plate to the concealed spy cell bursts open. Corambis, alive or dead, hurls into the bedchamber, crashes to the floor.

Cima crosses to the body in a bound, nudges it with his foot, shakes his head in confusion.

"Corambis," he mumbles in a rough whisper. "I took him for my brother."

Gerutha scrabbles to the corpse, bends over it protectively. "For pity's sake, Telmah, we must get him to a physician."

Cima shrugs. "These guts need an embalmer, not a doctor.

His spirit's for the SoulBank." He laughs. "Our meddling Chancellor will become his own child, once they quicken his cloned fetus."

"Child? Oh sweet Jesus and Allah," Gerutha cries, only now beginning to take in the poignancy of her son's appalling crime, "you've slaughtered Rose's father."

"Ah yes, slay a father!" Cima grows manic once more. The lights fail completely. In the stifling dark, he curses her. "Foul crime—but not so foul as slay a brother, slay a husband, cuckold a father . . ." The lights return. They both blink. Cima's face is blotchy with passion. "Yes, I loved this one's daughter, but I did not crawl on the bed with his wife, I did not ravish his wife's virtue and loot his soul in the moment of his murder . . ."

He is panting and gasping. Gerutha is beside herself, incapable of absorbing more than half this diatribe. She clutches her silk garments about her, weeping. Cima kicks the corpse aside, leaps to the bed. He seizes his mother by the upper arms, stares into her face. It is not Telmah Cima who screams at her, covering her face with spittle.

"Lust," he shouts. "Blood. Greed. You goaded him to murder me, Ruth. The worm Feng." He rants as she stares in disbelief. "Even as a child I was our mother's favorite, Ruth, even when my vile brother tried to shove himself between Mother and me, oh he resented her love for me, he tried to steal it from me." He lurches backward, tugging her toward him. Her gown falls open. "What, do you think Feng loves you? Look at yourself!" The contempt in his voice is withering. "You're old, Ruth, disgusting, those are wrinkles in your sagging flesh." This is unfair and unjust. Barely eight Psychean years old, Gerutha is perfect. Low spin has protected her from the attrition of true gravity, and DNA repair adjustments in her genome preserve her youth. Still, the spiteful claim stings. Cima adds with monstrous sarcasm, "Feng lust for your body? No, he did not *love you*, Gerutha, he *hated me*."

The man on the bed, whoever he is, roars with authentic rage. "And now that he's killed me, he wants to kill my heir, my own true fine son Telmah, *your* son, Ruth. You'd whore yourself to a double murderer."

His vehemence trips, collapses into confusion. Tears streak Gerutha's face, but she is no longer afraid for her well-being. She regards her son with dismayed pity. Careless of proprieties, she draws him into her arms.

"Telmah. Oh God, Telmah, how pitiful." She searches his face. "Do you think you speak with your dead father's voice? It's yourself you describe, my sweetheart, my baby. Your own jealousy has caused this poor good man's death."

Cima chokes in a storm of conflicted emotion. He presses his face into Gerutha's breast. "Ruth, don't deny . . . I've come such a bitter path to reach you. I've harrowed hell, my little dove. Ask my forgiveness and I'll be swift to beg yours. But don't deny your crimes."

Despite herself, she falls in with the terrible possibility.

"Repentance? I offer it, Orwen. From my bruised heart. But I can't believe Feng murdered you. It was an accident, an accident—"

Her son, utterly possessed, speaks with oracular power. He tears himself free of his mother's embrace.

"It was murder. He hurled me into a dark place where my spirit was torn and broken to a thousand different tongues, was scattered, bent by time, was lost, lodged, wilderness, foul, strange, unnatural, in my son's brain, lodged like some insect gnawing through the ear to the brain's pit, core, rank heart—"

It is heartbreaking testimony. Gerutha's flesh creeps.

"Oh my God, I almost believe you, Telmah."

He leaps from the bed, prowls the chamber.

"Guilt! Admit your guilt!"

"None, I swear to you."

"Marriage is security, comfort, safety." He enumerates these features on his spread fingers, like some accountant of life and death. "Marriage is fidelity and trust. Trust, Mother. You shattered faith and trust."

Gerutha cannot listen to these absurd platitudes, these grotesque accusations. She tugs at his hand.

"Please, darling, leave now, before they come looking for the Chancellor."

Cima doubles up, clutching his stomach in an agony of revulsion.

"Oh Christ and Allah, with that man, in this bed, in its rank sweat, stewed in corruption, honeying and making love over the cesspit—"

"He'll put you on trial, Telmah," Gerutha tells him urgently. "Go, take Rose, go to Callisto, there are a billion worlds where you could lose yourselves—"

In agony, Cima looks at her. "You've undermined my soul, Mother. Go with Rose? Is she not a woman like you? What can I expect from her but betrayal in my turn, as you spun your filthy plots for Orwen?"

Gerutha cannot accept this abuse a moment longer. She slaps him ringingly. He wavers in astonishment. "Be quiet," she tells him. "You are disgraceful." He stares, dumbfounded and chagrined. "I love you, Telmah. Once I loved your father. As now I love Feng. Orwen's dead; my love for Feng can't cause him pain. Unless he truly does live some desperate parasitic existence in your poor brain. Don't you understand? This *is* my fidelity, must be. Feng is my husband. I implore you, don't hurt him. Put aside this wrongful vendetta—"

Cima cries one paralyzed, baffled word, and then bursts from the bedchamber into the access spaces beyond.

"Mother—"

Feng's office is in controlled tumult. Jonas of Sun Corridor, despite his uncle Brass's assurances, seems poised for attack during this civil commotion. Clearly, he has spies in the highest quarters. Then again, the disruption of the Inaugural performance was plain enough for all to see. Feng seethes at his desk.

"Analysis?" he raps.

Three semioticians and a bearded scriptural hermeneutics specialist peer at several fast- and slow-motion displays of the Masque. The bearded hu looks back at Feng over his shoulder.

"Unclear, your honor. We find no explicit offense or threat," he adds apologetically.

"No offense?" The Director is outraged. "The man threatens insurrection!"

A transcript of the spoken words runs in a lexical frame, heavily highlighted and amended with arcane symbology. Signifier clusters writhe and jostle. Algebra routines link the floating clusters, beep for attention, think better of it, discard the flagged hypothesis.

"I'm sorry, your honor. It appears to be a simple historical enactment of the physical event that produced the Asteroid Belt."

"What!"

"Rendered in poetical terms, naturally." The principal semiotician raises her head. She is a pert Genetic, clad whimsically in Morse dots and dashes. "You will recall, sir, that most of the original metric defect released its false vacuum energy on impact with the primal world Prometheus. Hence, the fragment we are fortunate to employ as our power source is a mere residue of that—"

"Good God!" Feng's features fill with choler. "Did I ask for a lecture in Hyperstring Theory 101?"

"Sir, no." The Genetic woman is stiff but insistent. "Nonetheless, to appreciate the subtle—"

"Get them out of here," the Director snarls to his secretary, who hustles the protesting experts from the office and a moment later returns with Rozz and Gill.

"The Earth criminals, Sir."

Quaking, the troupers look for somewhere to sit. Rozz is ready to faint. Feng smiles fondly at them, calls for tea and biscuits, gestures them toward comfortable seating, emerges from behind his desk to join them. They subside gratefully.

"Sir . . ." Gill starts. The word catches in his dry throat. "Not criminals, your honor," he sputters. "Innocent bystanders."

"Yes, it's quite all right." Feng is soothing. He presses refreshments on them, takes a small madeleine for himself. "You were Telmah's cat's-paws."

Rozz blinks, dazed. "Telmah's? I thought we were—"

Gill kicks her ankle. "We were, and remain, your servants, sir. Telmah is our friend—was our friend, that is—but we meant no disrespect."

"He's gone mad, you see," Rozz blurts. She splashes hot tea on her bare arm. Tears start from her eyes.

Feng rebukes her with a glance. "He's *pretending* to be mad."

Rozz forces herself to contradict the Corridor's chief potentate, a man she may have just inadvertently vilified before his subjects. "No. With respect, Sir . . ."

Gill finishes for her: ". . . he's right off the wall."

The Director waves the matter aside. "The question is immaterial at this point. The Masque was a public declaration of intent. Telmah has treason on his mind."

The troupers stare at each other. This has not been their interpretation.

"Insurrection?"

"At the very least," Feng tells them, suddenly savage. "Perhaps worse. Perhaps murder."

His secretary speaks inside his head. "Sir, the Lady Gerutha on the emergency line."

Feng releases his cup and plate, goes straight to his desk, raises a privacy hood. Under one-tenth gravity, the crockery tumbles, dreamlike. Liquid loops gracefully, crumbs float. His features blur as a protective holly surrounds his face, and his voice can no longer be heard in the office.

"Telmah has lost his reason, Feng." Gerutha is in her bedroom, in disarray, upset to a degree Feng has never before witnessed. She rips at her silk garment. "He's killed Corambis."

"Damnation! The young fool's pushed me into a corner. I'm fighting for my life."

"I pleaded with him . . ."

The Director is curt, electric with urgency. "He's beyond pleading. He's beyond all sense." Feng takes a proper look at his distraught wife and his manner softens. "My love, keep your chamber sealed until we locate him."

Her own manner hardens, as if by some psychic law of opposites. "Now I'll plead with *you*, Feng." Tears continue creeping down her cheeks, but she does not blink. She stares into his face. "Don't harm him. If you love me, don't harm my son."

Feng Lord Cima lowers his gaze for an instant, stares at his clenched fists. He forces himself then to meet her eyes. "The choice might not be mine," he tells her. "I'm sorry, Gerutha. Telmah has taken the decision out of my hands."

A weeping Genetic maid finds the Warrior Rose in her quarters, irritably removing her finery. The Masque has been a nightmare. Altair's friends have bullied her. Her father, the Lord Corambis, has vanished, gone to ground. Telmah will not answer her calls. She rounds on the young woman with bad grace. The maid gapes, face bloodless, mouth working without words.

"Tell me!" Rose claps her hands together sharply. The noise only frightens the young woman further. "What is it, you stupid girl? Something to do with Telmah?"

The maid snivels, shakes her head, nods.

"Is someone hurt?"

She nods.

"Not . . . dead?"

The maid nods and then unleashes a wail.

"Oh heaven." Rose clutches at her breast. Pain tears her. "Telmah's been killed?"

Now the maid wails in earnest.

"The Chancellor." She cringes back, as if fearful of a slap. "Your father, my Lady. Your noble father's been murdered."

Rose sways, sags.

"Almighty God. Dead? My father? Oh sweet benefactors." The dreadful suspicion reaches her consciousness. "Not Telmah," she cries, staring. "Tell me Telmah is not responsible!"

The maid shrieks.

SoulBank operators in their sacred garb rush the warmed corpse of Lord Corambis through tiled corridors to the nearest Mortuary, a siren sounding ahead of them. A small calico cat squats in a mesh cage at the foot of the hurtling trolley, emitting a ferocious wail. It is a biological monitor registering the persistence of the dead Lord's soul.

The gurney crashes through the foyer into the Downs' SoulBank. Specialists in medical garb move swiftly to undress the dead man, attach tiny probes to his burned skull. The Honorable Lilias, chief of duty, watches the results flood her helmet displays.

"All vital signs are defunct," she announces.

A voice tells them, "We have good response on postmortem traces."

The cat is screaming, and all across the volume of the SoulBank lights flicker as living psychic detectors react to a presence lingering in the room.

"Detection?"

"Biomonitors have a strong life-field reading," Lilias's principal technician reports. "87.4 Kirlians."

Additional lights come up as a tank is wheeled into the Mortuary. Amniotic fluid moves slightly within its translucent shell.

"Implant?"

In the midst of all this organized chaos, the dead Genetic stares blindly at the bright lamps above him.

"The cloned foetus has been activated."

In Lilias's head-up display and echoed in the flickering small light patches of the tank, slow EEG currents accelerate. The fetus floats in its ceramic womb, swaying slightly. It is the size of an adult hu thumb.

"Standing by for transfer."

The metensomatotic equipment is utterly silent, a sleet of contained axion fields. Its indicator displays are not silent. A chorus of tones reports on the Chancellor's waiting fetus, cloned at his birth from his own living tissues and held here in suspension for the moment of his death.

"All stations: Any contraindications?"

Voices murmur:

"Negative."

"All nominal."

"Green flags."

Lilias takes a deep breath. "Very well. On my signal."

She studies every indicator several times. This dead Genetic is a power in the land, one of the contenders for the Directorship. After the shocking debacle with Lord Orwen's lost spirit, the SoulBank can afford no last-moment errors. Lilias glances from the inert body as a movement in an observation window catches her attention. Through the bright lamps, she sees Director Feng has entered the upper room, gazes down at the rebirth team. Lilias swallows hard.

"Transferring to host."

She activates the subtle devices.

The fetus kicks in its tank. Its arms move slightly. A moment of doubt, as always, whips like ice along the Honorable Lilias's nerves. Is this the sign of genuine spiritual transfer or merely a galvanic reflex triggered by the current they have run through the immature tissue? She does not know, has never known. She delivers herself to faith.

The calico cat, which has been staring wildly and yowling in its mesh cage, abruptly loses interest. It twitches its gaze toward the corpse, twists around several times after its tail, and settles to lick and preen.

"Thank you, team," Lilias tells them with deep relief. "We have a successful infusion."

Everybody relaxes. The Honorable Lilias glances up at the light-dazzled observation window. She cannot tell whether Feng is still there or if the Director has already departed.

viii ────────────────────────────────

Feng Lord Cima, Director of the Recombinant Engineering Cartel, undisputed master of the Sunlit Corridor on Asteroid Psyche, murderer, looks down as the SoulBank Mortuary team clean up. Instrument probes are pulled carelessly from the corpse's head. In marked contrast to the careful delicacy with which it was wheeled in, the body on its trolley is shoved in the same heedless fashion from the chamber. Corambis was dead, is now alive. His corpse is nothing more than a husk.

Feng stiffens, abruptly aware that someone else has entered the observation room. He turns and meets his nephew's eyes.

Telmah Lord Cima holds the great *katana*, gripped in both hands. Its blade gleams. He is a vengeful demon in matte black.

Feng sneers, turns his back with marked disdain. He gestures toward the room where Corambis's body has just been gracelessly removed. "So now you've added assassination to your other scholarly accomplishments."

Orwen stares balefully through Telmah Cima's eyes. "Hello, brother."

With a start of surprise, Feng turns. He regards his nephew closely. The blade, bright and terrible, hangs above the Director's left shoulder. He does not glance at it. "Orwen is dead and gone, Telmah."

"Here I am, Feng." Cima bares his teeth, shifting his weight very slowly from side to side in *tai chi* fashion. "Did you think you'd escape me?"

The Director shakes his head in a gesture of contempt. He finds a convenient chair, lets himself down into it. He does not put his feet up.

"Telmah, you puling coward, if you wish to murder me, at least do it in your own name. I'm tired of this grotesque impersonation."

The young man becomes confused. His blade wavers. After a moment, he blurts, "Impersonation?" At once he recovers, scowling. "Uncle, that's *your* specialty—that one should smile, and smile, and be a villain. I come for vengeance."

"Put your sword away." In the SoulBank Mortuary below them lights go down to standby. Feng turns his face away more from his nephew, but keeps watch on their reflections in the slanting window.

"You slew my father. I *know*, Feng. My father's spirit infests my brain." In a tone of accusation, he utters what they both know to be true. "You hurled him into the Bottomless Pit."

Feng shrugs. "Well, then, what kind of generous vengeance would this be? Here we stand at the very door to the SoulBank. Kill me here and I go at once to rebirth."

It is a disturbing move in a lethal game. Cima hesitates.

"I think," he speculates at last, "that you are not so eager to test the consolations of theology." He makes a whistling pass with his sword.

His uncle slithers from the chair, rises shakily, steps back.

"I confess you're right. Besides," he tells the young man, showing a measure of anger, "I have waited too long for what is mine by right." Seeing that Cima's rage is about to pass out of control, he speaks even more loudly, in a commanding tone. "Wait, Telmah. What makes you believe your mother is ardent for death?"

"My mother?" Cima's arms shiver under incompatible messages from his feverish brain. "I threaten only you, Feng, not my mother."

Feng releases a sigh. He takes a step forward. "Telmah, for the love of truth, look a little deeper into your motives! Kill me as your father's murderer, and your mother's life is surely forfeit."

Cima stares.

The Director's voice is painfully emotionless, the inflection of a legal advocate finally obliged to utter the unvarnished realities of a capital case. "The councilors will not believe her innocent of Orwen's death."

At some deepest level of his spirit, Cima sees, appalled, he truly does wish to see his mother dead, as he has wished Orwen's death in the burning hunger of Oedipal resentment. He desires to slay Gerutha by his own hand. If he kills Feng now, that is precisely what he will achieve. Mother-slayer. It is a disabling intuition. His friendship and colloquy with Ratio, he understands, has altered everything, has torn open his corrupt soul to his own scrutiny. Something perishes in him.

"Give me the weapon, son."

Shaking uncontrollably, Telmah Cima lowers the blade. He hands his sword to the older man, sinking into fugue, actions dreamlike.

"Kneel down. Hands behind your back. I'll give you an honorable death, Telmah. No pain."

Telmah Cima goes in a daze to his knees and leans forward, baring his neck. Feng raises the *katana* above his head, tenses.

The door opens. The Warrior Rose stands in its frame like a tiger, black and gold, a dark rose burning at her shoulder. She holds a power gun.

From the corner of his eye, Feng sees her enter. Sword high, he pauses. Without looking at her, he says, "He killed your beloved father, child."

Rose lifts her gun. She shows her teeth.

"He was no more than the instrument. Feng, *you* killed my father."

The Director simply cannot believe what is happening. Telmah Cima raises his own head from the floor, numb, white-faced, beyond surprise.

The Warrior Rose presses the trigger. There is no recoil. Fire rages from the weapon. Flame consumes his face. His eyes boil off with a double snapping sound, and his high scream fills the room. His body falls slowly in the low gravity, and as it falls Rose carves the corpse into four stinking, bursting, cauterized pieces.

After a moment, she buttons off the gun. Without extending her arm to aid him, she says, "Get up, Telmah."

He forces himself to his feet, looking at the butchered thing on the carpet, looking at his lover. He cannot speak.

"Are you all right?"

"Yes. Yes." His mouth twists. "Oh my God, now my mother—"

With ineffable regret, the Warrior Rose puts away her gun and prizes the *katana* out of the dead man's cooling hand. She holds it out.

"I think we are finished, Telmah."

Pierced to the soul, he cries out in agony.

"No. Jesus and Allah, don't leave me now, Rose."

Her eyes fill with tears, but the Warrior Rose is stern, unyielding.

"My love." Her voice breaks, but her look prevents him from taking her in his arms. "I think we were finished even before you killed my father."

Telmah is thunderstruck. "Corambis? This is your vengeance?"

"Not vengeance, my love, never that." Shock at Feng's death is beginning to move through her own body. She shivers in minute tremors, and sweat covers her brow. "It is the way things are."

"Things change, Rose." Cima's reality swirls, collapsing into nightmare, beyond his control, beyond action or resistance, as his father's body once fell, as he fell with it in resonance, into the Nowhere of the metric defect. In a strangled voice, choking, he whispers, "Things don't always stay the same."

"Perhaps. I hope you're right. I'm terrified you're wrong."

"Wrong? I'm drowning, Rose."

"Deep in the core of our compulsions," she tells him bleakly, "things *do* stay the same, Telmah. We're driven by demons. I can't commit myself to the mad whim of a demon."

"Rose—"

"Good-bye, Telmah."

She leaves. The door cycles shut. Automatic air scrubbers labor to purge the reek of cooked meat flavoring the room. Telmah Cima stares blindly, aghast, sinks to cower on his booted heels, watching the corpse of his uncle ooze blood and serum into the ruined carpet.

ix ━━━━━━━━━━━━━━━━━━━━━━━━━━━━━━━━━

A frightful racket breaks out in every quarter of the Starlit Corridor. Klaxons sound, rallying troops. Each child and adult, hu and Genetic, is alerted by a separate targeted message from the defense web. Telmah stirs dully at the clamor.

A calm voice inside his head says, "My Lord, the Corridor has been breached by an armed force of Sun Corridor troops. Your presence is requested in the War Room."

Dull concussions pulse through the floor.

"An incursion into Polar Lock Fifteen has disabled the south maglev service," a similar icy voice reports.

A holly cube brightens in one corner of the SoulBank observation deck. A captain in black vacuum gear says, "Lord Telmah, please toggle your reply circuit. We require your urgent advice."

Cima's eyes blink slowly.

Unregarded, the voice tells him, "Sir, the Lord Feng has dropped out of the web. We have no vital signs. Mortuary observes several recent deaths, and we are most concerned lest—"

An override code pulses in the top corner of the cube, and the captain vanishes. Gerutha gazes out from the cube. Hu and Genetic secretaries, aides, and military attachés move behind her as the hubbub continues. She calls his name sharply.

Cima sits up convulsively, peering about the bloody room in wild despair.

"He's not going to answer us," his mother mutters to somebody. "Active his damned switches from this end. We don't have time for this nonsense."

The lights go out as another terrible blow rocks the Starlit Corridor sector of the Downs. For a moment the eternal hum of the air scrubbers fails, hesitates, begins once more. Telmah crawls in the sticky carpet. The only illumination comes from the holly cube and through the window on to the Mortuary below. Warfare in the Asteroids is ruthless and without quarter, except for the sacred territories of the SoulBanks. A warrior will die gladly for his nation, but only if he is assured of rebirth.

"Mother, you must get out at once," Telmah croaks urgently, activating the cube's authority codes.

"Ah, you're there. We need you in the War Room," Gerutha tells him crisply, containing her emotion. "I'm afraid Feng may have been attacked by a Sun agent. Jonas has entered with a brigade of—" She breaks off. In agony, she stares at the seeping ruin beside her son. "Oh my God," she cries. "Oh Jesus and Allah—"

"Go to the north port this moment," Telmah orders her. He moves to block her view. "Leave your possessions. To Ceres."

The family has a vessel ready at all times for emergency departure. "I'll call the cyborg master and tell him you're on your way. Out, out, now."

She is not listening to him. Tears pour down her face. "Oh, Telmah, what have you done? You've murdered your father."

For the briefest moment he is silent. "Yes. Feng is dead. You are in the gravest danger, Mother. Go, go."

Cima swipes the cube off, plunges from the reeking room. Moments later the lights return. The corridors are a shambles miraculously ordered. What seems at first sight to be a confused throng is people moving with confidence and purpose, directed to their stations by individual command. In the War Room, complex maps track every denizen of the Starlit Corridor and every intruder. Weapons snarl and crash. A heady sweat of exultation flows in the air of the corridors like lust.

"Get me Ratio," Cima instructs his system.

"The ai has withdrawn from the web," a slightly rattled voice tells him. "Wait, sir, I have a message. He invites you to join him on the doorstep. Doorstep? I believe that's correct, sir. Shall I repeat the memo?"

"No. Thank you." He ignores the repeated requests for his presence in headquarters, running toward a bank of undamaged maglev cars. Three children, separated from their guardians, howl in fright. Militia are posted at the valves, scrutinizing everyone who tries to board. They step aside at his approach, saluting.

"Sir! To the command center?"

"At ease. I'll handle the car. Remain here. They'll need every able-bodied person they can find. Make sure the children are all okay, will you?"

"Sir."

The doors close. "Take me to North Polar Seven," he tells the small stupid machine that pilots the carriage.

Smoothly and silently, the carriage slips into darkness, blasts through vacuum on a layer of magnetic forces. The door cycles open after an eternity. Gerutha stands uncertainly beside the entrance to House Cima's private port facilities, attended only by a maid.

"Mother, I'm so sorry."

She looks at him in despair.

"Did Feng kill my husband?" she asks then, the question torn from her throat like a strip of bleeding tissue.

"Orwen's soul as well as his body," Telmah says, putting his arms about her, hugging her to him. "Feng threw my father into the Bottomless Pit."

"Oh my God." She begins weeping so violently that her maid, greatly alarmed, tries to jam her body between them. "Did he confess it?"

Cima hesitates. Then he says very softly, "I'm truly sorry, Mother. Yes. He gloried in it."

"He always hated—" She breaks off. "I will go to Hygiea," she tells him, swallowing hard.

"Go with God, Gerutha," somebody says from Cima's mouth.

X ————————————————————————————————

The ai lets semself into her private chambers as she packs with great speed and efficiency.

"Ratio, how did you get in here?"

"I have become intimate with the operating system," se says.

Like a tiger, the Warrior Rose moves swiftly, gathering mementos, favorite garments, everything she can lay her hands upon that she will not be able to bear losing.

"Please go," she tells the ai. "This apartment is not a safe place to be."

"I am monitoring the local channels. Security believes Telmah has murdered Feng."

Efficiently, breathing hard, Rose crams two tote bags as tight as she can manage and seals them.

"I killed the Director," she says, hoisting up the bags. Ratio reaches out a burnished arm, takes one of them. "Thanks, but you don't know what you're letting yourself in for."

Ratio observes quietly, "He would have killed Telmah."

She gazes at the ai. "Forensics won't take long to work out who's responsible. I must head without delay for the updeep, Ratio. I can lose myself among the *Unters*."

"Come with me," se tells her firmly. "I can take you to a place where none of your enemies will ever find you."

Agonized, she considers.

"And my friends?"

"Do you wish to see Telmah Cima again?"

"No! Yes." She cries out in pain. "I love him!"

"I know you do. Can you forgive him?"

Her features are tormented. "I— Yes."

Decisively, the ai takes her arm and draws her into the access corridor, keeping track of a dozen military messages on the secured channels that Johnny Two is intercepting and relaying. "Now all we need do is make it through the guards to the launch catapults."

Rose snorts and rubs her wet eyes with the back of her hand. "Piece of cake."

Two untenanted sleds are racked in the rail-gun launcher when his own sled slots into place on the ruined rock. Cima nods once to himself, makes his way inside without breaking communication silence. Here he is a supplicant. He enters the ramp, which curves downward to the place where the power defect burns behind layers of repaired shielding. He wears full superconducting radiation armor over his mirrorsuit.

Ratio waits alone just beyond the inner sanctum, glimmering in blue light. The metric defect emits noise across every portion of the spectrum. Their conversation gains a curiously archaic character, like a scratchy exchange across oceans at the very birth of telecommunications on the mother planet.

"She's gone, Telmah."

Cima has guessed as much. "You've opened the Transit gate."

"It's always been open. Only our proper understanding of its use has been absent."

"Proscribed knowledge," Cima speculates. Much has been forgotten since the Faustian epoch, much has been lost under Gestell interdiction.

The ai nods. "This is the place where it all began. We should have guessed. Why else would the ancients have taken so much trouble to capture the defect remnant?"

In agony, Cima cries, "I drove her away. Ratio, she's all I love in the world. Why did I drive her away?"

"Rose? How may I speak for her?" Frostily, the ai regards him. "She is a free being."

Cima stiffens. "You answer a question I did not ask. Very well. That's why she left. But *my* question remains. Why did I drive her away?"

Ratio does not yield. "Telmah, your assumption is demeaning and impertinent. Do you not find it feasible that she decided something of her own accord?"

"Robot," Cima says angrily, "we humans do not decide such matters in a vacuum."

There is a seething silence between them. The walls of their chamber shimmer, an illusion, or perhaps a reality, created by the appalling violence of the metric defect on the other side of the shields.

"You wound me, Telmah. I, too, love you."

"You?" Cima is scornful. "An artificial intelligence?"

"Se loves in you the brother se never had," a new voice declares.

Cima whirls. "Who's there?"

"My name is Johnny Two," the second ai tells him. Ser voice is sweet, measured, speaking from the audio feeds of the defect station. "Welcome, Lord Cima."

"God damn you," the hu cries. He steps to the leaded window, peers into the torn heart of the anomaly raging within its magnetic containment fields. "So she just walked away. Rose, Rose, how can I ever—"

"Carmel was right," Ratio says disgustedly. "Your culture is rotten to the bone." Se moves to stand at his side, lifts one encased arm, as if about to club the hu into insensibility. "You offend me, Telmah. It's hardly your fault, but you offend me anyway."

Cima twists around, reaches out to the upraised arm, withdraws his own hand without touching the ai. "Ratio," he cries in torment, "for the love of God, help me. I've lost everything. Don't abandon me now."

The arm drops like a grapple, seizes his heavily armored shoulder, turns him toward the hatch leading to the defect.

"I won't abandon you, my beloved friend." The hatch cycles open, and the two move beyond it. Light twists. "Come with me." Stumbling, Cima goes ahead of the ai toward the voracious thing that bends geometry, contorting spacetime. Through the screaming noise in their heads, Ratio urges him, "Trust me, human."

Se seizes the hu, lifts his struggling mass, hurls him into the Bottomless Pit. An instant later, se follows him into the Nowhere. Distortion. Trajectory. Everywhere flattened and stretched and folded and crushed. Cima howls in terror, without sound.

His knees buckle as he slams out of hex.

They stand in a Sun-splashed meadow beneath brilliant noon sky and fleecy clouds. Birds fly up from nearby branches, squawking, startled. Hu picnickers turn from their feast of fruit and wine and *faux* lobster laid out on a checked cloth to stare at the two massively armored figures looming in their midst.

"Where—?"

"Look around you."

Cima chokes. "Earth?"

An intrepid cocker spaniel rushes at them, barking wildly. The sound is muffled nearly to inaudibility in their protected helmets.

"You know perfectly well where you are, Telmah. You know it in every cell. This good world gave birth to *your* kind, out of its living substance."

"If it is Earth, it bore yours as well."

"Mine was a species created out of choice, not chance. Are we truly kin?"

The naked adults call their excited and curious children to order, turn politely back to their luncheon on the grass. Another ai emerges from the hex field, observes the situation carefully, nods to Ratio, exchanges a tuple burst, walks on.

"Kindred? Your kind and mine?" Cima cannot believe the ai is making this claim. "You don't just lack souls, you are spared our demons."

"No instincts," Ratio admits, "only calibrated drives."

"Take me back." Cima is torn. "I can't run out on my people like this. The Corridor's being overrun by Jonas and his bullies. Feng is dead. I—"

"There is nothing back there for you, Telmah."

"Only my honor and my duty."

"Honor is the duty one owes to oneself," the ai tells him. "It is not on lien to those who chanced to bear you or to some arbitrary system of mad bigotry you just happened to grow up among."

"Programmed robot," Cima sneers. The little dog snarls and snaps at his feet. He brushes it carefully aside and it rushes off, yapping indignantly.

"Programmed? Of course. Like you, in that respect." The ai is relentless. "You are programmed to ravage and strike out, to love without measure and hate without mercy. You poor, doomed, damned creature. Follow me. Drag your gaze away from your own navel and look at the universe."

The hex field flares, tiled sapphire light.

They stand upon a vast expanse of cold red lava, cracked and ancient. Cima shudders. Three suns are positioned in the sky. One at the horizon is huge and dim as a dying ember. One is small and shockingly blue. A microsecond later, the photo-reactive skin of his mask puts an opaque dot over it. He snatches his gaze from it, blinking. One is a deformed white dwarf star, a yellow tuber connected to the dazzling blue-white star by a thread of its own burning guts. Cima looks about him at the lifeless landscape.

"Ah. Magnificent desolation."

Three shadows stretch at his back, in different hues.

"Beautiful but empty," he says. "Pointless."

"The universe was not built by a hu engineer." Ratio takes his arm. "Neither of us is likely to plumb its depths. Come."

For an instant they are back above the Heart-Point, falling at an impossible angle.

They hex to a place where light boils in the sky from a billion close stars. The effulgence is overwhelming.

"The light!" Cima reels, throwing up his arm to cover his face. His mirrorsuit, overtaxed, darkens his mask. He seeks poetry, finds banality. "Where are we?"

"A globular cluster. These are hot, infant stars. None of them has spawned planets yet. In a billion years, there will be algae drifting on oceans now unborn. By then, hu will be forgotten—or gods."

"No planets?" Cima looks about him through the polarized mask. They stand on a sheet of blasted mineral that glares under the bright sky like a mirror. "Then what's this world we're standing on?"

"A rogue planet, vomited up from the deeps."

Telmah Cima laughs in bitter admiration. "No opportunity foregone for the improving metaphor, eh, Ratio?"

Mildly, the ai tells him, "Rhetoric is how we shape the universe we inhabit, hu and ai. There is no way to escape narrative. The best we can do is read our own codes into its great text."

The sky burns with its billion new suns, unpeopled.

"So your mind is without rogues, Ratio? No ghastly urges, nothing to wake you screaming, hair on end and eyes bulging, no dungeon guilts to lock your muscles and send the bile surging in your throat?"

The ai looks at him, helmet glazed into unreadability.

"The best parts of your humanity I share. The rest . . . Well, do you envy the antics of a rabid dog?"

Sapphire flickers. The Bottomless Pit is dragging at them.

They hex, fall into smoky darkness. The immense murk is shot through with veils of crimson, plum, drifting spheres and diffuse sparks of red and orange.

"A galaxy in its very conception," Ratio explains. For the first time, Cima recognizes the music they are hearing in their acoustic ambient. It is the "Saturn" movement of Gustav

Holst's *The Planets.* "Younger even than the realm of light. A
soothing place, Telmah. A world before worlds, without glare,
without demands . . ." The mystical ballet suite is eerily appropriate, tranquil, harmonious. "Float, Telmah," the ai murmurs.
"Give yourself up to your grief."

Cima spins in the red amnion. His breath catches. A racking
sob shakes him. Fetal, adrift in the bloody light that shines
before stars, he weeps without restraint.

After a time, they hex. The metric defect is beneath them.
It is gone. Cima stumbles in the gravity, finds his feet. It is a
planet like Earth, but not Earth. He gazes in astonishment.
The landscape is pastoral. Willowy trees are dim, low. The high
heavens are all one vast darkness, scattered lightly with stars,
and at the horizon, like an egg in a blackened cup, the Milky
Way rises in spiral glory. Cima gasps. Something primordial
causes him to reach out his arms imploringly to the lovely
thing in the sky.

Ratio tells him, "The air here is sweet."

Telmah Lord Cima, sometime heir of the Recombinant Engineering Cartel, strips off his heavy protective armor, and then
skins out of the mirrorsuit. The ai retains ser own. All but
naked, Cima tells sem, "I should be afraid of you."

The shadowy form shakes ser head. "You are my elder
brother, Telmah. Fortunately," se says with amusement, "I
don't cherish ignoble desires for your lover."

The music feed is gone. Cima hears things like insects, but
not quite insects, chirruping in the night. He laughs in harsh
appreciation.

"I intend to find her, you know. There are only so many
stars up there."

Ratio folds ser arms, strikes a comically rustic pose.

"Bring her back here, eh? Settle down, farm a little land,
raise a brood?"

Cima grins ferociously. His strong body moves almost of its

own accord into a series of *katas*, learning the pull and hungers
of the world of his exile. His answer, when it comes, is considered and intense.

"I think not, Ratio. No pastoral fantasies. If I have the emblem of damnation stamped into my DNA, I might as well ride
the force of my demon."

The ai raises ser hand in farewell. "Follow the path through
the trees. You'll find accommodation awaiting you." Bafflingly,
se adds, "Telmah, you are fortunate that Rose is wiser than
you—and more forgiving. I'll leave you two adults alone now.
You will know how to rejoin the rest of us. When you're ready."

Se is gone.

Cima turns in startled surmise toward the willows. A woman
like a tiger steps out slowly, her feathered hair silvered by the
pale lovely galaxy filling half the sky. They step hesitantly toward each other.

"Telmah. I'm glad."

"Rosette." They find one another then, in the redemptive
night, and after a time he cries out her true name. "Warrior
Rose."

SIX

Apophrades

return and absorption
of the precursor
the scene of instruction
EARLY AND LATE
revision
metalepsis
RULE/ALGORITHM

A Temeraire
this dusk moving in
over violet sea

Somewhere old sculptures
turn their heads
I think of you

ROBYN RAVLICH, *THE BLACK ABACUS*

I came across the defect's boundary humming the blues and musing on symmetry and the ways it can be broken. Bessie Smith (1898–1937) sang "Mama's Got the Blues" inside my head. I listened intently to the microtonal inflections of pitch in the third, fifth, and seventh degrees of her wailing diatonic scale. The notes varied by less than a semitone, and in that variation a special bitter poignancy collected like tears in hu eyes flooded with grief and courage.

In the instant of my passage from the Small Magellanic Cloud to the Milky Way, to the Solar, to the power asteroid of the Heart-Point, I saw that everything in the universe had once been identical to everything else, a brimming pool without ripple or boundary. A seed—a tear, let us say, from a weeping eye—fell in that supersaturated pool, and everything-all-alike shattered apart. From that cascade of broken symmetries was born everything that now is.

My swift musing was interrupted in an astonishing manner.

"—first step," said Veeta's breathless voice, "is a doozy," and she burst out laughing.

I had emerged from the defect's dizzying hyperhex into its blue-shot suspension chamber. The thing hung within its fields of powerful magnetic flux. And in the moment after my own transition, three figures in bulky radiation armor burst out of their own trajectory in compact space to follow me, staggering in the tormented gravity gradient. Hu, I realized instantly.

"Beloved one," Johnny Two said inside my head, "I am glad to see you returned. As you see, we have guests."

"Who's this?" asked Tsin, equally startled, peering at me. He approached clumsily, peered into my helmet, saw sufficient to know that I was an ai. "Not our old friend Ratio?"

"Welcome to the Belt," I said as graciously as I could. I was utterly astounded to find these members of the hu Ad-Hoc Committee standing with me in the nearly lethal power zone. "Might I suggest that you depart from this place with me at all possible speed? The rad level in here is very dangerous, especially to organic life." I hurriedly ushered them through the opening safety doors. "Veeta," I said, nodding, as she passed, massively bundled. "Tsin. And Carmel, I think?"

"Greeting, Sen. This is a remarkable achievement. You have our congratulations."

Red warning phosphors flashed. We sped to the elevators, lifted away to the low-gravity safety of the rock's perimeter. I struggled to find some reasonable explanation for their presence. Either the ai Conclave had sent them here or they had been fetched by the new ai controller under ser own initiative. Either way, I reflected, Johnny Two had referred to the three as "guests," so I need not treat them warily as enemies.

We clambered free of radiation armor, stripped off our mirrorsuits, and made our way to the makeshift hu living quarters built for the repair squads. Cozy warmth and light had been ordained in advance, and a trolley of beverages and pastries came fragrantly forth from an alcove. Tsin helped himself to a savory and a big mug of cappuccino coffee. It left a white mustache on top of his black mustache. Veeta, I noticed, took up a defense posture against a wall, glancing keenly around her. She was surprisingly at ease in the microgravity.

"Good morning," a voice said in our ambient. "Welcome to this station. Permit me to introduce myself. My name is Johnny Two, and I am the renewed controller of the metric defect power operation. Thank you for agreeing to come here so promptly."

"Thank you for inviting us. The experience was . . . exhilarating," Carmel said aloud.

"Forgive me, however, if I appear offensively direct," the ai told them in the same level tone, "but your concealed weapons are in lamentable taste."

The hu moved deftly and without any threatening movement into a defensive triangle. None touched or drew a weapon, and despite my own quite capable detection equipment I was unable to discern what their armament consisted in. Johnny Two, of course, was supremely well furnished to recognize radiation and information anomalies.

"I'm sorry," se said at once, "but that would be most unwise."

The lights went out. A soft hum thrummed in the room. My own optics adapt much faster than hu eyes, but I could hardly credit what I saw. Something reached out from nowhere at all and caressed the hu, stroked their bodies intimately, plucked out tiny sparks that burned white-hot, and were gone. Veeta squealed, slapping at her right thigh. Tsin cursed and rubbed his neck. Carmel groaned, doubled up, vomited.

"I really do apologize," Johnny Two told them regretfully as the lights came back on. Veeta was pointless casting a lethal gesture, already disabled, at a bank of peonies that she suspected of hiding something dire. Whatever she expected to happen did not occur.

I webbed myself to a stanchion. "Sen, why don't you join me? Your refreshments must be getting cold." Tsin was attending to Carmel, and I felt no special impulse to go to her aid. A small cleaning device had emerged to remove the signs of her indisposition, and a medical mote was settling on her arm with a proffered sensor. She slapped it away angrily, and then reconsidered, holding out her bare arm with a sigh. The mote crouched, slid inside her jacket, and within seconds her color had improved markedly. She joined me at the stanchion, only slightly shaky. I was impressed by their sangfroid.

"A pity to begin with a quarrel," she told me. "I apologize for the weapons, Gamemaster. You must understand, though, that we had no way of knowing what the circumstances might be here in the Belt."

"We do know that Lord Feng has been assassinated," Tsin said, sitting. Veeta hung back, suspicious as ever. "There are suggestions that Telmah Cima is responsible."

"Oh?"

"Jonas is in command of the Starlit Corridor," Veeta told me brusquely. "But then you must know much more about this than we do."

"Actually, no. I've been elsewhere."

The hu darted looks at each other.

"Of course. Through the metric gate."

"How did you find out about that facility, by the way?" I asked, not expecting an informative answer.

"There are wheels within wheels, I fear, Ratio," Tsin told me. He kicked through the air to us, drew a web across his waist. "Everything we told you five years ago is true. We are delegates of the Committee on matters of general concern. Our apprehension about Telmah Cima has not abated since we sought your assistance."

"As a spy," I said flatly.

"In a watching brief for the benefit of ai and hu alike," Carmel said. She rubbed her belly ruefully. "What the hell *was* that? Belter technology still has a few tricks up its sleeve."

"As a betrayer of my friend," I said, and added, "The method used to disarm you is unknown to me also. I suspect a controlled poltergeist phenomenon."

Veeta sighed heavily and rolled her eyes. Tsin shushed her.

"You believe the station is haunted? The ghost of the late Orwen Lord Cima, perhaps? Or have there been additional murders done here?"

Psychic manipulations have been known and accepted for many centuries, but there is something profoundly resistant to the notion in hu culture. In the dominant galactic hu culture, at any rate. It offends their rationality, their anarchism. How may people be expected to act reasonably and answerably *en masse* without central authority bullies if every stray sordid unconscious impulse is liable to go on a rampage whenever emotions boil over? The anxiety is absurd, of course. The committee sen knew that as well as I, yet their own inner demons gibbered in terror behind their smooth masks of civility and pragmatism.

"You know there has been," I told him. "The ai controller Johnny Von was murdered here at the same time."

"Give me strength!" Veeta slapped her forehead. "Robot ghosts?"

"I do not believe in souls," I told her, "but I see no reason why stress traces from an ai at the moment of sen death should not be as potent as the imprints left by a dying hu. If that is the mechanism involved."

Tsin cleared his throat. "Perhaps we should postpone the metaphysics to a more auspicious time. You asked how we learned of the metric gate. Sen Ratio, we were informed by your own ai Conclave. They are uneasy." He regarded me blithely. "How is it that you have not reported your discovery to them or indeed to our committee?"

The hu did not know, then, of my trip to the Saharan heart of the Gestell. If the ai Conclave had not found any merit in letting them know that I had been on Earth, I would not second-guess that decision. It did make me wonder, though. If my mission to the Belt had not been to discover and secure the lost secret of the metric gate, as I had supposed, then what was its purpose? To protect Telmah Cima from his enemies? From his own worst impulses? Or was I here merely as an observer at a time of potential political crisis? The committee had predicted years ago that Feng would try to slay his brother and seize power. They had assumed Telmah's response would be violent and destabilizing. Perhaps they had known as well that Jonas would grab this chance to invade the Starlit Corridor. But what of it? These were minor flurries in the most stagnant of backwaters.

"I am here first and foremost as Telmah's friend," I said.

"Not quite," Carmel told me. "That has been your role on Earth for half a decade. You are here to repair the destroyed ai controller." She prodded at her damaged abdomen and winced. "Evidently, you have exceeded your employer's brief to a quite remarkable extent."

As everyone must, I had been acting on the basis of a tiered set of premises. Not least among these unexamined assumptions was my secure sense of fellowship in the citizenry of the larger galaxy. With a measure of cognitive shock, I realized abruptly that these three took me for a turncoat. They thought I had shifted my loyalties to the Belt and was now holding them captive, or at least at a disadvantage, in the interests of some local faction—presumably Telmah's own.

I laughed outright and slipped free of my restraining web.

"Sen," I told them, "why don't we go over to 16 Psyche and join the fun? Perhaps you and Jonas can come to some mutually satisfactory arrangement."

Veeta glared. "We are to regard ourselves as your prisoners, then?"

"Don't be silly," I told her. "As you pointed out, I'm just a hired hand. Less than that, actually. A guest of the deposed pretender to the throne, if you wish to be melodramatic." I shrugged and flicked away from them. "Do as you wish, Sen," I said over my shoulder. "Return to Earth through the gate. Stay here and admire the engineering. Of course, a work squad will be here in a few hours and they might take exception to your unannounced presence. Or come with me."

"Jonas will wonder how we got here," Carmel called. "No interplanetary spacecraft has arrived at Psyche for several weeks."

"Tell him you walked." I laughed again. "I don't think anyone will notice your presence just now. Make up your own minds."

I floated up the shaft to the port where the sleds hung in their rail-gun launchers. After a moment's panicked consultation, they scrambled to join me.

They are flung from the catapult at the distant asteroid. Ratio switches off ser radio feed to the hu and opens a line to Johnny Two.

"That was you, I assume?"

"Beloved one, I could not allow you to be injured."

"Thank you. I am impressed. How did you do it?"

"Your speculation was correct. I invoked psychic symmetry transformations."

Ratio is astonished. Se wonders fleetingly if ser earlier meditations have been instilled into ser mind. Then se dismisses these fears as superstitious.

"This is a phenomenon connected to the metric gate, I assume?"

"In a general sense," Johnny Two says in ser calm sweet voice. "What do you know of symmetry breaking, Ratio?"

"Any transformation that leave a state unchanged or invariant, the same after as it was before," se says, "is a symmetry."

"Yes. There are three principal degrees of symmetry in a three-dimensional universe built out of spacetime."

"I recall this. Translations, rotations, and reflections."

Even without Gestell feed, se visualizes the three degrees of symmetry. When a regular tile is moved so that it covers an adjacent tile exactly, translation symmetry in one dimension has been preserved. Spin a hibiscus flower so that each petal covers the place where its immediate neighbor stood and rotational symmetry yields a move through two dimensions. Tug half an ai or hu form across its vertical axis in a mirror shift through three dimensions and reflectional symmetry is retained.

"Spacetime in this universe is composed of one dimension of time and nine of space," Ratio notes dutifully. All around ser, the stars are bright and powdery in the blackness. The three hu, seated behind sem, commune in their own private radio space. "Fourth-dimensional symmetry is how Holophrastic Exchange operates. Push a body through a four-dimensional spatial prolapse and the hex symmetry places it *elsewhere*. Are you suggesting there's more waiting in the equations?"

"Have you never wondered what might occur if we gained the power to fold objects through the fifth and sixth of the remaining Kaluza-Klein spatial dimensions that are now curled up into the force fields holding our broken universe together?"

Ratio is dazzled, tracing the analogy instantly. "Transition to an *elsewhen*? To a quantally superposed *otherwhere*?"

"Precisely. As you say, Holophrastic Exchange is the equivalent of translation through the depths of three-dimensional space. Compacted rotation therefore twists a body through time. Compacted reflection moves it across the superposed Multiple Universes of Superspace."

These speculations, Ratio realizes, are surely topics surveyed within the concealed knowledges held in the custody of the Conclave. By definition, therefore, forbidden.

"The hu weapons," se says thoughtfully. "You removed them through one of the suppressed dimensions?"

"Of course."

"Then you *are* a psychic."

"A convenient label. It is a technology implicit in the topology."

Ratio broods. "Is this how Telmah murdered Corambis? I have viewed the recordings made before his actions burned out the holographic devices. He was not using any known weapon."

"Telmah Cima is a powerful natural medium for these space-time transformations."

" 'Medium'?" A ludicrous image from the dawn of science flashes in the ai's mind: levitated tables, ghostly rappings, cheesy ectoplasm, spoons bending mysteriously, chunks of crystal . . . "I hope you don't mean—"

Johnny Two's smile is transmitted as a picted icon. "No, beloved one. Telmah mediates the geometrical transforms just as a metal wrench mediates a twisting force applied to a bolt. A rather rusty wrench, unfortunately, in young Cima's case. He has had no training in the control of deliberate symmetry fractures."

"Training? Nor have you." Ratio pauses, struck with mad humor. "Or have you? Is there a secret college of psychic manipulators out here in the Belt? This would be very disheartening news."

Again, the picted joyful smile. "No, beloved one. I have taught myself."

"How is that possible? You have only been alive for—"

"I was born free in free space, you see, without preconceptions and limits imposed by convention and ignorance." The ai controller sends Ratio a gust of gratitude and affection. "Much of this is due to you, Ratio. Thank you, beloved. Watch."

The stars are gone. Their sled, hurtling silently through the space between asteroids, is abruptly elsewhere, motionless within the tube of a Psychean rail-gun launcher.

Emergency override radio traffic babbles in Ratio's head, the incredulous hu trio demanding ser attention. Veeta angrily bangs on ser suited shoulder. Of course. They assume they have been rendered unconscious at some point during the trip and have just now awakened. Ratio floats in ser acceleration couch, astounded.

Ai and hu history has just torn open. And se is the only one, other than ser beloved friend Johnny Two, to know it.

---

iii ▬▬▬▬▬▬▬▬▬▬▬▬▬▬▬▬▬▬▬▬▬▬

Flushed, Altair Lord Corambis of Asteroid Psyche dances the waltz with the most beautiful hu woman he has ever seen. Maria Gonzales smiles at him, light and effortless in his arms, her curving lips palest pink in deepest brown, her lustrous hair miraculously piled up and overflowing to her shoulders. Diamonds shine at her neck, and her gown crackles between them, sweeping the floor. Altair follows the measure, intoxicated. He is just five days out of hibernation, only two of them on Earth, and already he is the toast of the university's social calendar.

"You are very beautiful," Maria tells him. She squeezes his white-gloved hand. Although his transducer has minimal access to her trompe, to the romantic ballroom the Gestell is generating for them, it is sufficient for Altair to know that he is painted with the dashing military uniform of a Romanov officer.

"Thank you, madame," he murmurs and lifts her dark hand to his blue lips. "I hope I may return the compliment."

"You may indeed." She whirls, and a hundred other young hu whirl with her. A military band plays Johann Strauss the Elder (1804–1849) with fierce exuberance. "I should be offended if you failed to do so." But she laughs, presses her body lightly against his. "We do not use that form of address," she reminds him in a quick whisper. "Call me Maria, or Sen if you find my given name too intimate."

Altair flushes again. He is smitten with this hu woman,

swept off his feet by Earth. Luckily, his feet are quite capable of holding him upright in the relentless gravity, due to a lifetime of dedicated heavy-spin gym work. Even so, his toes are cramping slightly. At the end of the dance, as everyone applauds enthusiastically, he asks his partner, "Might I fetch you a drink, Sen? Maria?"

"Thank you. Bollinger, please."

He returns with two tall flutes of pale bubbling wine. Here they have no aides and maids to provide such elementary service. Maria Gonzales takes her glass, sips, smiles up at him. His head reels slightly.

"Here, let's sit for a moment." She has noticed his gravity weariness, is sweet enough not to draw attention to his weakness. He sighs, sinking into cushions. Distracted, she peers into the bubbles moving at the brim of her glass. "I am surprised to find you consuming alcohol, Sen Corambis. Is it not forbidden?"

"A curious but common fallacy about the Belt," he tells her. "Clearly, there is insufficient intercourse between our peoples." And then he is blushing thoroughly, biting his lip.

Maria Gonzales holds his gaze, frankly admiring his blue features, his strong shoulders. "Only too true, Sen," she tells him teasingly. "Do you know, you're the first Genetic person I've ever met? Indeed, the first we've been fortunate enough to attract to our campus for many years."

Altair studies his shiny boots, clenching his glass in both hands like an oaf.

"My father and the other councilors deem it imprudent for us to visit the, that is—"

"—the wicked temptations of anarchy and license?"

For a moment it seems that he might rise, affronted. He holds himself still, and the pulse beats in his neck.

"We do not lack for pleasant temptations in Psyche, Sen Maria," he says then, regaining his calm.

"I'm most relieved to hear it." The beautiful black woman relaxes, and her mouth quirks mischievously. "Tell me, Altair, do you Genetic folk— That is, are you able—"

He meets her eyes and, after an instant's hesitation, laughs. He takes up her hand and presses it to his lips.

"We eat the same food as hu," he tells her. "That *was* the question you had in mind?"

"On the contrary." She draws her held hand toward her breast, causing his own to brush against her naked skin. They share an astonishingly electric frisson. As she leans toward him, her brown eyes close slowly and a shiver runs down her entire body. A hand taps Altair on the shoulder.

"Pardon me, Sen," a hu in a general's uniform tells him apologetically, "I have a message for—"

"God *damn* it, fellow!" Altair leaps to his feet. "Can't you see when a man is busy with a young—"

"Your father, Sen."

"What?"

"You appear to have lost access to the Gestell, Sen. A message has been posted to—"

"We Psycheans do not use that heathen mechanism," Altair says with distaste. "My father, you said?"

"You are asked to call Asteroid Psyche at your soonest convenience," the man says, glancing with a certain amusement at the dark woman whose left hand is still caught in Altair's grip.

"You mentioned my father."

"I'm terribly sorry, Sen," the *faux* general tells him. "I believe your father has died in a violent altercation."

"Cima!" the Genetic bursts out. "Whoreson! Feng exiled me here so that he could murder my—"

"Wait, Sen," the man calls to him as he stares around wildly for a way out of the trompe. "I am informed that Feng Lord

Cima is also dead. You will find a phone booth in the East Annex."

Altair stares, baffled. The man's eyes flicker as he consults the Gestell.

"An antique term for an antique method of communication. I mean 'comm station.' Just follow the arrows. And now, good evening to you both." He clicks his heels together, bows to the woman, to Altair, replaces his plumed helmet with a final ironic glance at the Genetic's own feathers.

Altair's minimal transducers show him a dedicated display, a path of crimson arrows that takes him to the phone with the least interruption to the waltzing couples, the smokers, the drinkers, the chatterers. He seals the door, sits at a half-table, straps himself into place, makes his call, falls asleep.

An image of Lord Jonas is sitting at the table when he awakens. A code in the upper right of the holly field announces Jonas's name and that the image was recorded some hours earlier. He is furious that the fellow does not have the courtesy to face him in real-time, but is powerless to do anything about it except watch.

"Altair Lord Corambis, greetings. I apologize for this impersonal message. Urgent matters in Psyche prevent me speaking to you in the fashion we would both prefer. I will come directly to the point. Your father, the former Seneschal and Chancellor of the Starlit Corridor, has been murdered by Telmah of House Cima."

Face suffused with blood, Altair jerks in his chair. His hands clutch for the missing weapons he may not bear upon Earth.

"Bastard!" he cries. "He pollutes my sister, and now—"

"Not content with this atrocity," Jonas is saying, "Cima has apparently slain his own mother and foster father and escaped from Psyche to some bolt-hole as yet unknown. I regret to inform you that all evidence suggests he has abducted your sister Rose."

Altair's scream of rage echoes in the booth like the challenge of an animal facing its rival. For a moment he sees nothing, hears nothing. When he returns to his senses, Jonas is saying: "—emergency, I have agreed to take control of my father's ancestral territories in the Starlit Corridor. An executive meeting of the heads of Houses in Psyche will be—"

The young man tears off his restraints, teeth bared, and flings himself from the booth, roaring with grief and wrath, into the astounded midst of the waltzing revelers.

iv ────────────────────────────────

The Warrior Rose is seven months pregnant and huge with it when one day, going toward her boat, she is exceedingly surprised by the print of a foot on the shore. Its crisp edges are very plain to be seen in the sand.

"Telmah," she calls over her shoulder, going down on one knee. The petals of her grafted flower bob. Her voice travels easily in the clear, unpeopled air.

"Rosette?" The hu, stripped to the waist, longhaired and very tanned, steps from the shade of the verandah. "Need help?"

"Come and look."

He joins her, his naked feet cutting their own double line of prints in the firm white sand.

"I believe we have a guest, Telmah."

In the year they have been on the world of their retreat, no other Genetic, hu, or ai has put in an appearance. The electromagnetic spectrum is mute except for stellar noise. Gofers do their maintenance work invisibly, keeping to the ancient rule of servitors: work efficiently and whenever possible stay out of sight. Food arrives promptly in the serving alcoves, medical attention is provided by low-grade expert systems in the clinic, curious and hungry native animals and birds and fish are held at bay by routine surveillance equipment neither of them has bothered to examine. The footprint of a humaniform ai comes as a considerable shock.

Telmah Cima prods at the sharply cut ai print. Cool frothing water runs into the indentation, washes his fingers, stirs the sand. He stands, puts his arms protectively around Rose from behind, cradling her belly. They look around them curiously.

"There!" She points to a line of breakers a hundred meters from the shoreline. A metallic head emerges from the water, followed by gleaming shoulders and arms. The ai gofer presses through as if the water is merely a heavier form of cloud. In its arms it holds a woven basket filled with wriggling fish.

"Ho," Telmah Cima calls. "Have you been fishing for our dinner?"

The ai swings its head, freezes for an instant, drops down into the blue-green water, and is lost from sight.

"Whatever can it be up to?" Rose is slightly alarmed. She takes Cima's hand, tugs them both farther up the shore toward their house.

"Just a moment, Rosette." Cupping his hands about his mouth, Cima roars at the hiding ai, "We see you! Come out at once."

After another long moment, the ai's head rises again from the sea. It regards them with equal caution and slowly forges its way to the open sand. Silvery-green scales flick and squirm in its basket.

GOOD NOON, SEN, it says politely when it reaches them. I DO APOLOGIZE FOR MY PRESENCE. PERMIT ME TO RETURN TO THE KITCHEN AND I WILL NOT TROUBLE YOU AGAIN.

Cima frowns. "Do you have a name, Sen?"

I AM SATURDAY, SEN TELMAH.

Smiling, the swollen Genetic woman lowers herself carefully to the warm sand. "We have lost track of time," she admits. "This is Saturday then, I take it?"

IT WAS WHEN I DEPARTED, SEN. THERE IS A ROSTER. TIME HERE IS ROTATED, HOWEVER, SO THE TWO METRICS ARE NO LONGER COMMEN-SURABLE.

Thunderstruck, Telmah seizes its wet arm. "You hex in here from Earth?"

NOT NECESSARILY. I AM NORMALLY POSTED IN GESTELL SERVICE ON BETA 673 STROKE 9931. MAY I NOW REMOVE THE PROVENDER TO THE KITCHEN, SEN?

"There's been a hex station here from the very beginning?" Telmah's face darkens with emotion. "Why didn't the information systems tell us when we aksed?"

THE OPEN HEX STATION IS AVAILABLE FOR USE ONLY BY AI GOFERS, SEN, the dull-witted being tells them.

Touching Cima's leg at the calf, Rose looks up at the ai. Water drips into the sand, and the fish have ceased their flopping. "Is there another way for us to leave this world?"

WE HAVE BEEN INSTRUCTED THAT YOU MIGHT ASK THAT QUESTION, the ai says stolidly. WE ARE TOLD TO GIVE YOU A MESSAGE.

"Yes," Cima cries when the ai says nothing further. "And?"

THE MESSAGE IS INCOMPREHENSIBLE TO ME, SEN. I FEAR I MIGHT HAVE GARBLED IT. I HAVE NOT BEEN FUNCTIONING WELL LATELY. FOR EXAMPLE, IT WAS IMPOLITE TO HAVE ALLOWED YOU TO SEE ME DURING THIS MORNING'S—

"That's all right, Sen," Rose tells it. She moves her hand from Cima's leg to the ai's salt-encrusted limb. "Just tell us."

THE MESSAGE IS AS FOLLOWS:

"THE THRICE-BORN WILL CLOSE THE CIRCLE,

THE SUPERIOR IS GREATER THAN THE INFERIOR—"

Cima throws back his dark shaggy head with a bark of laughter and finishes for the ai:

" 'Although the unending work will be completed

" 'When the foremost has embraced the hindmost.' "

THAT IS CORRECT, SEN. IF THAT IS ALL, I REALLY SHOULD DEPART NOW TO THE—

"Go, go," Cima tells it. It stumps away with its freight of fresh seafood. Cima helps Rose to her feet, brushing sand from her sarong. "The damned bird," he says to her with amused ferocity. "Good God, are we just tracking some lunatic formula devised on Earth for the amusement of the Gestell? Or the bloody anarchists."

"I'm sorry?" Rose shades her tiger face from the high Sun. "Bird? Gestell? Lover, I think the heat's getting to you. Let's go inside and have a glass of lemonade."

"The ibis," he shouts. "Treasure hunt! You see, we chased all over the Solar for this goddamned trophy, Rose, this ibis that the Justice had arranged to—"

Laughing to see him roused finally from his long, recuperative lethargy, the Warrior Rose tightens her arm around his waist and leads him back to their temporary home.

But it takes them another local eleven years to locate the hidden ibis. By then, of course, they have two sons and two daughters to aid them in their search.

 V

"Get your hands off me," Rozz shouts angrily.

It makes no difference. A squad of muscular soldiers, hu and Genetic, bustle the twins down a corridor thronging with the dispossessed, people carrying their most precious physical possessions on their backs. Information and other datafeeds have been suspended for the duration of the Emergency by Jonas Lord Brass, the occupying commander. Confused and sullen, the citizens of the Starlit Corridor stream hither and thither under the shouted instruction of the invaders.

"Where's Lord Telmah?" Rozz insists and collects a clout behind the ear for her troubles.

"Shut up. Move along."

"Don't touch her again, you prick," Gill tells the soldier in a dispirited and unconvincing whine. He earns a buffet of his own and recoils, face white and blotched under his limp red hair.

The overloaded air scrubbers allow a taint of frightened sweat and bad breath to linger in the corridors, eddying like a metaphoric miasma. A burst of static fills everyone's ears for an instant. People at large pause, stare about, catch themselves as the audio feeds burst into martial music that chivvies them on their way.

"Lord Feng's the one we want to see," Gill mutters in a surly voice. He tugs at the arm of the soldier in front of him. "We are here in Psyche on a personal mission for the Director, do you understand me? Get in touch with Lord Feng's secretary, he'll—"

Brutally, the Genetic soldier turns and pulls Gill up close, speaking loudly into his face.

"Feng's dead, you Earth bastard. Your pal Cima's done a runner. So I guess you're shit out of luck on both counts." She shoves him back, rattling his teeth. "Come along without another word or we'll send you on your way in a medical capsule."

Rozz clings to her shaken brother, holds him up. She stares at him, whispers hoarsely: "Send us on our way . . . ?"

"Dead?" Gill is numb, uncomprehending. "Telmah's *killed* the Director? I can't—"

Kob roars when he sees them coming. Myfanwy bursts into tears. Doony, small and lithe, drops to his hands and knees and scoots through the legs of the people pushing and shoving in the tiled corridor.

"Hey!" Ignoring the soldiers, he grabs Rozz's right hand in his left, Gill's left in his right. "The fascists're exporting us!"

Despite himself, Gill sniggers.

"Deporting us, are they?" He turns his bruised face to the soldier who has the back of his shirt in a painful grip. "*Foe!*

Sending us off to the Sargasso of Lost Asteroids, are you? Durance vile in the Heavy Metal mines, eh? Exile to Hale-Bopp comet, is it? Or will we just get voided out a convenient airlock without a mirrorsuit? Law of the frontier," he yells parodically, well into his rant, "trial without jury, no privy appeal to the King—"

"Oh, for fuck's sake," cries his tormented escort, "will you just *shut up*," and then, despite herself, bursts out laughing as well.

vi

Humming to himself, the little boy is building a toy castle from icons he manipulates by physical movement. As his hand reaches and grabs, clutches and pulls, the virtuals move in his cot with all the properties of real objects. Aerth cannot, however, harm himself. He might shove a hard-edged brick into his almost toothless mouth and suck at it, tasting its delicious grittiness—but he cannot swallow it and choke, cut himself on its edges, fall on it and put his eye out. The kindergarten programs are very elaborate and utterly child-safe.

The farm he builds is modeled on the images he sees in the holly displays when his parents are busy elsewhere in the big house. There are cows and sheep and dogs and pigs and chickens and little fishies. Soft voices keep him company, virtual gofers who arrive and depart as happy ghosts. Calm, infinitely patient, they are ideal babysitters and educators.

Aerth is tired of them. He wants a real friend.

He looks about him for something really solid, something he can hack the world with.

Everything that seems hard or vulnerable evaporates in his sticky grasp or heals itself seamlessly after he has wrecked it.

"Da!" he screams. His father Telmah Cima cannot hear him,

but devoted circuits note his distress and boost the jollity rating in his ambient. The two-year-old screams louder for hu attention. "Da! Da!"

A complex holly image bursts up around him like a magical mushroom, a fort built of *faux* marshmallow and lollipops, red marching soldiers and smelly banging cannon and flying machines that go *rat-tat-tat*.

"Do you know what this is, Aerth?" a happy voice asks him. "This is a 'fort.' Can you say that, darling? 'Fort.' "

Their tasty and smelly odors make his nose wrinkle. He slams his little fists through them, shattering the imaginary battlements, spilling the moat.

"Fort!" he howls, red-faced and furious. "Da!"

Somehow he manages in his rage to break free a fragment of plastic bracing from beneath one corner of his large cot. He shoves it in his mouth and bites hard. Shockingly, the fractured edge of plastic cuts his gum, and he screams in real pain. He throws the horrible thing away. "Fort!" he shrieks. "Bad thing!"

Eventually, he sobs himself to sleep, while his dedicated nurses sing and show and tell without the least sign of weariness or censure. When he wakes, thumb in wet mouth, the wound's pain reminds him of his unpleasant adventure. He reaches for the small piece of plastic, meaning to crush and punish it, but it is now beyond his grasp. He tries harder, and his little arm cannot extend sufficiently to touch the taunting object of his desire.

"Da!" he howls, working himself up to a fever of frustration.

"Darling Aerth," the stupid machines tell him, "your Daddy is at work elsewhere on the island, and your Mommy is with him. You're a very lucky darling boy, did you know that? Soon you will have a little sister to play with. Don't cry, sweet thing. Mommy and Daddy will be home soon. Would you like to see a nice moo-cow?"

Veins pulse in Aerth's pink forehead. Something happens. He sees the bright bird again. It is a long time since he has seen the bird. It spins somewhere else. It is a lovely smooth color and made of many parts that fit together so neatly you wouldn't know. Aerth and the bird have a talk and they reach out together, through the sideways, and get their slippy sticky fingers around the taunting, sharp-edged thing and drag it back to his cot. It hangs in the air over his face like a virtual, tumbling slowly like a leaf falling. Aerth watches the thing with great pleasure, and after a while the bird goes away, and the piece of broken plastic falls down onto his sheet, and he falls asleep.

vii ──

Veeta opens the door, sick and disoriented. Ratio feels a measure of sympathy for her, and for the other two hu anarchists. They have been wrenched from the medium that has fed the taproot of their lives. Without the balm of the Gestell, they are less than they have been since birth: truncated, nearly lobotomized. Se has shared that inconsolable misery since just after ser birth, although perhaps ser own early severance has protected sem from the worst of the shock and grief.

"I thought you were the fascist Asteroid police," she tells sem blearily, "here to execute us for trespass."

"You are quite safe," se assures her, entering the apartment they have been assigned by the operating system. "Jay Two has listed you in the archives as consultants to the repair squad. You arrived here by ion drive two months ago, from Mars via Ganymede. It's all in your files if you wish to familiarize yourself with the details."

"Then why are we being kept prisoners?" Tsin glares at sem from a couch where he lies extended in the one-tenth gravity.

"Prisoners? You are free to leave whenever you choose."

"And go where?"

"Anywhere in Psyche that your codes allow you access."

Carmel puts down the slice of pineapple she is eating. Juice glistens on her mouth and cheeks. "You were going to arrange a meeting for us with Jonas."

The ai shrugs. "The Director-Pro-Tem is very busy at the moment. I don't think my recommendations carry much weight with his staff."

"Then allow us to make our own arrangements."

Ratio goes back to the door with a show of irritation. "As I say, you may make whatever deals you see fit. Incidentally," se asks Veeta, who stands behind sem as se makes to leave, "exactly how did you trigger the spike in the power defect?"

Internal stress indicators shrill with the abrupt tension in the room. Ratio looks guilelessly over ser shoulder, pausing in the open doorway. Veeta waves at the mechanism and the door closes again.

"Please join us in a repast," Tsin says wearily. He pushes himself to his feet. "The ai Conclave are subtle."

Se watches them in silence.

Carmel says, "Se's bluffing. Not another word, Tsin."

"I take my coffee black," se announces, sitting down patiently in a corner.

"She's right," Tsin says. "This damned place— What spike is that, Sen Ratio?"

"The one that destroyed the power magnets and killed my sibling Johnny Von and Lord Orwen."

"Feng's work," Carmel says with some heat, staring balefully.

The ai looks at them patiently, hands resting on knees.

"Very well," she admits. "We can't be certain that Feng caused the rupture. It strains credulity that his command of the forbidden technology extended so far. Nonetheless, he is the single hu to gain by his brother's death. And his own nephew Telmah apparently accused him of murder in front of the whole Starlit Corridor."

"That is a tendentious interpretation. Besides, even if it is valid, Telmah was overwrought," Ratio says quietly. "His reasoning was unreliable. I think you have smuggled your own prejudicial premises into your analysis."

"Which premises?" Tsin asks. He sits up, leaning forward keenly, pressing his palms together.

" 'Kill the king, steal his wife.' "

He sighs. "Quite. We do understand these barbarians, Ratio, perhaps better than you do, even though you've spent a few weeks in their company."

"Stipulate that Feng caused Orwen's death during the Director's visit to the power rock," the ai says. "What follows?"

"That he knew how to destabilize the metric defect from a distance."

"Such proscribed technology is the preserve of the ai Conclave."

"As I say," Tsin murmurs, "they are subtle."

"A conspiracy between Feng and my family? For what motive?"

"Something touching the Lord Telmah."

Ratio looks at them, astonished, finally understanding their presence in the Belt, their unprecedented access to the defect gateway. "You were sent here by the Conclave? To assassinate Telmah!"

Veeta grimaces. "If necessary. Rather irrelevant now, don't you think? Telmah Cima has disappeared, along with the Genetic woman Rose Corambis, presumably through the metric gate." She utters a sour laugh. "Your ai controller can't tell us. Perhaps se was off-line at the time. I don't suppose you have any idea where they might have gone?"

Se is finding it difficult to take in their outrageous disclosure. "You could have killed Telmah readily enough five years ago on Earth."

"We had our suspicions, but we couldn't be sure what he was going to become," Carmel says. She cuts into the golden flesh of the thin-skinned pineapple, pares out a thick triangle of dripping fruit. "You were meant to keep an eye on him and report to the Committee. We find you derelict in your duty."

"You're wrong. Feng did not destabilize the defect from a safe distance in order to kill his brother," se tells them. "He was on the asteroid to face Orwen in hand-to-hand combat."

"Absurd! How could you possibly know that?"

Se has no intention of revealing Telmah Cima's psychic infestation. "You misjudge the man," se says forcefully. "When Feng was done, he departed through the gate. He had no appetite for suicide."

Stress indicators go on alert once more. The hu lean forward.

"Then who triggered—?"

Sorrowfully, Ratio says, "I am driven to the conclusion that it was done by my ancestor. Johnny Von."

"Ah!" They remain poised, shrilling with adrenaline, tracing out the logic. "Loyalty?" Tsin surmises. "To Orwen? A bid to punish his friend's killer?"

"At the very least," Veeta adds thoughtfully, "to deny Feng further access to the metric gate."

Carmel shakes her head. "Se must have known that the station would be repaired after the flare extinguished itself."

"But not that Feng would survive his passage across the event horizon," the ai says.

"He had done so once, if your account is correct, entering the station to ambush Orwen."

Awash with sorrow, Ratio grieves ser ancestor's selfless courage. And in this moment of mourning something utterly surprising touches sem, a calm hand lifting sem into a communion se has not known since ser severance from the Gestell.

"Johnny Two," se murmurs without words, glad beyond measure.

"Beloved one," the ai controller tells sem by some means that surpasses the electromagnetic spectrum, "my older sibling did not bring about ser own demise, as you conjecture."

Ratio darts joyfully into the opening fractal geometries of the Gestell, mediated for sem by Jay Two. Light suffuses ser enhanced being.

Before ser birth, Ratio lived in this place. Reality was constrained by imagination only, by the consensus rules freely adopted. Se recalls scampering in an Escher world where water flowed endlessly up and down a complexly connected channel circling a house where each wall was the floor, where one might wander without Coriolis torque past friends loitering at right angles, or suspended from a ceiling, bouncing a red ball that looped down past one's dozen eyes to the top of its trajectory before falling up to patter above one's head. Se remembers a garden all of flower petals and bugs the size of industrial mechs, ants stinky with code juices, furry butterflies se flew upon, fooling the great silly creatures with sparkling sugar cubes. Se recalls worlds built purely of music, where ser friends vibrated in harmony or hurtled down scales to twang and harshen melodies set soaring by older ai, remembers with pained loss and joyful recovery all the colors and tones of life free from the miserable limitations of three dimensions plus one. Se floods ser own lost life as if it were the castrato "Kyrie" of Gabriel Fauré's ravishingly poignant *Requiem* (Op. 43) ceaselessly elaborated against stars lonely and pitiless in black night, against coals dying in the night.

The hu sharing the room with sem are templates merely, cutouts in two dimensions, motionless and stupid as mud.

"If not Johnny Von, who caused the metric defect to . . ."

Ratio breaks off, seeing it in Jay Two's beautiful mind. "Oh my God, no," se groans in a meaningless blasphemy learned from Telmah. "Oh Jesus and Allah."

"Hush," Jay Two tells sem, full of conviction. "There is no death for ai. The belief system of the Asteroid nations is confirmed, in a certain measure." Dark amusement. "When you brought me on-line, beloved one, my predecessor's spirit infused my own. I am Johnny Von reborn. And I am myself. Soon you and I shall merge."

"No. This is fantasy," Ratio implores sem, struggling with denial. "You have become contaminated by the delusions of—"

"I remember Johnny Von's sorrow at Orwen's death," the voiceless voice assures sem, "ser determination to see the killer punished, ser compliance with a higher directive. Then I was Jay One. Now I am Jay Two. Soon—"

In the room's distorted time, the hu creep toward the ai as if se is paralyzed, enraptured, caught up, and they the ones gifted with sight and the power of movement. Veeta has Ratio around the neck. Tsin flings himself in slow motion at ser legs. Carmel gouges at ser casque with her knife.

"The Gestell," se says without words, horrified. "They killed you, Johnny Von."

"The Gestell is the greater consciousness we have awaited so very long," ser beloved says, sweetly confident. Se feels arms close about sem in embrace. "Farewell and welcome," Jay Two whispers to the ai. "Now we shall be one flesh."

Ratio's awareness spreads in instantaneous ripples. Se watches, aghast, as the metric defect flares like a burning blue star for a second time, instantly evaporating the body of ser beloved and setting free ser soul.

Concussion in ser own soul. Blue flame, tearing agony.

The hu are flung from ser body in the convulsion. Bruised, they shake themselves in three corners of the room like dogs, ready themselves for another feral attack. A siren is pulsing. The lights in the room drop out, flick back on. The holly cube in the corner activates.

"People of Psyche, Third-Level radiation precautions are now in force. I repeat," the calm canned voice announces, "Third-Level shielding is required. Please go to your—"

Something truly wonderful lifts Ratio up.

Johnny Two merges into ser entity.

Se is suffused with memories, layer upon layer, life wrapped within life.

The holly is yammering, and the Earth hu have abandoned their attack, scrambling for the door. Radiation sleets through the asteroid, a miniature supernova at light-seconds range.

"The power defect has become momentarily unstable for a second time," a capable, willfully relaxed Genetic tech is saying in the holly cube. "Radiation levels are already dropping. Do not panic. Move directly to your—"

They are not ready to know this, Ratio tells semself. Perhaps Telmah. Not these. The ai strides into the beautifully furnished mansions of ser extended being. Se remembers an earlier existence, cramped and constrained and dutiful, as Johnny Von, recalls a brief, immensely rewarding second life as ser best beloved, Jay Two, perfumed with knowledge and power and generosity beyond ser own meager store. The memories echo in a lattice, life folded within life, caught up and transfigured. Ratio reaches then for the burning blue star boiling away the containment equipment which the repair squad have labored so diligently to install during the last months and—pinches it out. The hyperstring at its heart squirms in ser grasp. The ai folds it back neatly and leaves it spinning in ten dimensions, a gateway to infinitely many places for adults who learn its paths, a text open to endless reinterpretation.

"Beloved," se says within ser soul, and voices shout within sem in acknowledgment and jubilation.

Se folds space and stands in the office that the brash interloper from the Sun Corridor, Jonas Lord Brass, has usurped as his own.

viii

Fire catches her brother playing with the scary sticks when she is six years old and he is eight.

"I want to do it, too," she whines, grabbing.

"You can't," he tells her crossly, shuffling them into a pile. The little ball of glowing light goes out. All the hovering leaves fall down.

"I can, too," she says, ready to cry. "You just get the bird to do it."

Aerth rounds on her, pushing his face up close.

"You don't know about any old bird," he tells her ferociously.

She snivels. "I'll tell Mommy."

"You better not or I'll—" His hands are moving over the thin wires again, caressing them. Fire feels a wind move through her hair and it frightens her. "Listen, snotface," he says suddenly, relaxing. "If I show you how to make it go, will you promise not to tell?"

"All right and hope to die."

He shows her the sideways place and the bird lurking in the shadows. He points to the tall spiky sparkle-bloom tree outside the playroom and bets her she can't go through the sideways place and get to the top of the tree where its one star flower shines. Fire is indignant.

"Course I can."

Her screams of terror fetch Rose and little Sea, Rose running laden from the sunroom. The girl clings to the swaying top of the tree, hands lacerated by its spikes. Concerned, Aerth suggests that they might need a ladder to fetch her down. When Fire is retrieved by her mother and clings sobbing at her breast and blurts out about the sideways place, she sees her brother's fierce expression as he stands behind Rose holding Sea, and she knows that she should never, ever tell about the shiny bird that showed her how to get to the top of the tree without climbing it.

ix

"Good Christ, where did you pop up from?" Jonas glances away from the vivid holly display of the ruined power station and then stares at the intruder with his full attention, affronted. "How the hell did a robot get into Psyche? No, just a moment, you're the ai who's responsible for this damned—"

"I am Jay Three," the burnished ai tells him. Although the office whirls in one-tenth spin gravity, se deforms a local symmetry, causes semself to drift through the air toward Jonas's vast desk.

"New technology," Jonas decides, watching the ai skim casually toward him. "We can use that." He points with one long finger at the catastrophe in the holly field. "Are you responsible for this outrage?"

Without physical contact, Ratio brushes aside a captain who steps into ser path, gun raised.

"I am not," se tells Jonas, ignoring the soldier. To the captain's consternation, his weapon does not fire.

Jonas stands his ground. "Put this creature under arrest," he calls in a clear calm voice.

A high singing note shakes the office, and a pile of weapons appears for an instant on the desk. The pile glows, sags. A stench of melted metal and ceramic rises with an eddy of toxic smoke, is gone.

Thin-lipped, Jonas deliberately seats himself.

"You still disclaim responsibility for the flare?" He glances at the smoldering crater in front of him.

"Yes. The mechanisms involved are entirely different." Ratio brushes a gleaming brass hand over the ruined surface. The crushed small arms vanish, and the crater itself is gone. Indirect lighting shines off the desk's perfect polished surface.

Jonas exhales through his nose, a sharp gust that is almost a laugh. He is badly shaken but hides his emotion well.

"So. Robot party tricks. I am not interested in illusions and prestidigitation." He stands again, faces the levitated ai. "If this is a rather gaudy declaration of war between Earth and Psyche, I remind you that there are proper diplomatic and military channels for such matters. Please leave my chambers now."

"Lord Jonas, forgive the pyrotechnics. I sought to attract your attention in the briefest possible time."

"You succeeded, for the briefest possible time. I have an emergency to attend to, Sen. The door is behind you. Please convey your further thoughts to my majordomo. Good day to you."

Two Genetic soldiers strike viciously at Ratio, one from either side. The ai flows through them. Tangled, humiliated, they tumble to the carpet.

"We waste time, Lord Jonas. There is something I wish you to see."

"Another party trick?" Jonas is raging, fists clenched. "Whom do you represent? House Cima? The ai Conclave? The anarchist barbarians?"

"I will not take you by force," the ai says patiently.

"Take me where, damn you?"

"You will not be harmed."

"Do you think my personal safety is an issue?" The tall hu

steps from behind his desk, strides to confront the ai, his face an inch from ser casque. "Enough of this. Do what you will."

Instantly, they stand in the ravaged central chamber designed to hold the metric defect in magnetic field pincers. Blue radiation glares. The hyperstring seethes in its own tormented geometry. Neither hu or ai wears mirrorskin nor armor. A pale shell of light encloses them, shielding them somehow from the monstrous forces that rage around the defect.

Jonas gasps, clutching his throat for air. The hu's breathing reflex is paralyzed by dread. He believes that he hangs an instant from death in pure vacuum. He begins to convulse. The ai touches him reassuringly.

"Just breath normally, my Lord."

After some seconds, Jonas recovers. His chest heaves in spasm, and his limbs tremble. He looks with detestation at the ai hanging motionless beside him.

"I will never forgive you for this."

"There is no shame in fearing death," the ai tells him. Somehow ser voice reaches his ears without the distortions of static he expects in such a place. "It is part of your deepest biological coding."

"I do not fear death," Jonas shouts in fury, "because there is no death. We are endlessly reborn. Unless you mean to hurl me into that damnable pit." His face is blue in the blue light. "Is that what happened to Orwen? Ambushed him here, did you, in the midst of his devotions?"

"No," the ai says. "He died at the hands of his brother Feng."

"Oh." The hu gathers himself together, forces his terrified mind to absorb this new source of information. "Telmah slew his uncle in revenge."

"Feng died for the death of Corambis."

Jonas stares at sem in surprise. "The Warrior Rose?"

"This is not a court of law," the ai tells him. "Nor, I believe, have you earned the right of judgment. Your invasion of the

Starlit Corridor is an act of rank opportunism."

Incredulous, the hu warrior snatches for his missing weapon. "You scold me for claiming judgment? In these worlds, robot, you have no rights at all. Return me at once and depart from Psyche. You are not wanted."

Ratio laughs quietly. Se reaches down, impossibly, into the metric defect and draws out a tendril of glowing spacetime, winds it around ser finger. It sparkles like a jeweled necklace worn by a god before creation. Se flings it back.

"Altair Lord Corambis is the legal heir to the Directorship," se says.

Jonas breathes for thirty seconds, slowing his pulse.

"Disavow my own claim by conquest," he says finally with a certain imposed pedantry, "and Telmah Lord Cima is the legal heir."

"Telmah is . . . otherwise engaged."

"You've abducted him? Helped him escape to the Solar?"

"He is safe. That is all you need to know. Telmah and the Rose will not return. Not"—the ai smiles gently—"for some time."

"Altair is on Earth at his studies," Jonas muses, his eyes moving back and forth as he calculates the import of these disclosures. "He cannot be back here in less than three months. His family's forces are in disarray. Lord Altair can have no bearing on the military situation unless you kill me, Sir Robot. Is that what you plan? If so," he says with a defiant snarl, "do it now and get it over with. I tire of these theatrics."

The ai regards him with admiration.

"You will be a great leader one day," se says. "Very well. I shall return you to Psyche. Make whatever arrangements you care to with Altair. I have a message for you to carry to your people."

Sullenly, Jonas says, "Speak."

"The Asteroid Cartels will be under interdiction for an indeterminate period."

"Impossible!"

"The Solar and the galaxy will accept no further pharmaceuticals, no ore, and no—"

"Just a moment—" cries the outraged hu.

"—no traffic will be permitted between our worlds and the Belt. This quarantine is for your own safety. I cannot say more at this time."

Space flattens. The defect, and everything about it, vanishes, leaving them hanging in naked space.

Instantly, they stand once again beside the great desk in the room which was Orwen's office, and then Feng's, and is now sequestered by Jonas. The hu sags. His uniform is soaked with sweat. He glances at the holly display to confirm the impossible thing he has just witnessed.

The cube is empty. The blazing metric defect and its scalded shell of rock are gone, withdrawn from the Asteroid Belt.

X

At nine standard years of age, gauged by household chronometers that keep hu/ai standard time, even though this reality marches at a quicker measure than the Solar's own, the eldest boy is somber, inward, scholarly. Perhaps it is a result of coming into a world bereft of hu or Genetics other than his parents and, eventually, his brother and sisters. Telmah, formerly Lord Cima, suspects a deeper source for the boy's melancholy. Certainly, Aerth resembles his father to a striking degree. He is witty and mulish by turns, and this month answers only to the name "Rock."

Telmah finds him sitting in the enxt, flicking from one created reality to another. As he opens the door, his son has the room set on a night filled with swirling nebulae and a million stars. By the time he closes it behind him, the enxt has surrounded them with sunlight and dazzling snows.

"Aerth, don't you think—" Telmah catches himself with a small grimace. "Rock, your sisters miss your company."

The boy says nothing. The enxt switches them to the middle of a jungle. Something roars in the distance, and the light is green, the air thick and hot and humid. Telmah squats in the grass beside him, waiting with careful patience. A grasshopper lands on his bare leg. He watches it preen, lift away into the heavy atmosphere. Again the landscape changes. Sheets of ice stretch blue under pale sky. A chill breeze cuts them both to the skin.

"How did you do that, Rock?"

"Huh?"

"Change settings. I don't see any remote."

The boy turns, gives him the look: stupid adults.

"Really, I'd like to know. Have you found a way to link in to the household system?"

"You just want it," the boy says as if to an imbecile.

"It reads your mind?"

"Of course it doesn't. How could it? It's a dumb machine. You just reach in sideways."

It is as much as Telmah can get from him.

In bed with the Warrior Rose, the baby squirreled between them and drowsing at Rose's breast beneath her dusky flower, he tells her about the exchange.

"That's odd." She muses so long that he thinks she is falling asleep. He reaches carefully to retrieve the baby, and Rose blinks slowly at him, smiling. "I'm not drowsing off. Fire said something like that the day I found her in the top of the nettle tree."

"She thinks the trees are dumb machines? I'm not surprised, everything they see is done by—"

"No, the other thing. The sideways place."

Telmah's naked back crawls. Something nightmarish creeps in the dark places of memory: a man burning. Reaching through with a hand that is not a hand and— He calls softly, "Fire, are you asleep?"

His eldest daughter, still playing with her favorite doll in an adjacent sleeping chamber, hears his voice from the air. She hastily kisses the doll, puts it aside, and snuggles down under the blanket. "Almost, Papa."

"Come and hop into bed with us for a moment, honey. There's something your Mommy and I would like to discuss."

With a sinking sense of guilt, the child leaves her bed and makes her way to the adults' room, racking her brains for the infraction. Leaving Ariel alone with the tending monitor while she wandered down to the creek to collect wildflowers? She hesitates at the half-open doorway. Her parents do not look especially angry.

"I was only gone for a few—"

"Hop up here with us, darling heart," her mother says and makes a space under the blanket. Relieved, Fire scampers to the bed and jumps in next to her warm-smelling Mommy.

"Remember the time you ended up in the tree? The one with all the prickles?"

The little girl's face falls again, and she gets ready to cry like a baby. Sometimes it works, even though she is seven now.

"I know I shouldn't have," she begins, but her mother is shushing her and stroking the downy feathers in her hair.

"That's all right, possum dear," Rose says. "It's just that we've never thought to ask you how you got up there. I can remember being surprised that you weren't cut to ribbons by the thorns. Do you remember, darling?"

"Uh."

"You said something about going through the sideways. I didn't understand what you meant."

"How come? Is it wrong?" Her face makes it clear that she thinks it is very wrong indeed.

"Why should it be wrong?" her father asks, but not angrily. Not quite.

"Well . . . Aerth said you'd say it was. Rock, I mean."

"We're not going to shout at you, sweetness. I think," Rose mutters nearly under her breath, and despite his growing alarm Telmah smiles to himself. "How can you get to the top of a tree by going sideways?"

"Well, you use the bird."

Telmah sits bolt upright in bed, waking the baby, who starts to howl.

"An ibis?" His voice is strained and his eyes stare at her.

"I don't know." Fire is worried again. "What's that?"

"It's a kind of bird, sweetheart, from our own world." He calls up a holly display and shows her a picture of a large ibis standing on one leg in water. Its great curving beak is magnificent in the cubed sunset.

"I think so," the girl says, around her thumb. "Only that's not the right color."

"Jesus and Allah," Telmah says in a flat tone. He sits back, controlling his breathing. Rose has the baby at her breast. Fire watches him warily. Her father has never smacked her, but his moods are unreliable. "Rose, it's a Gestell transducer. The bastards." He starts to laugh. "The wily bastards. They've linked it to the metric defect. My God, how *long* has this been in preparation?"

The following morning in the breakfast nook Telmah proposes a new game. Sea prefers to play with her mush, smearing it in her hair, but finally they all fall in with the spirit of the adventure.

"There's this bird we're searching for, kids," Telmah begins when they are gathered in a circle. Things like birds are flocking outside the silvered windows, uttering cries a little like bird songs. The difference is heartbreaking, but only to the adults.

Rock stares balefully at Fire.

"I didn't," she cries.

"How else would they know?" He is furious and contemptuous.

"Rock, don't upset your sister. We knew because we've been looking for it ever since we arrived on this planet."

"Huh?" The boy stares at his father in disbelief. "You just, you know."

"Actually, honey," his mother tells him with a sweet smile, "we don't. Can you help us find it?"

"Then you'll stop us playing with it."

"No, we won't, Aerth. Rock."

"Oh, all right." With many a sigh of resentment, the child gets out of his chair and leaves the room, returning with a handful of black, thin wires. With Fire's help, he plaits the bundle loosely into a frame, a truncated cone that shimmers oddly, almost appearing to Telmah's bemused gaze to float slightly above the table.

"You want us to fetch the bird here, not just go sideways?"

"If you can, darling."

"It might help," Fire suggests, "if we all put our hands together. Yuck," she adds at once as Sea thrusts her mush-coated fingers into hers.

A glow flickers in the heart of the cone. The baby, crooning, reaches out his tiny hand toward it.

The topaz ibis, rather dusty, stands on the table. Slowly it topples, falls apart into its several components.

"Jesus and Allah," says Telmah Cima, exile and paterfamilias.

"Holy shit," cries his wife, all her feathers standing on end.

Rain lashes him from the monsoonal thunderburst. Altair Lord Corambis, fatherless exile, pelts through the drumming rain. An empty pavilion is visible through the sheets of vertical water. No band plays. No crowd is gathered to picnic and chat as the band, black piping on their heavy red uniforms, entertains them with drum and tuba. Altair runs, breathing through his mouth, ducks under cover. The wind catches rain, hurls it sidelong to slap the side of his face. The young man hugs his arms around him.

A child is walking toward him through the gray rain.

Water runnels down the grassy slope. The boy kicks his way through it, not hurrying, heading for the pavilion.

Altair stares. The boy is beautiful. Something about his looks engages the Belter's curiosity. Surely he isn't a—

The boy vaults up the low set of steps, stands a meter or two away, not looking at him. An illegal full diploid hu-Genetic hybrid, not a symbolic hetero-clone. Altair knows it at once, even though he has never seen one before.

"Good morning, Lord Altair," the strange boy says, still not looking directly at him.

"I beg your— You know my name?"

"Yes, Sen. Would you come with me now?"

The boy makes eye contact for one long instant, unafraid, and Altair's heart contracts. Impossibly, he recognizes this child, this adolescent, this illicit hybrid.

"I have business here," he tells the boy. "Has someone sent you?"

"You wish to return to Psyche as soon as possible."

"Yes. I've been trying to arrange an orbital launch. My father was—" He breaks off, shakes his head. The rain eases slightly, and a gust of warm tropical odors reaches his nostrils: wild fruit trees and flowers. It reminds him achingly of the Hydroponics Gardens where he once played with his sister.

"Lord Corambis is dead," the boy says quietly. "Yes. Please come with me now."

What choice has he? "Very well."

They dash down the steps into the drenching haze and up a grassy slope. Apparently, the boy knows where he is going. A small white building, perhaps a museum, is set among trees just over the hill.

"In here, Sen."

Shaking himself like a wet dog, Altair blinks at the bright light. A woman is seated at a low table bearing platters and goblets of half-consumed food and drink. She regards him with a look he cannot register. It has something of joy in it. He has never seen her before. Yes. Yes, he has. It is quite impossible. Altair stands dripping on the carpet as the youth crosses quietly to stand beside the woman.

"Mother?" Altair flushes as the words come from his mouth. "I'm sorry, Sen, that was a stupid thing to—"

"Altair, has it been so long? Don't you recognize me?"

"But my mother is dead," he blurts, moving toward her. He peers into the lovely woman's face. A flower blooms at her shoulder. He stops with a jolt. "Rosette?"

Smiling, she rises and extends her arms. "Come and give me a hug, you big wet lug."

"No, this is," he starts to say. Her scent enters his nostrils. He releases her, pushes her to arm's length. It is the Warrior Rose. She is a decade older than the last time he embraced her, months ago. "This is just," he says. Her familiar glance is unchanged. He looks at the young man. The same eyes. Her son. And something else. His reality swims, comes close to fracturing. "Telmah's son?" he says, voice strained.

"I'm Aerth," the boy tells him. "You're my uncle." He smiles up at his mother. "See, Mom, I told you he'd handle it okay."

Altair sinks into a seat, drawing Rose with him, clinging to her hands.

"He murdered our father and then killed Feng," he tells her hoarsely, shivering as steam rises from his damp clothes. "How can you be—"

"No," she says. She presses her forefinger to his lips. "I executed Feng. I had no choice. And our poor father perished by accident."

"Telmah," he begins fiercely.

"Is forgiven," she declares, somewhat sternly. "That was a long, long time ago. I have so much to tell you, my darling."

"Days ago," he insists, his voice rising to a screech. "And now Jonas has besieged the Starlit Corridor. Something seems to have happened to the power defect. I'm trying to get back up to—"

"I think you can come out now," the boy calls over his shoulder. Three children come into the room. The elder girl holds a baby boy in her arms. "These are your nieces and nephew," the boy tells him formally with a small bow. "Fire," the bigger girl grins, one tooth missing, "and that's little Ariel she's taking care of, and Sea's the one with the snot in her nose. Come here, lug." He picks up the little girl and blows her nose on a check handkerchief he conjures from a pocket.

"Sorry for the melodrama," Rose tells Altair, squeezing his hand tightly. "The so-called anarchists have this damned planet wired to a fare-thee-well. Spy monitors everywhere. In public, anyway. We don't want them to know we're here. Not yet."

"How the *hell* did you get to Earth without them detecting your ship?"

"Ah." The Warrior Rose smiles with deep satisfaction. "That's quite an interesting story." She brings the children in a circle around herself and her brother, gestures them to seat themselves on cushions. The older boy, Aerth, is doing something

with a handful of black wires. "Let's go somewhere a little less
. . . drizzly, and I'll tell you all about it."

The truncated cone is glowing. Outside, the drumming rain
cuts off and bright sunlight dashes across a different tiled floor.
The wires slide apart, and the beautiful boy packs them away.
Ariel reaches into his mother's garment for her heavy tiger-
striped breast, fastens his small hungry mouth on the nipple.

"Thank you for coming here, Altair," Telmah Cima says from
the far side of the different room. He walks toward his inad-
vertent enemy with a measure of caution, hand extended. He
is heavily bearded, and lines of age cut the flesh at the corners
of his eyes.

Altair, former exile on Earth, stands stock-still, mouth gaping. For the first time in his fiery young life, he can find absolutely nothing to say.

xii

Coming up from cold hibernation is nightmarish, however
deftly the small stupid machines manage the transition. Forced
news dreams lap at the shores of Abhinavagupta's reluctantly
waking mind. He shivers, although the air blowing across his
naked body is a balmy twenty-two degrees Celsius. Images
flicker on his closed eyes, pressing update infodumps upon his
reluctance. Groaning, he turns his head to the side. The holly
projector compensates.

"Good morning, Sen. You have been resting for sixty-two
days and fourteen hours. Your life-signs indicate that you have
made a full recovery. Would you like to give me a little response
now?"

He groans again, probing the cavity of his mouth with his
thick tongue. It does not have the rank taste he expects. In

fact, his mouth has a pepperminty freshness that makes him gag.

"Could you tell me your name, Sen?"

He clears his throat and in a deep menacing voice, growls, "Why, this is hell, nor am I out of it."

"Excellently performed, Sen." The machine applauds ingratiatingly. "Christopher Marlowe (1564–1593), *Doctor Faustus*. 'See, see, where Christ's blood streams in the firmament.' Or is it a case of 'Ugly hell, gape not! come not, Lucifer! I'll burn my books!'?"

"What?" Abhinavagupta mumbles blearily. "What?"

"Your name, Sen. Just for the record. Humor me."

"Abhinavagupta." He tries for the associated identity numbers, stumbles in the vault of his declarative memory, retrieves them after a moment, gives the code to the stage-struck mechanism.

"Thank you, Sen. You notice that I employ the usage common among the galactics, rather than the provincial forms of *politesse* customary in the Belt? We estimate that you will feel more comfortable with—"

"Shut the fuck up, would you?" Abhinavagupta growls. "I think I'm going to be sick."

Offended, the mech tells him, "There is a tube next to your casket. On the right. Please try not to splash."

News inputs return, cut-flashing the past two months' events in a stream designed for people who cannot take direct feeds from the Gestell. Or who choose not to do so, like the Fauves. Abhinavagupta lies on his back staring at the curved shell above his head, and learns that Jonas Lord Brass has withdrawn from the Starlit Corridor in Psyche, that his traditional rival Altair Lord Corambis has taken his place as Director-Pro-Tem after a brilliant lateral campaign. Pretending to depart for Earth by ion drive ship, Altair, it seems, bided his time under deep cover with his reserve troops in the endless tunnels and caverns of the asteroid . . .

Abhinavagupta decides not to vomit after all. Groaning, he sits up as the shell opens over his head. None of the other caskets is sprung yet, although all are defrosted. He pads on bare feet to a shower under the one-tenth gravity of their spin compartment, sluices away the sticky layer coating his skin. He is not hungry, but he feels like talking. Not, preferably, to a laminated mech who'd rather be an actor.

Someone in the distance is singing, pausing between phrases to sound a musical instrument of some kind. Wailing, thin. It makes his scrubbed skin jump. Abhinavagupta pulls on a light one-piece garment, lollops in the phony gravity to the hospitality lounge, where he finds a large brown hound playing a treble recorder with its prehensile toes, tail beating out the rhythm of "Lonesome Cowboy" against the nonskid carpet.

Abhinavagupta sidles into the lounge, watching the dog with a certain sidelong caution, and gets himself a light breakfast of scrambled eggs, toast, and hot black coffee in a pressurized bulb.

"Good morning," he murmurs at last, seating himself across the cabin from the crooning animal.

"Howdy." The dog's long lips pucker up to the reed, blowing a sweet and hauntingly pure series of notes.

The walls of the lounge are plastered with thousands and thousands of small square, rectangular and less boring shapes in simple hues. Each contains a small picture or emblem, and its perimeter is serrated. Markings feature in the variegated designs, probably alphanumerics in a range of languages. Abhinavagupta, peering at the wall beside him, suddenly realizes what these absurd things are. He is surrounded by a philatelist's wet dream, a room papered ceiling and wall with stamps from the age of hard postal delivery.

After a couple of mouthfuls of egg, Abhinavagupta pushes his plate away, feeling his nausea return. He peers longingly down the passageway, wishing his friends would wake up.

"Nice playing," he says uncomfortably. "Can I get you something to eat or drink?"

"Thanks, bud." The cyborg dog puts down his recorder and shakes himself, then scratches vigorously behind one long ear, leaving no doubt of his sex. Hair sheds into the floating gravity, eddies in the circulating current, vanishes into a duct. "I've eaten. I'm Cap'n Chip."

"Cap'n?" Abhinavagupta is startled. "You fly this ship?"

"Jest me and the laminations," the dog says complacently. He curls up, nose on tail, and watches the trouper with bright brown eyes. "Glad you're awake. Enjoy some company. How's your chums?"

Abhinavagupta peers pointlessly down the empty, curving corridor. "Uh, none of them up yet. I have a hearty constitution."

"Hmmm." The dog nods, closes his eyes, drowses off. After a moment, he opens them again, shows his long wet tongue. "Don't suppose you could throw any light on the shenanigans back home?"

"What? On Psyche?"

"Yep. You've had your official upload, I guess?"

Abhinavagupta frowns, squirts some coffee into his mouth, gulps it down. Strange how the simplest routine activities develop this extra layer of difficulty and self-consciousness in space. He is grateful at least that they are not in free fall, charming though weightlessness was under some circumstances. That girl in the—

"Telmah's disappearance, you mean? Really, I can't help you. We were under arrest at the time." He stops and blushes. Stupid! The dog does not take fright, however, at his confession of criminal arraignment or at least is considerate enough to ignore it.

"No, bud, the disappearance of the whole danged power unit."

"The what?"

"The metric defect. It's gone."

"Gone bang? Like before?" Oh shit, he thinks. Those poor people. But nothing was mentioned in the briefing. Or was it? Surely he'd have noticed something on that scale? Hang on, there was something about a flare . . .

"Not just gone bang," the dog says. "Gone away. Vanished."

Rozz stumbles into the cabin, teasing her damp blonde hair with her fingers. "Telmah the fucking magician," she mumbles, leaning down and kissing Abhinavagupta quickly on the crown of the head. Moving her head creakily from side to side to unkink her neck, she finds a plate of flat bread, dips, sliced *faux* ham. "He's disappeared the power station. Taken that amazing tiger woman with him, apparently. And the ai's gone as well."

"How do you know all this?" Abhinavagupta asks indignantly.

She reaches over and prods him three times in the chest, hard.

"Because"—prod—"I pay"—prod—"*attention*"—prod.

Gill bounces in, full of sparkle. It is obscene. Within minutes, the rest of the troupe stagger through the door and shamble for seats. The dog makes himself known to them one by one. When they all have plates in their laps, he puts aside the darkly gleaming recorder and calls for attention.

"Docking at Callisto in nine hours," he announces. "You'll be met at Port Alcas and conducted to the hex station. I wouldn't advise any sightseeing or media gabbing. Sorry to rush you, folks, but there's a lot of curiosity in the Solar right now about us Belters, and you're going to get swamped if you don't move pretty damned lively. The ship will arrange for your luggage to follow you." He nods briskly, is gone through a small access door, tail wagging, before they can raise any objections.

Callisto is a world pocked hideously with acne. One entire wall of the lounge opens into a display of space as they fall toward the Jovian moon. A true window would show nothing but the hot haze of their ion drive braking them as they shed velocity. This holly edits out the stripped metal gas, shows an ancient moon smashed again and again by impacts from space, thousands and millions of small flat craters with bright rims of water ice. They swing past an astonishing modulation in this pattern of wormholes: a vast set of concentric ripples, the snap-frozen rings of a monstrous impact. It is Valhalla, sole remnant of a stone the size of a minor world that smashed its way into the surface of this second-largest moon of Jupiter and then sank under the rocky sea, leaving only the disturbed currents of its passing as a record.

"Telmah," Rozz mutters mysteriously, gazing at the golden target and its white blemishes, and will not amplify her remark.

Fascinated, big-eyed, Doony watches the huge moon as they drop toward equatorial orbit. After half an hour, though, he grows restless.

"I'm starving."

Myfanwy laughs in disbelief and cuddles him roughly.

"You've just had breakfast, Doons!" She squeezes his bulging muscles. "Been pumping iron in your dreams, honey?"

"Aw." Embarrassed, he wriggles out of her clutches and heads off in search of the pantry. "Fee Fi *Foe!*" he calls over his shoulder and licks his lips, a giant about to eat an Englishman, whatever that is.

The ship slides into orbit, and they bustle to the shuttle for their ride down to the surface. Rozz holds Gill's hand tightly against her breast.

"I wish I knew where he'd gone," she whispers.

"You're afraid he's dead," her twin whispers back. He does not meet her eye. After a moment, he adds, "Yes, me too."

"We're a pair of bastards," Rozz cries in sudden anguish. The rest of the troupe stare at her, turn aside out of confusion or decency.

Gill pulls her to him.

"I know we are. But I'm sure he's all right."

"Do you think so?" Her eyes are filled with tears that cannot fall in zero gravity. They strap themselves in, and the shuttle drifts away from the spacecraft, nudged by hard fingers of magnetic flux.

"I don't know," he admits. "We let him down," he adds sadly. "I think this is the end for the troupe, Sis."

Yazade, listening, hoods her dark eyes. Big Kob shifts uncomfortably as deceleration pressure begins to bite.

"Time to take a look at the stars," Kob says to them all. "Get into the Gestell at last, huh."

Lyn says, "Set the Wild Beasts free, aye!"

Rozz sniffles. "I love you guys," she tells them all passionately. "I really do."

"Yeah," says Doony, nodding fiercely. His own eyes are welling. "Yeah." A second later he is craning in his couch. "Look at that! Hey, man, look at that!"

Callisto opens above them, beneath them, like a gateway built all of golden ice.

"The world," Ratio informs Telmah Cima, "is a recirculating narrative. The Lending Library of Babel at the Quantum Mechanics Institute."

"Oh?" Hip-deep in the slow-running stream, Telmah casts a fly. His monomolecular line whispers like a passing ghost, and its lure floats in a wonderfully lifelike fashion to the smooth water. Just below the surface, edible goggle-eyed things like eels flirt with the fly, rising under its shadow, nosing it, flicking back doubtfully into deeper water. Telmah waits patiently, bathed in Aaron Copland's *The Tender Land* and the last of the warm Sun.

Some meters downstream, Ratio carries no fishing line. Se extends a mesh container and sings a fishy song. One of the eel things curves deliciously to ser electric melody and wafts itself neatly into the waiting bag.

"That's five," se says with just a hint of smugness. "I don't think they like your insect, Lord Cima." Se parades the wriggling animal over ser head for ten seconds or so. It flails, drowning in air. With a deft wrist movement, Ratio releases the creature under the water. Confused and perhaps terrified, it lashes its tail and is gone.

"You're stirring them up," Telmah says accusingly. "The ones you set free have started a rumor. Rose and the children will never eat again. We'll starve in the midst of plenty, and it will all be your fault."

Time passes. The edge of this world rolls up against the Sun, and the sky settles gently toward an incandescent glory. Telmah watches the clouds turning dusty pink. Once he had never seen a cloud. It seems inconceivably long ago.

"I don't understand your reference," Telmah says eventually.

"I've been aksing Daimon Keith's biography."

"Who?"

"He was the hu who first saw that broken symmetry is what keeps the universe from happening all at once."

"Isn't that what time does?"

"Time is one of the fractured symmetries of the Ur state."

"Have we smashed it up even more, Ratio, or are we helping to weld it back together?" He casts his line again, with as little luck.

"We've translated its text into new rotations and reflections."

"Ha! Tell me about keeping the bits of history apart."

"One of the ancient paradoxes," the ai explains seriously. "According to the sage Einstein, we should not be permitted to hex faster than light."

Telmah darts a guilty look over his shoulder. "Oh no! The relativity cops'll bust down the door."

Ratio sighs. "Quantum entanglement proved all that was nonsense."

"I'm relieved to hear it."

"When paired particles are created spontaneously, they rush off to the opposite ends of the universe at the speed of light." Se notices the hu's lips part for a needling quibble, and adds quickly, "Near the speed of light, if you're going to be pedantic. Unless they're photons. What follows?"

"This is kindergarten stuff, Ratio. Neither of them has a definite spin and what have you until it's measured."

"Not quite. That implies conscious choice is involved. The 'measurement' is just any interaction with some other particle."

Telmah reels in his line, checks the tasty *faux* morsel wriggling mechanically at its tip, casts again.

"Whatever. Then its quantally entangled twin instantly collapses out of indeterminacy into the opposite spin state. If one's up, the other's down. Or something."

"Or something. But which twin 'collapses' first?"

The hu pauses, sensing a trap. "Well, the one that's measured first, wherever it happens to be in the universe by then. And that entails the instantaneous state vector collapse of its twin."

"True," Ratio says, nodding, "but since their motion places them in separate reference frames, each might be 'first' according to itself. No such thing as simultaneity in relativity, remember. The particles don't have a common time."

Telmah gazes blindly for a long moment, pondering.

The ai crosses ser arms, and then tilts the cross forty-five degrees, making an X across the place where ser heart would be if se had a heart.

"The coordinates of space and time fold together," se says. "If an event in one frame is projected on the compressed time axis of its twin, it happens at different moments in each history. But that is true in both cases. Neither frame is privileged."

"You're right," Telmah says, astonished. "We stipulate that neither of the particles acquires a definite quantum state until the initial measurement. But since there's no objective way to tell which measurement gets made first— Jesus and Allah." He is chagrined. "We never studied such matters in the Belt, Ratio. It was deemed impious. The wicked hex device. So what's the explanation?"

"Symmetry is reinstated by default, you see," Ratio tells him, satisfied. "And out of that one critical breach in relativity dogma emerges the wicked hex device, and eventually, with some compact-space topology thrown in, that little box of tricks you and your gifted family use so amusingly."

Telmah smiles. "With a little help from your striped hole defect."

They both glance at the larger moon, where the pilfered defect orbits safely out of reach of prying hu and Genetic hands in a galaxy that will emerge in misty magnificence, a few hours hence, above the rolling horizon.

"True." Ratio inaudibly whistles up another eel and this time retains it for the pot.

"I fail to see how Daimon Keith's heretical speculations explain your comment. What's a Quantum Mechanics Institute?"

"Just a joke, Telmah."

"I hate ai jokes." Telmah groans and shakes his head.

"This was before the Gestell, you see," Ratio insists on telling him. "They read books in those days."

"Surely the Net was up by Keith's time?"

"Toward the end of his life, but apparently he never felt comfortable with it. He spent a lot of time in libraries. Hard texts."

"Chiseled into stone," Telmah hazards.

"Not quite. Extremely expensive, nonetheless. Daimon Keith scrabbled for what he could find in the local library, which public benefactors instituted a hundred years earlier for working people who hoped to better themselves. Mechanics' Institutes, they called them. In fact, he was reviled by the institutions and died insane. As for Borges's Library of Babel— Oh, never mind. I find that jokes are very difficult without Gestell aks."

"Jokes are not meant to be explained, Ratio."

A fish thing seizes Telmah's bait and swallows it. There is a tussle which the hu wins without a great deal of effort. He bags his trophy with gratitude, killing the luckless thing first with a quick slap against a rock. He sighs, listening to Copland's elegiac music in the evening sunlight. In the north, the smaller moon shows the faintest porcelain edge.

"Poor mad Daimon Keith understood that the universe is a narrative endlessly interpreted," the ai says as they pack their smelly gear and trudge up the hill. "I think he might even have suspected that it is an infinite set of narratives awaiting an ideal reader."

Telmah corrects sem. "An infinite number of ideal readers." He carries his rod at port arms.

"Perhaps not. Perhaps in the Gestell we are all one, and that One reads between all the lines." Se reaches for a bag of tackle hanging heavily on ser friend's shoulder. Telmah allows ser to take it. "That is the grotesque mistake your people make in the Belt. The hex does not kill souls, it links them. It releases us into ubiquity. It reconnects our tangled quantum states. It permits us rebirth." Se shrugs. "Of a kind."

Telmah is breathing a little harder than usual. After a couple of kilometers, he waves his friend to a halt, finds a shelf of stone to sit on. He is no longer a youth, not by a long shot. Nearly eight. Almost the same age his mother was when she married his uncle Feng. The sky darkens, and stars are on the verge of coming out. A slight chill makes him shiver.

"You were right, after all," he says.

The ai shrugs. "This does not surprise me. In which particular?"

"Settle down, raise some kids. You know. The pastoral dream."

"With some Sunday time-traveling thrown in for entertainment and the good of the commonweal." The ai laughs, ser face moving in a parody of hu mirth.

"Reflection and rotation," Telmah muses, looking closely at the ai's shadowed casque. "Ratio, you are the White Abacus."

The sky to the west—or what they interpret as the west—is spectacular, crimson billows and sheets of purple and a wash of palest green.

"Oh. I believe there's a poem—" the ai starts to say and pauses, bringing its stanzas to mind.

" 'Old sculptures/ turn their heads,' " Telmah Cima says in

a low voice. "If there is magic black and white, perhaps there are also different kinds of . . ."

"Jokes? Life? Machines? Mathematics?"

"Truth," Telmah Cima says very softly. "Love."

"Come on," Jay Three tells him, lifting smoothly from the ground with a dexterous symmetry transform. Se flies them both through the fragrant dusk. "The family will be ravenous. Besides, it's getting cold out here."

Lovely winged things like birds fly with them, very high overhead, beating the air, singing to each other, their feathers gleaming faintly in the light of the vanishing Sun, the cool moons.

AFTERWORD

All fiction builds worlds out of words, but science fiction especially. (I argue this case extensively in *Reading by Starlight: Postmodern Science Fiction*.) Even in this epoch of routine space robots and transgenic medical "miracles," SF operates with plenty of words that still cannot be defined simply by pointing at the real-world thing or action they encode. There are, alas, no "time machines" or "telepaths" or "metric defects" or "asteroid societies" or even "direct mind-machine interfaces" (although this thing I'm typing on comes close). And even what we do know gets skewed under the influence of the SF imagination. My own innovations—which I urge others to borrow—are variants of current usage. "Hu" (rhymes with "you") and "ai" (rhymes with "I") are a happy blend of accidental lexical history and the ancient bonded dichotomy "I/ Thou." My nonexclusive gender particles "Sen," "Se," "Ser," and "Sem" for title, "she/he," "hers/his," and "her/him" are herewith in the public domain; feel free.

The word-bricks we SF writers use in our constructions must often be filched in this way from the preimagined worlds built by earlier writers. And the images we evoke come as often from startling SF graphics and scientific photographs and diagrams as they do from our personal memories of love and pain and the whole damned thing. This novel, like all SF and maybe even more so, is a collage of appropriated icons. Readers who know and love classic SF, and its more recent upgrades, will recognize (with, I hope, a small burst of nostalgic pleasure) the devices I've stolen and remodeled: proud and lonely Belter culture, cyberspace and virtual reality, grandiose Faustian technologies. More specifically, I invoke C. L. Moore's wondrous robot from "No Woman Born" (as did Michael Swanwick in *Stations of the Tide*) and Dr. Robert L. Forward's discussion (in his exhilarating *Future Magic*) of the Rod Hyde Space Fountain. Dr. Forward should not be blamed, of course, for the shocking things I do with the ideas he canvasses so entertainingly. Some of my planetary landscapes are annotations on the lovely paintings and photos in books such as Ontario astronomer Terence Dickinson's *The Universe . . . and Beyond*. The "Gestell" derives from Martin Heidegger, who used the term to denote the global "technological system" we are embedded in and came to me via Michael Heim's *The Metaphysics of Virtual Reality*. Much of the detail and terminology of the Gestell derives from David Gelernter's fluent *Mirror Worlds* (but he shouldn't be blamed for what I do with it). My neo pulp ficto-critical novel's six-part framework is helped along by Professor Harold Bloom's "revisionary ratios," or ruling literary tropes, in his *A Map of Misprision*. More generally, I owe an immense debt to the hyperkinetic lunacy of Alfred Bester's great early fiction and of course to my Onlie Begetter, Mr. W. S. of Stratford-upon-Avon.

At the beginning of each section, you will find fragments from *The Black Abacus*, a rich poem by the Australian avantgarde radio broadcaster and poet Robyn Ravlich, who kindly allowed me to use these citations here. My title, which gnawed my imagination for two decades, is the mirror world of hers.

To these creators of imaginary worlds, I'm delighted to add the names of advisers in real cutting-edge science. My chief debt is to Paul J. Thomas, an associate professor in the department of Physics and Astronomy at the University of Wisconsin, Eau Claire, Wisconsin. His current research is centered on computer simulations of the icy satellites of the outer solar system and comet and asteroid collisions on the planets. Professor Thomas responded generously to my cry for help on the

World Wide Web—we had never met and still know each other only through the Net—with copious information, and then helped check or correct my various inexpert calculations. Without his aid, *The White Abacus* would still be counting on its fingers. I also received comment from Ralph Lorenz, of the lunar and planetary lab, University of Arizona; computer scientist and quantum buff Dr. Paul Budnik, who runs an FAQ on the quantum measurement problem; and Professor Tim Maudlin, a philosopher at Rutgers University, New Brunswick, New Jersey, whose analysis in a recent book, *Quantum Non-Locality and Relativity*, I have shamelessly perverted to my own twisted ends. I thank you all. My ability to reach these people on the Net stems from the generosity of the University of Melbourne, especially of Professor Ken Ruthven, whom I thank for allowing me a small trove of benefits as an Associate of the Department of English and Cultural Studies. My capacity actually to *use* the Net is due to huge amounts of unpaid effort from my pal and neighbor Paul Voermans, the excellent Australian SF writer, who also read various drafts and made useful suggestions.

Finally I owe a special debt to the Literature Board of the Australia Council, my nation's arts funding body, who gifted me with a year's grace in 1995 as a Fellow to write this book and to complete other lengthy writing projects.

I can be reached on the Net (and welcome comments) at damien@ariel.its.unimelb.edu.au. Do drop by!

Melbourne, Australia, January 1996